Cynthia Harrod-Eagles was born and educated in Shepherd's Bush and had a variety of jobs in the commercial world, starting as a junior cashier at Woolworth's and working her way down to Pensions Officer at the BBC. She won the Young Writers' Award in 1973, and became a full-time writer in 1978. She is the author of over fifty successful novels to date, including twenty-five volumes of the Morland Dynasty series.

Visit the author's website on
www.twbooks.co.uk/authors/cheagles.html

Gone Tomorrow

CYNTHIA HARROD-EAGLES

timewarner
paperbacks

A *Time Warner* Paperback

First published in Great Britain in 2001
by Little, Brown and Company

This edition published by Time Warner Paperbacks in 2002

A CIP catalogue record for this book
is available from the British Library.

ISBN 0 7515 3227 4

Typeset in Amasis by
Palimpsest Book Production Limited,
Polmont Stirlingshire
Printed and bound in Great Britain by
Clays Ltd, St Ives plc

Time Warner Paperbacks
An imprint of
Time Warner Book UK
Brettenham House
Lancaster Place
London WC2E 7EN

www.TimeWarnerBooks.co.uk

Author's Note

Shepherd's Bush and White City are real places, of course, but this *is* a work of fiction, so if certain liberties have been taken with the geography, please don't write and complain. None of the characters is based on a real person; and though there is a police station at Shepherd's Bush, my Shepherd's Bush nick is a made-up one, as are the Phoenix and the Dog and Sportsman pubs, which have no relation to any hostelry living or dead.

CHAPTER ONE

Too Much Like Aardvark

By the time Detective Inspector Bill Slider got to the scene, the rest of the circus was already there: the area had been closed off with what always struck him as inappropriately festive blue-and-white tape, the screens were erected, and uniform had got the crowd under control and space cleared for official cars.

Detective Sergeant Hollis held his car door open for him.

'You're very kind,' said Slider, climbing out.

'I used to get hit if I wasn't,' Hollis said. He was a scanty-haired beanpole of a Mancunian with a laconical delivery.

'Atherton not in yet?' DS Atherton, Slider's bagman, was due back from holiday that morning.

'Not when I left.'

Slider nodded towards the screens. 'Who is it?'

'Dunno, guv. He's not saying much. Large bloke, no ID. I don't recognise him.'

'Who found him?'

'Parkie. He doesn't know him either.'

Hammersmith Park was a long, narrow piece of land which lay between the White City estate and Shepherd's Bush. It had a gate at either end. One was in South Africa Road – home to the stadium of Queen's Park Rangers football team, known locally, for their horizontally striped shirts, as *ve 'oops* (or, if they had been having a successful run, *superoops*). The other gate was in Frithville Gardens, a cul-de-sac turning off the main Uxbridge Road which also led to the back door of the BBC Television Centre. Between the two lay the moderately landscaped green space of lawns and trees, with a sinuous path from gate to gate which was used as a cut-through for estate dwellers to and from the Bush.

Slider had been called to the South Africa Road gate. Just inside it, to the left, was a children's playground, whose amenity had been much reduced over the years in the retreat before vandalism. There was a paddling pool with no water, a sandpit with no sand, two rocking horses which, in the interests of safety, had been bolted to the ground and no longer rocked, and two sets of swings, one for babies and one for children.

Between the playground and the road was a small two-storey building which had once been an office and residence for a park keeper. It was now unused and all its orifices had been sealed up with breeze-block – the only way these days to keep out vandals, who had the tenacity of termites and would set fire to their own left legs in pursuit of a thrill. The only purpose of the building now, Slider noted a little glumly, seemed to be to conceal activity in the playground from anyone passing by in the street.

The body was on one of the children's swings. Slider passed through the screens to take a look. The swings were of a simple, municipally sturdy design, suspended from a framework made of scaffolding poles by chains thick and heavy enough to have towed a ship. The seats were made from short, thick chunks of wood that might have been chopped from railway sleepers, and the one was bolted to the other with sufficient determination to have resisted mindless destruction.

Deceased was seated, slumped forward, head and arms hanging, legs bent back and feet resting pigeon-toed on the ground. He had been a large, muscular man, otherwise he would probably have slipped off; as it was, he was kept in place by his own weight pressing against the chains, the bulge of the deltoids to one side and the pectorals to the other making a sort of channel for each chain to lie in snugly.

Hollis ranged up silently beside Slider.

'When was he found?' Slider asked.

'Park keeper came to open up at half seven. The gates are open between seven-thirty in the morning and dusk,' he added, anticipating Slider's question. 'Dusk is a bit of a movable feast, o' course. Sunset's around nine o'clock, give or take, this time o' year. But in practice the parkie shuts up when he feels like it, or when he remembers.'

Slider grunted, staring at the body. It was a fit-looking man, probably in his thirties, dressed in an expensive leather blouson-type jacket and a thin black roll-neck tucked into tight blue jeans, Italian leather casuals and a gold chain round his neck.

'The Milk Tray man's uniform,' Slider commented.

'He looks like an up-market bouncer,' Hollis agreed.

The hair was light brown and cut very short, the face was Torremolinos tanned, and he had a gold earring in the top of his left ear, small and quite discreet, the sort that said *okay, I'm cool, but I'm also tough*.

It was strangely hard to tell with corpses, when the face was without expression and the eyes closed, but this man probably would have been quite good-looking in life, of the sort a certain kind of woman fell for. Only his hands let him down: they were ugly, with badly bitten nails and deep nicotine stains. He wore a heavy gold signet ring, unengraved, on the middle finger of the right hand – the place fighters wore it, where it would do most damage.

Hollis reached out with a Biro and delicately lifted aside one side of the jacket to show Slider the stab wound below the left breast. 'Single blow, right where he lived. The only one as far as I can see, without moving him.'

'Not much staining,' Slider said. There was a stiff little patch around the wound, but nothing had gushed or dripped. 'Probably killed him instantly. If the heart had gone on pumping for any length of time there'd've been a lot more blood.'

'That's what I thought. Professional?' Hollis suggested.

Slider did not commit himself. 'No sign of the weapon?'

'Not so far.'

'And no ID?'

'Nothing in the jacket or the back trouser pocket. I've not gone in the front trouser pockets, o' course, but they feel empty.'

'Those jeans are so tight there can't be room down there for much more than his giblets,' Slider observed.

'Anyroad, all I found was money and fags.'

'Oh well, there might be something more when we can strip him off. Doctor been yet?'

'No, guv. Held up in traffic.'

Slider stepped back out to look around. What had brought this man here to his death? A meeting? Or perhaps he had been killed elsewhere and left here on the swing as a nasty kind of joke? At all events, it was a fairly private place, hidden from the road by the bulk of the defunct building. The park was overlooked only from the right-hand side by the upper floors of the flats in Batman Close, and then only in winter. At this time of year the foliage on the well-grown trees baffled any view of the ground. Yes, provided a person could get into the park in the first place without attracting attention, the spot was well chosen.

Beyond the park railings a small murmuring crowd had now collected, the usual mix of the idle, the elderly, and truanting kids. Slider scanned them automatically, but he didn't recognise anyone except Blind Bernie and Mad Sam, a well-known couple round the Bush. Mad Sam was Blind Bernie's son, and was not mad, only mentally retarded, a round-faced, smiling child of forty. He was Bernie's guide, and Bernie looked after him. They each kept the other out of A Home, the thing both dreaded with Victorian horror. Slider could see Sam's lips moving as he told Bernie what he could see, and Bernie's as he translated what Sam told him. Now he came to think of it, they lived in Frithville Gardens, so they naturally would be interested in something that happened in what was virtually their front garden.

Along the roof of the disused keeper's house a row of seagulls sat, shuffling their wings in the small breeze and turning their heads back and forth to see if all the unusual activity portended food. Once, they had come up into the estate from the Thames only in bad weather, to shelter, but now they seemed to live here all the time. Probably the large area of high buildings reminded them of cliffs; and there was plenty of rubbish for them to pick over. They had forgotten the sea; but on a quiet day their raucous squabbling cries brought it near in Slider's mind.

It was quiet here today, with the road temporarily closed to traffic. Somewhere out of sight a car horn broke the gentle background wash of distant city sounds, a composite murmur like the 'white noise' of silence; a crow cawed in one of the park trees, a fork-lift truck whined briefly behind the wall of the TVC, and far above a jumbo growled its way to Heathrow, flashing back the sun as it crawled between clouds.

All around, for miles and miles in every direction, in streets and shops and houses, real life was going on, oblivious; but here a dead man sat, the full stop at the end of his own sentence, with a little still pocket of attention focused fiercely and minutely on him. Why him? And why here? Slider felt the questions attaching themselves to him like shackles, chaining him to this scene, to a well-known process of effort, worry and responsibility.

He had a moment's revulsion for it all, for the blank stupidity of death, and longed to be anywhere but here, and to have any job but this. And then the doctor and the meat wagon arrived simultaneously, one of the uniforms asked him about press access, the police photographer came to him for instructions, and one of his own DCs, Mackay, turned up with the firm's Polaroid. Extraneous feelings fled as the job in hand claimed him, with a familiarity, at least, that was comfortable.

Detective Superintendent Fred 'The Syrup' Porson looked exhausted. He'd had this nasty 'summer flu' that was going around – seemed to have been having it for months – and his face looked grey and chipped. The rosy tint to his pouched eyes and abraded beak was the only touch of colour in the granite façade.

The HAT car (Homicide Advice Team) had been and gone, assessing the murder.

'We're keeping it,' Porson told Slider.

'The playground murder?'

'What did you think I meant?' Porson snapped irritably. 'Queen Victoria's birthday? And you don't know it's a murder yet.'

'Single stab wound to the heart and no weapon on the scene,' Slider mentioned.

'When you've been in the Job as long as I have, you'll take nothing for guaranteed,' Porson said darkly.

Slider almost had been, but he let it pass. The old boy was irritable with suffering.

'Anyway, it's ours,' Porson repeated.

'The SCG doesn't want it?' Slider asked.

The SCG was the Serious Crime Group, which had replaced the old Area Major Incident Pool, or AMIP. No doubt the change had brought joy to some desk-bound pillock's heart, and SCG was one letter shorter than AMIP which must be a great saving on ink; but since the personnel in the one were the exact same as had been in t'other, Slider couldn't see the point. It was hard for a bloke at the fuzzy end to get excited about a new acronym, especially one that did not trip off the tongue.

'SCG's got its plate taken up with the Fulham multiple,' Porson answered. 'Plus the Brooke Green terrorist bomb factory – to say nothing of being short-handed, *and* having four blokes on the sicker.'

Slider met The Syrup's eyes and refrained from reminding him that they too were short-handed. What with chronic under-recruitment, secondment to the National Crime Squad – not to mention to the SCG itself – plus absence on Roll-out Programmes and the usual attrition of epidemic colds, IBS and back problems – the ongoing response of over-stretched men to a stressful job – there could hardly be a unit of any sort in the Met that was up to strength. But Porson knew all that as well as he did. The SCG were supposed to take the major crimes, which these days generally meant all murders apart from straight-forward domestics, but the fact of the matter was that Peter

Judson, the head fromage of their own particular SCG, was a cherry-picking bastard who had obviously logged this case as entailing more graft than glory and tossed it back whence it came.

'After all,' Porson went on, trying to put a gloss on it, 'when push comes to shovel, it's a testament to your firm's record of success that they want to bung it onto us.'

'Yes, sir,' Slider said neutrally.

'You ought to've got a commendation last time, laddie, over that Agnew business. It was pure political bullshine that shot our fox before we could bring it home to roost. So here's your chance to do yourself a bit of bon. Brace up, knuckle down, and I'll make sure you get your dues this time, even if I have to stir up puddles till the cows come home.'

The allegories along Porson's Nile were more than usually deformed this morning, Slider thought, which was generally a sign of emotion or more than usual stress in the old boy. But he knew what he meant. He meant that Slider should put his nose to the wheel and his shoulder to the grindstone, a posture which inevitably left his arse in the right position to be hung out to dry if necessary; and Slider had a feeling, from the preliminary look of the thing, that this one was going to be a long, hard slog.

When he got back to the office, Atherton was there, looking bronzed, fit, rested and generally full of marrowbone jelly. Slider felt a quiet relief at the sight of him. Atherton had been through some tough times recently, including a near nervous breakdown, and there had been moments when Slider had feared to lose him altogether. He'd had other bagmen in a long career, but none that he would have also called his friend.

Atherton did not immediately look up, being engaged with the *Guardian* crossword. DC McLaren was hanging over his shoulder, a drippy bacon sandwich suspended perilously on the way to his mouth.

'I can't read your writing,' McLaren complained. 'What's that?'

'Aardvark.'

'With two a's?' McLaren objected.

'It's a name it made up for itself when it heard Noah was boarding the ark in alphabetical order,' Atherton explained kindly. 'The zebras were exceptionally pissed off, I can tell you. That's why they turned up in their pyjamas – as a kind of protest.'

'Now I know you're back,' Slider said. Atherton looked up, and McLaren straightened just in time for the melted butter to drip onto his front – which was used to it – instead of Atherton's back. Atherton was a classy dresser, and it would have been an act of vandalism akin to gobbing on the Mona Lisa.

'No need to ask if you had a good time,' Slider said. 'You're looking disgustingly pleased with yourself.'

'Why not?' Atherton agreed. 'A fortnight of sunshine and unfeasibly energetic sexual activity. And now a nice meaty corpse to get our teeth into.'

'Some people have strange tastes. How did you know, anyway?'

'Bad news has wings. Maurice was talking to Paul Beynon from the SCG while you were upstairs.'

'I knew him at Kensington,' McLaren said. 'He rung to give me the gen.' His time at Kensington was his Golden Age, source of all legend. Amazingly, it seemed he had been popular there. At all events, they were always ringing him up for a bunny, and vice versa.

'So it seems I just got back in time,' Atherton said.

'Yeah, from what you said, another day'd've killed you,' McLaren said lubriciously.

'How's Sue?' Slider asked.

Atherton smiled. 'You'll never know.'

McLaren pricked up his ears. 'Oh, is that who you were with? That short bird I saw you with that time? Blimey, you still going with her?'

His surprise was understandable, if tactless, for Atherton had always demanded supermodel looks as basic minimum, and Sue – a colleague of Joanna's – was neither willowy nor drop-dead gorgeous. She had something, however, that melted Atherton's collar studs. But he didn't rise to McLaren. He merely looked sidelong and said, 'You know the old saying, Maurice: better to have loved a short girl than never to have loved a tall.'

'Right, shall we get on with it?' Slider interposed. The rest of his team, bar Hollis and Mackay who were still at the scene, had come in behind him. 'With no identification on the corpse, we've got more work even than usual ahead of us. In fact, I expected to find you all hard at it already,' he complained.

'We have been. Hive of activity, guv,' McLaren said smartly. 'Just waiting for you to get back to see how you wanted it set up.'

'Never mind that Tottenham. When did I ever want it set up any differently? Here's the Polaroids from the scene. And I shall want a sketch map of the immediate area up on the wall. Get on with it, Leonardo.'

McLaren stuffed the last of the sandwich in his mouth. 'Right, guv,' he said indistinctly. 'Get you a cuppa first?'

'From the canteen? Yes, all right, might as well. It'll be a long day.'

'Get me one too, Maurice,' Anderson said.

'Slice cake with it?'

Anderson boggled. 'You what? Turn you stone blind.'

McLaren shrugged and hurried off.

Atherton shoved the newspaper into his drawer and unfurled his elegant height to the vertical. 'He probably thought you meant DiCaprio,' he observed to Slider.

The park keeper, Ken Whalley, was in the interview room, his hands wrapped round a mug of tea as if warming them on a cold winter's day. He had a surprisingly pale face for an outdoor worker, pudgy and nondescript, with strangely formless features, as if he had been fashioned by an eager child out of pastry but not yet cooked. Two minutes after turning your back on him it would be impossible to remember what he looked like. Perhaps to give himself some distinction he had grown his fuzzy brown hair down to his collar where it nestled weakly, having let go the top of his head as an unequal struggle.

He looked desperately upset, which perhaps was not surprising. However un-mangled this particular corpse was, it was one more than most people ever saw in a lifetime, and finding it must have been unsettling.

Slider, sitting opposite, made himself as unthreatening as possible. 'So, tell me about this morning. What time did you arrive at the park?'

Whalley looked up over the rim of the mug like a victim. He had those drooping lower lids, like a bloodhound, that showed the red, which made him look more than ever pathetic. 'I've already told the other bloke all about it,' he complained. 'Back at the park. I told the copper first, and then I had to tell that plain-clothes bloke an' all.'

'I know, it's a pain the way you'll have to keep repeating

the story,' Slider sympathised, 'but I'm afraid that's the way it goes. This is a murder investigation, you know.' Whalley flinched at the 'M' word and offered no more protest. 'What time did you arrive?'

Whalley sighed and yielded. 'Just before a'pass seven. I'm supposed to open up at a'pass.'

'At the South Africa Road end?' A nod. 'And what time did you leave home?'

He seemed to find this question surprising. At last he said, as if Slider ought to have known, 'But I only live across the road. I got a flat in Davis House. Goes with the job.'

'I see. All right, when you got there, were the gates open or shut?'

'Shut. They was shut,' he said quickly.

'And locked? How do you lock them?'

'With a chain and padlock.'

'And were the chain and padlock still in place, and locked?'

'Yeah, course they were,' Whalley said defensively.

'And what about the Frithville Gardens end?'

'I never went down there. Once I saw that bloke in the playground I just rang you lot, and then I never went nowhere else.' He looked nervously from Slider to Atherton and back. 'Look, I know what you're thinking. You're thinking I never locked up properly last night.'

'I didn't say that.'

'Well I did. I done everything right, same as always. It's not my bleedin' fault 'e got done!'

'All right, calm down. Nobody's accusing you of anything,' Atherton said. 'We just need to get it all straight, that's all. Once we've got your statement written down we probably won't need to bother you again.'

Whalley seemed reassured by this. 'All right,' he said at last, putting the mug down and wiping his lips on the back of his sleeve. 'What j'wanna know?'

'Tell me about locking up last night,' Slider said. 'What time it was, and exactly what you did.'

'Well, it was about a'pass nine. I'm s'pose to lock up at dusk, which is generally about arf hour after sunset, but it's up to me. I generally lock up earlier in winter, 'cause there's not so many people about. It's a cut-through, but there's no lights in the park, so we can't leave it open after dark. Course, people still want to take the short cut, and they used to bunk over the gate, so we had them new gates put on down the Frithville end, with all the pointy stuff on top.'

Slider had seen them: irregular metal extrusions, vaguely flame-shaped, topped the high gates, looking as if they were meant for decoration but in fact a fairly good deterrent. Of course, a really determined person could climb over anything, but the flames prevented 'bunking' – hitching oneself up onto one's stomach and then swinging the legs over – which would deter the casual cutter-through.

Whalley went on, 'But in summer it stays light longer and it depends what I'm doing what time I shut up. But anyway, I went over a'pass nine with the chains and padlocks. What I do, I shut the South Africa gate but I don't lock it, then I walk through telling everyone it's closing. Then I lock the Frithville gate, and walk back, make sure everyone's out, then lock the South Africa gates.'

'And that's what you did last night?'

There were beads of sweat on Whalley's upper lip. 'That's what I'm telling you, inni? I did everything just like normal and then I went home.'

'Have you ever seen deceased before?'

'No, I never seen him before in me life,' Whalley said emphatically. 'I don't know who he is, and that's the truth.' He wiped his lips again.

'Did you see him in the park anywhere before you locked up?'

'What, j'fink I wouldn't a noticed a bleedin' dead body?' Whalley said indignantly.

'No, I meant did you see him alive? Was he hanging around, perhaps?'

'I dunno. No, I never.'

'Was there anyone in the park who took your notice? Anyone unusual or suspicious-looking?'

Whalley drew up his shoulders and spread his hands defensively. 'Look, I don't go checking up on people,' he whined. 'It's not my job. I just go through telling 'em it's closing. Everyone was out before I locked up, that's all I know. You can't put it on me. F' cryin' out loud!'

'It's just,' Slider said gently, 'that you said you didn't go down to the Frithville gate this morning, but when one of our constables went down there, there was no padlock and chain. The gates were shut, but they weren't locked.'

Whalley stared a long time, his lips moving as if rehearsing his answer. Then at last he licked them and said, 'Someone must've took 'em.' Slider waited in silence. Whalley looked suddenly relieved. 'Yeah, someone must've cut through 'em. You could cut that chain all right with heavy bolt-cutters.'

Walking away from the interview room, Atherton eyed his boss's thoughtful frown and said, 'Well?'

'Well?' Slider countered. 'How did you like Mr Whalley?'

'Thick as a whale sandwich, and more chicken than the Colonel. What did you think of him?'

'I don't like it when they start supplying answers to questions they've no business answering,' Slider said.

'That stuff about bolt-cutters?'

'If you were breaking into the park for nefarious purposes, would you bother to take the padlock and chain away with you? Or having cut through them, would you just leave them lying where they fell?'

'I see what you mean. So you think Whalley's lying? He's nervous enough.'

'In his position I'd be nervous, whether I was lying or not. When a corpse is found on your watch it doesn't bode well even if you're innocent. It's possible he merely forgot to lock the gates, and doesn't want to admit it in view of the consequences.'

'Point.'

'The other possibility is that he's in on it in some way. But what "it" is, we can't know until we can find out who deceased is.'

'Well, I can't see Whalley as a criminal conspirator,' Atherton said. 'He's a pathetic little runt.'

'I expect you're right. It's just the padlock and chain not being there that bothers me. Our corpse was too nattily dressed for climbing over gates. Especially gates with pointy bits on the top.'

'You think he had an appointment in the park?'

Slider shrugged. 'Whatever he went there for, he went there. Alive or dead, he went through one of the gates or over it, and I can't make myself believe in over.'

CHAPTER TWO

Opening the Male

In the post-mortem room of the hospital's pathology department, Freddie Cameron, the forensic pathologist, presented to the world an appearance as smooth as a race-horse's ear. It was his response to the unpleasantness of much of his work to cultivate an outward perfection. His suiting was point-device, his linen immaculate; his waist-coat was a poem of nicely calculated audacity and his bow-tie *du jour* was crimson with an old gold spot.

All this loveliness, of course, was concealed as soon as he put on the protective clothing, but still he was positively jaunty as he shaped up to the corpse.

'Anything's better than facing another pair of congested lungs, old bean,' he said when Slider queried his pleasure. 'I'm even beginning to eye my bath sponge askance. This flu epidemic seems to have gone on for ever. Good to see you back,' he added to Atherton. 'Good holiday? You're looking very juvenile and jolly.'

'Fully functioning on all circuits,' Atherton admitted.

'So, you've no ID on our friend here?' Cameron asked.

'Not so far,' Slider said.

'Well, I'll take the fingerprints for you, and a blood sample. Chap looks a bit tasty, to my view.'

'I agree. Everything about him suggests there's a good chance he'll feature somewhere in our hall of fame.'

'Right. Well, as soon as my assistant arrives, we'll begin. Ah, here she is. Sandra, this is my old friend Bill Slider. Sandra Whitty.'

Slider shook hands. She was an attractive young woman, sensationally busted under her lab coat. Her lovely profile preceded her into a little pool of held breath which had gathered round the table; broken a moment later as McLaren muttered fervently, 'Blimey, she takes up a lot of room!'

Why is it we're all so childish about bosoms, Slider wondered. He wasn't immune himself. Charlie Dimmock had a lot to answer for. He met Miss Whitty's eye apologetically. 'Excuse the reptile.'

Fortunately, she only looked amused. 'That's all right, I keep pets myself.'

She obviously knew what she was doing, and handled the body with an easy strength as she and Freddie removed the clothing and put it into the bags McLaren held out. There was nothing in any of the pockets to identify the deceased. One jacket pocket yielded cigarettes – Gitanes, a rather surprising choice – and a throwaway lighter. The other contained a quantity of change and a crumpled but clean handkerchief. The inside jacket pocket contained a fold of notes held with a elastic band. When McLaren unfolded and counted them, it came to over a thousand pounds, in fifties, twenties and tens.

'Now there's a thing you don't see every day,' Freddie said. He breathed in deeply. 'Ah, money! I can almost smell the mint.'

'Evidently robbery from the person was not a factor,' Atherton said.

'But there's no wallet, driving licence, credit card, or any of the gubbins a man carries about,' Slider said. 'Was he unusually self-effacing, or did the murderer cop the lot?'

'If he did, why wouldn't he take the money?' Freddie added. 'Only fair, after taking the trouble to kill the chappie.'

'I'd have taken the jacket,' Atherton said. 'It's a lovely piece of leather. I wonder where he got it?' He looked at the label sewn inside just under the collar. '"Emporio Firenze",' he read. 'Never heard of them. Still, it's very nice.'

'Nice watch, too,' Sandra said.

'Is that a Rolex?' Atherton asked, leaning forward.

'It only thinks it is,' she said succinctly. 'Good fake, though. Date, phases of the moon, two different time zones, alarm, stopwatch function and integral microwave oven and waffle maker. Not cheap.'

'How do you know so much about men's watches?'

'I've handled a few,' she said. Slider could see Atherton working it out and felt a mild urge to kick him. When it came to women he had all the self-restraint of an Alsatian puppy on a bowling green.

'Look here, Bill,' Freddie said a moment later. 'Someone has been into the pockets. You see here, the left inside pocket is stained with blood where it rested against the wound. Now, over here, a tiny smear of blood on the *right* inside pocket. Someone's checked the contents of the left pocket and then transferred the blood on his fingers to the right.'

'While looking for something,' said Slider.

'Which presumably he found,' Atherton added. 'Any chance of a fingerprint?'

'I'll have a look under the microscope, but I wouldn't hold my breath,' Freddie advised. 'It's a very tiny smear.'

When the jumper was removed, it revealed a tattoo on the right forearm.

'Nice,' Sandra commented tartly. It portrayed a plump red heart with a steel-blue dagger thrust through it. There was a realistic drip of blood falling from the tip of the dagger, and around the heart was wrapped one of those heraldic ribbon scrolls bearing the word 'Mary'. It was an unpleasant and disturbing combination of sentiment and violence. 'Mary's a lucky girl,' Sandra said.

'It may help to identify him,' Slider said.

Atherton was not impressed. 'He could have got it done anywhere, any time.'

'Not any time,' Cameron said. 'I'd say it was quite recent – within the last couple of years.'

'All right, but anywhere. If we've got to start trawling the tattoo parlours of the world—'

'It's better than nothing,' Slider said.

'Not by much.'

Slider knew what he meant. A tattoo was a bit like finger-prints – good for confirming an identity when you already knew who you had; but for plucking an identity out of the void, it was as useful as a fishing net on a stick for retrieving a ring you'd dropped over the side of the cross-Channel ferry.

When the body was naked, Cameron made his external examination, reporting as he went. There was a little click every time he activated the tape recorder by means of the foot button; that and his cultured voice were the only sounds that disturbed the hum of the air conditioning. Slider thought it was a bit like being in his office, with the coo of a pigeon on the windowsill and the murmur of traffic outside. Strangely soporific. He found himself drifting a little.

'Deceased is male Caucasian, height five feet eleven, age apparently mid-thirties. He appears to be well nourished and in good health. Good musculature. No skin lesions, no surgical scars. No sign of any drugs usage.'

He measured and described the knife wound in the chest, and continued, 'No other visible wounds. Some evidence of bruising on the left side of the jaw, on the left upper arm and to the knuckles of the right hand. Bruising is not fully developed, suggesting that it was inflicted a short time before death.'

Slider jerked back to the present. 'What sort of bruising?' he asked when the recorder clicked off.

'Looks as if he was in a scrap of some sort. This one on the arm, you see, shows the shape of knuckles: one, two, three lobes and a fainter fourth, the little finger, which has less impact because of the curve of the fist. A right-handed punch, delivered with great force.'

Slider looked, recreating it. 'Probably turning away slightly, fielding it on his arm instead of his face.'

'Well, that should help us identify him,' McLaren said. 'A man with a tattoo who was in a fight.'

'Narrows the field wonderfully,' Atherton agreed.

'Right,' said Cameron, 'let's open him up. Mints, Sandra.'

Sandra Whitty pulled out of her pocket the obligatory tube of Trebor and passed them round. Reaching for his long scalpel, Cameron began to whistle softly, a habit he hardly knew he had. The tune, Atherton recognised after a moment, was 'Some Enchanted Evening'. Whistling, he slipped in the blade and opened the body like a man opening his mail.

A post-mortem is not a pleasant thing to witness, and it was good to have something else to focus on at partic-ular moments. Slider found the lyricism of Miss Whitty's moving torso very soothing. It was plain to Slider that she was quite well aware of the effect she was having. He liked a woman to enjoy her own prowess – why not? – but he couldn't help thinking that it was not the best thing for a newly revitalised Atherton to be exposed to. *One* of them ought to have his mind on the job.

'Well, what can I tell you?' Freddie Cameron said at last, with a certain sympathy in his eye.

'Some good news,' Slider said.

'If I had any of that, I'd open a shop,' Cameron said. 'Deceased died from a single stab wound from a double-edged, narrow blade, about five inches long, maybe longer – there's always a certain amount of compression – which penetrated the heart. There's no sign of any chronic disease or any other contributory cause.'

'And there wouldn't have needed to be?'

'Oh, no. That wound is quite sufficient. Death would have been instantaneous.'

'There's no reason to think he was poisoned or drugged, is there?'

'Nothing in the pathology. The stomach contents are well digested. It looks as if he hadn't eaten for several hours, though I fancy he had a pint not too long before death. Do you want them analysed?'

'Not at the moment. There's the budget to think about, and we might have to have the DNA analysed. Any way of telling whether he was killed where we found him or moved after death?'

'Not really. The hypostasis is consistent with the way he was found, but as you know it can be two or three hours before it settles, and even if the body is moved after it appears, it may well slip down to the new position anyway.'

'And the time of death?'

'Well, old dear,' Freddie said cheerfully, 'I can give you an educated guess. Based on the temperature, I'd say anything up to eight hours before I first saw him.'

'That means some time after midnight,' Slider said. 'I could have told you that.'

'But it could have been earlier,' Freddie went on, ever more cheerfully. 'He was a muscular chap, and it wasn't a cold night; and if he'd been kept bundled up or in a sheltered position – indoors, or in the boot of a car, for instance – he wouldn't have cooled so quickly.'

'I can't think,' Slider said with dignity, 'why they call it forensic *science.*'

'Ah, if only I were a fictional character,' Freddie said, 'I could take one squint and tell you he died at exactly twenty to three on Tuesday-was-a-week.'

'If *he* were a fictional character,' Slider capped him, 'his watch would have stopped at the moment of death and I wouldn't have had to ask you.'

Freddie took pity on him. 'Absolutely best guess, between four and eight hours. But don't quote me. And if you finally discover he was done at eleven pm or five am, don't come crying foul to me.'

'King Death hath ass's ears,' Slider said.

'Sounds like one of those tongue twisters. "The Leith poleeth dismisseth us." Not easy to say with a mint in your mouth.'

'Well, guys and gals, the bad news is that the fingerprints have come up with no match. Our deceased friend has no previous.'

There was a murmur. Atherton, sitting on a desk contemplating his shoes, said, 'I must say that does surprise me. He looked like a villain.'

'Maybe he was a successful villain,' said DC Swilley. Her given name was Kathleen, but for phonetic reasons, as well as her ability to look after herself, she had always been known as Norma. For as long as Slider had known her she had been engaged to a man called Tony whom no-one had ever met. Swilley had always been reticent about him to the point of mystery; some – generally those who had tried to make her and failed – had even said he did not exist. Then a couple of months ago she had electrified the department by actually getting married. Tony's surname turned out to be Allnutt, and it had not taken much agonising for Swilley to decide to keep her maiden name while she was in the job. Life was hard enough, even for a tall, Baywatch blonde like her, without adding unnecessary problems.

Atherton for some reason had been very upset about Swilley getting married. He had told Slider he couldn't bear to think of any man defiling her. Slider had pointed out that Mr Allnutt had of a certainty been defiling her for years, but Atherton claimed illogically that she was different since the wedding: less unattainably godlike, somehow diminished. Annoyingly, Slider knew what he meant. There was a strange ordinariness to Mrs Allnutt, a glow of domestic contentment, which was like polished pewter to her previous burnished silver. He didn't, however, go as far as Atherton and blame her for it.

So when Swilley said, 'Maybe he was a successful villain,' Atherton immediately contradicted her.

'There's no such thing.'

'Don't be such a dick,' Swilley said impatiently. 'Of course there is.'

'Criminals are basically stupid. They always give themselves away in the end. We'd have had him through our hands.'

'Yes, and if we'd had to let him go for lack of evidence or whatever, he wouldn't have a record and the prints would've been destroyed,' Swilley pointed out.

'Well, if that's what you call successful—'

'Children, can you wait until playtime if you want to quarrel,' Slider said. 'Now, I must say I was rather counting on a record to identify him. What we're left with is a blood sample which we could have checked against the DNA database, but that's expensive and—?' He looked round like a friendly lecturer.

'If he's got no fingerprint record, there'll be no DNA record,' Mackay filled in obligingly.

'Give that man a coconut. If all else fails we may have to fall back on his dental profile—'

'God forbid,' Atherton said. 'He was pre-fluoride. The bastard had teeth like Madeira cake.'

'It can take months to get a match on dental,' Mackay said.

'Exactly. So before we tread that despairing route, there are other things to do.'

'Mispers,' McLaren suggested.

'It's probably a bit early for that, but check it anyway. And meanwhile, we do it the hard way. Knock on doors, show his face and the tattoo, until we find someone who recognises him.' There was a composite moan. 'Start with the flats and houses nearest the two park gates and work outwards. You know and I know that it's twelve to seven he wasn't from outer space or the Outer Hebrides. He'll have been a local, and chances are he's used the park before for whatever he was using it for.'

'What if he was dumped there dead?' Anderson said.

'Well, that's probably even better from our point of view. It's impossible to move a large dead body around without somebody noticing something. But it's my belief he went to the park alive and was killed on the spot – for the same reason, that it would be a ludicrously difficult place to dump him without being seen.'

'Guv,' said McLaren, 'he was stabbed, had all his ID lifted, but his money left, and no attempt made to conceal the body. That looks like a punishment thing, dunnit? Or a gang thing. He was involved in something and they caught up with him, sorted him, and left him there as an example.'

'That's one theory.'

'I just can't see why they didn't take the wonga,' McLaren urged. 'Who's gonna leave well over a K in folding when it's sitting up and begging to be took?'

Mackay agreed. 'We've got Doc Cameron's evidence that his pockets were gone through, so it can't just be they missed it. But if it was a punishment thing, why not take it anyway?'

'To make it scarier,' Atherton said.

'What?' Swilley challenged derisively.

He shrugged. 'A villain who's not interested in money? It scares the shit out of me.'

'All right, let's get on with it,' Slider intervened. 'While we've got all the uniform help with the doorstepping, I'd like you people to try for a short cut. That's pubs, clubs, cafés, anywhere you can think of on our ground that the lowlife gather – remembering that he might only have been a fringe player. Don't forget your snouts – they're probably the likeliest to know him. Swilley, get the pictures off to the other boroughs. Most likely he's local but he might have strayed at some time or other: it's not as if we've got border control. McLaren, check Mispers. Atherton, have a go at our own dear Criminal Intelligence System to see if there are any matches on single stab wounds to the heart or anything connected with the park. And,' he added through the scrape and rustle of troops rising, 'let's not forget the obvious. Show the pictures to our own. Who's on downstairs?'

'Paxman,' someone said.

'Oh, well, he knows everyone who's ever lived. I think I'll pop down and have a word with him myself.'

Sergeant Paxman was a great solid bull of a man, his curly poll growing a little grizzled now, like an elderly Hereford. He had a bull's massive stillness too, a complete lack of fidget, which spread out around him in waves. It made him invaluable when they brought in belligerent drunks or drug addicts with the screaming abdabs: in a room full of thrashing arms and legs he was a kinetic black hole.

His relationship with Slider had sometimes been uneasy. Paxman was a devout Methodist and disliked any form of moral laxity, particularly in policemen, who he felt ought to set an example to society at large. PCs on his relief tended to find themselves getting married to the people they were living with almost without their own volition. His current favourite in the Department was Norma, whom he favoured, when she passed him, with his rare smile.

Slider had once been one of Paxman's okays, but he had fallen from grace when his marriage to Irene broke up and he went to live with Joanna, who had been a witness in one of his cases. Paxman would never say anything, of course, but his disapproval of hanky-panky spread around him in the same palpable ripples as his stillness. However, Irene had remarried, and Joanna had gone abroad. She was a professional violinist and had been offered a lucrative and prestigious position in an orchestra based in Amsterdam. With work so scarce at home, she had felt she had to take it. Slider missed her with a horrible hollow sucking emptiness; but at least now that he was living alone, hankiless and without a shadow of panky, he thought he had detected a breath of rehabilitation with Paxman.

Paxman stared at the photographs for a long time, stationary as a ton of paper. Slider waited, feeling the dust of aeons sifting down on him, soft and implacable. Then at last the sergeant lifted his head and said, 'No. I don't know him. Not been through my hands. But you said he'd been in a barney?'

'Apparently. He was sporting some knuckle bruises.'

'Hm. Well, there was a bit of a frackarse last night down at the Phoenix.'

'Really?' This was the pub in South Africa Road, a little way along from the park gates. 'Who went down there?'

'Oh, we weren't called,' Paxman said. 'It wasn't anything major. Just a bit of a barney. Two blokes throwing punches. Over before it started sort o' thing. Dunno if it's anything to do with your bloke.'

Slider wondered, if the police weren't called, how Paxman knew about it; but the question would probably only be answered with a shrug, so he didn't ask it. Sometimes he thought even Paxman didn't know how he knew things. Osmosis, probably.

'Well, thanks, Arthur,' he said. 'It might well be something. I'll point one of my lads at it.'

'Right,' said Paxman. He laid an enormous hand over the photos. 'I'll keep these, show 'em around. You never know.'

You never did, Slider agreed. 'And pass them on when the relief changes? Thanks.'

In the event, Slider went down to the Phoenix himself. He wanted another look at the immediate surroundings. The

White City was a large estate of five-storey blocks of council flats, built in the thirties. It had originally been created to be a complete community, with its own shops, park, playground and public house, the General Smuts. However in the sixties there had been a small expansion on its southeastern border, where the new park had been opened; and there an infant school, another row of shops and a second pub had been added.

Created in that unloved period of architecture, the Phoenix was everything a pub didn't ought to be, a featureless pale-brick box with picture windows. It inspired no affection or loyalty as a local, and almost from the beginning the rougher types had been tempted there. Now most of the picture windows had been bricked up to avoid temptation, and the interior was as dark as an American bar – so dark the security cameras Slider noted at the angles of the ceiling must have worked on infra-red. The prevailing design motif was the avoidance of anything that could be picked up and thrown. The bar stools and tables were bolted to the floor and the only other seating was the banquettes round the walls, covered in red leatherette gaping open to its foam filling in numerous wounds. The brewery that owned it had recently yielded to this fashion trend and restocked with plastic beer glasses. It was that sort of pub.

On this sunny day, however, it was peaceful. The door was standing open to let some light into the interior, and the three customers it could boast were sitting up at the bar over their pints not bothering anyone. The landlord was a moody-looking bald man with a glass eye. He looked about fifty, but was mega fit for it, with a weightlifter's vast shoulders and nipped-in waist, which he emphasised by wearing a clinging black teeshirt and jeans with a heavy

leather belt cinched tight in between. The fact that he was
only five foot six somehow made him seem more, rather
than less, dangerous, as a terrier is more unnerving than
a Great Dane.

His name, according to the licence notice over the door,
was Colin Collins – which Slider reckoned was enough to
jaundice a man from earliest childhood – but he was always
known as Sonny. Slider assumed it was spelt with an 'o':
a 'u' would have been too needlessly cynical. He had old,
faded tattoos on his forearms and left biceps; and at some,
presumably drunken, point in his merry life he had had a
dotted line tattooed right round the base of his neck. In
the gloom of the far reaches of the bar his black-clad torso
was almost invisible, and his pale throat and gleaming ivory
head floated eerily above the dotted line as if someone had
already obeyed the implicit instruction to cut along it.

Slider introduced himself and passed the photographs
over the bar. Collins looked down at them with his good
eye, while the glass one continued to stare furiously at
Slider. It must be something that came in handy when
dealing with the obstreperous, Slider thought, and was
briefly beguiled by the memory of a story Tufty Arceneaux,
the forensic haematologist, had told him about his time in
Africa. It was about an up-country estate boss Tufty had
frequently drunk with, who had a glass eye. When he
couldn't be in two places at once the bloke used to take
the eye out and leave it to supervise, the natives believing
that he could thus see what was going on *in absentia*. Once
a man had been brought to him for discipline, but he had
been called away urgently in the middle of the interview,
so he had left his glass eye on the desk and told the man
to stay put. In dealing with the emergency he had forgotten
to go back, and the miscreant had sat in the office facing

the eye for four days. His relatives had taken turns bringing him food and water.

Sonny Collins didn't take four days about it, but it seemed to Slider an uncomfortably long time to wait under the basilisk gaze. 'I understand there was a bit of a barney outside last night,' he prompted. 'Two men throwing punches. I wondered if this was one of the men.'

'Might be,' Sonny vouchsafed at last.

'Can you tell me about it,' Slider asked patiently.

'About what?'

'About the fight.'

Sonny shrugged, and his massive muscles manoeuvred about under his skin like Volkswagen Beetles trying to pass in an alley. 'Not much to tell. Two blokes started arguing.' He closed his mouth tightly after each sentence like someone switching off unnecessary lights to save electricity. 'One's throwing his lip. Effing and blinding. Told 'em to take it outside.'

'And they went.'

'In my pub,' Sonny Collins said, suddenly expansive, 'when I say take it outside, outside it goes.'

'I believe you,' Slider said, trying a bit of flattery. It melted Collins in the same way a one-bar electric fire melts a block of granite. Both eyes were as yielding as marbles as they stared at Slider. 'What time was this?' he asked, humbled.

'About closing time.'

'And what happened outside?'

'Didn't see it. Heard about it. Not much of a fight. Couple o' punches thrown. Then it all goes quiet.'

'And who were the two men? You think this was one of them? What's his name?'

Sonny Collins stared as if Slider were being irrational. '*I* don't know,' he said impatiently. 'He's not a regular.'

Slider picked up an inference Collins perhaps didn't intend him to. 'But the other man *is* a regular,' he said, not making it too much of a question. 'What's his name?'

Collins seemed to weigh the pros and cons of co-operation. At last he said, 'Eddie.'

'Eddie what?'

The impatience again. 'You don't ask surnames,' he said. 'Pub like this, you don't ask names at all. Heard him called Eddie, that's all. Lives local. Comes in two, three times a week. That's it. That's all I can tell you.'

'And this other bloke,' Slider said, gesturing to the photograph, 'had you seen him before?'

Collins shrugged. 'May have. He looks a bit familiar. That's all I can tell you.'

'Can you describe this Eddie?'

'Tall, dark hair. Fancies himself. Always talking about how many women he's had.' Collins grew impatient. 'Is that it? Only I can't stand chatting to you all day. I got customers to serve.'

None of the other three people in the pub had moved a muscle since Slider had entered. They hunched over their half-empty glasses like three Mystic Megs staring into their crystal balls. Slider thought Collins knew more than he was telling, but he knew he wouldn't get any more out of him now, and if he pushed him it would spoil the chances of getting more next time. With naturally irritable people like him, going against their grain could be counter-productive.

CHAPTER THREE

A Load of Crystal Balls

'You should have let me go,' Atherton said.

'He wouldn't have told you even as much as he told me,' Slider said.

'Why not?' asked Atherton, ready to be offended.

'Because you're tall and he's short. That's psychology,' Slider added kindly. 'So we've got our man having a fist fight outside the pub some time after eleven, and being stabbed in the park a few dozen yards away at any time between then and seven-thirty the next morning.'

'The obvious inference is that they took the quarrel, whatever it was, into the park, and it turned to murder.'

'Hmm. But I always like to resist the obvious,' Slider said. 'And it wasn't the South Africa gate that was unlocked, it was the Frithville gate.'

'That could be nothing to do with it. You said yourself Ken Whalley might just have forgotten to lock up.'

'Yes, and that's more likely than that someone cut through the lock and chain and then carried them away,' Slider said.

'I wish you wouldn't always argue both sides at once,' Atherton complained. 'Still, the simplest solution is that Eddie and deceased had a row, deceased maybe got scared and legged it, nipped over the gate into the park, Eddie followed, caught him up in the playground, and stabbed him.'

'Except that with that gate, you wouldn't be doing any nipping. Climbing carefully would be the order of the day. And if he was running away from a homicidal Eddie he'd make better time sprinting along the road. Eddie must have been right behind him, and he'd have been able to grab him before he got over the gate.'

'You don't know that. Anyway, fear lends wings. Stuffed full of adrenalin, he might have nipped.'

'Fear would have had to lend him a lot of luck, too, not to have torn his clothes on those pointy bits. Anyway, if he did climb over the gate he will have left his fingermarks on it somewhere, so we'll soon know.'

'As will Eddie. Unless they were wearing gloves.'

'Yes, a wise man always puts gloves on to have a fight outside a pub.'

'I get the feeling,' Atherton said with dignity, 'that you aren't taking my suggestions seriously.'

'Oh, did you mean me to?' McLaren appeared in the doorway. 'Yes, what is it?'

McLaren looked pleased with himself. 'Guv, I've had a nibble!'

'Must we discuss your sex life?'

'The betting shop just up the road – corner of Loftus and Uxbridge Road. They recognised the mugshot *and* the tattoo.'

'Betting shop? That was a good idea of yours. What made you think of it?'

McLaren writhed slightly. 'Well, I didn't exactly – I was just passing and I thought—'

'All right,' Slider said hastily. If McLaren had gone in to

place a bet while on duty Slider didn't want to have to
know about it just now. Later, when all this was over . . .
'So they recognised him.'

'Yeah, they said he used to be a heavy punter until about
a year ago. In every day, got through a shitload o' money.
Then he just stopped coming. They reckoned he either
gave it up or went elsewhere.'

'It took brains to work that out,' Atherton commented.

'Did they give him a name?' Slider asked.

'Said his name was Lenny. They called him Unlucky
Lenny. Said he was so unlucky, if Liz Hurley had triplets,
he'd be the one on the bottle. He was a foul-mouthed,
violent bastard an' all, they said, but he lost so much money
with 'em he was worth keeping. When he stopped coming
in they didn't know whether to be glad or sorry.'

'Lenny what?'

'Dunno, guv. That's all they knew, Lenny. But they said
he was local – lived somewhere local.'

'All right, it's a start, I suppose. You'd better get someone
to go round all the other betting shops in the area, see if
he changed allegiance.'

'I can do it,' McLaren offered.

'I wouldn't put you in temptation's way,' Slider said
kindly. 'Tell Anderson, will you? He's a steady chap.'

'As long as you don't send him to B&Q,' McLaren said
darkly, departing.

'So now we've got two people to look for,' Atherton said.
'The pony-mad Lenny and the woman-mad Eddie. Both
local and neither with a surname.'

'Sonny Collins said Eddie was a regular. I think there's
a case for someone going into the Phoenix tonight to see
if he comes in. No, not you,' he anticipated. 'It's got to be

someone who fits in at a dump like that. Better be Mackay,
I suppose.'

'I won't tell him you said that.'

The full report came in from Freddie Cameron, but he had
nothing to add to what had been said at the post-mortem.
'The weapon was a two-edged, non-serrated blade, about
five inches long and not more than three-quarters of an
inch wide, and with very little taper. The blow was given
with sufficient *force* to leave bruising where the hilt or cross-
guard struck the skin. However, it does not follow that
great *strength* was needed: if the point of the weapon were
sharp enough it would penetrate the skin relatively easily
and the rest of the blade would follow without effort. I
would estimate from the clean edges of the wound that the
point in this case was sharp.'

Slider put down the report and imagined the blade.
Straight and double-edged like a dagger, but only three-
quarters of an inch wide. It sounded like a flick-knife. Add
that to the pockets being searched and the money left and
it began to sound very much like a gang or professional
killing. And if there was one thing that depressed Slider
more than another it was gang killings.

He read on. The blood smear on the right inside pocket.
No hope of anything from that, it was too small for a fingerprint. Inkstain on the inside bottom of the same pocket.
Well, people did carry Biros about, though none was found
on the body.

The phone rang.

'Hullo,' said Joanna. 'I've been ringing you at home.
Wasted calls are expensive from Frankfurt, you know. What
are you still doing there?'

'We've had a murder.'

'Oh dear. I'm sorry to hear that.'

'You sound as if I said I'd got a headache.'

'I should think you have, figuratively.'

'Especially as the corpse is still unidentified. It's hard to find out who dunnit when you don't know who they dunnit to.'

'Still, you oughtn't still to be there. It's a quarter to nine, you know.'

'I've got a man out in a pub, trying to track down a drinker who was seen with deceased. It's a rough pub and I want to be on hand if he gets into trouble.'

'You're a loony,' she said affectionately. 'What're you going to do if he does, rush round and punch noses? That's a job for uniform.'

'I suppose so,' he said reluctantly, and then, 'I do miss you!'

'Me too,' she said briefly.

There was a silence, through which he heard a distant clash of voices. 'Where are you?'

'Backstage. We've just finished the first half. Beethoven fourth piano concerto. Sigmund Manteufel.'

'First half? You make it sound like a football match.'

'With a soloist like him it was like a football match.'

'What was the score?' he asked.

'Beethoven four, Manteufel nil. So now it's the interval. Wolfie's getting me a drink. I wish you were here. Even gin and tonic loses its savour.'

'How d'you think I feel? Going home to that empty flat—'

'Ah, now I know the real reason you're still there at this hour. Are Jim and Sue back?'

'Just. I spent the night there once while they were away,'

he confessed. 'On the sofa with the cats. Couldn't face going home to that big empty bed.'

He heard her sigh. 'Bill, you don't make this easy for me.'

'Who said I wanted to?' he answered, but he put a smile in his voice, not to pressure her too much.

'I'd better go,' she said. 'There's a queue waiting for the phone, and the interval's only twenty minutes. You do know why concert intervals are only twenty minutes, don't you?'

'Tell me, tell me,' he said obediently.

'So you don't have to retrain the violas.'

'I love you,' he said.

'I love you too.'

'Phone me tomorrow.'

'If I can get to a phone.'

'And watch out for that Wolf person.'

'Don't worry, Wolfie's not that sort of girl.'

'Ha!' he said. 'You forget, I've met him.'

It wasn't really, he thought as he put the phone down, that he was jealous or didn't trust her. His fear was that she could live without him much more easily than he could without her; and that if she got used to being away from him, she might eventually fall for someone else, especially if someone else was a musician. It was a thing that happened all too easily among people whose jobs isolated them from the rest of humanity, like musicians and policemen. You fell for someone you worked with, however unsuitable they were in every other respect, because they understood your way of life. They knew what you were talking about.

This job Joanna had taken with the Orchestra of the Age of the Renaissance was a permanent position, though she had taken it for the moment on a six-month trial. It was a very good job for her, too good to have turned it down – and not just from the money point of view: it was prestigious, and artistically satisfying as well. But could they continue their relationship on the basis of seeing each other once a month? Could that even be said to be a relationship?

He suddenly realised that he was very hungry – absolutely ravishing, as Porson might say – and that he was doing no-one any good sitting here by the phone, Mackay least of all. Nicholls, who was the uniformed sergeant in charge of the night relief, knew all about it and could be trusted to send in the infantry if there was any trouble – and why should there be, after all?

There was an all-night café under the railway arch next to Goldhawk Road Station where the taxi drivers noshed. Taxi drivers always knew the good places. He had a sudden, golden vision of sausage, egg, chips and beans, tea and a slice, and his mouth watered. Atherton would shudder with horror at the thought, but Atherton had Sue. A man whose love was in Frankfurt needed the comfort only a greasy fry-up could provide.

Morning brought disappointment. Mackay had manfully done his duty and consumed four pints of deeply indifferent beer, but no-one who might be Eddie had shown up, and the other drinkers with whom he had managed to scrape up a conversation had shown blank incomprehension when presented with the names Eddie and Lenny or the suggestion that there had been a fight.

'I don't know whether they clocked me for a copper and that shut 'em up, or they're just naturally stupid,' he said. 'Bit of both, I expect. I couldn't push it too hard or ask too directly or the barman would've clocked me and that would've been that. Maybe if I went in a few more times, built up a pattern, they might open up.'

'I hate to put anyone's innards through that punishment, but it might be necessary,' Slider said. 'Hold yourself in readiness. Anything from anyone else?'

It all added up to a big, fat zero. 'Nobody jumped at the mugshot or the tattoo,' Norma summed up. 'And my snouts deny all knowledge.'

'Tattoo parlours in the area turn up blank,' said Hollis, 'but that's not surprising. There's no reason it had to be done locally. He could have had it done in Brighton on a day trip for all we know.'

'Nothing from the other betting shops in the area,' Anderson reported.

'Don't you think that *is* surprising?' Atherton said. 'Does a betting man just give up like that? McLaren's source seemed to be suggesting he was a heavy and regular punter.'

'Smokers give up. Alcoholics even. Why not a gambler?' Swilley said.

'I know it's possible,' Atherton countered, 'but is it likely?'

'There's offshore betting these days on the Internet,' McLaren put forward.

'Bit sophisticated for Laddo?' Atherton suggested.

'We don't know how sophisticated he was,' said Swilley.

'He had that swanky watch and that expensive jacket,' Hollis put in.

'Yes, what about that jacket?' Slider said. 'Any chance of tracing it to its source?' He looked at Atherton. 'You're the one who knows about clothes.'

'I don't recognise that brand name,' Atherton said. 'I doubt whether it was from this country, and if it was sourced abroad we'd never track it.'

'Have another look at it,' Slider said, 'and see what you can do. What else?'

'The door-to-door has come up with nothing so far,' Hollis said. His was the enviable task of overseeing the reports. 'The usual crop of mysterious strangers but nothing that looks like our man. Trouble is, that park isn't over-looked from anywhere in summer, when the trees are covered with leaves.'

'Except from the BBC building,' Swilley said.

'Only from the very top, which is a long way off for recognising anyone, even say someone was bothered looking; and even then, you can't see into the playground.' He met Swilley's raised eyebrows and added, 'Yes, I did go in and try. What did you think I was doing down there all day?'

'So our hope really is from someone who happened to be passing when Lenny went into the park,' she said.

'Or when – to stretch a point – someone carried his body in there,' Atherton added. 'What about the people living in Frithville Gardens?'

'Nothing so far,' Hollis said, 'though there's still some doors to knock on. Trouble is, it was late and most people are in bed by half past eleven.'

'What an indictment of the most exciting, frenetic, cosmopolitan city in the world,' said Atherton.

'Did you turn up anything on the CrimInt?' Slider asked him.

'Nothing to put in the diary.'

Slider rubbed his hair up the wrong way in frustration. 'I can't believe this bloke's never been in trouble before. Maybe we'll get a nibble from one of the other boroughs. Meanwhile, everybody keep asking around. Not just your snouts, but anyone you've ever had contact with who's local, or knows the area. Don't forget that the park is less than half a mile away, and Frithville Gardens is the next road along from here. It won't take the press long to start asking why we can't get a handle on a murder right in our own back yard.'

'I don't see why that's supposed to make it easier,' Swilley said indignantly.

'Police-bashing is their favourite sport,' Slider said. 'When has logic ever come into it?'

It was time, Slider thought, to follow his own advice and talk to a few of his contacts. It was something he had to do in person. In the Job, a man's snouts are sacrosanct; generally they would not talk to anyone else in any case. He had already tried a few phone calls to his usual informants, with no result. Now it was time to spread the net wider.

He bethought himself of One-Eyed Billy, a small-time thief who had latterly managed to pull himself together and go straight. He lived in one of the tiny Victorian terraces in Ethelden Road, but this time of day he ought to be at work; or rather – he checked his watch and registered with routine surprise that it was lunchtime already – in the British Queen having a pint of Bass and a pork pie. This, indeed, was exactly where Slider found him, sitting up at the bar with the paper folded open at the racing pages, pie and pickle part consumed, pint glass usefully almost empty, down to a golden half inch at the bottom and a white line like soapsuds marking the level before his last swig.

'Hello, Billy. What is it?'

He looked up sharply, registered Slider's presence and the absence of anyone at his shoulder, and answered the nod in the direction of his glass. 'My usual, ta very much. Pint o' Bass.'

Slider gestured to George the barman and did the honours. One-Eyed Billy watched him with slight reserve but no hostility. He had two perfectly good eyes to do it with. His name did not denote any ocular deficiency, but was a sort of patronymic, his father having been known as One-Eyed Harry, a well-known local trader with a pie-and-eel shop in Goldhawk Road. Harry had lost an eye in Korea, having been too young, to his intense regret, to be called up for the Second World War – 'the real war', he called it. 'Korea was a bloody mess,' he used to say, 'but dooty is dooty, and I'm proud to have served my Queen and country.' He always kept a framed picture of 'Her Maj' prominently on the wall of his shop and Mrs One-Eye had a large scrapbook of royal family cuttings; they prided themselves on being old-fashioned honest traders and had given generously to various charitable efforts got up by the police.

So it had been a dreadful shock to them when their youngest son, Billy, had turned out bad. Harry often said they must have dropped him on his head when he was a baby; Mrs One-Eye blamed the sixties. 'What a world for a lad to grow up in!' However it happened, Billy had early refused to show any interest in the family business, and had ducked out of helping in the shop. Harry had stopped his pocket money as a quid pro quo – 'You don't get anything in this world without working for it, my lad!' – to which challenge Billy had risen by stealing the sweets and comics he could not now buy.

The dropped-on-head theory gained ground with the gathering evidence that Billy was not just a thief, he was a very bad thief. His career developed, if that was the right word, into a succession of easy cops for the police; his villainy was so petty, so inept and so plain daft it was hard for them to take him seriously, and he was slapped on the wrist more times than was good for him. Slider well remembered the occasion when One-Eyed Harry came, in agony of soul, to ask them not to let Billy off any more. 'I reckon if he doesn't get a shock and see where it all leads, he'll be past hope. Me and Gladys are very grateful for what you've tried to do for our boy, but he's got to learn, the hard way if necessary. He's bringing shame on the whole family.'

So when Billy stole a Magimix from Curry's for his mum's birthday and was caught because he took it back to complain that one of the fixtures was missing, the boom was lowered on him, and he went down. The lesson did not immediately strike home. It took several more years, and sentences to a progressively longer spell in jug, before the shock of his mother's death (hastened by shame, his brothers said) changed his ways.

He was now employed by an uncle who had a greengrocer's stall in the Shepherd's Bush market, and was working off his forgiveness in this world by hard labour and co-operation, when it was asked for, with the police. His quick guilty glance beyond Slider's shoulder suggested that he was still up to something, but Slider thought it was probably something very mild and on the fringe, like illegal betting or buying hookey fags, which was best left alone. It was not so much turning a blind eye to crime, but the necessary price that had to be paid to have Billy just on the sticky side of the line that divided the real world from the criminal world, where he could be useful.

The pints came. Billy said, 'Cheese mite,' and drank off a good quarter, and Slider said, 'Well, Billy, how are you keeping?'

'Straight, Mr Slider,' Billy answered quickly. 'Straight as

a die, I promise you. Uncle Sam'd kill me if I wasn't.'

Slider smiled. The guilty man, etc. 'I didn't mean that. Are you well?'

'Gawd, yes. Never been ill in me life.' He was perhaps a little undersized, but stocky enough, with a curiously young face, given that he must be forty by now. It was smooth, almost unlined; small-featured, and pleasant enough under bristle-cut light brown hair, only a little vacuous, and with eyes that were just too far apart, which gave him a slightly glassy look, like a stuffed toy. 'Yourself?' he returned politely.

'Oh, I'm fine. Busy as always.'

'Yeah. This murder up the New Park.' This was what locals had always called it – to distinguish it, of course, from the old park, Wormholt. 'I've been reading about it.' He gestured vaguely towards the newspaper.

Slider saw that it was the *Daily Mail*. 'Bit up-market for you, isn't it?'

Billy smirked. 'I got this young lady now,' he said. 'Bit of a looker, she is, if I say it myself. She's dead posh. Works in that hairdressers on the Green, The Cut Above, it's called. Qualified and everything.'

'Good for you,' Slider said. 'Thinking of settling down?'

'Maybe,' he admitted. 'Anyway, she wants me to better meself, so she's started me reading this instead've the *Sun*.' He looked at the paper a bit hopelessly, and then said, 'Well, I never was one for reading. It's got the racing in it all right, though.'

'I didn't know you were a betting man,' Slider said. 'Fond of the ponies?'

'Oh, I always done a bit. It's an interest more than anything. Me mum didn't approve of betting, but she liked watching the races on the telly. Liked the horses. Same with me, really. Me uncle Sam what I work for now had a horse and cart when I was a kid, did a round on the White City estate. I used to like helping round the stable an' that.'

Slider took a leisurely drink of his pint, feeling Billy relax at this reassuring lack of hustle. 'Funny thing,' he said, 'this bloke that got murdered in the park, he was a betting man. I wonder if you've come across him any time. Unlucky Lenny, they called him.'

Billy chuckled. 'Unlucky Lenny? Gawd, yes! I've heard about him all right. Is that who it was?'

'Seems so.'

'Gaw, what a mug! Talk about good money after bad! Always picked the long odds, daft outsiders, mug doubles, you name it. And if he ever did pick a good 'un, it got scratched or fouled or fell down. He 'adn't got,' Billy added instructively, 'no science. If you're gonna bet on the ponies, you gotter have luck or you gotter have science, one or the other. He didn't have neither.'

'And what have you got?'

'Me? I don't do much, just a bob or two. It's more an interest, like I said. What I got is a sort of instinct. It comes over me every now and then, almost like I can see into the future. I look at a certain horse, and I just know. Then I stick a tenner on its nose and sit back. You'd be surprised how often it comes off.'

Slider would have been surprised. It sounded like crystal balls. In his experience betting men forgot their losses almost instantaneously, but remembered their wins for ever – a function which greatly improved their overall statistics and the bookies' profits. He took another drink and said casually, 'So about this Lenny – what was his surname?'

Billy shook his head. 'Now that I can't tell you. Never knew him personal. Everyone just called him Unlucky

Lenny. He used to punt at the shop on the corner o' Loftus Road. Just up the road from you,' he added on an after-thought.

'Yes, I know,' Slider said. 'Know anything else about him? What was he up to, Billy? He looked a bit tasty to me.'

'I dunno exactly, but he was up to something all right,' Billy said, flattered by the assumption of his omniscience. He desperately wanted to give value for money, and Slider could almost hear his brain creak as he strained to remember something worth delivering. 'I see him around the estate a bit,' he said at last.

'Is that where he lived?'

'I reckon he did. I dunno for sure.' A light went on inside his head. 'What I *do* know,' he said triumphantly, 'was he lived with a tom. What was her name? Tanya or Terry or something like that. No, Tina, that was it. Definitely. I heard some geezers talking about her.'

'She was a prostitute?'

'Oh yeah, she was definitely on the game. Lenny knew all about it.'

'Was he her pimp?'

'I dunno. Maybe. He wasn't a professional pimp, I don't mean that. He didn't have no other girls. I reckon he just lived with her. Maybe he like organised it for her. And got it for free himself – you know. They say she's a bit of a sort an' all. A cracker. Goes like a train.' He dropped a man-to-man wink. 'So maybe old Lenny wasn't so unlucky after all, eh?'

CHAPTER FOUR

Tart with a Heart

The tailor's shop was just off Shepherd's Bush Green – a few yards down a side turning, Caxton Street, which made all the difference to the rent and rates. It also made all the difference to the drop-in trade, but one glance at the window showed that drop-in was not the mainstay of this emporium.

Over the window was the name *Henry Samson* in chipped gold-painted plastic letters screwed to a black fascia. The window was exceedingly dirty and contained no display, only some bales of cloth wrapped in brown paper, a couple of old biscuit tins full of odds and ends, and three plastic roses in a vase *circa* 1973.

Atherton pushed the door open, and an old-fashioned bell on a strap tinkled pleasantly. It was dim inside after the sunshine in the street. The shop was tiny, and most of the space was taken up with the shelving round the walls on which bales of cloth were stored. A wooden counter with a glass front was covered in professional litter: scissors, tape measures, boxes of pins and a neglected sea of invoices, orders, correspondence and – probably – final demands from utility companies. The display element of the counter contained cardboard boxes of buttons and zip-fasteners. The tiny unused space in the middle of the floor revealed bare, dusty floorboards and a small square of old carpet on which the customer might stand to view himself in the cheval mirror which stood beside the curtain into the back shop.

The curtain moved now, and the proprietor poked his head out like a stage manager checking the House. The broad, fat, wrinkled old face creased into a smile of welcome, revealing the porcelain uniformity of the National Health's finest.

'Mr Atherton! Welcome, welcome! Just one moment and I'll be with you!'

The curtain dropped, there was a sitcom rustling and thumping of hasty activity, and then it was thrust aside with a rattle of curtain rings, and the tailor came out. His head had first come through the curtain at Atherton's level, but that was because he did his sewing in the back room sitting on a table (which kept the cloth off the dusty floor). Now he was on his own two legs his head was hardly more than five feet from the ground; but what he lacked in height he made up for in girth. He was wide all the way round, with tiny feet and quick, pudgy hands; rimless half-glasses poised halfway down his nose; surprisingly fine eyebrows, and a scantling of hair combed carefully over his bald top and dyed soot black with a tailor's vanity. He wore old-fashioned striped morning trousers with a black waistcoat over a white shirt with the sleeves rolled up. The waistcoat glittered with the needles and pins thrust into both fronts, and a tape measure hung round his neck like a garland of honour.

He advanced, beaming, on Atherton, his hand out, and when Atherton gave his, enfolded it in both his own and pumped it up and down rhythmically as if he hoped for water. 'Good to see you! Good to see you! Are you well? You look well.'

'I'm in the pink, thank you,' Atherton said. 'I don't need to ask you how you are.'

'Never better!' the tailor cried boastfully. 'I'm never ill, you know. Hard work is the best medicine.'

His name was James Mason ('No relation!' he cried gaily on first introduction) but since he had escaped with an older sister from Germany during the war, that almost certainly was not his real name. He admitted to seventy-five, but Atherton would not have been surprised to discover he was eighty-five. With the wrinkles, the vitality and the swift, plump movements it was impossible to tell.

'So what does my favourite customer want this morning?' Mr Mason asked, relinquishing Atherton's hand and drawing the tape measure off his neck with anticipatory relish. 'Favourite customer' was less of a hyperbole than usual with such titles. There was a small group of cognoscenti who treasured Mr Mason as he should be treasured, but he eked out a living with alterations and repairs to clothes it pained him to handle. 'You've come at just the right time, as it happens. I have some cloth here – come, come and see. Let me show you. Just came in this morning, and I thought of you right away.'

He twinkled over to the window and heaved a wrapped bale, with astonishing strength given that it was nearly as tall as him, off the stack and over to the counter, dumping it on top of the clutter with a fine disregard for administration. Quickly he unfolded the brown paper and drew out a length of the cloth. 'Look, look how beautiful. Feel. Lovely, isn't it? I wish I could get more of it, but I thought of you first. I said to myself, "Mr Atherton must have a suit out of this. A pair of trousers, at the very least."'

Atherton stepped forward to finger the cloth. It was charcoal grey with a faint stripe which was not colour but merely in the weave. Mason gazed up into his face, nodding and beaming.

'Yes? Beautiful, isn't it?'

'What is it?'

'You tell me.'

'It's very soft,' Atherton suggested.

'But very hard-wearing. It's a mixture, of course. Wool, cashmere – mostly cashmere – and just a little mink.'

'Mink?' Atherton said, bemused.

'I joke you not. Very hard, mink hair. Cashmere alone would not cope with all the sitting. But mink—!' His eyes screwed up with anticipation of a coming jest. 'When did you ever see a ferret with a bald patch?'

Atherton laughed dutifully, and prepared to break his tailor's heart. 'It's very nice, but I'm afraid I didn't come here for anything to wear.'

Mason took it well. He knew Atherton's calling. He spread his hands a little and said, 'Sandwiches I don't do, it must be information.'

'That's right.' He brought the leather jacket out of the bag he had carried it in, and held it out. 'I hoped you could tell me where this came from.'

Mason looked serious. 'Leather? Leather is something else. I am not an expert on leather.' But he took it anyway, his fingers seeming to do their own examination, separately from his eyes. 'Nice, nice quality skin. Off the shelf, of course, but the tailoring not bad, all the same. An expensive piece, I would say.' He turned to the inside. 'Good-quality wool lining.' It was tartan, but of no clan or sept known to Scotland: a mixture of caramel, cream and milk-chocolate shades. Subtle and attractive.

Mason examined the label, and snorted. 'Not Italian, of course! All the world wants Italian this, Italian that. Why? I can't tell you. Italian food, Italian wine, yes, but when did you ever hear of an Italian tailor? Mean jackets, tight trousers, shoes too narrow – you want to look like a barrow boy? So choose Italian. You want to look like a gentleman . . .' He left a space there for his most generous shrug.

'If not Italian, what is it?' Atherton asked patiently.

'American,' Mason said promptly. 'The cut, the quality of the stitching. And the name I've heard of before.' He examined the two tiny tags sewn into the seams near the bottom. 'North-east America. These code numbers you get in New England, stock control. Not for export.'

'So it was probably bought over there?'

'Yes, but they sell such things also in PX stores. That's export as far as we're concerned, but to an American the PX is United States soil.'

'I see. Well, thank you. I knew you'd be able to pin it down for me.'

'Does it help?' The bright eyes scanned his face keenly.

'I don't know that it does,' Atherton said. Purely in the name of thoroughness he drew out the photographs and showed them to the tailor.

'He's dead, nuh?' Mason said, looking closely at the mugshot. 'It was him who wore the jacket? No, I don't know him. And the tattoo – very few people with tattoos come to me. Or at least, not tattoos of that sort.'

'Ah well, I didn't think you would know him. Thanks anyway. At least I know he got the jacket from America.'

'Or maybe an American gave it to him,' Mason cautioned. 'In payment for a debt, maybe. He doesn't look the kind to get birthday presents. And now, from business to pleasure,' he went on beguilingly, displaying the cloth again. 'A pair of trousers, what do you say?'

'That's business, surely?'

'To make trousers for you is a pleasure,' Mason said seriously. 'I tell you no lie. A pure pleasure, Mr Atherton.'

'Getting information on this case is like pulling teeth,' Slider grumbled. 'Now we know that Lenny lived with Tina, but not where, and no surnames for any of the blasted crew. And an American jacket. Where does that get us?'

'Nowhere,' Atherton acknowledged. 'We don't know that they were never imported. Or he could have gone on holiday to America and brought it back. People do, all the time.'

'Or bought it in a pub from an American,' Norma added. She was leaning against the door-jamb of Slider's office, her arms folded across her chest like a housewife. Marriage had really changed her, Atherton thought. Any minute now she'd be getting a perm. 'Or from someone who nicked it from an American – that's more likely. So what now, boss?'

'We try and find a tom called Tina,' said Slider.

'Needle in haystack time,' Atherton commented.

'If this were Ruislip it might be worth investigating a possible American connection, but there are no bases near here,' Slider sighed.

'What about the cultural legation or whatever it's called in Holland Park?' Swilley said. 'That's only just up the road.'

'Culture?' Atherton said. 'A bloke called Unlucky Lenny who lives with a tom?'

'Maybe he provided a service of some kind. Even an embassy needs cleaners and dustbin men.'

'That's very profound, Norma.'

'All right, you can look into it,' Slider told Atherton. 'I don't suppose it's anything, but it's better to leave no stone unturned. Meanwhile, it's on with the clubs, pubs and especially door-knockers. If Lenny lived on the estate, he must have been someone's neighbour.'

'Have you any idea how many flats there are on the estate?' Norma said with horror.

'I daresay in a couple of weeks you'll be able to tell me exactly,' said Slider.

Porson was sitting down – in itself an unusual thing. His usual torrent of restless energy seemed to have been staunched. He sat at his desk reading, looking grey and old. Even his wig seemed limp and spiritless. Normally Slider's fascinated fear was that it would go flying off with one of the old boy's rapid changes of direction, but today it seemed to huddle close to the bony pate for comfort like a dog sensing disaster. Slider would have liked to ask if he was all right, but sympathy was not a thing you could show to The Syrup.

'So,' he said, looking up at last, planting a finger to mark where he had stopped reading. He had big, knuckly hands with an old man's chalky, ridged nails, but they pinned down the paper firmly, just as, however random his vocabulary, his mind would pin down the facts of an investigation. 'What have you got?'

'More reports than a balloon-popping contest,' Slider said, 'but nothing to go on yet. We've got a first name, but no surname or address. An informant says deceased lived with a prostitute, but we've only got a first name for her as well, and of course there's no knowing it was her real name anyway.'

Porson looked at him steadily from under eyebrows so bushy they always made him appear to be frowning. 'You know we're going to be under the microscope from the press with regard to this one? Our own back yard, and et cetera?'

'We're doing all we can, sir,' Slider said.

'I know, laddie,' Porson said, unexpectedly kindly. 'But

I think we'd better go public all the same. Can't do much investigating if you don't even know who he was, can you?'

'When, sir?' Slider said, with a shrug in his voice. Going public was always a two-edged sword. It might bring in information, but it also warned people you might hope to take by surprise; and it spread knowledge of your weakness across the widest audience.

'Too late today. I'll talk to Mr Wetherspoon, get something in the morning papers, and arrange an item on the early evening news tomorrow. The local.'

'Yes, sir.'

'What d'you feel about doing it?' Porson asked unexpectedly.

'Doing it?'

'The broadcast. I know we've got a press officer, but the journos always want to talk to a warm body. A real copper. Plays better in the one-and-nines.'

'Me, sir?' Slider looked his horror. 'But you always do the broadcasts. I'm not – I've never liked cameras.'

Porson looked annoyed. 'Do you think any of us do it for fun?'

'I always thought you looked such a natural, sir.'

'What, seeing myself plastered all over the screen like a blasted Spice Girl? I shake like an aspirin, every damn time! But needs must, laddie. Only this time, what with this cold and—' He paused. 'Other considerations – I'm not really up to it. You've got a nice, friendly face. You'll look good on camera. You might find you like it – being the sinecure of all eyes.'

'Atherton's a handsome chap—' Slider tried in a lastditch defence.

'No bon. You know it's got to be a DI or better. No, you're it, Slider.'

'Is it an order, sir?' Slider asked.

'No, it's not an order, it's a request,' Porson said, growing impatient. 'But if you refuse a perfectly reasonable request from your senior officer, I'll have to make it an order, won't I?'

'In that case, I'll do it,' Slider said glumly. As long as I know where I stand. I never craved the limelight, the fierce doo-dah that beats upon the thingummy, but if that's the way the runes fall, it is a far, far better thing and so on. Joanna always said he ought to go on the box; and the children would be thrilled. They were of the generation that felt nothing was real until the TV validated it. But he had never wanted anything about himself to be public property. To him it was a violation. He didn't even like to see his name in the telephone directory. And anonymity was not just a personal preference, it was one of the tools of his trade. He was the Alec Guinness of Shepherd's Bush Nick.

'Brace up, laddie,' Porson said, reading his face. 'Most people gape at the telly with their mouths open and their brains in neuter. You'll slip in one side and out the other. It's deceased they'll be interested in, if at all.'

True, thought Slider, but not much comfort to the reluctant performer.

Atherton put his head round Slider's door. 'Anything else before I go?'

Slider came back from a long distance. 'Are you off?'

'It's after seven.'

'Is it? Blimey, doesn't time fly when you're having fun?'

'Everyone else has gone. Why not have an early night? You look tired.'

Slider shrugged. 'I don't sleep well in that bed when

Joanna's away. It needs a new mattress. It's like the slopes of Mount Etna. Strange, though, somehow I never notice the lumps when she's there.'

'Sleep on the sofa,' Atherton suggested. Slider got the impression he wasn't taking his plight seriously.

'What are you doing this evening?' He didn't like to ask, but if Atherton invited him back for a meal he wouldn't say no.

But Atherton said breezily, 'Oh, I've got plans. Well, if there's nothing more, I'll be off. Night!'

'Goodnight,' Slider said, concealing his disappointment as Atherton whisked away. He stared at the empty doorway a moment, and then turned to look out of the window. A warm, slightly hazy evening was spreading its buttery light over the streets, quiet in this time between commuting home and going out on the town. In the old days, he and Atherton would have gone for a pint in a pub with a garden, and maybe for a curry afterwards. Now women had come between them; which was fair enough when the women were all present and correct. But all that beckoned him now from his desk was an empty flat and, he was pretty sure, an empty fridge.

Oh, well, he thought, there are plenty of restaurants in Chiswick. He pictured them – a long and varied row, French, Italian, Chinese, Indian, Thai, Black Tie, new British, Old Greek, Middle Eastern – and wondered what he fancied, trying to whip up some enthusiasm for the notion of a meal out alone. Or he could take fish and chips home and eat in front of the telly like a sad divorcé. He so rarely watched it, he hadn't the faintest idea what was on. And if he had known it wouldn't have helped much. All television was a bit like a serial, he thought; or like science fiction, based on the assumptions of everything that had gone before. If you didn't keep up with it, you couldn't understand what they were on about, and lost interest.

And then the thing that had been bothering the back of his mind swam to the forefront. Atherton had said, 'I've got plans.' Not, 'We've got plans.' He wondered if it meant anything, or if it was only a slip of the tongue. He hoped the lad wasn't up to something.

When he got outside, he thought better of the whole idea of going home. He left his car where it was and walked up Abdale Road. The air was warm and still, and there was a smell to it, not entirely unpleasant, but a little used and smeary, like the smell of one's own bedsheets after they'd been slept in. The houses in Abdale Road were terraced cottages, two storeys with the tiniest front gardens – you could have leaned across from the street and knocked on the window. They had been built for Victorian workmen but owing to the increasing desirability of Shepherd's Bush they were being gentrified out of all recognition. You could tell the ones that were now in middle-class hands: they had freshly painted front doors, lots of pot plants, and no net curtains.

Round the corner in Loftus Road the houses were much bigger, three storeys plus a basement, with steps going up to the front door over a wide, well-lit 'area'. By an odd reversal of fortunes these houses, which had been built for the servant-employing class, were now on the whole occupied by people lower down the social scale than were the tiny cottages in Abdale. They were mostly split up into flats and bedsitters, and were shabby and peeling. One or two, however, had been spotted for their potential by the newly affluent and were being done up regardless. Skips, scaffolding and contractors' vans marked them out for work in progress.

There was one, towards the end of the road, in which the process was complete. Its sooty brick had been cleaned back to the original pleasing London yellow; new double-glazed sash windows, new paint, new roof slates, even new railings proclaimed its status as a beloved object. The time-nibbled edges of the steps up to the front door had been repaired so that they were as sharp as the day they were born, like a freshly unwrapped bar of chocolate; the area had been paved with expensive Italian tiles. Slider slowed his pace so that he could look appreciatively as he passed. It was a pleasure to see an old house properly taken care of, and it just showed what good houses these could be. The Victorians knew how to build all right. Someone had sunk a lot of dosh into this one, but they had got a fine and very large property out of it, which would probably have cost them three times as much in Fulham or Notting Hill.

Loftus Road was a cul-de-sac, but there was a cut-through into South Africa Road through the courtyards of Batman Close – one of the later additions coeval with the Phoenix. It was very quiet everywhere. Hardly anyone was about. The door of the pub was open, and the subaural thump of its background music issued forth like a dragon's heartbeat. In the small flight of shops the newsagent was still open and a couple of kids on bikes were hanging around the door, evidently the best use they felt they could make of the golden hours of childhood. Two men were in the launderette, reading newspapers at opposite ends of the bench before the row of machines; and there was a queue of three in the fish-and-chipper. The smell of frying, sharpened with vinegar, drifted out on the warm air. Slider's stomach growled a warning. He hadn't eaten since a meagre egg-and-cress sandwich Anderson had brought him in at lunchtime. He felt grubby from the day's work, and his feet felt the pavement too keenly, as though his shoe soles had got radically thinner since this morning.

He was heading for Buller Close – all the blocks of flats were named after Heroes of the Empire, the estate having been built on the site of the old Commonwealth Exhibition. Who was Buller, he wondered as he trod the chewing-gum-pocked pavement, trawling his schoolboy history lessons. The name Redvers Buller sprang to mind, but it came with no information attached and pretty soon sprang out again.

The flat was on the first floor. There was a long pause after he had knocked on the door, and he turned his back to it and leaned on the balcony wall, staring down at the yard and wondering where all the children were. It was the great advantage of the estate that it was ideal for 'playing out' – enclosed yards, large greens, no through-traffic, and the blocks were low-rise enough for even a top-floor mum to shout down to her children and be heard. But the yards and greens were deserted. All indoors watching telly, he supposed sadly.

Behind him there was a sound, and he turned quickly to find an eye peering at him through the merest thread of a crack. At the sight of his face, the crack widened enough to reveal most of a face and a hand clutching a pink dressing-gown at the neck.

'Hullo, Nichola,' he said. 'It's all right, it's not trouble. I'm alone.'

Nichola Finch opened the door fully. Her face looked puffy and creased as if she had been asleep, but otherwise she was a pretty girl, wafer-slim, with full lips, big brown eyes and thick, curly dark hair. With her smallness and slimness she looked at first glance almost like a child, but on closer inspection – at least in daylight and without make-up – the ravages of time were apparent. As far as Slider knew, she was in her late twenties or perhaps early thirties. She admitted to nineteen; but that was not surprising in a person who spelled her name Nikki on her calling-cards. He thought she had probably admitted to nineteen since she was fourteen.

'You woke me up,' she complained.

'I'm sorry,' said Slider humbly.

She was instantly mollified. 'S'all right. I had to get up anyway. What j'want?'

'Just a talk.'

Her eyes narrowed suspiciously. 'What about?'

Slider made a small outwards gesture of his hands. 'Do we have to do it here on the balcony? Can I come in?'

'Have to do what on the balcony? 'Ere, have you come for a freebie?'

'I'm a happily married man. I just want to talk.'

'Most of my customers are happily married men,' she said with unusual acuity. She yawned right back to her fillings, closed down with a smack of the lips, and said, 'I need a coffee.' She turned and went in, leaving the door open – all the invitation he was going to get.

In the tiny, chaotic kitchen she fumbled about for the kettle, shook it to gauge its fullness, and switched it on. She sorted through the dirty crockery for a mug, waved it at him in enquiry, and when he shook his head, shrugged in reply. A woman of few words, was Nichola. She rinsed the mug meagrely under the cold tap, put it down by the kettle, spooned in powdered instant out of an industrial-sized tin, added sugar, and settled down to wait, folding her arms across her chest as women do when comfort is their priority rather than allure.

'So, what's it all about?' she asked, though without much invitation.

'I want to pick your brains,' he said.

'Not a bloody gain,' she said with huge exasperation, rolling her eyes theatrically.

'Come on now, Nichola, I haven't seen you for months.'

She tacked off, easily distracted. 'Why ju always call me that?'

'It's a pretty name.'

She stared at him, trying to fathom whether he was being ironic, or kind, or had some other devious ploy too subtle for her to grasp. In the end she gave it up and said, 'You're a funny bastard, you are.'

He smiled. 'But I'm okay,' he suggested, as if that would have been her next sentence. She only shrugged. 'I looked after you all right when you had that bit of trouble—'

'And you never let me bloody forget it!' She responded again with the disproportionate, withering sarcasm that seemed to be the only mode of communication with girls like her. He supposed it must come from the soap operas, and perhaps the tabloid headlines – a continual artificial outrage whipped up about the most trivial of 'offences'. Slider had always got on well with prostitutes, having cut his teeth on Central Division, which covered Soho, but the younger ones were hard to talk to. Apart from the automatic stroppiness, they seemed to have huge and baffling areas of ignorance about quite basic things, so that at any moment a perfectly ordinary conversation suddenly became the equivalent of discussing the fine detail of a Test cricket match with a middle-aged farmer from Iowa who'd never left his home town.

'So you're all right now?' he pursued. 'You haven't had any more trouble?'

'No, he's buggered off. Much you'd care!' she added, as if afraid she'd been too gracious. 'So what j'want, anyway?'

'Some information.'

'I ain't the bleedin' Yellow Pages.'

'You know the estate and you know lots of people. And you're a clever, noticing sort of person.' He was afraid he might have gone too far with this, but she didn't react. 'You've got what you might call specialist knowledge.'

She tilted her head a little sideways, and smiled. 'You don'alf talk funny,' she said. 'But you got a nice voice. I always said that, din' I? I always said you got a sexy voice.'

She never had said anything of the sort, but he saw she was building a scenario for herself in which she would help him, so he went along with it.

'We were always good friends,' he said. 'And that's what friends do, help each other.'

'Yeah,' she said. The sentiment sounded right to her, and she had no concept of logic. The kettle boiled and clicked off, and she turned away to make the coffee, and then, taking up the mug, said much more pleasantly, 'J'wanna come and sit down? It's a bit of a tip in there, but—'

Given the kitchen, he could imagine. He said, 'Whatever you like. I'm all right here, but—'

'Okay,' she said, settling again to lean against the work surface, folding one arm and propping the other elbow on it so that the mug was within easy reach of her mouth. 'What's it about?'

'There was a man murdered in the park on Monday night,' he began.

'Oh, yeah, someone said,' she agreed. He remembered she didn't read newspapers. Come to think of it, he had no evidence that she *could* read. She had had eleven years of progressive education at a State school, after all. 'I don't know nothing about that,' she said.

'No, of course not. But not long before that, Monday night about eleven, this man had a fight outside the Phoenix with—'

'Eddie Cranston, yeah,' she finished for him.

Slider managed not to jump as the missing surname was provided so easily and casually. 'Oh, you know about the fight?' he said.

'People are talking about it. I never knew it was this bloke what got murdered, though. He give Eddie a black eye.' She grew enthusiastic. 'Eddie's ballistic about it. He fancies himself rotten, and he thinks it spoils his fabulous good looks, know't I mean? That's why he's not been out of the 'ouse since. Lying low until his eye goes down. Plus, he don't like being made a fool of, and this bloke's got the better of him, en't he? I mean, Eddie's picked a fight with this bloke to show 'im who's boss, and he's come off wiv a black eye, and this other bloke's walked away wivout a scratch, right?'

'Well, not exactly,' Slider said. 'The other bloke's dead.'

'Oh, yeah.' Her eyes widened and the mug was arrested on its way to her lips. 'Yeah,' she breathed, 'you're right. You reckon Eddie done him in, then?'

'It's a possibility,' Slider said. 'So tell me about this Eddie Cranston.'

'He's a git,' she said simply. 'He thinks he's God's gift, know't I mean?'

'And is he?'

'What, God's gift? Well, he's good-looking, I give him that,' she said grudgingly. Slider made an enquiring noise and she responded, 'Tall, black hair, suntan. Sharp dresser. He's all right-looking, but he's a total bastard.'

'In what way?'

'Treats you like dirt,' she replied shortly. She sipped her coffee, her eyes over Slider's shoulder, as if the interview was finished.

'So where does he live, this Eddie?' he tried next.

She snorted so hard she did a nose job with the coffee and had to wipe her face on her dressing-gown sleeve. 'Where *doesn't* he live?' she said eventually.

'What does that mean?' Slider asked patiently.

She put the mug down, the better to tackle his ignorance. 'Listen, he's got this scam. He's got women all over the estate, all round Shepherd's Bush.'

'You mean they're working girls, like you?'

'Nah!' Huge withering scorn. 'That'd be too much like hard work for Mr Eddie Bloody Cranston! No, they're all on benefit – most of 'em have got kids – and he just comes round and takes his cut.'

'Why do they give it to him?'

'Why j'think? Cause he's a smooth-talking bastard. They all think he's *their* bloke. It's love, innit? Plus, he'd knock their teeth in if they didn't.'

That covered the bases, Slider thought. 'How do you know about this?'

'I know one of 'em, Karen. She used to be a mate at school. I've told her, I've said you're dead stupid, you are! But she says he's the farver of me kids – well, one of 'em. She says she loves him. I've told her, I've said to her you ain't the only one, you know. I've told her he's got women all over. But it don't make no difference. She thinks it's her he really loves, and he'll give the others up one day and settle down. Gaw!' She rolled her eyes skywards at the stupidity. 'I said to her, I said at least I get paid for it. And I don't have to have'm hanging round afterwards. Quick in an' out and cash in me 'and, and the rest of me time's me own. But *she* pays *him*, the dozy cow. Cuh!'

She drank some more coffee while Slider let this sink in.

'You say he's a sharp dresser,' he said at last. 'But where does the money come from? Taking women's social security doesn't add up to much, even if he has got a lot of them. I suppose he'd have to leave them enough to live on. He couldn't take it all.'

She didn't seem much interested in this. 'Oh, he's got other scams,' she said. 'Bound to.' Evidently she didn't know what they might be. Slider changed tack.

'This bloke he had the fight with, Lenny. Unlucky Lenny, they call him. Do you know him?' She shook her head, her eyes blank and far away. 'Some said he lived with a working girl.'

'I don't know him.'

'Do you know what the fight was about?'

'Nah. I never heard.'

She had plainly grown bored with the whole process and any minute now would yawn and send him away. He said, 'You've been really helpful to me, Nichola. I shan't forget this. Your friend Karen – Karen what, by the way?'

'Karen Peacock. Why?'

'Do you think she'd talk to me? Where does she live? Have you got her address?'

Nikki's face sharpened. 'You barmy? Talk to the cops about Eddie? He'd break every bone in her body if he found out.'

'I'd make sure he didn't find out.'

'She'd never do it,' Nikki said certainly. 'Anyway,' with a look of cunning, 'I don't know where she lives, so I can't tell you.'

'Fair enough,' Slider said peaceably. Nikki's black hole

of ignorance was working in his favour now. It simply didn't occur to her that if Karen Peacock was drawing benefit there would be an official record of her whereabouts which Slider could consult. It would save time if Nikki would tell him, but saving time was as nothing weighed against not alienating a useful informant and not having her warn her friend that he was coming.

And when it came to Karen Peacock's safety, he thought Eddie Cranston was less likely to find out he had been asking questions from him than from Nikki herself. When Nikki had been expounding her philosophy of life she had said, 'and I don't have to have'm hanging round afterwards.' Slider was pretty sure the ''m' had been 'him' rather than 'them'. That, plus a certain something in the quality of her scorn for her friend, persuaded him that Nikki knew Eddie Cranston rather more Biblically than she was letting on.

He took his leave and stepped out into the fading evening. He was tired and hungry, but he had got a handle on the case at last, a first step towards identifying Unlucky Lenny. He couldn't get through to social security until the morning, so he was free now to go and get something to eat, and relax for what was left of the evening. He walked back to the station more cheerfully than he had left it. By the time he drove out onto Uxbridge Road he had decided on Alfredo's for his supper, a big bowl of pasta with lots of tomato and garlic in the sauce, and a couple of glasses of Apulian wine. And then home, bath, bed. And the possibility that Joanna would phone from the hotel, after the concert and before sleep. Talking to her in bed was one of the great joys of life – even if she was in a different bed at the time.

CHAPTER FIVE

The Eyes Have It

Hollis appeared in Slider's doorway. 'Edward Cranston,' he read from the printed sheet. 'Age thirty-eight, height five foot eleven, eyes brown, hair brown, mole on right cheekbone. Last known address in Ladbroke Grove four years ago.' He looked up. 'Any money on him still being there?'

'It's not far across the fields from White City,' Slider said. 'A mile, if that.'

Hollis snorted derision. 'As to his record, well, he's not Robbie Williams. Not even top fifty material. All small-time stuff. He's got possession of a controlled substance, possession of stolen goods, dah-di-dah-di-dah. Living off immoral earnings. Drunk and disorderly, affray – five Public Order offences altogether. And one assault and actual. That was his finest hour. Broke the cheekbone of the girl he was living off. Our brothers in conflict at Notting Hill caught her at the hospital when her guard was down and got her to prefer charges. Wanted to run him off their ground. Reckoned he was up to a lot of stuff they couldn't nail him for. But his brief coached him, he pleaded guilty, sobbed contrition, and the judge gave him a suspended, on condition he went through anger management counselling.'

Hollis blew out through his scraggy moustache in disgust. 'Where do they dig 'em up from?'

'Did he go?'

'What, guv? Oh, to the classes. No, he ducked out after the first, but Notting Hill reckoned they'd scraped him off their shoe so they weren't too bothered. He's got nothing since the assault, so he's been keeping out o' trouble, or at least out of their hands. Dave Tipper at Notting Hill said if we can find him, we can have him. Joke, unfunny, officers for the use of.'

'Well, if we can find him, we can slap him for breaking the terms of his suspended,' Slider said. 'That'll make things easier.'

'If we can find him.'

'Check with the old address, just in case. Someone there might know. Then look in all the usual places. Most likely he's claiming benefit – you might try there first.'

'If he's offed Unlucky Lenny he's probably done a bunk.'

'Oh, I don't know. These overripe types who fancy themselves often think they can't be caught. He might lie low for a bit, but if he's got good scams set up round here he won't want to abandon them.'

'If he's that cocky, he'll probably turn up at the pub again, once his black eye's gone down.'

'Yes, but that could be four or five days. It strikes me that Sonny Collins probably knows more about Eddie Cranston than he's letting on. I think we might get him in and lean on him, see if he creaks.' Slider frowned in thought a moment. 'Run him through the system, will you, see if he's got any form.'

'What, Collins? Righty-o, guv.'

'Anything will do. Parking tickets, smoking in the lav. And someone can go round and have a chat with Karen

Peacock – though if she's as wet as Nikki says she is, she probably won't know anything about Eddie worth knowing.'

It was common wisdom that women preferred to unburden themselves to other women, but Slider had always begged to differ. It was one thing for a female to Tell All to her bosom chum, but in his experience they had a basic animal suspicion of women who were complete strangers, whereas they would spill the most astonishing intimacies to a strange man if he were sympatico enough. Atherton said it was all to do with sex, and proved that women, even more than men, were always potentially on the pull. 'At least men stop for football,' he pointed out.

So Slider didn't send Swilley to interview Karen Peacock. He toyed with the idea of sending Anderson, who was a nice, unthreatening family man, but remembering her penchant for handsome bastards, plumped in the end for Atherton.

'I suppose you mean that for a compliment,' Atherton said.

'It's all to do with sex,' Slider said serenely.

Karen Peacock lived in Evans House, almost opposite the park and a plastic pint glass throw from the Phoenix. Atherton tried not to get too excited about this fact. Nowhere on the estate was *that* far from the Phoenix. He trod up the stairs like a cat avoiding something spilt, and found Karen Peacock in. She was a depressed-looking woman who was probably in her early twenties but looked older because of her draggledness. Her face was pale, her eyes defeated, her hair dyed black with a luminous red streak, which defiant punkery went with the rest of her appearance like liver and custard. She was not more than usually overweight, but everything about her seemed to droop baggily, from her face to her shoulders, her bust, her belly and her clothes, as if they were all despairingly giving up the fight and sinking to the ground. She was dressed in unforgivable Lycra leggings and an enormous mauve teeshirt, her bare feet in flip-flops revealing chipped burgundy varnish on the toenails. She had three silver studs in the rim of one ear, and three small children, the middle one of which had obviously been sired by a black man and didn't match the other two. Atherton wondered which one was Cranston's. He supposed the youngest, unless the man was unnaturally forgiving, or merely businesslike.

If Cranston was as tasty as reputation had him, Atherton expected difficulty in getting anything out of one of his women, but when Karen opened the door to him she looked up at him with a mixture of fear and submission, and it only took a moment or two of smiling charm before she invited him in. Soon he found himself sitting on her dreadful sofa in her clean and tidy but dreadful lounge. For the purposes of furthering their relationship he expressed an interest in her children, though unfortunately attention only encouraged the eldest, Bruce, a boy of four, to show off, and their subsequent conversation was punctuated by shouts, loud bangs as he whacked furniture with various blunt instruments, and weak pleas from his mother not to put his toys down the toilet or torture his little brothers.

Atherton's charm worked on Karen so well that her submission was soon tinged with a fluttery sort of pleasure rather than fear. She responded to his generous labelling of Cranston as her husband by saying, 'Well, we're not actually married. Not as such. Really, I'm still married to Vinnie's father – that's my middle one – but Eddie is Eric's father – that's my baby.'

'He's a lovely little boy. Does he look like Eddie?' This

line removed the last traces of Karen's reserve. It also prompted an offer for Atherton to hold the baby, but he supposed that was a small price to pay. Baby Eric was placid enough – indeed, almost inanimate, like a large lump of flesh that had been excised from somewhere or other. It sat on Atherton's knee and stared at nothing. He thought of his trousers and prayed its nappy was leakproof.

After this diversion, Atherton brought the conversation back to Eddie. 'But he does live here with you?'

'Well, not as such. You see,' she looked sidelong, almost coyly, at Atherton, 'you get more from the social if you don't live together. Eddie's got his own place.'

'I see. But I expect he's often here.'

'Oh yes,' she said, but her eyes filled with tears. A bit more probing and she spilled it out, that Eddie had other women – well it was only natural, he was so handsome and everything – but it was her he loved really. 'He's told me so, ever so often.' This was the clincher, Atherton mused with a sort of sad disgust. If he said it, it must be so.

'What about this fight he had with Lenny over at the Phoenix?'

'Oh, that was terrible!' she said. 'Lenny give him a black eye. I mean, Eddie! He's got such beautiful eyes.'

Eddie had been with her that evening. He'd dropped in around nine, nine-thirty. He'd come to bring her some things he wanted washing. She did his hand-wash for him, his nice jumpers and that. She'd been putting the kids to bed. She'd made him something to eat – a fry-up, that was what Eddie liked, with baked beans, and then one of them jam roly-polys and custard that you do in the microwave. Eddie had bought her the microwave. He got it from a pal of his, cheap. She used it a lot. It was really useful for warming up the baby's bottles and that.

Where had Eddie been before he visited her? She didn't know. She never asked Eddie where he'd been or where he was going. He didn't like her to ask questions. He just liked her to be ready for him whenever he dropped in. After he'd had his supper he watched telly a bit and then he went. He said he was going over the Phoenix for a drink. That would have been about a quarter past ten. No, he hadn't come back afterwards. He hadn't said he was going to so she didn't expect him. In fact, she hadn't seen him since.

'But you heard about the fight? Do you know what it was about?'

Now for the first time she seemed reluctant to answer. But after a pause, she whispered, 'It was about a woman.'

'That must have been really upsetting for you,' Atherton sympathised. Bruce, the eldest child, was standing behind his mother amusing himself by pulling faces at Atherton. He was using both hands to get some of his effects. Atherton made an effort and shut him out of his consciousness. The application of a little more lard soon eased Karen out of her shell, and her long-buried sense of grievance surfaced.

Eddie, she confessed as much to herself as him, did not just see other women on a casual basis. She wouldn't have minded that – much. After all, men couldn't help themselves, could they? And when he did have women like that, it never meant anything to Eddie. He said so.

What hurt was that he had other women like her, regular, settled women like wives, and at least one of them had children by him.

It must have shocked her when she realised, Atherton crooned. How it must have hurt! To know he had treated her so badly, lied to her, double-crossed her—

Oh, but he still loved her, Karen cried hastily, leaping to the defence of her tormentor in time-honoured fashion. It was just he was so good-looking and everything, women wouldn't leave him alone, and she supposed he'd got trapped and that.

Some natural tears she shed – or at least, her eyes moistened. She blew her nose dismally and he eased her back to the fight outside the Phoenix.

Eddie had found out this Lenny was bothering some of his other women. That's what he had gone over the Phoenix for, 'cause he knew Lenny was going to be there and he wanted to have it out with him. And they'd started arguing, and that Sonny had chucked them out, and then they'd got into a fight outside and Lenny had give Eddie a black eye.

How had Karen found all this out?

Because that cow Carol Ann had told her. She was one of Eddie's women. She claimed to be his real one, but Karen knew better. It was her Eddie loved; Carol Ann was nothing. She was just a slag. But Carol Ann had phoned her up the Tuesday to tell her about the fight and that Eddie had gone to her after, as if that proved anything.

Where did Carol Ann live?

'I don't know,' Karen said crossly, 'and I don't want to know. He doesn't live with *her*. He's got his own place. He told me. Because of the social money.'

'What's Carol Ann's other name?' Atherton asked. But Karen didn't know that either. It was Carol Ann Lying Cowface as far as she was concerned.

'And what about Lenny? Where does he live?'

She had never met Lenny. She'd only heard Eddie talking about him Monday night, that was all. She didn't recollect hearing his name before, but Eddie didn't talk much about his friends or anything. He didn't talk much at all, really.

Atherton could see in his mind's eye the amiable Eddie dropping in for food, sex and washing, taking the first on the settee in front of the telly and the second probably in seconds, a practical thing like blowing his nose. His idea of foreplay was probably, 'Brace yourself!' No, conversation would be way, way down on his list of wants from his woman.

Outside again, and anxiously inspecting his trousers for damp, Atherton wondered how Eddie had known that Lenny would be at the pub that night if he was not, *apud* Sonny Collins, a regular. He also reflected that if Eddie had gone to Carol Ann Cowface after the events of the evening, she would probably know whether he had killed Unlucky Lenny or not. She would probably be required by Eddie to provide his alibi, and she would probably know who Lenny was too. She was an extremely important part of the jigsaw. Unfortunately, like everyone else in this case, she came without the basic courtesy of a surname. He sighed. Like ants, they were, shifting a mountain of sugar grain by single grain.

Sonny Collins was not a happy rabbit. His barely contained rage swirled round the interview room like a tiny tornado in a bottle, and his good eye moved about so much it met up with its partner only rarely, like a frightfully mismatched pair of ballroom dancers.

'Can I get you a cup of tea?' Slider offered daintily.

'I haven't got time for all that,' Collins snarled. 'You asked me to come here, and I've come. I'm a busy man and I haven't got time to mess about. So what do you want?'

'Eddie Cranston,' said Slider.

'What about him?'

'Oh, you know who he is? Last time I spoke to you, you said you didn't know his surname.'

'Maybe I'd forgotten it.'

'And maybe you hadn't. So let's have a bit more co-operation now. Tell me everything you know about him.'

'He comes in my pub. That's it.'

'Where does he live?'

'I dunno.'

'You said he was local.' Sonny shrugged. 'What's he up to, Mr Collins? What's his scam? Where does he get the money to buy his nice clothes?'

Both eyes fixed on Slider for once. 'Is that what you dragged me in here for? I told you I don't know him. All right, I know his name, but that's it. He comes in my pub two-three times a week and I've heard him called by it. Why should I know anything else about him, or any of my customers? I'm a publican, not a bloody lonelyhearts agency.'

Time for the thumbscrews, Slider thought. He held out his hand to Atherton, who gave him, with a nicely judged solemnity, a buff wallet-file, from which Slider extracted a piece of paper, allowing a glimpse of a not inconsiderable wad of other papers within. It was the file on the long-defunct Shepherd's Bush Nick football team (osp) but Collins was not to know that.

'So, you're a publican, are you? For how much longer, I wonder.'

Collins tried not to look as if he was looking at the file. 'What's that supposed to mean?'

'It means that my colleagues in uniform have had their eye on the Phoenix for some time. Drinking after hours is only the least of the things that worry them.'

'Rubbish!' Collins snapped.

'Oh, I don't think so,' Slider said, running his finger down the page in his hand. 'You've been under observation. Dates, times, number and description of people seen drinking in your fine hostelry after closing time *and*,' he tapped the sheet with his fingernail, 'the names and addresses of those who've been apprehended leaving your premises at inappropriate times. Would you be willing to place a small bet on the likelihood that they wouldn't give you up to save their own skins?'

'That's total bollocks,' Collins said calmly; but suddenly he was beginning to sweat. Slider could smell it; and his bald crown was shining. 'If you've got anything on me, charge me. Otherwise—'

Slider shook his head. 'As I said, that's the least of your sins. Observation suggests there's a great deal going on that we'd like to know about.' All this he had from Nicholls, the uniform sergeant in charge of the observation. The file might be bogus, but the suspicions weren't. 'People passing drugs to one another. Illegally imported cigarettes—'

'I don't know anything about that,' Collins interrupted. His voice was still calm, but the tension in his body was almost tangible. Slider was afraid he might blow apart any minute, filling the room with thousands of tiny cogs and springs. 'If people take drugs, I don't know anything about that.'

'Yes,' Slider said with broad sympathy, 'but if it happens on your premises you're still responsible. It's a bugger, isn't it? Now so far we haven't pushed the investigation because, frankly, you're fairly low down on our hit-parade of villains. But you can always be moved up the list—'

'You can't prove anything against me.'

'And,' Slider went on as if he hadn't spoken, 'it wouldn't take a moment to send off this list of after-hours offences to your brewery. Have you got a second career lined up, Mr Collins? Any other job you've always had a secret desire to try out?'

The mobile eye went very still as Sonny Collins indulged in some deep thought. It was staring at the wall over Slider's left shoulder. Because of the angle of his head, the glass eye was staring over his right shoulder. It was unnerving.

'What do you want from me?' Collins asked at last in a low growl.

'Just a little information,' Atherton said. He had been standing all this while. Now he pulled out the chair beside Slider and sat down as if they were all coming to business.

'What, about Eddie Cranston?'

'That'll do for starters,' Atherton agreed. 'What's he up to, Sonny? What's his scam?'

'He's just a poncey little slag,' Collins said with large contempt. 'He hasn't got the balls to get into anything big-time. Listen, he's got a string of women he lives off, takes a cut of their benefit money – that's the kind of toe-rag he is.'

'Yes, we knew that,' Atherton said. 'What else does he get up to?'

Collins seemed to have a little difficulty with moving his lips, as though the next confession was harder. 'He gets hold of a lot of iffy stuff, flogs it off to mugs.'

'Receiving stolen goods?'

'I never said stolen,' Collins said.

'Of course you didn't,' Slider said. 'How could you know?'

'What sort of goods?' Atherton asked.

'Electrical stuff – microwaves, CD players.' He shrugged. 'And a load of other crap. Umbrellas. Toys. Aftershave once. Anything. You know, the sort of gear you get at flood damage sales.'

'Of course. He's a regular little Del Boy, isn't he?' Atherton said. 'Cigarettes?'

'No,' Collins said sharply. 'He's never had cigarettes as long as I've known him.'

'What about drugs?'

The lip curled. 'Him? I told you, he's not got the balls. He's strictly small-time.'

'So what were he and Lenny getting into together?'

The eyes went still again. 'Who's Lenny?'

Slider leaned forward a little. 'Oh, come on, Mr Collins. Unlucky Lenny, the man who had a fight with Eddie at your pub and ended up dead a few yards from your doorstep the very same night? What a short memory you've got.'

'I told you,' Collins said, working up a spurt of anger, 'I don't know him. He's not a regular.'

'But you'd seen him before?'

'No. Never seen him before in my life.'

'Oh, really?' Atherton said. 'But Eddie came to your pub on purpose to meet him. Why was that, if he wasn't a regular?'

Collins stared a moment, and then was suddenly calm, as if he'd thought of something. 'You'd better ask him. No use asking me, is it?'

'We'll do that. So where does he live?' Slider asked.

'I don't know,' Collins said, and this time he anticipated the protest. 'It's the truth. I don't know. It's somewhere local, that's all I know.'

'Where does Carol Ann live?' Atherton asked, quickly and lightly.

Collins looked surprised. 'Carol Ann? The barmaid at the Boscombe?'

'That one,' Slider confirmed without missing a beat.

'*I* dunno,' Collins said, and it sounded genuine.

'How do you know her?' Atherton countered.

'She's a barmaid,' Collins said as if it were self-evident. 'We all know each other. What's she got to do with it?'

'You're getting confused,' Atherton said. 'I ask the questions, you give the answers, right?'

'All I know about Carol Ann is she works at the Boscombe Arms. If you want to know any more, ask them. But she's straight as far as I know. Is that it now? Have you finished? Only I got work to do.'

'Just for the record, where were you between eleven Tuesday night and eight Wednesday morning?'

He stared thoughtfully. 'I was in the pub clearing up till about a quart' to twelve. Then I locked up and went down the Shamrock Club for a drink. Barman there'll tell you. Liam.'

'And you stayed until when?'

'Must've been about ha' past two, quart' to three. Then I went home. Took a taxi. Got home fourish, give or take.'

'Anyone at home to confirm when you came in?'

'Do me a favour,' he said scornfully. 'I live alone, above the pub. Let me know when they make that illegal. Anything else?'

'That's all for now,' Slider said. 'Thank you very much for your co-operation.'

Atherton stood as Collins stood so that he could look down at him. 'Isn't it much nicer when we're all friends?' he enquired sweetly.

Collins managed to stare at both of them at once. 'I could break you in half with my bare hands,' he told Atherton with horrid confidence. He was wearing a black sports jacket over his usual kit, but still Atherton could see the muscles squirm under his skin-tight vest. He looked like an unusually well-dressed sack of ferrets.

'Well, that was very nice,' Atherton said as they trod upstairs. 'And almost painless.'

'I wonder why he decided to co-operate,' Slider mused.

Atherton gave him a look. 'Because we threatened him. Have you forgotten?'

Slider shook his head. 'That wasn't it. He was frightened all right, but I don't believe he was frightened by anything we could do. The way it looked to me, he decided to give up Eddie Cranston in the hope it would deflect us from something else.'

'Yes, the drug dealing or whatever else he's got going that can lose him his licence. I think you're making it too complicated.'

'Maybe. It's just he didn't seem worried by the suggestion of drugs, either passing in his pub or Eddie being mixed up with. It wasn't that that made him sweat. And I still think he knows Lenny.'

'You think he gave up Eddie to keep us away from his connection with Lenny? But why?'

'Maybe. I don't know. It's just a feeling.'

'We all love your feelings,' Atherton assured him.

'His alibi's all just a bit too pat, isn't it?'

'If it checks out.'

'It'll check out. He wouldn't have offered it otherwise. I wish we'd asked him for it yesterday, before he'd had a chance to get it organised. I don't trust a man with an alibi ready for the asking like that.'

'There's no pleasing some people. Anyway, it doesn't cover the whole night. Maybe Lenny was killed at five am after all.'

'Don't humour me. Anyway, I thought it was Eddie we were after?'

'True, oh king. And now we've got a handle on Carol Ann, which ought to lead us to said Eddie, and that's enough to be grateful for for one morning.' Slider was silent, still in thought. 'We can always get Collins in again later and beat him up some more.'

Now Slider looked at him, amused. 'Funny how when

you both stood up, he looked the taller of the two.'

'Those muscles are all for show,' Atherton assured him airily. 'I have the subtle but amazing trained strength of the master of eastern martial arts. My whole body is a lethal weapon.'

'Quite a few women have told me that,' Slider agreed.

CHAPTER SIX

From Err to Paternity

The Boscombe Arms, on the corner of Percy Road and Coningham Close, was a very different sort of pub from the Phoenix: one of those tall, handsome High Victorian efforts, all wood panelling, mirrors and elaborate engraved glass. It attracted a different kind of clientele, did a lot of food, and would have recoiled in horror from the mere suggestion of plastic glasses.

The guv'nor was a youngish, stocky, sharp-eyed man with a taller, older and even sharper-eyed wife who came up behind him like a shadow as soon as she realised he was answering police questions. She didn't say anything, but you could tell her husband was speaking with her in mind.

'Carol Ann Shotter. No, she's not in today – called in sick on Tuesday. Said she had the flu. What's she done?'

'Nothing that we know of. We just want to ask her about a friend of hers. Has she worked here long?'

'Oh, about six, eight months. Nine maybe. She's a good worker. Never given any trouble. She had good references. Used to work in the Elephant in Acton.'

'Why did she leave there?'

'She said she got fed up with the buses, wanted to work

nearer home. She only lives in Abdale Road. She wasn't in any trouble,' he assured them earnestly. 'This is a respectable house. We don't have any trouble here, and we don't take on dodgy staff. All my staff are very good people. Can't afford otherwise. We get a nice class of customer in here – lots of money. They wouldn't come in if we had riff-raff behind the bar.'

'So it sounds as if the Eddie–Carol Ann romance might be a recent thing,' Atherton said. 'If Sonny Collins hadn't heard about it, and she's only been working locally for a few months—'

'Maybe. And if she's a fully employed barmaid she isn't one of his benefit babes,' Slider said.

'No wonder Karen Peacock got all uppity about her. Nothing like real superiority to get under a person's skin.'

'It wasn't very superior of her to phone Karen Peacock up just to boast.'

'She probably didn't. I don't gather that Karen is very bright. I expect she phoned with a message from Eddie about his alibi and Karen heard what she expected to.'

'You can be quite psychological when you try, can't you?' Slider said.

The house in Abdale Road to which they had been directed was not one of the done-up-regardless ones. It was not a slum by any means, but it had the tell-tale marks of a rented rather than an owned property – the cheap paint job, the cracked concrete in the front patch, the chipped coping of the garden wall and the missing gate, the gay tussock of grass growing in the roof gutter. Landlord was written all over it. It had heavy but clean nets in the downstairs window, and the upstairs window had its curtains drawn.

'House of sickness,' Atherton observed. 'Is she in bed, or has Eddie gone to ground up there? Or both?'

'Why do you always ask rhetorical questions?'

'Do you think we need back-up?'

'Let's hold our horses. We're just asking questions at this stage. We don't even know he's in there. She might really have the flu.'

'A flu that conveniently started on Tuesday morning. Suppose he panics and runs out the back?'

'He can't get anywhere. All the gardens back onto one another. He'd have to scramble through every garden right down the row and then shin over a ten-foot wall at the end. I think we'd hear him.'

'I love your confidence.'

'It's not mine. I'm looking after it for a friend. Look, if she's his alibi, he's not going to run away, is he? If his story is he never done nuffing and she can prove it, he wants to be found in her house, doesn't he?'

'It's a lot of "ifs".'

'Just knock on the door.'

Atherton still didn't really expect the knock to be answered. He expected the upstairs curtain to twitch, followed by a muffled sound of feet running down the stairs and a rattle of the back door being opened. But after quite a short pause the door opened and a woman stood there with the half enquiring, half suspicious look any normal person wears in the circumstances.

'Miss Shotter?' Slider asked, showing his brief. 'I'm Detective Inspector Slider and this is Detective Sergeant Atherton. Would you mind if we had a little talk with you?'

Carol Ann Shotter was in her late twenties or early thirties. She was a dyed blonde with a good figure, and her face missed being attractive by such mere millimetres that

at a quick glance or in a poor light she'd have passed as
a bit of a sort. There was a tension about her as her eyes
moved quickly from one face to the other, but it was more
a readiness for action than fear or guilt. She seemed not
nervous, but watchful, expectant.

'What's it about?' she asked, inevitably.

Slider smiled. 'Just a few questions. I'd rather not ask
them on the doorstep, if you don't mind. Can we come
in?'

She yielded. The house was laid out in classic London
Dogleg – stairs straight ahead, narrow passage hooking
round them, one room at the front, one at the back, and
the back-addition scullery beyond. But it was all on a tiny
scale, like a human doll's house. The front room into which
she led them was about nine feet square, so that the small
sofa, two armchairs and television arranged round the
miniature fireplace (blocked in and fitted with a gas fire)
took up all the available space, and four people sitting in
the four available places could have linked hands for a
séance without leaving their seats.

The furniture was old and had been cheap to start with,
as had the carpet; and there were no pictures or ornaments
to soften the furnished-let look. One of the shallow chimney
alcoves had been filled in with shelves, which were stacked
not with books, but with videos. The only reading matter
in sight was a heap of holiday brochures dropped on the
floor at the end of the sofa. The other feature of the room
that jumped to Slider's attention was that though the television set was at least five years old, the video player under
it was brand new.

Carol Ann Shotter sat down, nervously tugging at her
skirt. She had good legs in sheer black tights, Atherton
observed, but she was too old by ten years for a mini that

short. Perhaps it was professional kit. Her stretchy cotton top emphasised her bust, and she was well made up for a woman at home on sick leave. But the purported flu was not in evidence. Not so much as a sniffle.

'I understand you're Eddie Cranston's girlfriend,' Slider opened, not making it a question.

'I – well – yes, I suppose so,' she said with less than a whole heart. 'I mean—'

'He lives here with you, does he?' She hesitated, and Slider pushed her a little. 'Well, does he or doesn't he? You must know, surely?'

'Well, he sort of does and he sort of doesn't,' she said. 'He's got his own place, but he stays here a lot.'

'I see. He's here now, is he?'

'He's upstairs in bed,' she said. 'He's not well.'

'Oh dear,' Slider said, 'not this awful summer flu? You've got it yourself, haven't you? But no, wait, there's been a miracle cure!'

She looked at him with dislike. 'Are you being funny?'

'Your boss says you phoned in sick on Tuesday, and you've been off since. But here you are, bright as a button, not a soggy tissue in sight.'

She roused herself to fight back. 'What right have you got to go round asking my boss about me? You want to lose me my job?'

'Not at all,' Slider said politely. 'I just wondered if your absence from work could possibly have anything to do with Eddie's little adventure on Monday night?'

'Look,' she said – the first word in the vocabulary of capitulation, 'I don't know what this is about, but Eddie's not done anything.'

'Then there's no reason he shouldn't talk to us, is there?'

'He's ill in bed.'

'Oh come on, love,' Atherton said. 'Do we go up there, or do you get him down? It's up to you.'

She sighed. 'I'll go up and tell him.'

'Just call him down,' Atherton amended.

One more burning look, and she stalked past him to the foot of the stairs and shouted, 'Eddie! Come down here. Come on!'

There was a long pause and then the murmur of a voice from above. Atherton, from his angle, could see a pair of male feet in socks at the top of the stairs.

'Who d'you think? It's the police.'

Another murmur.

'Oh, for God's sake, get down here! I'm sick of this.'

After a hesitation, the feet began to descend, and slowly a pair of black tracksuit bottoms joined them, and then a blue teeshirt with some dark hair peeking out at the neck, and then the face and head of Eddie Cranston, visible at last. He had the dark, ripe good looks and thick, black, swept-back hair of a complete bastard, along with a narcissistic suntan and the obligatory gold jewellery, including a watch so vast and covered in knobs it looked like a mine on a strap. The identifying small mole on the cheekbone was there, along with a fine black eye. Judging by its state nearly three days on, he mustn't have been able to open it at all on Tuesday.

He reached the foot of the stairs and stopped, looking at Slider and Atherton, trying to be the hard man, though it's not easy for a man to appear cool when he's obviously recently lost a fight. Carol Ann plainly felt the same. She stepped aside to give them a clear view, and said in that withering tone women reserve – Slider never understood why – for men they were sure of: 'Look at him. Didn't want anyone to see him with a shiner. I ask you!'

'I think it's a little more serious than that,' Slider said. 'Isn't it, Eddie?'

Eddie's eyes flitted about, and he licked his lips. 'I haven't,' he said faintly, 'done nothing.'

'Where were you on Monday night, Eddie? After you had the fight with Lenny, I mean?'

'He was here,' Carol Ann said quickly, before he could answer. 'He came round here, and he's been here ever since.'

'Yes, I thought that might be the case,' Slider said. 'It's the bit in between we're interested in, though.'

Atherton took it up. 'Between the fight and coming here. The bit where Lenny got stabbed to death. The Lenny you'd just had a fight with, I mean – just to make that quite clear.'

'I never,' Eddie said. 'I never. I wasn't me.' He still tried to strike the defiant pose but his eyes – or eye, to be more precise – was conscious and afraid.

'Why don't you come down to the station with us and tell us all about it?' Slider said.

Eddie pulled himself together. 'Are you arresting me?'

'Well, I could if you like, but don't you think it would be nicer if we did it on a friendly basis?'

'You got nothing on me,' he said.

'Then you've got nothing to worry about, have you?' As Eddie still did not move, Slider added, 'You broke the terms of your suspended. I can nick you for that, if you like, if it'll make you feel happy.'

Eddie swallowed. 'No,' he said. 'All right, I'll go and get my shoes on.'

As he started up the stairs, Slider looked at Atherton and flicked his head, and Atherton went up after him. Turning, Slider found Carol Ann's eyes burning him. 'Just a precaution, in case he tries anything silly,' he explained.

'He's daft enough for that,' she said bitterly. 'Look, he

never killed Lenny. He's not the sort. If you knew him, you'd know he's not got the balls to kill anyone.'

'I would like you to come down to the station as well and make a statement,' Slider said.

'No,' she said. 'I'm not getting mixed up.'

'I'm afraid you already are. Come on, love. Better get it over with.'

'I told you,' she said, working herself up and losing her refinement in the process, 'I'm not going down *no* station to make *no* statement, so you can stick that where the sun don't shine!'

'Don't make it hard for yourself,' Slider advised.

'If you want me down that station, you're gonna have to arrest me,' she said with supreme confidence.

He looked across her shoulder into the sitting room. 'That's a nice video you've got there,' he said. 'New, isn't it? Have you got the receipt?'

'No, it was a—' The next word forming was 'present', but before it reached the air understanding came to her. A strong emotion crossed Miss Shotter's face; her nostrils flared and her lips tucked themselves down tightly. A child within range of an expression like that would have known it was likely to be followed by a wallop. 'Oh, my good Gawd,' she said in soft fury. 'The stupid bastard!' She met Slider's not unsympathetic eye and it burst from her. 'I said he was daft: he's a bloody dipstick!' Slider was inclined to agree with her.

Eddie Cranston was sweating freely, and the interview room was filled with the miasma of his body, his cigarettes, and his chain coffee drinking. Interview room coffee came from the vending machine and to Slider's mind smelled like dirty socks. He sometimes wondered if it could be banned under the United Nations protocol on torture.

'Lenny Baxter,' Cranston said, giving them so lightly the piece of information they had been yearning for from the beginning. The spectre of a television appearance retreated from Slider a pace or two.

'Where does he live?'

'I dunno,' Eddie said. 'Somewhere local. He lives with this tart, Tina. That's all I know.'

'How do you know him?'

'Oh, I seen him around.'

'At the Phoenix?'

Eddie shrugged. 'Just around. Everybody knows Lenny.'

If only that were true, Slider thought. 'So what was your beef with him?'

'Look,' Eddie said, 'I never had no problem with him. I hardly knew him. Just seen him around. He was all right as far as I was concerned. I mean, we all got to live, right? But then he started messing with one of my women. I couldn't have that, right? I mean, that was well out of order.'

'Messing with one of your women?'

Eddie Cranston lit another cigarette and leaned back a little in his chair. 'All right, Carol Ann's not my only bird,' he said, as if modesty almost forbade him admitting it. 'I can't help it if women throw themselves at me, can I?'

'You could move out of the way,' Atherton murmured, but only Slider heard him.

'How many women have you got?' Slider asked mildly.

He shrugged. As well ask a sultan for a tally on his harem. 'Oh, quite a few. I get around a bit.'

'You're not married to any of them?'

'Nah! What ju take me for?'

'I wouldn't take you for a king's ransom,' Slider said, but it went past Eddie. 'But some of them have children by you?'

He shrugged. 'Well, it keeps 'em happy. Women like kids.'

'And you get more from the Social Security if they have children,' Slider concluded. 'So in what way was Lenny messing with one of your women? You mean he was having sex with her?'

'Nah!' Eddie said broadly. 'A git like him? Leanne wouldn't touch him with a bargepole. I tell you, my birds are all crazy about me. When you've had the best – forget the rest, right?'

'And besides that,' Slider said, 'to quote a friend of yours, you'd knock their teeth in if they didn't toe the line?'

He looked taken aback. 'What friend? Who said that?'

'Never mind. So if Lenny wasn't poking your woman, what was he doing?'

'He was taking money off her. Been round threatening her to pay up. She didn't want to tell me, but I got it out of her. So, as I say, that was well out of order, wasn't it? I had to give him a smacking, didn't I?'

Eddie was leaning so far back now the two front chair legs were off the ground. His smirk was interrupted only by the need to put a cigarette between his lips. Atherton thought of the draggled Karen Peacock and her three children and his palm itched. He looked pointedly at Eddie's black eye and said, 'Except that it seems Lenny was the one did the smacking, right?'

The chair crashed back to earth, and Eddie scowled. 'He got a lucky punch in, that's all.'

'And having come off worse in the first encounter,' Slider said, 'you followed him and got your revenge by stabbing him through the heart.'

Now he paled, seeing where he had been led. 'I never! I went straight to Carol Ann's.'

'Why do I find that so hard to believe?'

'I never killed him! I swear!'

'What, a hard man like you, whose women have been bothered by a git like Lenny? You had to show him who was boss.'

'Look—'

'You're a big name in the criminal world.'

'No, I—'

'You'd lose your cred if you didn't off him, wouldn't you? I can see that. People would say you'd bottled out. So you had to kill him.'

'No, it's not like that!' Eddie's bubble was well and truly burst. He was almost pleading now. 'Look, it's not me that's the villain. I never done nothing wrong. It was Lenny upsetting my bird. I had to make him leave her alone, that's all.'

'You didn't want him taking money from her, because that's what you do.'

'It's different,' he said, wiping sweat from his upper lip with his forearm. 'Look, Lenny's a runner for a loan shark. Golden Loans in Uxbridge Road. Old Herbie Weedon, he's his boss. He got Leanne into it. Give her a loan against her benefit. You know what the interest is like on them sort of loans! She's getting further and further into debt, and Lenny's going round muscling her—'

'Getting at her money before you can,' Atherton suggested.

'He was frightening her!' Eddie protested. 'You never saw it like I did. Leanne was crying her eyes out. She didn't want to tell me at first, but I got it out of her. She was worried sick about it. So I went after him.'

'How did you know he'd be in the Phoenix that evening?'

'I didn't, not for sure. But he often was. Anyway, he wasn't there when I went in. I had a few pints and waited, and he come in just before closing. So he goes up and talks to Sonny Collins, and I wait till he's finished, and then I goes up to him and says, "You've been messing about with my woman, and I'm not having it." So he tries to pretend he don't know what I'm talking about and we start having a shouting match and Sonny Collins says, "For Gawd's sake take it outside, Lenny," so Lenny legs it for the door and I follow him. And outside I grab him and I say, "You're not getting away that easy," and we start rowing again, and then I lose me rag and throw one at him, only he puts his arm up, and the next minute he's hit me right in the eye.' Eddie paused for breath and put an unconscious hand up to touch the bruise tenderly. 'Gawdamighty, you'd never think it could hurt that much. Otherwise I'd have had him. As it was, I went kind of dizzy for a minute, and while I'm standing there swearing off a blue streak, waiting for me vision to clear, right, he legs it, the mouldy little coward.'

'Which way?'

'Down past the football ground. Time I could look around, he was out of sight. So I went straight to Carol Ann's.'

'Why did you go there?'

'Well, I got me own place, but she was nearer.' He drooped a bit further. 'I didn't want to walk about looking like that. You never know who might see. If it got out—! And I didn't know how bad me eye was. I didn't know if I ought to go up the Casualty. I thought she could have a look at it.' He looked at them pathetically. 'And I been there ever since. That's it and all about it.'

'Why didn't you go home on Tuesday morning?'

'I told you, I didn't want anyone to see me with an eye like that.'

'Come on, Eddie. You were scared, weren't you? You'd killed him and you were lying low.'

'No, I never!'

'What did you do with the knife, Eddie? A flick-knife, was it?'

'I've never had no flick-knife.'

'Did you make Carol Ann get rid of it for you? It wasn't right to get her involved. That makes her an accessory, you know. She didn't deserve that. But then you're a bit of a bastard when it comes to women, aren't you? You don't care what happens to them as long as you can save your own miserable hide.'

'It wasn't like that! I never killed him! I haven't got a knife!'

'I'm sure you haven't got one now,' Slider said, and with a glance at Atherton, passed the ball over to him.

'Tissue of lies?' Atherton said when they left him.

'Full box of Kleenex,' Slider responded, but he sounded thoughtful.

Swilley, who had been having a go at Carol Ann, met them back in the office. The rest of the team gathered round hopefully. 'Nothing,' she said. 'She's got her story tight in her head and she's sticking to it. She says he arrived on her doorstep about half past eleven Monday night with a black eye, saying he'd been in a fight, and he hasn't left the house since. He was so upset she called in sick to stay home and look after him. She says he's a real baby about hurting himself, like all men. Well, that bit rings true at least.'

'Ta muchly,' said Hollis on behalf of them all.

Swilley ignored him. 'I found out how Karen Peacock knew about it, by the way. So much for Carol Ann phoning her – it was her phoned Carol Ann. She'd heard about the fight and wanted to know if Eddie was all right. Eddie had given her Carol Ann's phone number, the dipstick. Any luck with yours, boss?'

Slider shared the result of the interview with them. 'Trouble is, we haven't got any exact times,' he said. 'The fight took place just about, or just after, closing time, which could mean anything from eleven to twenty past. And he got to Carol Ann's house at about eleven-thirty.'

'Which is five minutes' walk from the Phoenix,' Atherton put in.

'But Lenny was stabbed – we assume – in the park,' Swilley said, 'which means they either went over the South Africa gate, or went round and through the Frithville gate, which has got to be ten minutes' walk. And then another five, probably, back to Abdale Road.'

'It doesn't take long to stab somebody,' Mackay said. 'Even with fifteen minutes' walking, it's still enough time if the fight happened anything up to ten past.'

'But *why* would they go all that way round?' Slider complained. 'If they wanted to go into the park it would make more sense to climb over the gate only yards from where they were standing.'

'Because if they climbed over someone might see them,' Anderson suggested.

'And we know there were no fingermarks on the gate to match Lenny's, so we can assume they didn't go over,' Swilley said.

'The fingerprint evidence doesn't help at all,' Slider said. 'There was nothing clear on either gate, but it doesn't mean some of the smears weren't one of them, or both. But why would they go into the park at all?'

'As I see it, guv,' McLaren said, 'Lenny runs off, climbs the gate to get away, meaning to run through the park and out that way. Cranston follows him, catches him up by the playground, they have another tussle, and he knifes him.'

'Your brain's come unstuck again,' Swilley said impatiently. 'Why would Lenny run away from Eddie? He's already won the fight.'

'All right,' McLaren said comfortably, 'Eddie runs away from Lenny, bunks over the gate in a panic, Lenny follows him to finish him off, corners him, Eddie's got his knife out and – bang.'

'It makes more sense that way,' Hollis agreed.

'Right,' said McLaren, encouraged. 'Then Eddie goes back over the gate and round to Carol Ann's. Five minutes the lot.'

'Why not through the park and out through the Frithville gate?' Atherton asked.

'The way I see it, he wants to get under cover as soon as poss,' McLaren said. 'Why would he go the long way round?'

'Sometimes,' Atherton conceded, 'you almost sound like an intelligent life form, Maurice.'

'I'm still not happy about all this climbing over gates,' Slider said. 'For one thing, there'd be some sign, surely, on Lenny's clothes? And for another, if this was closing time there ought to have been people on the street. *Someone* would have seen them.'

'Maybe they did and just aren't coming forward,' Atherton shrugged.

'And another thing,' Slider said, 'Eddie said he'd seen Lenny in the Phoenix. Why did Sonny Collins say he'd never seen him before?'

'You want a *reason* for Sonny Collins to lie?' Atherton said incredulously.

'And,' Slider went on, 'Eddie said that Collins said "Take it outside, *Lenny*."'

'I refer the hon member to my previous answer.'

'It looks straightforward enough to me, guv,' Hollis said. 'And a right squalid little story it is. Nasty small-time lowlife preying off women. Benefit fraud, loan shark muscle-men. Two bits o' scum squabbling over their miserable pickings like two dogs with a mouldy bone. And it ends like usual with one dead and one in the slammer where he belongs.'

'What a poetic way you have of putting it,' Atherton said.

'The trouble is,' Slider said, 'that we haven't got a shred of proof. Eddie doesn't deny the fight, but that doesn't prove he's the murderer. We've no witness, no weapon, no timetable. All we've got is a motive.'

'That'll do it, nine times out of ten,' Mackay said.

'You know and I know the CPS won't move without a cast-iron case, and so far this one's as sound as a card-board canoe.'

'But it's a start?' McLaren pleaded.

'It's a start,' Slider allowed kindly.

'It's more than that,' Atherton said. 'We started off this case with a sack of people who all had one eye, no surname and no address. I think we've worked wonders to get this far.'

'Yes, well, now we've got to start finding some evidence,' Slider reminded him.

'What are we going to do with Carol Ann, boss?' Swilley asked. 'I think we'll have to let her go pretty soon. She's coming over all operatic. Dying duck in a thunderstorm.'

'Ah yes, duck *à l'orage*,' said Atherton.

'She can go any time she likes,' Slider said. 'She's here voluntarily. I'd like to search her house though.'

'They've had two days to tidy up.'

'But we might spot what he used as a weapon, or there

might be a bloodstain on something. It's surprising what they miss.'

'I don't think she'll agree,' Swilley said doubtfully.

'She will. There's that video recorder, remember.'

CHAPTER SEVEN

Bra-Tangled Spanner

'You'll have to rewrite your TV statement,' Porson said.

Slider's heart sank. 'I was hoping I could get out of that, now we know Eddie's and Lenny's surnames.'

'You don't know Lenny's address.'

'Yes, but we've got a lead on that. His employer's bound to have it.'

'Fair enough. But you said yourself there's got to be witnesses. I agree with you. All this fighting and climbing over gates – someone saw something, that's crystal, but no-one's come forward. Got to shake 'em up. Once the community starts turning a blind ear to crime, you're walking down a thin blue line. I'm not having any part of my ground turned into a no-show area. Nothing emerged from the door-to-door?'

'Not so far.'

'Local TV news, then. That's the ticket. And you're the man. Nice sympathetic face. Not a crumbling old ruin like me.' If it was a joke, he didn't laugh, and Slider thought better of smiling, even sympathetically. Strike the wrong note with Porson and he could take your head off clean as a vole with an earthworm. 'What do you want to do with Cranston?'

'Now we've got his address, I'd like to search his drum. Either he can give permission or I can arrest him, whichever way he wants to play it.'

'Not shouting, is he?'

'Mute as a swan. Seems to have resigned himself.'

'Don't nick him unless you have to. Got enough to do without realms of paperwork.'

'Right, sir,' Slider said, grateful for small mercies.

'All right, Bill,' Porson said, suddenly kind, 'better go and work on that statement of yours, get yourself in the right frame of mind. You'll be doing it over at Hammersmith, of course.'

'Will I?' Slider hadn't expected that.

'They've got a proper press suite all set up. And the press officer wants you there an hour beforehand to prepare you. Check your nose hair, give you electrocution lessons, that sort of thing.' He surveyed his junior. 'Had any lunch yet?'

'No, sir.'

'Thought you looked a bit fagged out. Go and get something to eat, and get your statement drafted. Your mind'll work better on a full stomach.'

Slider, as he trudged off, wasn't sure there'd be room for food with all the butterflies.

Golden Loans occupied one of those dusty-windowed offices above a hardware shop in Uxbridge Road. Access was via an extremely battered door which stood between the hardware shop and the deli next door. The smell of paraffin and salami competed on the air. The door was on the latch and pushed open to reveal long and steep flight of stairs covered in green marbled lino which sported a collection of muddy footmarks that would have delighted

the heart of a Holmes or early Wimsey. Since it hadn't
rained in over a week, it was plain that office cleaning was
not high on the list of priorities.

At the top of the stairs was a half-glazed door through
whose hammered glass it was perfectly possible to see the
outline of the high toilet cistern and its dangling chain. No
female staff then, Atherton concluded. The passage led
back towards the front of the building and another half-
glazed door on which the name in gold paint had been
partly scratched off so that it now read GOI DEN L AVS.
From the Bakelite doorknob hung a cardboard-and-string
home-made sign on which was written in irregular capitals
KNOCK AND ENTER.

Atherton knocked and entered. The door swung only
ninety degrees, stopped by the massive desk which domi-
nated the room. Between the door and the wall to Atherton's
right was an empty square of lino'ed floor about two feet
square, but that was the only empty space in the room.
There were two small, hard kitchen chairs against the right-
hand wall, for customers, presumably – or applicants or
supplicants or whatever the correct term was in the loans-
to-the-unthrifty biz. The rest of the room was filled with filing
cabinets, a large metal stationery cupboard, a table cluttered
with paperwork, the huge desk, and the man behind it.

Herbie Weedon was vast and almost shapeless: if it
weren't for his head you'd have been hard put to it to swear
he was human. He seemed penned behind his desk like
something dangerous, for the files and papers which
covered the desk had stacked up in interlocking piles like
a dry-stone wall, those furthest from him the highest, in
teetering columns. He looked dangerous, but to himself
more than the world: his blood pressure appeared to be
well over into the red zone and almost off the gauge. His

nose was spread, bumpy and purple, his eyes sunken and congested, his cheeks an aerial map of tiny red veins. His hair was sparse, as if it had been pushed off his skull by the terrifying forces within; his breathing filled the office, rivalling the traffic sounds from outside. He was like an ancient steam boiler with a jammed safety-valve, ready to blow at any moment. Yet by contrast his pudgy hands were pale and almost dainty, with well-kept nails. One rested on the desk top; the other was occupied with conveying a small thin cigar to and from his mouth. They looked as if they were quite separate entities from the rest of him: milk-white handmaids serving a bloated old sultan.

'Mr Weedon?' Atherton said gently, on the principle that one doesn't shout in an avalanche zone.

'The same,' he wheezed. 'Do for you?' Behind the puffy lids the little dark eyes were as knowing as a pig's. 'Police?'

'Is it that obvious?'

'To me,' Weedon said, pleased with himself. 'When you've been in this business as long as I have . . . I've seen them all come and go. All sorts. Spot a copper a mile off.'

Atherton was upset by this. He knew what coppers looked like: cheap suits, big bottoms, thick-soled shoes. Had his standards slipped so far?

'It's the eyes,' Herbie explained just in time for Atherton's self-esteem. 'Which nick are you from?'

'Shepherd's Bush. Detective Sergeant Atherton.' He showed his brief but one of Weedon's hands waved it away magnanimously.

'Who's The Man up there now? Can't keep track since old Dickson died. Great bloke was your Mr Dickson. Many a brandy and cigar we had together down at the club. University graduate he was not, but he was what I *call* a copper. There's many a fine degree earned in the great School of Life.'

'It's Mr Porson now,' Atherton said, hoping he wasn't going to throw up. But he knew what Weedon was really saying: *I'm older than you, laddie, and I know important people. I can get things done.* And also, *You and I are on the same side of the law.* If he had ever supposed Golden Loans was a squeaky-clean outfit, he would have revised his opinion after that.

'Porson? No. I don't know him,' Weedon said thoughtfully, accepting a suck of cigar from right-hand maid. 'So what can I do for you this fine day? An advance against your salary? You wouldn't be the first copper to come through that door for that. Shocking badly paid, you blokes. Wouldn't do your job for all the tea in Wigan. Siddown, siddown.' Left-hand maid waved Atherton to a kitchen chair. 'Standing around like that, give me a crick in my neck looking at you. Make yourself comfortable. Smoke?'

'Thanks, I don't,' said Atherton.

'Very wise. I'm giving it up myself.' He began to make a terrible noise and Atherton, who had almost sat down, almost leapt up again, his mind on resuscitation techniques. Then he realised Herbie Weedon was laughing at his own joke. The laugh ended in a racking, phlegmy cough that bounced his whole body, and left-hand maid dashed to his pocket for a handkerchief and tenderly wiped his face.

'I'm interested in an employee of yours,' Atherton said, thinking he'd better get the questions asked before it was too late.

'Oh yes?' gasped Weedon.

'Lenny Baxter.'

The eyes sharpened. The breathing slowed. 'Oh, yes,' said Weedon in a very different tone. 'What's he been up to?'

'He's dead,' Atherton said kindly. 'I rather thought you might have noticed.'

Weedon smiled a little. 'I might have, if he'd died in here. But as it happens, he hasn't worked for me for a couple of months. He was one of my collection agents, but I had to turn him off. He was coming up short.'

'You mean he was stealing the money he was supposed to collect?'

Weedon looked away towards the window and waved his cigar gently. 'Oh, I don't like to use a harsh word like that. He might have lost the money. He might never've *had* the money. It might have been stolen off him. But a collection agent who doesn't deliver I don't need. So I said thank you Lenny and bye-bye.'

'And when was this?'

'Like I said, a couple of months ago.'

'From what I hear, he was still collecting much more recently than that. Like maybe last week or early this week.'

Weedon shook his head, quite unmoved. 'Not for me.'

'Did he collect for other people, then?'

The hands spread in a little gesture. 'He was a freelance, he could work for anyone he liked. I didn't enquire.'

'I thought he was employed by you.'

The little eyes gleamed. 'Self-employed.' Aces over tens. Beat that. All the possible leverage of employment legislation down the tubes.

Atherton had no choice but to become the supplicant. 'So what else was Lenny up to, Mr Weedon? You're a sharp man. You must have an idea.'

Weedon leaned forward a little, and for a moment Atherton thought he was going to come across. But he said only, 'It's a big bad world out there, Mr Atherton, and full of dark deeds. I wouldn't be at all surprised if Lenny Baxter was into something too big for him and it turned round and bit him. He was a cocky sod and he thought he knew it all. But what that thing he was into might have been I can't tell you.'

'You must have a suspicion.'

'Maybe I have. Maybe you have. But if it comes to guessing we can each guess for ourselves. Maybe Lenny Baxter had it coming. That's all I can say.' He blew out smoke and leaned back in his chair. 'Anything else I can do for you this fine day?'

Atherton sighed inwardly. Without some leverage he would not get any more out of this old trouper, and any threats he uttered would have to be well filled to work. No use just hinting Golden Loans was crooked. He acknowledged himself beaten. 'Lenny Baxter's address,' he said.

'That,' Weedon said graciously, 'I can do for you.' Both hands were placed flat on the desk and he began heaving himself up. It was a terrifying process. The vast white-shirted torso melded into a vast black-trousered behind propped on short thick legs as big round the thigh as the average man was round the chest. The colour in the face deepened, the wheezing became a roar. Once up, Weedon clamped his cigar firmly in his teeth and waded round to a filing cabinet to pull out a drawer. At close quarters Atherton could hear a whole extra symphony of breathing sounds resonating within the clogged chest, as if he had a family of meercats living in there.

Weedon returned to his seat and wrote the address down on a slip of paper. Atherton pocketed it and thanked him, and rose to go. At the last minute, as if taking pity on him, Herbie Weedon said, 'Dark deeds, Mr Atherton. It's a jungle out there. Young Lenny thought he knew it all. He thought I was an old fool. But he's dead and I'm alive.'

Only just, was Atherton's uncharitable thought as he went out into the dark passage and shut the door behind him.

The search of Carol Ann's house and of Eddie Cranston's flat in Scotts Road revealed nothing of any interest as far as Lenny Baxter's death was concerned. Cranston's place was a tiny one-bedroom conversion, and looked as though he used it for little more than to get changed in, for it was chaotic and short on conveniences. The kitchen showed no sign of being used for food preparation, and, indeed, there was nothing in the fridge except for eight cans of Stella, a pint carton of milk gone solid, with a 'best before' date of two months ago, and a part-used tub of low-fat spread wearing an interesting blue fur cape under its lid.

The other thing Cranston evidently used his flat for was to store things. Just as it was deficient in home comforts, it was over-endowed in other areas: packs and packs of cigarettes, an unopened boxed dozen of vodka, several boxes of assorted used CDs, a large cardboard box containing about fifty shortie umbrellas, another of shocking-pink nylon fur soft toys with the sort of button eyes on pins that any self-respecting toddler would have out and swallow before you could say 'peritonitis', and three cases of imitation leather wallets from Slovakia. A right little Del Boy he seemed indeed.

It was going to be a whole separate investigation to find out what, if anything, was nicked and what was genuine stock in trade, especially as Cranston didn't seem the sort of man who bothered much with paperwork. Fortunately the search team also found a lump of cannabis resin wrapped in kitchen foil in the bedside cabinet drawer, which was enough to keep Eddie under wraps should he feel like legging it.

All this, plus the result of Atherton's interview with Weedon, Slider learnt when he returned in somewhat of a foul mood from Hammersmith, where he had done his statement and appeal for witnesses before both local TV channels, three local radio channels, four local newspapers and the *Standard*. It would add up, he reckoned, to about one and a half minutes of air time, and had used up nearly three hours of his day. And who knew if it would yield any results?

He stamped up to Porson's room to report, and found it empty, to his surprise. Porson's mac and briefcase were gone. He made his way down to the shop where Sergeant Nicholls was in charge, patiently filling in prisoner report forms. 'Nutty' Nicholls was a handsome Scot from the far north-west, where they speak a pure English, and the accent is soft with the wash of sea and rain. He had some surprising talents. Once at a police charity concert, got up by the egregious area commander Mr Wetherspoon, Nicholls had sung the 'Queen of the Night' aria in a fine, true falsetto and brought the house down.

'Nutty, do you know where Porson is?'

'He's away home,' Nicholls answered.

'*Porson?*' The old man never went home early. Slider wouldn't have been surprised to learn that he never went home at all.

'Went through half an hour ago.'

'I thought he'd have waited for me to do my bit on TV.'

'I think his wife's not very well,' Nicholls said.

'Oh. Hard to think of him having a wife, really.'

'How did it go? Your piece.'

'All right, I suppose. According to that press female over at Hammersmith, anyway.'

'Amanda Odell. Aye, I know her.' He eyed Slider cannily.

'What's eating you, Bill? I know you don't like the press, but they're a necessary evil.'

'It's that Odell female mostly. She's supposed to be one of us, but she has a completely different set of priorities. We're trying to deal with a murder case, and all she cares about is how I place my hands and whether my tie is sympathetic enough.'

Nicholls shrugged. 'It's her job,'

'There shouldn't be a job like that,' Slider said, the exasperation bursting through at last. 'What kind of a people are we, for God's sake? Everything's judged by appearance. It doesn't matter what people do any more, only what they look like.'

'You're upset, laddie,' Nicholls said wisely. 'You didn't like being in front of the cameras.'

'I hated it,' Slider said. 'I felt exposed and – invaded. I feel as if I need a very long bath.'

'You need a very long drink,' Nicholls corrected. 'I bet you came across just fine, anyway.'

'Well, I tell you, never again! Porson can do it. They don't pay me enough to go through that.'

'When's Joanna coming over?' Nicholls asked, cutting to the chase.

Slider looked at him. 'You think that's what's wrong with me?'

'If I was only seeing Mary once a month I'd be climbing the walls.'

'It's a bastard of a situation,' Slider admitted.

'Aye. Listen, I'm due a break. D'ye want to have a cup of tea and a chin? Two ears, no waiting?'

'No. Thanks, Nutty, but I've got to go and do the search of Lenny Baxter's drum, now we've got the address.'

'No minions?'

'No overtime. It has to be me, as the song says.' He sighed. 'Not that it's likely to yield anything, after all this time.'

'He was living with someone, wasn't he?'

'According to sources.'

'Why didn't she report him missing?'

'Word is she was a tom, so I don't expect "co-opera-tion" and "police" ever come together in her vocabulary.'

'A-huh. Who're you taking with you?'

'Swilley, in case the female's there.'

'Atherton's gone home to the wife, eh?' Nutty smiled.

'I certainly hope so. If the present set-up doesn't curb his wandering spirit we'll have to think seriously about getting him neutered.'

'Well,' said Nutty, going back to his paperwork, 'if you're at a loose end later, I'll have a drink with you when the relief's over.'

'Thanks,' Slider said. 'I might keep you to that.'

'Friendship's the next best thing to love,' Nutty pronounced.

'You've been at the *Reader's Digests* again,' said Slider.

Lenny Baxter's flat was in Coningham Road, the basement floor of a large Victorian house. It had its own entrance via the area steps; the flats on the three floors above were reached by the stairs up to the front door.

'Nice and private for coming and going,' Swilley remarked.

There was no response at the door and no sound from within. It proved surprisingly easy to break in, however, for although there was a deadlock on the front door, it was not engaged.

'I wonder why he didn't lock up properly when he left?'

Slider said. 'He was obviously careful – serious locks on the windows.'

'I suppose the woman, whoever she is, was the last to leave and she didn't bother,' Swilley said.

The flat was not large. The passage from the front door ran straight to the back. Off it to the left were the sitting room with the window onto the area and a rather dark bedroom, with a tiny windowless bathroom between them. The passage ended in the kitchen, which had a window onto the rear area. There was no access to the garden, and the area had railing round the top of its wall to prevent – or at least discourage – access from the garden. All the window locks were engaged and there was no sign of break-in.

The whole flat was a mess: the occupants plainly had not believed in tidying up. Clothes, papers, dirty crockery: whatever was used seemed to be left where it dropped. But gradually through the casual mess emerged something else: the disorder left by a hasty flight. In the bedroom, drawers had been emptied and most of their contents were missing. A pair of black, flimsy nylon panties lay on the floor halfway to the door and half a pair of sheer black stockings was tangled in the crumpled sheets of the unmade bed, mute witnesses to the hasty packing. The dressing table had marks in the dust to show where toiletries had been swept off it wholesale, and a bottle of eyeliner had fallen down into the limbo between it and the skirting-board. The wardrobe stood open, and there was a suitcase-sized space in the high shelf; one end of the clothes rail was empty, wire hangers were scattered on the floor, and a strappy dress hung askew where it had resisted arrest.

A man's – presumably Lenny's – clothes were still present, on the rail and in drawers, and men's toiletries and an electric razor were still in the bathroom. 'His girl-friend's done a runner,' Swilley concluded.

'And in some panic, by the look of it,' Slider said. The air in the bedroom was strong with her scent. *Paris*, he thought. Yes, there was an atomiser, left behind with a bottle of body moisturiser on the dressing table.

The sitting room smelled of Lenny's French cigarettes.

'He wasn't short of a bob or two,' Swilley observed, noting the hi-fi gear, the very latest wide-screen TV, the new video recorder. 'I suppose that's why he had the window locks. Well, there's nothing for us here by the look of it.'

'That's it,' Slider said. 'The look of it. Just stand still a minute, get an overall picture.'

She obeyed, but after a minute she said, 'What, boss?'

'Someone else has been here. There are things missing.'

'We know that. She's packed and run.'

'Yes, and that's disguising it to an extent. But apart from her frantic scrabbling about, someone else has been through the house. A professional.'

'I don't see it,' Swilley said.

'Remember the bedroom: her dresser drawers are on the floor, but his have been pulled out and left out. Why would she do that? She must know where things are kept. Someone searched his drawers, and a professional starts at the bottom to save wasting time pushing them back in. And in here, the stuff on the lower shelf of that table has been taken out and roughly stacked on the floor. Why? And look, there by the telephone, there's a gap in the mess on the top. Smallish, square – an address book?'

'Maybe,' Swilley said unwillingly.

He looked at her. 'All right, a little bet. Try last number redial. I bet you a tenner it's the speaking clock.'

She didn't accept the bet, which was just as well, because he was right.

'An amateur wouldn't be likely to think of that. We'd better try 1471, but I'll bet that's been blocked too. It'll probably be a public phone box number. These people know what they're doing.'

'But what were they after?'

Slider knew a rhetorical question when he heard one. 'We'd better have a search team in to go over the place, but I doubt if it will yield anything. They'll have taken anything incriminating, and they'll have worn gloves. And we'll have to interview the neighbours, and see if anyone knows who the girl is and where she's likely to be.'

'Boss, if this place was done over by an expert, could it really have been Eddie Cranston? I mean, he comes over as such a plonker.'

'Yes, and if he's only acting the idiot he should be up for an Oscar,' Slider said.

'Carol Ann's no fool, though. Sharp as a packet of needles, that one.'

'But she's got no form.'

'That we know about. Maybe we ought to look into her background. She did shield Eddie.'

Slider gave a tired smile. 'Maybe she's not that bright, after all, then.'

He went for the drink with Nutty. They walked round to the Crown and Sceptre in Melina Road where they served Fuller's, which was worth the extra distance; and, since Nutty didn't want to drink on an empty stomach and Slider didn't know where his next meal was coming from, they ordered toasted cheese sandwiches as well. When they came, Slider noted without surprise that even pub sandwich garnish had succumbed to the cherry tomato mania. He had nothing against cherry tomatoes except that any attempt to cut them shot them off the plate with a velocity that could lay out a gemsbok at fifty paces, and putting them in the mouth whole and biting down was a not entirely pleasant experience that could result in doing the nose trick with tomato seeds.

'It's presentation again,' he said to Nutty. 'Trying to find a new way to make you buy something you've got used to.'

'People like miniatures,' Nutty said. 'God knows why. It's a fad, like those selection boxes of tiny wee Bountys and Mars Bars. Mary's got a friend who collects doll's house furniture. She hasn't a doll's house, you understand. She just thrills to Welsh dressers and Regency chairs small enough to stand on the palm of her hand.' He shook his head in wonder. 'She seems normal enough otherwise. But everybody seems to collect something nowadays.'

'I seem to be shedding rather than collecting,' Slider said. 'Wives, children, homes . . .'

'So what's going to happen with you and Joanna?' Nutty asked, licking the foam from his upper lip. 'I have to tell you, Bill, that's one of the great relationships. Antony and Cleopatra, pork pie and mustard – you two just go together.'

'It's like that when she's back,' Slider smiled. 'Last time – well, not to go into details, but it was like the first time we met. Couldn't keep our hands off each other.'

'Aye, a-huh,' Nutty said wisely, 'but a relationship's not all damp hands, is it? Nice though that is.'

Slider agreed. 'I want her there all the time. I want to do everything with her. Even the shopping – that's how far gone I am! God knows we've got little enough time to be together anyway, with her job and my job.'

'But this new job of hers – it is temporary?'

'She's doing it on a trial basis, but it's a permanent job.' He turned his glass round and round on the bar top. 'I keep thinking, if she stays away, maybe she'll meet someone else.' He looked up, met Nutty's eyes, and shrugged. 'It happens.'

'Maybe you will,' Nutty said.

Slider shook his head. 'I'm starting to think maybe I will have to chuck it in and go over there. I'll have got my twenty-five in at the end of this year.'

'That's only half final salary. You can't live on that.'

'I might be able to find a job where the language isn't a problem. Tourist guide or something. Of course, she'd be travelling, but I'd see more of her there than I will here.'

Nicholls thought it all sounded hopeless. 'You'd miss the Job,' he said unemphatically.

'Like the toothache,' Slider said with a swift smile. 'Still, it helps to pass the time.'

'How did your search go?' Nicholls asked, taking the offered exit from the tender subject. 'Was Baxter's lassie there? Did you find the murder weapon in her underwear drawer?'

'Why should you think that?' Slider asked, startled. He thought of the flimsy knickers, abandoned on the floor. Was Nutty psychic?

'That's where women always keep things. First place your professional burglar looks for the jewellery – you know that.'

'But do you think she did it?'

'Christ, man, don't look at me!' Nutty protested. 'I've not been following yon soap opera. It's just a lifetime's conclusion that women are at the bottom of most things. Are you going off Cranston, then?'

'Cranston leaves a lot of questions unanswered,' Slider

admitted. 'It's starting to look more like a professional job, and Cranston doesn't come across as that organised.'

'Well, I hope it is him,' Nicholls said. 'He's a nasty little creep, and from what I've observed, a professional getter-away with things. I don't like freeloaders. Another pint?'

'That sounded like a very pointed juxtaposition,' Slider said. 'It's my round – same again?'

While he was waiting for them to be pulled, his mobile rang. He had to go outside to get the privacy and the quiet to answer it.

'Hullo, Mr S.' It was the husky tones of Tidy Barnet, one of his snouts – though nowadays they were supposed to call them CHIS: Covert Human Intelligence Sources. Some boy wonder destined for great things spent his days in his comfy office at the Yard thinking up things like that.

'Hullo. You got something for me?'

'Seen you on the telly,' said Tidy. 'You was good.'

'You think?'

'Manner born. The wife reckons you could be a pin-up.'

'It can be my second career. I'll need one if I don't get a break soon.'

'Got a bit of gen for you. That Lenny Baxter – lived down Coningham, right?'

'That's right.'

'He was seen outside his house Mundy night, about half eleven, quart' twelve, talking to a pair o' right tasty bastards.'

Slider's pulse quickened. 'Got any names?'

'Nah. My bloke don't know 'em, but he knows the type. Muscle-men for some big wheel. Top-price minders. Baseball caps, shades, leather jackets. Wearing gloves, and it was a warm night. Well nasty. Unlucky Lenny was in over 'is 'ead all right, right?'

'You don't know who killed him, I suppose?'

'Nah. Nobody don't seem to know.' Tidy sounded slightly surprised at this. 'I've 'ad me ear to the ground, but there's nuffink going round.'

'Well, thanks anyway. Keep listening, and thanks for the tip. Oh, by the way, this stuff about the minders – is it good?'

'It's A1, Mr S.'

'You're starting to sound like one of us,' Slider said. Police graded intelligence using the four-by-four system, starting at A1 at the top, for reliable information from a proven source, down to X0 at the bottom, for something gleaned from an alien from outer space.

CHAPTER EIGHT

Bet your Bottom Deux Lards

The main office was full of sunshine, the smell of McLaren's fried egg sandwich and the murmur of voices. Atherton strolled in with a bag of doughnuts for everybody.

'What are you so happy about?' Swilley demanded suspiciously.

'Can't I just have a generous impulse?' He opened the bag under her nose and shook it gently. 'That one's got cream in it. Go on, Norm, you know you want to.'

'Oh, all right. Ta.'

'The woman tempted I, and she fell.'

'Where d'you get 'em?' Anderson asked, edging up and pincering in.

'The baker's under the railway bridge,' Atherton said. He held the bag out to Mackay. 'There's a Scottish girl serving in there. I said to her, "Is that a cream cake or a meringue?" and she said, "Ye're no wrang, it is a cream cake."'

'Your Scotch accent's bollocks,' McLaren said as he was passed by. 'Here, don't I get one?'

'For Chrissakes, you're already eating a sandwich.'

'Well, I can have it for later, can't I?'

'Surely an oeuf's an oeuf?'

McLaren didn't get it. 'I can have it for afters,' he said,

finishing his sandwich in one goose-throttling swallow.

'Maurice, I love you, and I want to have your babies,' Atherton said. 'Here, take one, then. And one for little *moi*, and that just leaves one for teacher.'

'Where is he, anyway?' Mackay complained.

'He's gone upstairs to see Mr Porson,' Hollis said.

'Porson's not in,' said McLaren through the sugar sticking to the egg yolk on his lips. 'His old lady's sick. I heard Sergeant Paxo on the dog about it when I come in.'

'What is it, the flu?'

'Dunno. I never heard. But she must be bad for the old Syrup to stop home.'

Slider came in. 'Are we ready to go? Did anyone get me any tea?'

'Over here, guv.'

'What's up with Mr Porson's old lady, guv?'

'Word spreads in here like a virus in a hospital ward. I don't know. I was only just told he hasn't come in this morning. I expect we'll hear later. Let's get on, shall we? Any minute now the SCG will have sickies coming back on duty and they'll want this case back.'

'And we don't want the sceptre of failure stalking us,' Atherton said, quoting Porson. Norma glared at him. 'What? It's affectionate,' he protested.

'Some of you may know,' Slider said loudly, 'that we got a call last night after my TV appearance—' He waited for the outbreak of whistles and catcalls to stop. '—from a lone community-minded member of the public who was passing the Phoenix on his way home on Monday night and saw the fight between Cranston and Baxter. That's the good news. The bad news, from our point of view, is that his account largely agrees with Cranston's. It was between ten and a quarter past eleven, our witness estimates. The men were standing outside arguing when he first noticed them. He was on the other side of the road, approaching from the Bloemfontein Road end, and kept an eye on them in case they came his way.'

'Your nervous type,' said Mackay.

'Sensible,' Swilley corrected.

'Anyway,' Slider continued, 'as he drew nearer there was a scuffle and the taller, darker one reeled away, swearing and clutching his face, apparently hurt. The other one immediately made off, not running but walking fast, down South Africa Road past the football ground towards Bloemfontein Road – which I don't need to tell you is the opposite direction from the park. Our man went past quickly, not wanting to appear too interested, but when he'd put a bit of distance in he looked back to make sure he was safe, and saw the taller one heading for the cut-through by Batman Close.'

There were murmurs of comment, over which Hollis said, 'We're getting witness in today to look at mugshots just to be sure, but the descriptions fit all right. It seems like the goods.'

'And I had a bit of information from one of my snouts last night,' Slider went on, and repeated what Tidy Barnet had said.

'Coningham Road's more or less opposite the end of Bloemfontein Road,' Mackay said, 'so Baxter was probably heading home when he left Cranston.'

'If he was seen alive at a quarter to twelve, that lets Cranston out anyway, doesn't it?' Anderson said. 'His alibi's from half past eleven.'

'Only if you believe it,' Swilley said.

'They could have met again later, we don't know,' Mackay said.

'Let's go through things in order, shall we?' Slider said. 'Lenny Baxter was stabbed to death some time between eleven forty-five Tuesday night and eight o'clock Wednesday morning. That's a fact. His body was found in the children's playground in Hammersmith Park. That's a fact. Eddie Cranston had a fight with him at about ten past eleven. That's a fact.'

'I think we could assume he was killed in the park,' Atherton said. 'The general public may be unobservant, but you can't carry a dead body through the streets like a roll of lino.'

'My own feeling is that he was killed where we found him,' Slider said, 'but we have always to bear the other possibility in mind. It's possible he was taken in a van up to the Frithville gate, though I think someone would have noticed that. No-one's come forward, but of course that doesn't mean it didn't happen.'

'You're not your usual cautious self today, guv,' Atherton complained.

'If he was killed elsewhere, wouldn't that let out Cranston?' Anderson asked.

'Not at all. As Swilley says, we don't know that his alibi is true. And I'm afraid the new evidence that Baxter was seen alive at eleven forty-five doesn't let him out either. We've got a wide leeway on the time of death. We don't know exactly when Lenny was killed. It would be nice to be able to rule Cranston definitely out or definitely in, but life ain't like that, ladies and germs.'

'I just hate having anything Slob Eddie's told us turn out to be true,' Atherton complained.

Slider continued. 'Now, the case against Cranston, such as it is – and let me remind you we don't have any evidence against him – has the merit of simplicity, but it leaves questions unanswered. What did he do with the weapon?'

'No problem there,' Swilley said. 'Even if he really didn't leave Shotter's house between then and the time we found him, it still gave her two full days to get rid of it.'

'Which would make her an accessory and an accomplished liar,' Slider said.

'I've put some enquiries in train about her,' Swilley said. 'She's got no record, but DC Hughes at Acton owes me one. He's going to sniff around the Elephant for me.'

'You conjure up some dainty images,' Atherton said.

'The pub, dickbrain.'

'Second question,' Slider intervened, 'if it was Cranston, why did he go through Lenny's pockets, what did he take, where is it, and why didn't he take the money?'

No-one had any suggestions to offer. After a pause, McLaren said, 'Well, it's still Cranston for me.'

'That's the kiss of death to any theory,' Atherton said.

'You're such a snot,' Swilley snapped, and turned to McLaren. 'Go on, why?'

McLaren blinked in her sudden warmth. 'Well, we've got nothing else. And he did have a fight with him.'

The warmth switched off. 'You've got to lay off those stupid pills, Maurice. Boss, if it wasn't Cranston, what was Lenny doing in the park? Was he meeting somebody? If he was, maybe it was him that used the Frithville gate. We know he went home, and that would be the logical way for him to come back.'

'But where are the bolt-cutters?' Hollis asked. 'And where's the padlock and chain?'

'Most likely the park keeper just forgot it and it never was locked,' Mackay offered.

'To back up the Cranston Is Innocent theory,' Slider went on, 'we've got all these dark hints that Lenny Baxter was mixed up in something bigger than collecting loan repayments from women on benefit.'

'Herbie Weedon got quite apocalyptic about it,' Atherton said.

'Yes, but he wanted to get you off his tail,' said Swilley. 'On the other hand, there's the evidence that Baxter's pad was searched by a professional. They didn't take his goods and chattels so they must have been after something else. Something that would incriminate someone, maybe.'

'And he was chatting to two heavies outside his house,' Anderson said.

'They might just have been friends of his,' Atherton said fairly.

'But someone who wasn't interested in money went through his pockets,' Slider reminded them.

'And that's definitely sinister,' Hollis said. 'Contempt of money is the root of all evil.'

'I've heard that,' Atherton said.

'To me, the single stab wound to the heart always looked more like a professional killing than the result of a drunken fight,' Slider said. 'But even a drunk can get lucky, and we've got to keep open minds. So what lines have we got to follow up?'

'Check on Carol Ann Shotter and keep an eye on Cranston,' Swilley said. 'If he knows he's being watched he might do something stupid.'

'Right.'

'Put pressure on Herbie Weedon about who Lenny might have been annoying,' Mackay said. 'Cranston might not have been the only one of his customers out for his blood.'

'Right.'

'And there's Sonny Collins,' Anderson said. 'He's a loose end, isn't he? Said he didn't know Lenny but according to

Cranston called him by name. He and Lenny might have been into something together.'

'Right,' said Slider again. 'We must see what we can find out about Mr Collins. And let's not lose sight of Lenny's missing girlfriend.'

'Yeah, what's the story with that?' Mackay asked. 'She came home, found the pad had been searched, knew Lenny had been offed, panicked and ran?'

'Maybe she came home and surprised them at it,' Swilley said, 'and they snatched her to keep her quiet.'

'Maybe don't feed the bulldog,' Atherton said.

'Either way, we need to find her,' Slider said. 'Ask around, boys and girls. Get your snouts on that, and on who those two heavies were, seen chatting to Lenny outside his house. And keep cracking on with the search for witnesses. Everybody in west London can't be deaf, blind and dumb!'

'Sonny Collins has got no criminal record, guv,' Hollis reported.

'I didn't think he would have,' Slider said. 'Breweries have to be pretty careful.'

'Right. I've had a quiet word with them, and they said they checked him up when he applied. He'd had three other pubs before, and nothing against him. Before that apparently he was in the navy.'

'Oh? How traditional.'

'The brewery didn't know anything about his service record. Didn't check it up, apparently. Do you want me to?'

'Might as well. May give us an insight.'

'They were a bit antsy about me asking about him,' Hollis said. 'I said it was just routine and we had no reason to suspect him of anything. Well, we don't want to ruin his life if he is innocent, do we?'

'You're a regular boy scout. Did they believe you?'

He grinned. 'Would you believe me if you were them?'

'Not if he was him and I'd ever met him,' Slider said.

'But we've covered our arses either way,' Hollis concluded with satisfaction.

'That's the kind of bet I like,' Slider said.

'Are you in tomorrow?' Atherton asked from the doorway.

Slider looked up. 'No.'

'Sunday off? Blimey, is that a two-headed calf I see baying at the blue moon?'

It said a lot for Slider's state of mind that he actually began to turn his head towards the window.

'I'm having the kids,' he said. 'It was arranged ages ago, and if I miss my turn it's hell's own job to set it up again.'

Atherton spread his hands a little. 'You don't have to justify to me. No reason why you should work Sundays.'

But Slider went on, feeling guilty out of habit. 'There's nothing to be achieved by my being here. And they can call me in if they have to.'

'Be sure they will if they want to,' Atherton said.

A detective inspector, whatever agreement he thought had been reached after the Sheehy Report, was expected to be available on a 24/7 basis, as the jargon was. As chief inspectors left and were not replaced, and sergeants like Atherton cannily refused to apply for promotion, inspectors, like Issachar, were the asses couched down between two burdens, inheriting work from both directions. And inspectors were not paid overtime, either, which made them cheaper labour in these budget-conscious days.

'D'you want to come over for a meal with Sue and me tonight?' Atherton asked. 'I'm doing that chicken and rice dish you like.'

Slider hesitated wistfully. Atherton was a noted gourmet and he cooked as good as he tasted. 'I've got all this stuff to finish,' he concluded. 'I don't know how long it's going to take me. Thanks, but I'll grab something on the way home.'

'You'll get ulcers,' Atherton predicted. 'Ah well, you know where I am if you change your mind.'

He left, the office quietened, and Slider sank into his paperwork. Outside on the street Saturday night was winding itself up, and down in the shop they'd be bracing themselves for the influx, later, of drunks and druggies, the combative and the intellectually altered; barmy old gin-dorises wanting a maunder down memory lane, and stinky winos who'd performed their own lobotomies with decades of cheap booze and falling down on their heads; electric-haired conspiracy theorists; smudge-eyed lost teenagers scooped temporarily out of harm's way; morally vacant youths who thought crime was a lifestyle choice. Black eyes, bleeding noses, wandering wits, sullen silences, vicious insults, foul language, an unstaunchable stream of repetitive stupidity masquerading as cool; smell of fear, smell of feet, smell of beer, smell of pee; and vomit, and blood. All the glamour of the eternal cops 'n' robbers story.

In his office, in the pool of his desk light, Slider wrote in silence like a don in his tower. All policemen start in uniform. He knew what it was like down there. And once you've been on the right side of the counter, it changes your mind-set. You look at things differently. That was how old pro's like Herbie Weedon could spot a copper: the eyes are the window on the soul, and what's soul if it isn't mind?

He'd gone so far down that he didn't hear the phone until it had rung four or five times, as subconscious memory told him as he picked up the receiver.

'Did I interrupt you in the middle of somebody?' Joanna said.

'That's my line.' Just the sound of her voice made various parts of him tingle. What was it with her? Most of the blood in his head packed up and headed south, leaving him wanting wits but definitely *homo erectus*. 'Is it the interval?'

'We've not started yet. Ages to go. Concerts here don't begin until nine. The Spanish like to dine first.'

'The Spanish?'

'You get a lot of them in Barcelona,' she reminded him.

'Oh. I'd forgotten. I was thinking of you being in Frankfurt.'

'That was Wednesday. Keep up, Inspector!'

'Duh,' he said obligingly.

'Hey, did I ever tell you the story about the trumpet section in Frankfurt?'

'You mean with your old orchestra?'

'Yes, the dear old Royal London Philharmonia. We'd been doing one of those lightning tours, six capitals in seven days, and we'd all got a bit punch-drunk. Anyway, we were doing Shostakovich Five, and there's a long, long passage in the third movement when the trumpets aren't playing. It's second trumpet's job to count, so Bob Preston, who was playing first, had sort of drifted off. Not asleep, you understand, but just totally vacant. You get that way on the road. Anyway, suddenly he comes to himself, grabs Brian's knee – that's the second trumpet – and hisses, "Where the fuck are we?" So Brian whispers, "It's all right, Bob, we've got fifteen bars to go." And Bob grips harder and hisses desperately, "Not that, you dork, which *town*!"'

Slider snorted. 'I know the feeling.'

'I know, my darling, I've seen you like it. You shouldn't be there at this time of night.'

'I've nearly finished.'

'Then what are you going to do?'

'Go home, I suppose.' He heard how glum that sounded and made an effort. 'Atherton did invite me over for dinner, but . . .'

'And you refused? Have you been bungee jumping off short buildings again?'

'Well, he's got Sue now. I don't want to play gooseberry.'

'Jim's a big boy.'

'What?'

'So I've heard. Anyway, he wouldn't ask you if he didn't want you.'

'Oh, well, it's too late now.'

'No it isn't. It's only half past seven.'

'Is it? I thought it was much later than that. Well, maybe I will, then.'

'Yes, do. Pack up and go now. Then I can stop worrying for one night at least that you aren't eating properly.'

'I wish you were here,' he mentioned.

'If I were, eating would be the last thing on your mind.'

'Or any other part of my anatomy. What time do you get in on Monday?'

'Ten-fifty. I suppose you won't be able to meet me.' It was not a question.

'Come straight here and we can have lunch,' he suggested,

'And I suppose if you've got a murder case on we'll have hardly any time together,' she sighed. 'Why can't people hold off from killing each other for two minutes together? Interfering with my love life! I could kill them.'

'It's a pity you couldn't have come tomorrow, when I'm having the day off.'

'Saturdays and Sundays are when they have concerts,

dear,' she explained kindly. 'Besides, you'll have the children. Never mind, we'll just have to catch as catch can. I'd better go. This is costing a fortune.'

'Off you go, then. Play well.'

'I always do. Go and get fed.'

'Did you say "come to bed"?'

'As Monica said to Bill, "Close, but no cigar." I'll see you on Monday. Bye.'

Slider replaced the receiver, stretched mightily, stacked his papers together, and got up. Half an hour later he was knocking at the door of Atherton's small house in Kilburn, a gussied-up Victorian artisan's cottage – or artesian cottage, as Joanna called it, on account of the damp. Here Atherton had always lived the flighty bachelor life, with a rusty black tom called Oedipus who could be trusted to make himself scarce out by the catflap when his master eased prime totty through the front door.

But things were changing. Oedipus had died, gently of old age under the ceanothus, and – unwisely, Slider thought, but probably with some urging from Sue – Atherton had bought not one but two teenage Siameses to fill the gap, on the basis that they would keep each other company while Atherton was out working. However, what Sredni Vashtar and Tiglath Pileser mostly did while Atherton was out was to egg each other on to ever greater feats of vandalism. A couple of mobile shredders was what they were. No toilet roll was safe, and Atherton now had lace curtains in every room.

The other new thing in Atherton's life was Sue Caversham, a violinist friend of Joanna's. She opened the door to him now, a kitten teetering on each shoulder, their tails straight up as though they were suspended by them from the ceiling. Music was throbbing gently behind her, a violin concerto. Slider was getting better at recognising classical music but he couldn't place this one. Modern-ish. Not Tchaik or Mendelssohn or Brahms, anyway.

'Hullo,' she said, and the kits – Tig and Vash as they tended to get called – said 'Mwah' and 'Ftang' respectively. The smell of chicken wafted from the kitchen. 'Jim thought you might come.'

'Joanna rang and broke my concentration,' he confessed, following her in and shutting the door. 'She said you wouldn't mind if I turned up.'

'Of course not.'

'Thanks,' said Slider. 'What is that?'

'The music? Prokoviev. How is she?'

'Okay, as far as I know. She told me a story about Bob Preston.'

'Oh, well, that's all right then. Glass of wine?'

'Thanks.'

'Have a cat,' she said, and scooped Sredni Vashtar from her shoulder to his. The cat purred, kneading bread with a fine pinging of jacket threads, head-butted him affection-ately; and then did one of its disconcerting flying-squirrel leaps, kicking off lightly from Slider's shoulder and sailing through the air to land five feet away halfway up the curtains, where it clung, looking back over its shoulder as if waiting for the applause. Sue had missed it, having turned away to pour Slider's wine. At the same moment, Atherton appeared in the door to the kitchen and nodded a greeting.

'I'm glad to hear you're taking the day off tomorrow,' Sue said to Slider, still with her back turned. 'At least that means Jim gets some time off too. I know it's overtime for him, but for a wonder I was free on Wednesday and Thursday, and it's a pain when he has to work on my evenings off. I get so few of them.'

Atherton's face was inscrutable, but as Sue turned back with the glass of wine, he met Slider's eyes over her head.

Slider adjusted seamlessly. 'Yes, I'm sorry about that. Needs must.'

'You're a bleeding slave-driver,' Sue told him genially.

'Dinner won't be five minutes,' Atherton said, disappearing again.

Slider sipped some wine to avoid having to think of anything to say. What was Atherton up to? Or rather, who? Slider had thought all that was behind him. Damn and blast it, what was this self-destructive streak in him? He itched to kick his bagman's well-tailored bags.

'So which Bob Preston story was it?' Sue asked. Her blue eyes were merry and sympathetic, and Slider couldn't help feeling she knew exactly what had just been passing through his mind.

Sod's Law said that if you got an urgent call it would always come at the time when you were least able to obey it. O'Flaherty called Slider when he was heading in exactly the wrong direction with a carful of children. Well, there were actually only two of them, but it felt like a carful when he was trying to have a telephone conversation through one of their routine did-didn't quarrels.

'Issat you, Billy?'

'You rang me. Who did you expect? Jodie Foster?'

'Ah, that's a sexy female,' O'Flaherty breathed. 'Is she there, then?'

'If you've called me just to talk nonsense I'm going to kill you, next spare moment I get.'

'I'm safe then,' said O'Flaherty. 'You'll have forgotten by then. Listen, I've got Billy Cheeseman in here looking for you.'

It took Slider a moment to remember that was One-Eyed Billy's surname. 'Has he got something for me?'

'He might have. He says he wants a meet.'

'Wants a *meet*?' Slider hated that pseudo-cool expression, especially in the hands of a terminally dopey specimen like One-Eyed Billy.

'He won't tell me what it's all about. Says he can only tell you. Seems fidgety, eyes flittin' everywhere like a virgin at a wake.'

'That's not like him,' Slider said. 'He's too daft to be nervous normally. Maybe he has got something. I'll be there as soon as I can.'

'And when'll that be?'

'Half an hour, forty minutes.'

'Sure God, he'll have gone off the boil by then!'

'I can't help it. I'm on the way to drop the kids off at school. I can't tip them out on the dual carriageway, can I? You'll have to hold the fort until I get there.'

As he holstered the telephone his brain wanted to race off and speculate, but he yanked it back. He saw so little of the children, they deserved his full attention. He examined them as he tried discreetly to speed up. Matthew, slumped in the front seat with the aggressive relaxation of adolescence, looked as if he had slept in his clothes. It was an effect he could achieve within minutes of putting them on freshly laundered. The same mysterious alchemy could turn a tidy bedroom into something resembling Dresden, while Matthew had apparently been lying completely immobile on his bed.

Kate was bouncing up and down on the back seat like one of those Furbies on elastic. Her school uniform looked like a fashion statement. Her brown hair was the same heavy, shiny texture as her mother's, and like Irene she wore it short, the better to set off her sweet face and blue eyes. They were his eyes, but otherwise she looked the image of Irene when he had first known her: neat, pretty, self-contained. Any minute now, he thought with a father's pain, she would start on the boy business, and these days that didn't just mean exchanging sentimental notes and static, breathy kisses. Various scenarios slouched like rough beasts towards his imagination and he flinched from them. Would Irene advise her effectively? Would Ernie Newman, the new step-father, protect her? Could Slider have, had he and Irene not split up? Children these days were exposed to so much so early.

He was aware that Kate had asked him a question and was waiting for an answer.

'What's that, sweetheart?'

'Can I take fencing lessons?' she repeated with the huge, elderly patience she often assumed when talking to him. She already had that habitual eye-rolling exasperation that marks out young womankind. 'At school.'

'I didn't know you were interested in fencing.'

Matthew roused himself from his matutinal torpor. 'She's not. She just fancies the fencing teacher.'

'I do not!'

'Yes you do. Mr *Brierly*,' Matthew mocked, as though Brierly were an intrinsically ludicrous name.

'And I suppose you're not in love with your precious Mrs Wolfton!' Pleased with herself, Kate expanded. 'Oh, Mrs Wolfton, Matthew's so in *lurve* with you. He wants to *marry* you.'

Matthew blushed richly, bringing his spots into high relief. He was going to be a nice-looking boy once his skin settled down – not handsome, any more than Slider himself was, but just nice-looking. Girls would like him. But at the moment he was going through the worst period in a man's life: he was a war zone of rampaging hormones, and his face was the visible battlefield. Slider wanted to jump in and defend him, but that would be to hurt his pride. Instead, neutrally, he asked, 'Who's Mrs Wolfton?'

'Violin teacher,' Matthew muttered.

Kate bounced harder. 'I don't know why you want to learn stupid old violin. It's so *dorky*.'

'It is not!' Matthew retorted.

'It is. It's stupid. Only a pathetic saddo would play the violin.'

'What about Nigel Kennedy?' Slider said mildly.

'Oh, puh-lease! He's an ancient, boring old saddo! All violinists are nerds!'

'You shut up!' Matthew said with sudden fury, swivelling round to make a menacing face at her. She stuck her tongue out as far as it would go, and then, apparently satisfied, reverted to her normal tones and the previous question.

'So can I, Daddy? Take fencing?'

'What does your mother say?' Slider hedged.

Kate cut to the chase. 'It's *extra*,' she said succinctly.

Slider blenched. This fee business was a minefield, what with male pride, and Ernie's income being twice Slider's. 'Oh. Well, we'll see. I'll talk to Mummy about it.'

'I suppose that means no,' Kate said, but without grief. They had turned into the road where her school was, and her attention was on the other girls being dropped off. 'There's Melanie,' she said suddenly. 'Let me out here, Daddy.'

She ran off, bag over her shoulder, with that strange impervious completeness of little girls, perfect miniature grown-ups as boys never were. In seconds a group of them had their heads together: all alike with their long straight legs and glossy hair, like foals. It tweaked at Slider's heart with the devastating accuracy of a cat pulling a thread out of fine suiting.

He drove off. Now he had just a few minutes to devote to Matthew, and perversely could not think of anything to say. After a moment, however, Matthew spoke, seemingly from the depths of a long train of thought.

'Dad, are you and Joanna – you know?'

'Am I and Joanna what?'

'Well, is she – you know – coming back?'

Matthew was staring straight ahead and his blush, though less violent than before, evidently came from the same cause. There had been more going on earlier, Slider realised, than mere sibling teasing.

'She's coming back today,' he said.

'Yes, but that's just a holiday, isn't it? I mean—' He struggled with his unwillingness to name demons. What Matthew wanted to know was whether her and Slider's relationship would survive the distance now between them.

Slider would have liked to know that too. 'I don't know what's going to happen,' he said. Matthew moved restlessly, thinking he was being fobbed off, and Slider said, 'Really. I just don't know.'

'I like her,' Matthew said, surprising Slider. Matthew was at the age when any expression of affection was exquisite torture. But all was explained as he went on painfully, 'Mum said it wasn't surprising Joanna went, that no-one could live with you, because of your job.' His spots flared anew.

'She didn't say that to you.' Slider knew that much about Irene.

'No, she said it to Ernie, but we heard. Kate and me. We were just coming into the kitchen.'

All was now explained. A great protective sadness rolled over Slider for his son, who loved him, as painfully and perilously as Slider loved him back. He was not like Kate, who skated lightly and scornfully through life. Matthew's world was a minefield of angst. He expected every step to blow up in his face; he feared for those he loved as much as for himself.

'That's not why Joanna went,' Slider said. 'We didn't quarrel or anything. It was just her job.'

Matthew hunched lower. 'But she might not come back?'

Slider turned into Matthew's school road. 'We'll work something out,' he said. 'Somehow.' He hoped he sounded surer than he felt.

He found a space and pulled in. Matthew reached over to the back seat for his bag and began to get out.

'G'bye then, Dad. Thanks for the lift.'

'Have a good week,' Slider said. 'And – Matthew?' The boy paused and turned his face to his father, with all the troubles of the world on his shoulders. It was a bugger being a teenage boy. Girls had no idea. 'You don't have to take sides,' Slider said. 'Mummy and I are all right now. She didn't mean anything bad.'

'Kate's an idiot,' Matthew said, jumping a stage of logic; but his face had lightened.

'She's just a little girl. She'll grow out of that.'

'I wouldn't bet on it,' Matthew said. He grinned suddenly, letting Slider see for a moment what he would look like in five or six years' time (how that smile would melt the girls!) and then was gone.

As soon as Slider was alone, his mind snapped him instantly from his domestic into his professional persona. When he was engaged with either one, the other always seemed slightly fantastic. Which was real life, he wondered?

He knew what Irene thought. Probably all police wives –
unless they were in the service themselves – resented the
Job. He shoved the thought away and concentrated on
finding the fastest route through the morning traffic back
to Shepherd's Bush.

CHAPTER NINE

Arctic Role

Billy Cheeseman had not only gone off the boil by the time
Slider got back, he had gone off.

'I couldn't keep him,' O'Flaherty said. 'Said he'd to get
to work.' He raised his eyes ceilingwards. 'To think I've
lived to see the day when Billy One-Eye says he's to get
to work. But he's left his mobile number, says you're to
ring him. Every man and his dog's got a mobile these days,'
he added, shoving the piece of paper across. 'Sure, when
you think o' the crap floatin' about the airwaves – and they
say no sound ever dies. What they'll make of it all out on
Neptune . . .' As if to illustrate the point, he let out a ripping
fart, one of his specials, born of last night's Guinness and
his wife's famous steak-and-kidney pudding. Some bug-
eyed monster would be swivelling his finger round in his
antenna over that one in about 4.18 hours' time, thought
Slider, heading for his room.

When One-Eyed Billy answered, there was a babble of
background noise which Slider identified, with the aid of a
Metropolitan train bashing past on the viaduct, as
Shepherd's Bush market.

'Hang on a sec,' Billy said, and there was an interval of

indeterminate noise, together with the whistling of Billy's breath, and then at last a low, cryptic, 'Hullo?'

'I'm still here.'

'I've gone round the back for a bit of quiet,' Billy explained. 'I'll have to be quick, only Uncle Sam'll be after me.'

'So what have you got for me?'

'Well,' he said, obviously deeply reluctant, 'about this Lenny bloke what got offed in the park. I don't like getting mixed up in it. My young lady wouldn't like it. Dead posh she is. But me dad said I'd got to help you, so I been asking around.'

'Good for you.'

'But you got to promise to keep me out of it, 'cos of my young lady.'

'Keep you out of what? Spit it out, Billy. What've you got?'

'This geezer what I know, knows Lenny,' Billy murmured, and Slider could imagine the hand cupped round the mouthpiece for security. 'Knows what he was into. It was somethink heavy. He's scared shitless, this geezer. He won't come in the nick and talk to you. So it's gotter be a meet.'

'All right. Where and when?'

'It's gotter be off the manor. He's scared someone'll see him.'

Slider sighed. 'This had better be the goods, Billy. If I find you've been wasting my time—'

'It's the goods all right,' Billy said, faintly resentful. 'I'm tryin' twelp, like me dad said. But this bloke's scared for 'is life.'

'All right, so where?' Slider said again. Off the manor? He hoped it wouldn't be anywhere too exotic.

'You know the Dog up the North Pole?'

Slider translated this encryption effortlessly. It was a pub called the Dog and Sportsman (or as Atherton called it, the Dog and Scrotum) on the corner of North Pole Road. It was only surprise that checked him. North Pole Road was about three-quarters of a mile from the White City. If that was 'off the manor', the unknown informant had a very parochial standard of geography.

'Yes. I know it,' he said.

'I'll get him in there,' said Billy. ''Smorning, about eleven. I got to go up Willesden for me uncle, so he won't know. All right?'

'All right,' Slider agreed.

'But you gotter come alone,' Billy said. 'He'll talk to you, 'cos I told him you was straight, but if you bring anyone wiv you he'll scarper.'

'All right, Billy. I'll be there,' Slider said. All told he was getting off lightly. It could have been midnight under the railway bridge in Huddersfield, with all its attendant problems. But if the unknown informant really was scared, wouldn't he have wanted somewhere a bit more private and a lot darker than a pub on a main road at eleven in the morning?

Before heading out for the 'meet', Slider snatched a moment to ring Irene to let her know he had dropped the children off as arranged, otherwise she'd be ringing and accusing him of thoughtlessness and not caring about his children's safety. Materially she was very comfortable with her new man, but he had found that the less she had to worry about at home, the more she sought out a *casus belli* with him. He supposed it used up her spare energy – and Irene was one of those whiplash-thin women who never sit still. It was a pity Ernie Newman had a cleaning-woman:

Irene had no Hoovering to do any more to work it off.

'Oh, by the way, Kate was asking me about taking fencing lessons,' he said.

'Fencing?' Irene sounded blank.

A lifetime's knowledge made him familiar with her thought processes. He smiled. 'With swords. Not garden fencing.'

'Oh! Well, I know they do teach girls woodwork these days . . . Fencing? They say it's good for the figure,' Irene dredged up from the wide-ranging sagacities of 'Them'. 'It makes you graceful. As good as ballet, that way.'

'She can hardly be said to *have* a figure yet. Anyway, I just thought I'd warn you, so she didn't take you by surprise.'

'Why, are you against it? It must be all properly supervised or they wouldn't offer it.'

'I'm not against it. Fencing's a big thing in the Met – a lot of coppers do it. But it's Extra.'

'Oh! Well, that's—' She stopped, and Slider divined from the intonation that she had been about to say, 'That's all right, Ernie can afford it,' but caught herself just in time. 'I expect it's just a passing fad,' she said instead. 'You know what she's like.'

'If she's really serious about it . . .'

'We'll see,' Irene said comfortingly. 'She'll probably have forgotten by the time she gets home.'

Which meant, he translated when he had hung up, that if Kate really wanted to take fencing, Ernie would cough up and they would all try not to mention it to Slider. His former marriage had become like a game of bridge, where you had to translate codes to discover the true state of your partner's hand. He thought fencing would be good for Kate, but he simply couldn't afford it on his screw. That was a fact. Now all he had to decide was whether he minded more denying her the pleasure, or letting Ernie Bloody Newman be Father Christmas – again! Life! he thought. Hate it or ignore it, you can't love it.

The Dog and Scrotum was unreconstructed fifties, an arterial road giant too large for its clientele now that they all had more comfort at home and didn't need to seek it outside. In defiance of the national trend it served no food but crisps and pork scratchings, so at the lunchtime session it was the haunt of equally unreconstructed old keffs of the sort who wore a cap indoors and rolled their own cigarettes, plus a sprinkling of undesirables who had been banned from all the other pubs in the area.

The Dog occupied a corner spot, with two doors, one in each street. One-Eyed Billy and his friend were sitting at the table beside the main door, a position in which, on account of the way the door opened, they could see anyone coming through before *they* saw *them*, and could also keep an eye on the subsidiary door onto the side street. This positioning did not escape Slider's notice, and he was very sure it could not have been Billy Cheeseman's idea. His friend, then, had something of the pro about him.

Billy waved Slider over and introduced the other man with a hint of awe. 'This is my mate Everet Boston. Him and me was at school together.'

'Yeah, for one year. Long time ago, Bill,' the other said, as if distancing himself from that happy time. His eyes scanned Slider and darted away to check the rest of the pub again. He was a tall black man who, if he was a contemporary of Billy's, looked a lot younger than he was. He could have passed for mid-twenties, and had an air of flexible slenderness which was belied, on closer inspection, by the power in the arms and chest.

Beside him on the seat was a very fine suede jacket which Slider could smell was new. He wore his hair in four long dreadlocks caught into a bunch behind, his clothes were casual but sharp and expensive, he had the obligatory gold crucifix and chain round his neck, and he sat at an angle with one leg crossed over the other, clasping the ankle with the hand that was not occupied with his smoke. The word 'cool' sprang to mind, and then slunk away, acknowledging its inadequacy. No wonder they were meeting 'up the North Pole'.

'Get you a drink?' Slider asked, mindful of the proprieties.

'Yeah, I'll have a pint, please,' One-Eyed Billy said quickly, happy as if it were a social occasion.

Everet Boston seemed to hesitate a breath, and then said, 'Captain Morgan. Straight up.'

Slider got them, and a tonic water for himself, and when he brought them back to the table, Boston shifted along the banquette to the next table, giving Slider his seat and keeping the clear getaway for himself. He tossed back half the rum without speaking, and then said, 'You wanna know 'bout Lenny Baxter.'

'Anything you can tell me. I'm very grateful to you for coming forward.'

Boston waved the kindness away with a short sweep of the hand. 'I ain't done it for you. Billy ast me an' I owe 'im one. An' there's another reason.' He waved that away too. 'But I shoon't be here. Make it quick, right? An' no *names*,' he added, with a fierce look at Billy. 'You can't say it's me, right?'

'Who are you afraid of?' Slider asked.

Boston shrugged. 'If they find out, I'm brown bread. I ain't tellin' *you*.'

They all watched too much television these days. 'Okay,' Slider said. 'Any way you like it.'

One-Eyed Billy was evidently deeply impressed with his friend. The rum, the dreadlocks, the cryptic utterances, the hint of violence in the air: it all added up to one supercool dude. He beamed with proprietorial pride, so that with Everet's flickering caution and Slider's professional reserve they made a thoroughly mismatched trio.

'I won't quote you,' Slider said. 'Tell me about Lenny Baxter. What was he up to?' To prime the pump he added, 'I know he was in financial trouble. He used to play the ponies up to a year ago, and lost heavily. And he lost his job at Golden Loans because he was fiddling the takings.'

'Yeah, old Lenny was in trouble,' Everet Boston said. 'He was a rotten gambler, man! Never 'ad no common when it come to 'orses. You fink he stopped playing the ponies? But 'e never. He just stopped going to the bettin' shop, right? That's when I got 'im the job, yeah?'

'What job?'

'He wasn't just runnin' for ol' Herbie Weedon,' Boston said, with a scorn in his voice that suggested if Slider didn't know that, he didn't know *nuffin'*, man. 'He was a bookie's runner.'

'Illegal bookmaking,' Slider said, enlightened.

Boston shrugged. ''At's right, man. On the street. No tax, no pain, right?'

It was big business these days, Slider knew. If you bet at a betting shop, you paid tax either on your stake or on your winnings. Bet with an illegal bookie and it was all tax-free, as were the bookie's profits. And he would give you credit, which William Hill would not. Of course, it was on his terms, and the exaction of dues and interest on such loans could sometimes be a stressful process, which was why runners had to be big, fit men – like the late lamented Lenny. Like Everet Boston, perhaps?

'Is that what you're into, son?' Slider asked, trying to catch the flitting eyes.

'I ain't no son of *yours*,' Boston said scornfully. Slider was pretty sure he was right.

'But you work for the same boss?'

'What I do is my biz, okay? I'm tellin' you about Lenny.'

'Fair enough,' Slider said. 'How did you know him?'

'I met 'im down the snooker hall down Harlesden High Street. Must be two-three years ago. I fought he was all right, sort of. Guess I didn't know 'im that well,' he added broodingly.

'So who is this boss Lenny was running for?'

Everet shook his head. 'I ain't tellin' you *that*,' he said, as if amazed at the stupidity of the question. 'What ju fink, I'm nuts? You find out for y'self if you wanna know. Look, Lenny was in bovver. He was runnin' for Herbie an' he was runnin' for this other boss. He was suppose' to fix the bets and take the money, that was all, but 'e couldn't keep off the ponies 'imself, right? An' 'e was unlucky. He started owin' more'n he could pay. So he started crossin' the money, usin' Herbie's money to make up what he was short on the bettin' money.'

'And Herbie found out and sacked him?'

'Yeah. Then he was really in the clarts. So he went round some of Herbie's customers, try to get 'em to pay him like before, told 'em he was still workin' for Herbie.'

And one of them was Eddie Cranston's bird and he objected, sought Lenny out, and got into a fight, Slider thought. But Lenny could look after himself, and the fight was over before it began. So who killed him? Did Eddie go back for a second crack?

He tried a wide shot. 'What was Lenny doing in the park that night?'

'He used to do some business there,' Boston said. 'He used to sell shit an' poppers – maybe white, I dunno – and that was where 'is customers met 'im, right?'

'How did he get in?'

Boston shrugged. 'Froo the gate, man, how should I know? But everyone know that's where 'e is certain times.'

'Was he selling drugs for this same boss?'

'Nah. I don't fink so. He never done the serious stuff, just bhang an' amyl, y'know? I fink it was just like a side-line. I dunno where he got the gear. Lenny, 'e was mixed up in a lot of stuff. He liked to freelance. Maybe that's why he got in trouble.'

Slider felt a certain weariness coming over him. If Lenny Baxter was selling cannabis and amyl nitrate poppers it opened up a whole new cast of potential murderers. Eddie Cranston had a lump of cannabis in his flat. Maybe he had been one of Lenny's customers and knew him, therefore, a little better than he had let on. And if he was a customer, he'd have known where to find Lenny to kill him. The trouble was, so would everyone else.

He struck out again, hoping for shallower water.

'How was Sonny Collins mixed up in it?'

Everet Boston looked surprised, and suddenly fright-ened. 'How d'you know about Sonny?' Slider got his own back and merely shrugged. 'I don't know what Sonny's into,' Boston said. 'He does some biz for the—' He stopped himself, and went on, 'for the Man. I dunno what, though. Lenny run messages sometimes. We all do. Sonny passed 'em on.' He stopped again. His eyes flickered nervously. 'I don't know nuffink about what Sonny does. The Man keep everything very private. We don't ask an' he don' tell. That way he stay ahead an' we stay alive. You don't wanna get on the wrong side of 'im, I tell you.' He slugged back the rest of the rum and said, 'Look, man, I gotta go. It's dangerous talkin' to you.'

'You think the Man might be watching you?'

'He watches everybody,' Boston said.

'Tell me who he is.'

'You fink I'm mad? I shoon't be here.'

'Yes, why are you here?' Slider asked. 'I'm very grateful, but what made you do it?'

The supercool pose altered subtly as a different Everet peeped through the tightly drawn curtains of street atti- tude. 'There's this bird Lenny lived with.'

'Tina,' Slider supplied. 'You know her?'

'I knew her before.' Everet looked suddenly ferocious. 'Lenny was a bastard! He was a total ratfuck bastard an' he got what was comin' to 'im. I'd a killed 'im myself if I could a got away wiv it.'

'I suppose you didn't kill him, did you?'

'I jus' told you. Wojer fink, I'm comin' here givin' myself away? You fink I got shit for brains? I come here to help you, and no way you goin' to stick this on me, you bastard copper! I'm gettin' out of here.' He half stood, and glared at Billy. 'Last time I do anyfink for you.'

Slider spread his hands. 'Calm down. Of course I don't think you did it. But it would help if you could tell me where you were that evening, just so we can cross you off the list. Between eleven Monday night and eight Tuesday morning.'

'I was down the Snookerama all night, from about ten till they shut, about one o'clock,' Everet said, head back in a defiant pose. 'Then I went home. If I'd've knew what was goin' down I'd've been there in the park givin' 'em the

Mexican Wave while they done it, all right? But I never.'

'I believe you,' Slider said. 'Do you know who did kill him?'

Boston hesitated. 'Lenny, he trouble. He don' play by the rules, right? I reckon he had it comin'. And nobody won't shed no tears for him. Not Tina, that's for sure.'

'Do you know where Tina is now?'

The innocent question seemed to shock Everet. He stared at Slider, his eyes widening. 'I fought she was at 'ome.'

'She's not, and her clothes are gone. Where is she?'

Everet's lips parted, and for a moment Slider thought he was going to get something, but he only licked them and then, as if coming to a sudden decision, got up with a violent movement and said, 'I gotta go.'

'If you want to tell me any more,' Slider said desperately, 'you know where to get me. If you give me names, I can protect you.'

'No-one coon't protec' me against the Man,' he said bleakly, and with a sidling speed, like a threatened snake, he headed for the door. At the last minute, he turned to say, 'That night Lenny got done – it wasn't 'is night for dealin' shit.' And then he was gone.

Slider would have liked a moment's silence with his thoughts, but One-Eyed Billy wanted notice and recognition.

'He's brill, innee? Ol' Ev was always a right one. He was always in trouble at school. I got you the goods, didn't I, Mr Slider? You'll tell Dad I helped you like he said I had to?'

'What puzzles me,' Slider said, to Billy since he had to, 'is if he's so scared of his boss finding out he's been talking to me, why meet here in broad daylight?'

Billy looked pleased. 'He told me that. He said anyone

can go in a pub, and in daylight you can see people coming. He said if you meet down an alley after dark they know you're up to something.'

'That's very interesting,' Slider said. Stupid, possibly, but interesting. No, to be fair, it was probably true. Maybe Everet Boston really was as cool as he tried to appear. 'What was this Tina to him?' he asked. 'An old girlfriend?'

'I dunno,' Billy said. 'He never mentioned her to me.'

But he obviously cared strongly about her, Slider thought, and he was obviously alarmed that she was missing. He thought of the two heavies outside Lenny's house. Had she been abducted? Or was she fleeing this tiresome Mr Big Everet wouldn't name? At all events, Boston's moment of humanity warmed Slider to him just a degree, while poor old Unlucky Lenny, the victim, was becoming less lovable the more was discovered about him.

As Slider approached his room his nostrils began to twitch, but he was so deep in thought and speculation that he didn't realise what it was he was smelling until he turned in at his open doorway and saw Joanna sitting on his desk swinging her legs. It was her scent, of course. Her face lit up like a pinball machine awarding two thousand bonus points and an extra game, and he was across the room in a Cartlandesque single bound.

When they paused for breath, Atherton said, 'Ahem. Cough cough.' He was standing by the door into the office, and on the Everet Boston principle had been masked from Slider's view by the open door onto the corridor.

With large portions of Joanna still pressed against him, Slider could afford to be lenient. 'What are you doing here? Come to ask about that career move to the stolen cars unit?'

'I was keeping her entertained until you got back.'

'Well, you can go away now.' He turned back to Joanna. 'It's so good to see you. You look well.'

'She looks more than well,' Atherton said. 'She looks glowing.'

'Are you still there?'

'Apparently,' Atherton said blandly. 'How did your interview with One-Eyed Billy go?'

Slider moaned. 'At a time like this, he wants me to think of work.'

'Shall I go?' Joanna offered helpfully.

'No, no, stay. I don't have any secrets from you.'

'We could go and get some lunch while we talk,' Atherton suggested. 'Joanna's hungry.'

'Of course, you must be. It'll have to be the canteen, though.'

'Okay by me,' Joanna said.

'Has Porson come in?'

'No, he's not coming,' Atherton said as they headed out of the office. 'He phoned in to say he'll be out for a couple of days. I hope it's nothing serious.'

'So do I. He's a funny old duck, but I like him.'

As it was Monday, the canteen had bubble and squeak on.

'They like to keep up these little traditions,' Atherton said, handing Joanna a tray.

'It's quite good,' Slider said. 'It goes with the cold roast pork.'

'And wiz zat, madame,' Atherton hammed, 'Ah recommend ze rock 'ard carrots and ze soggy cauliflowair.'

'Oh brave new world, that has such menus in it,' Joanna said. 'I'll have the cottage pie, please. What?' she protested, catching Atherton's expression. 'I've been living on horse and chips and Wiener schnitzel for weeks.'

'Same for me,' Slider said to the server.

'Chips an' gravy, love?' she offered Joanna. And to Slider, 'No gravy for you, isn't it, sir? Would you like some of the bubble on yours?'

Atherton took a salad. 'I don't know how he does it,' he said as they sought a table. 'One look from his sad-puppy eyes and he has 'em eating out of his hand.'

Joanna batted her eyelashes at Slider. 'I'd eat anything out of your hand. Even cottage pie. Do you know,' she added in a normal voice, 'the worst thing in the world to watch someone eat?'

'McLaren's fried egg sandwiches?'

'Worse than that.'

'*With* tomato ketchup?'

'Worse than that. It's what Brian Harrop – second trumpet in the Phil – used to have at the Clarendon Arms after concerts. A cottage pie sandwich. It's true. A great big wodge of cottage pie, with gravy, between two slices of white Wonderbread. It's something you never forget. Like doing the nose job with porridge.'

'Thank you for sharing that with us,' Atherton said, sliding into a corner seat. 'So, dear old guv o' mine, what about this new lead from One-Eyed Billy? Tell us, Entellus.'

'One-eyed—?' Joanna began, but Atherton stopped her with a quick gesture.

'Not important. Who's the informant?'

'It was a dude called Everet Boston,' Slider said, unloading his tray.

'A *dude*?' they chorused in protest.

'No other word for it,' Slider said. 'A slick, smart, street-wise, slinky-shouldered black with a Willesden accent you could slice and bottle. He was as painfully hip as a hospital waiting list.'

'I'm getting the picture,' Atherton said in disparaging tones.

'Yes,' Slider said, 'but for all his attitude, he wasn't standing behind the door with One-Eyed Billy when they were passing out the brains.'

'Please,' Joanna begged, 'stop with all this one-eyed stuff. It sounds like a black-and-white B film from the fifties.'

'Billy Cheeseman,' Slider elucidated. 'His dad owned a pie and eel shop down the Goldhawk Road.'

Joanna put her head in her hands and whimpered. 'No more! I'm coming over all Jack Warner.'

'I'll talk to Atherton,' Slider said kindly, and between forkfuls, told what he had heard that morning, adding a swift blocking in of the rest of the case for Joanna's benefit.

'And you didn't bring him in?' Atherton asked when he had finished.

'I'd have needed at least eight wild horses,' Slider said. 'But Billy obviously knows him, and where he lives. If need be we can go and fetch him, but I'd rather not at this stage. He was genuinely scared, and if we want him later in court we'd better cherish him now.'

'You believed all this bollocks about a Moriarty lurking in the shadows?'

'*He* believed he was in danger,' Slider said. 'I said from the beginning it looked more like a gang killing to me.'

'You did,' Atherton allowed.

'If the boss, whoever he was, ordered Lenny's killing for some unspecified crime against the organisation, the same could happen to Everet.'

'So you think it was an execution?' Atherton said.

'How many times do I have to tell you—'

'He doesn't speculate ahead of his data,' Joanna finished for him. 'He likes to keep an open mind. Don't you, beloved?'

'What she said,' Slider nodded.

'The thing that strikes me, as an outsider, as significant,' Joanna said, 'was saying Monday wasn't Lenny's usual night for selling drugs. Which suggests he must have been meeting someone there by arrangement, who, presumably, killed him. So doesn't that rather rule out this other bloke, Eddie Whatsit?'

'Unless he followed him,' Slider said. 'He might have been out looking for him, spotted him on his way to the park and followed.'

'On that basis, it might have been anyone,' Atherton said.

'Quite. But there's also the possibility that Eddie was also working for the boss, whoever he was. We know he's stupid, but he might be useful as a blunt instrument, if he takes orders well.'

'Maybe that's why he stayed indoors for two days. Maybe he was told to lie low,' Joanna said. 'The stuff about being too vain to go out with a black eye sounds a bit thin to me.'

'You've not met him,' Atherton said. 'He's more vain than a blood donor clinic. I can't believe anyone would use him, even as a blunt instrument, if they had any choice. Well,' he concluded, spearing the last quarter tomato, 'it's obvious that Sonny Collins is the man to lean on.'

'I thought you'd had two goes at him,' Joanna said.

'Yes, but now it's time to take the gloves off,' Atherton said. He noted her expression. 'I can spout worse clichés than that in a good cause.'

'You're right,' Slider said. 'We'll get him in again, and this time he stays in until he comes across.'

'I suppose that means you want me to scarper,' Joanna said with barely a sigh. She knew the score.

'I'll try not to be late tonight,' Slider said, 'but you know—'

'I know. Don't worry about me. I'll ring you later and see how you're getting on.'

'What will you do?'

'I'll go and see Sue. Is she at her place or yours?' she asked Atherton.

'Mine, as far as I know,' he said.

'Oh good. I'm longing to see your cats.' She kissed Slider goodbye with her eyes, respecting his dignity. 'Go get 'em, tiger! See you later.'

CHAPTER TEN

Chicken Ticker

This time Sonny Collins came in accompanied by his brief, none other than the famous David Stevens, who represented all the worst villains in west London. Stevens was a small man with a well-lunched figure, smooth hair and a smooth face. He had merry twinkling eyes, the unfailing cheerfulness of one of life's higher earners, and suits so expensive and beautiful they would make a boulevardier faint.

Slider's heart always sank when he saw Stevens turn up with someone he wanted to question. They had crossed swords many times, and Stevens usually came off better. Behind his bonhomie he had a mind like the labyrinth of Knossos, and any argument he put up had more clauses than Santa's family tree; but Slider couldn't help liking the man. He beckoned, and Stevens turned aside willingly to chat with him.

'How can Collins afford your fees?' Slider asked, after they had exchanged the amenities. Stevens only beamed at him. 'Don't tell me the brewery's paying his bills?'

'A famous brewing firm would naturally want to protect its reputation,' Stevens said.

'So it is them?'

'I didn't say that.'

'I can't believe they'd lash out that much on a bloke who runs the Phoenix. Have you seen the Phoenix?'

'No. But I can't believe it either.'

'More likely they'd just sack him if they wanted to keep their hands clean.'

'Much more likely.'

Slider whimpered. 'Five minutes talking to you and I feel like a dog trying to bite its own tail.'

'But where can you get one at this time of day?' Stevens said genially.

'So you aren't going to tell me who's paying you?'

'Not in these trousers.'

'You know we're investigating a very serious crime?'

'Of course. And if my client is suspected of committing a very serious crime I'm sure he would like to hear your evidence.'

'I just want to ask him some questions,' Slider said. 'Why does he feel the need for a high-powered brief? Has he got a guilty conscience?'

'My client has already co-operated with you on two occasions. Taking him from his legitimate business for a third inquisition almost amounts to harassment, and he felt he needed a friend at his side to guide him.'

'I love the way you talk,' Slider marvelled through his frustration. 'I suppose what that means with the peel off is that he's not going to tell me anything?'

'That depends on what you ask him,' Stevens said, obviously enjoying himself hugely.

'I'm glad someone's having fun,' said Slider. 'All right, let's get this over. I wish you'd remember sometimes,' he added as they headed for the interview room, 'that we're supposed to be on the same side.'

'Not we,' Stevens said. 'Only you.' He patted Slider on

the shoulder. 'You need a holiday, old son. Cruise in the Caribbean, maybe. I've just come back from one and it's lovely there this time of year.'

Sonny Collins sat almost bursting out of his jacket with subdued power and emotions, but – interestingly to Slider – seemed less at ease with David Stevens beside him than he had seemed without. At every question he looked at the solicitor for instructions on how to answer, which seemed to inhibit him, especially as for the most part the sublimely relaxed Stevens merely twinkled at him.

It was as Slider expected: Collins would tell him nothing.

'Mr Collins,' Slider said patiently, 'we know that you knew Lenny Baxter, so why do you keep denying it?'

'Never seen him before in my life,' Collins repeated.

'You called him by name in the presence of Eddie Cranston.'

'Eddie told you that? He's a lying toe-rag.'

'I agree with you,' Slider said. 'Eddie's scum, but in this case he's telling the truth. You and Lenny Baxter did business together.'

'Prove it.'

'I have a witness who says you did.'

'He's lying too.'

'I don't think so. He worked alongside Lenny.'

'So where is he, then?' Collins said defiantly. 'What's his name?'

Slider put his hands flat on the table. 'Look, Sonny,' he said, 'you know that we've got an ongoing investigation into your little doings. If you don't start co-operating with me—'

Stevens intervened. 'Sounds like the opening phrases of a threat. You will be careful not to threaten my client, won't you?'

Slider tried to ignore him. 'Lenny Baxter was killed, and I think you know a lot more about it than you've said. Who was Lenny working for? Tell me that, and maybe it'll be enough from you for now. We're looking for a murderer. I don't want to clutter up my desk processing you for whatever little games you're mixed up in. Buy yourself some time, Sonny. You can clean up your act before we come after you. Tell me who Lenny was working for, and go back to your pub with an easy mind.'

Collins, sitting up straight as a ramrod, looked scornful. 'Easy mind? What do you know about it? You don't know who you're dealing with.'

'My client has nothing more to say to you,' Stevens intervened smoothly.

'Who, Sonny?' Slider urged. 'Who am I dealing with?'

'You got nothing on me!' Collins said. 'I'm saying nothing. I want it on record. I know nothing and I've said nothing.'

'He must be a pretty big shit if he can put the frighteners on you,' Slider said with interest. 'What can he do to you, Sonny? Lose you your job? I can do that. If you know something and don't tell me, I can have you for obstruction. Maybe perverting the course of justice. You can go down for that. How would you like a spell inside? Plenty of people inside would admire your fine physique. I'm sure you'd make lots of new friends.'

'Do it then. I don't care. It'd be a piece of piss compared with—' He stopped himself, and his good eye swivelled round to Stevens. 'I want out of here!'

'Unless you are intending to charge my client . . . ?' Stevens said on an interrogative note, looking at Slider, who waved a negative hand. 'Then my client is free to go.'

Slider looked sadly at Collins. 'You leave me with no option but to bring forward the investigation into your other activities. Everything's going to come out. All the little bits of business going on at the back door. We've got plenty on you already and if you don't think we'll get the rest you overestimate the loyalty of your customers. You're going to go down, Sonny – and all for want of a name. That's all you have to do, give me the name.'

Collins, already on his feet, paused, clenching his fists down by his sides. It seemed a curiously involuntary gesture. 'You don't know what you're talking about,' he said again. 'If I gave you his name—'

'This interview is over,' Stevens said.

'He'd never know it was you,' Slider said, holding Collins's gaze.

'Over,' Stevens repeated.

'*I'd* know,' Collins said with finality. 'Do what you like, I'm saying nothing.'

It was an odd little emphasis that puzzled Slider.

Atherton sat on the windowsill, backlit by the sunshine like a Dutch old master. 'So he's tacitly admitted that he works for the same boss – or at least, does business with him.'

'But he's too scared to give the name,' Slider said. 'Scared or – something.'

'Something? I'm dazzled by your eloquence.'

Slider frowned. 'There was something odd going on there. Some emotion or concern I couldn't guess at, but it was stronger than the fear of prison.'

'And Everet Boston's scared blue. This man provokes powerful loyalties.'

'Oh, so you believe in the big boss now?'

'Do me a lemon.'

Slider looked worried. 'I'm wondering about David Stevens.'

'Don't. That way lies madness and destruction.'

'But I can't believe Collins would have the money or the know-how to hire him, and if it's not the brewery—'

'Then it's Mr Big retaining him for defence of one of his minions?' Atherton said.

'Shoring up a potentially weak place in the organisation,' Slider concluded. 'But if that's the case then Stevens knows who he is.'

'As I said, that way lies madness,' Atherton repeated. 'Anyway, it's all pure conjecture. You know my feelings about this whole Mr Big story.'

'You think I've got a Moriarty complex.'

'I think small-time crooks like to talk big. If Boston's right about Lenny dealing drugs, it's more than likely he was doing a spot of trade in the park and one of his customers was blasted and did him to avoid having to pay.'

'But then why didn't they take the money?' Slider objected. 'And where's the lock and chain?'

'I think you can get too hung up on the lock and chain. They'll turn up somewhere.'

'They irritate me.'

'Maybe the park keeper's got them.'

'Maybe. I think we'd better have another word with him, at least clear up how Lenny was able to use the park as his office. Tell Mackay to go and fetch him in. He'd better check with the council first to find out where he is. I don't suppose he spends his entire day hanging around the one park.'

The telephone call established that Ken Whalley had not been in to work. It was natural enough, said the woman in the parks department, after such a terrible shock. Two weeks' compassionate leave, they'd given him, the same as you get for a close-family bereavement. They were going to arrange counselling for him, as soon as he phoned in to say he was ready for it. He was at home as far as she knew. She didn't think he had any family or anything, so unless he'd gone away for a holiday . . .

'Found him cowering indoors with the chain on,' Mackay reported when he had brought him in. 'Wouldn't answer the door at first, and even after he'd seen my brief it took me ten minutes to talk him out. He thought I was from the council, come to tell him he'd got the sack.'

'But they've given him leave,' Atherton said. 'Why would they do that if they were going to sack him?'

'I don't think he's very bright,' Mackay said. 'Apparently they offered him counselling and he thought that was something to do with a solicitor. Thought it meant they were taking him to court.'

'What for?'

'Dunno,' Mackay shrugged. 'He's not making much sense.'

When Slider went downstairs he could see why. Ken Whalley had gone downhill since Tuesday. He was unshaven, his hair was a wild bush, and he smelt as if he hadn't washed in as long as he hadn't shaved. He was wearing a pair of black shell-suit bottoms and an indescribably grubby teeshirt, and his bare feet were shoved into flip-flops. His pudgy face seemed to have melted into a shape of woe and the hair sprouted from it in irregular patches like mould. His droopy basset-hound eyes raised themselves to Slider's face in abject misery. He was a bad dog, and he had come to be punished.

'I never meant it to happen. I never meant no harm,' he whined before Slider had spoken. 'I sweartergod, if I'd of knew, I wouldn't never of done it. But when he ast me, I didn't see no harm in it. I never knew what he wanted it for.'

'All right, just calm down and we'll go through it from the beginning,' Slider said.

'Am I gonner lose me job?'

Slider sat opposite him, wishing there were a way to stay upwind of Whalley's miasma; but in a small enclosed space all directions were down. 'Never mind about your job now,' he said with measured sternness. 'This is much more serious than your job. If you're going to stay out of prison, you're going to have to co-operate with me fully, tell me everything.'

'Oh Gawd,' Whalley said faintly. 'What—?'

'No, I ask the questions, you answer. That's the way it's going to be. Do you understand?'

'Yessir,' Whalley said. Being managed seemed to brace him a little, as Slider had guessed it would.

'Now then, how did you first meet Lenny Baxter?'

Whalley licked his lips. 'I never—'

'The truth! You lied to me before. You said you'd never seen him before in your life. But that wasn't true. You knew him very well. That's why you were so shocked when you found him dead.'

'I fought,' Whalley said in the same wisp of a voice, 'I fought I'd get the blame for it.'

'How did you meet him?'

'He come up to me in the park one day. Got chatting. Wanted to know about me routine, locking up and that.'

'And he made you a proposition?'

'Not then. Not right away. I see him in the park a few times. Sometimes he comes over and chats. Then one day he comes in when I was locking up—'

'When was that?'

'Last year. In the summer. I know it was summer 'cos it was a late lock-up. 'Cos it gets dark later in summer,' he added helpfully.

'I understand. Go on. What did Lenny say?'

'He ast me to go for a drink. So I says yes. We went down the Coningham. That's his local, he says. So we goes for a pint.'

'And he made a proposition to you,' Slider asked, hoping to speed matters up a bit. 'What did he want you to do?'

Whalley looked down at his dirty fingernails, coming to the moment of shame.

'He wanted me to borrow him the key.'

'The key?'

'To the Frithville Gardens gate. He said he'd give it back. I said I couldn't, 'cos of opening up in the morning, so he said he'd come the next day after I opened and he'd have it back to me before I had to lock up.'

'And what did he want it for?'

'I dunno,' Whalley said, still looking down.

'I think you do,' Slider said.

'He never said.'

'He wanted to get it copied, didn't he? So he'd have a key of his own. So he could get in and out of the park when he liked. Isn't that right?'

Whalley nodded. 'Maybe. He never said, but – well, what else'd he want it for?'

'Why did he want to get into the park?'

'I dunno. He never said.'

'You do know.' No answer. 'Look at me!' The reluctant eyes lifted, full of fear and guilt. 'What did he want to use the park for?'

'I swear I dunno. It's the honestroof.'

'You must have known he was up to no good. Why did you go along with it?'

'Well, he ast me.'

'You could have said no.'

Whalley looked as though he might cry. 'I was scared,' he admitted. 'He was big. You never saw him. He was a big bloke. I fought he'd do me over if I said no.'

Slider looked at the pathetic lump of putty. Ken Whalley was such a coward you could have held him up through the post.

'So what did he offer you for letting him borrow the key? Was it money?'

'No,' Whalley said. 'I never took no money off him, not a penny, only the drink he bought me.'

Slider detected a note Whalley was probably unaware of. 'Not money. But he did give you something, didn't he? What was it?'

'I can't,' Whalley said, bowing his head. 'I can't say.'

'You will say. What did he give you? Come on, Ken, I can sit here all day if I have to. You're going to tell me. What did he give you in exchange for the key?' Whalley muttered the answer, and Slider couldn't catch it, it was so low. 'What? Say it again. Louder. What did he give you?'

'It was a woman,' Whalley said, and from the slump of his shoulders, it was clear they were coming to the bottom of this sad creature. 'It was this bird he lived with – Tina, he called her. She was gorgeous. A real cracker. Well, I'm – you know. I mean, look at me! I'm no good with women. They don't fancy me. I've never had a proper girlfriend.' Out with the plastic waterweed and the miniature gothic castle, they were down to the gravel now. 'If you wanna know,' he said abjectly, 'I'd never done it. Never in me life. I'd never done – you know – with a woman.'

It was a sad confession, and as a man with plenty of you-know under his belt, Slider pitied him.

'Are you gay, Ken?'

'No! I'm not like that. I like women. Only they don't like me. They laugh at me. And Lenny – he was such a big handsome sod. He could have all the women he wanted. He treated 'em rough and they loved it. But me . . . He got it out of me, when we had the drink, and he said if I'd do that little favour for him, he'd set me up with a woman. I mean, set me up like – have sex with her. He said she'd do anything I wanted. I thought she'd turn out to be this real dog, you know what I mean? But he said no, he said, she was gorgeous. And she was,' he finished simply.

'So when did this meeting with Tina take place?'

'Next night. After he give me the key back he said he'd meet me at locking-up time and take me to her. I never fought he'd be there.' He looked at Slider to see if he understood.

'You thought once you'd done your part of the bargain he'd have no reason to stick to his? You thought he'd stiff you?'

'Yeah. Why wouldn't he? He'd got what he wanted. But he was there. He played straight with me.' The gratitude was pathetic. This, Slider saw, was one of Lenny's many holds over Ken Whalley's loyalty, that he had had the chance to cheat him and hadn't taken it. 'So he took me to a place – his flat, I suppose it was – and she was there. This black bird, Tina. A real cracker. And young and everything. He left me with her and – and we done it.' He was silent a moment, perhaps reliving the moment. Then he said, 'After that, I never see him again, not to talk to – only the once.'

'When was that?'

'About a fortnight ago. He come in the Smuts, where I drink, and he took me outside and he said, Ken, he said, have you been talking? And I says no, I swear – which I hadn't. I'd never mentioned it to a soul. Why would I?'

'To boast about the girl, maybe?'

'What, tell everyone I'd never done it in me life till then? Anyway, who would I tell? I haven't got any friends,' he said with simple truth. 'No, I never mentioned it to a soul. Anyway, he believes me, and he says, you just keep it that way, he says, 'cos he says if I ever say a word to anyone, he'll know, and he'll get me. He'll beat me up, he says, so's my own mother won't know me. So I never said nothing.'

'Even after he was dead?' Slider said. 'Why didn't you tell me the truth when I first spoke to you? There was nothing he could do to you then.'

'I fought you'd fink I did it. And I fought – all right, he was dead, but someone else would get me. I mean, he musta been in it with someone else. Like – a gang or summink.'

He lit a cigarette with fumbling hands. Slider noticed absently that it was a Gitane, unusual choice for a dork like Whalley. Then his attention sharpened.

'Where did you get those cigarettes, Ken?'

'Lenny sold 'em me cheap. I don't usually smoke this kind. I don't like 'em much, but he let me have 'em so cheap it was worth it.'

'Where did he get them from?'

Whalley looked slightly surprised at the question. 'I dunno. Abroad, I s'pose. Maybe that's what he does – import and that.'

'Illegal import,' Slider said. 'Otherwise known as smuggling.'

Whalley looked frightened again. 'I dunno. He never

said. I didn't know they was illegal. I just – I just—'

'Oh come on, Ken, you know how that game's played. Don't tell me you didn't know they were smuggled.'

'I never ast him. You didn't know Lenny. You never saw him. You wouldn't ast him questions. You just wouldn't.'

'So what was his game? What did he do in the park? Come on, don't say you don't know.'

'I don't, I swear. I didn't want to know.'

'If he was up to something really bad, like dealing drugs, that makes you an accessory. You can go down for that – jail, Ken. Think of that. Locked up for years with a bunch of big ugly tough bastards like Lenny, only not so kind-hearted. You help me out, tell me what Lenny was up to, and I might be able to keep you out of there.'

'I don't – I didn't – I'd tell you if I could, but I *don't know*!' Whalley wailed in fear.

Slider shook his head and sighed. 'Bad choice, Ken. Seriously bad choice. If you won't help me, I can't help you. I'm not going to put myself out for you. You're going down. Not just accessory to Lenny's game, but accessory to his murder. How does that sound? You're going to prison for a long, long time.'

Whalley turned so white Slider thought he was going to throw up. The cigarette shook in his fingers and fell, rolling off the table into his lap; but he didn't notice. His cowardly heart had tried to do a runner: his eyes fluttered upwards and he slumped into a dead faint, his head hitting the table top with a sound like a judge's gavel.

'I think you went a bit too hard on him, guv,' Mackay said impassively.

Joanna sat up, her short, thick hair madly tousled.

'Wow,' she said. Succinct, but heartfelt.

'Why, thank you, ma'am,' Slider said. 'And wow yourself.'

'Food now,' she pronounced.

'No, no, you stay, I'll go. I've had this planned for days.'

'All right,' she said, settling herself back on the pillows, 'I'll do the sultan bit.'

'Sultana,' he corrected, heading, naked, for the door.

'I know, I'm your currant entanglement.'

'More my raisin d'être,' he said.

He was back soon with the tray: the best pâté de fois from the deli in Turnham Green Road, a ripe and creamy Gorgonzola, crusty French bread, fat Italian olives.

'Wow,' she said again.

'Nothing but the best for my lady.' He kissed her, getting back into bed.

'And what's this? Rocket?'

'Dressed with lemon juice and black pepper, à la Atherton.'

'You really did think this through! And what's in the bottle?' She shifted the cooler sleeve upwards to look at the label, and then turned a deeply impressed look on him. 'Meurseult?'

'Uh-huh,' he said modestly, tearing bread.

'I think I love you,' she said. 'This is not the most practical meal to eat in bed. We're going to have serious crumbs in the sheets.'

'I give you my personal promise to grind them to dust later on.'

'Swank-pot.'

'Pâté first or cheese?'

'Pâté, please. Oh, yum! Pour me some wine, also. Thank you.'

Slider lifted his own glass to her. 'To us.'

'To us.' They drank. 'You come very obligingly to the point,' Joanna said; but the phone rang.

'Frolicking bullocks,' said Slider, quite mildly in the circumstances. It was Atherton. 'Good evening, Detective Constable,' Slider said.

'Sorry, guv. Did I catch you in the act?'

'Never mind what I'm up to. Just make it quick.'

'Your wish is my command. They've had a phone call at the office from Herbie Weedon, the Golden Loans geezer. He wants to talk to me. Apparently got something interesting to tell.'

'Good,' said Slider. 'Anything else before I hang up?'

'Slow down a bit. I rang him back and he sounds as nervous as a dog in a Korean restaurant. He said he couldn't talk on the phone. He has to meet me, and he wants it to be now, tonight.'

'Is he serious?'

'I think so. I got the impression when I met him that he's an old pro. He knows which way is up. If he's decided to spill he'll have something worth sticking the bucket under.'

'I wonder why he's changed his mind?'

'I suppose I rang his bell,' Atherton said modestly.

'He could be working for the other side, hoping to find out what you know.'

'I don't think so. That wouldn't frighten him. And he was frightened.'

'All right,' Slider said. 'I'll authorise it. Go and get him while he's hot. But be careful. Don't walk into a trap.'

'Tell your grandmother. I'm the pump, he's the pumpee.'

'I didn't mean that sort of trap.'

'You and your Moriarty complex!'

'I mean it. Be careful. I like your face the way it is.'

'I'm not that sort of girl,' Atherton said, and rang off.

'What was all that about?' Joanna asked, and he told her, and filled her in on the interview with Ken Whalley. 'God, what a sleazy lot,' she said at the end.

'What did you want, glamour? All crime is sleazy,' Slider said, 'and murder's the sleaziest of all.'

'Never mind glamour, you might once in a while investigate some people with nicer habits,' Joanna said. 'This Lenny, lending his girlfriend out like a bicycle!'

'Yes, he's not turning out to be a very lovable chap, our Lenny. Still, he did give Ken Whalley the only happy memory of his life.'

'You men!' Joanna said. 'How can there be any pleasure in having sex with a stranger you'll never see again, knowing they're doing it purely as business? And she probably didn't even get paid!'

'Oh, that'd make it better, would it? If she got paid?'

'Better for her, anyway.'

'And less of this "you men" business.'

'It's a man thing.' She eyed him askance. 'You don't do it, but you understand it.'

'Academically. It's my job to. Are you working up for a quarrel?'

'What, me?' She leaned across and kissed his cheek contritely. 'It's just that the world is too much with us.'

'Late and soon, when you're a detective inspector,' he agreed. 'Have some more wine. Shall I put some music on, to soothe our ruffled breasts?'

'Yes, that'd be nice.'

'I'm getting good at this music business,' he said, getting out of bed. 'When I went over to Atherton's the other day he had the Prokoviev violin concerto on, and I very nearly recognised it.'

'I'm impressed,' she said. When he returned from putting

on the CD, she said, 'Have I told you the story about the Jewish lady in New York, who took her son to the Carnegie Hall? She went up to the box office and asked if they had any tickets for the Isaac Stern concert. The ticket man said no, they were sold out weeks ago. So she says, "How much would they have cost if you had any?" and he said, "I'm afraid the cheapest seat was eighty-five dollars." And the lady whacks her kid round the ear and says, "Now will you practise?"'

Slider laughed, easing himself in under the tray. 'D'you want to try the cheese now, or shall we do a little more practising of our own.'

'The night is young,' said Joanna. 'Let's see how we get on.'

It was much later, after both food and practice, when they were lying in each other's arms talking in a desultory way that she said out of a brief and relaxed silence, 'I'm glad we've got this time together, Bill, because there's something important I want to discuss with you.'

His scalp prickled at the words and the tone of her voice. 'Oh yes?' he said helplessly.

'I don't know if you've guessed what it is. Oh, damn it, I suppose I'd better just come to the point.'

Here it comes, he thought, and would have given anything to put it off. It was another man thing, dislike of this woman thing of always wanting to 'have things out'.

'Go ahead,' he said, bracing himself; and the telephone rang again.

'Oh, bloody Nora,' Joanna said. 'What is it with your telephone? Have you got a symbiotic relationship going with it?'

'Sorry,' he said, reaching for it.

It was Nicholls, and sorry was the first word he said,

too. 'Sorry to interrupt your evening in paradise, but we've got an emergency.'

'It had better be good,' Slider said. 'Or rather, it had better be bad.'

'Oh it's bad,' Nicholls assured him. 'Herbie Weedon's dead, and it's not natural causes. Can you come right away?'

'Shit,' said Slider, not for the first time in his career.

CHAPTER ELEVEN

Herbie Brown Bread

'He didn't turn up at the meeting place,' Atherton said, looking unexpectedly pale.

'Which was?'

'Shepherd's Bush station – the Hammersmith and City line. I was supposed to get a ticket and wait somewhere discreetly until he came through the booking hall, then follow him and get on the train with him. It was his usual ride home. Sit or stand next to him and he'd give me the information under cover of the train noise, but not to look at him or appear to know him, and not to react to anything he said.'

'He really was cautious. Where did he go to on the train?'

'Ladbroke Grove station. He lived in Lancaster Road.'

'That's only two stops. He couldn't have had much to tell you.'

'Maybe it wouldn't have taken long. Maybe it was just the name you've been wanting. Anyway, I waited about twenty minutes past the time and then rang his office, but there was no answer. I thought maybe he'd had some business come in or he just thought better of it, so I gave it up, but as I was walking back to the nick – I was still parked in the yard—'

'Of course.'

'—I passed the building and there was a light on in the Golden Loans window. The street door was on the latch so I went up. The office door was unlocked too. And there he was.'

There he was, thought Slider, and he was not a pretty sight. Herbie Weedon was still sitting in his chair behind the vast and cluttered desk, where he had lived so much of his life, and from which he was not parted even in death. When the forensic teams had finished and the mortuary van came for him it was going to be hell's own job getting him out, like prising an enormous crab from its shell.

There had been little struggle: a few papers scuffed to the floor, that was all. Maybe he'd tried to get up: Slider imagined him putting his hands on the desk top, grunting as his breath shortened, trying to push himself to his feet. But they'd have been between him and the door, so even if he got upright, where could he go? No, more likely he'd have tried to talk his way out of it. Not the physical sort, Herbie. He must have talked his way out of – and into – a lot of things in his life.

It didn't work this time. The red and purple face Atherton had described so graphically was congested, the little bloodshot eyes bulged like those of a stuffed toy, and round his neck was a thick iron chain with a padlock hanging from it like a pendant, resting on his chest, as if they'd made him Lord Mayor of some very industrial city. The marks in the swollen flesh of his neck exactly matched the links of the chain. There was no doubt he had been stran-gled with it.

'Though it probably wouldn't have taken much,' Atherton said. 'He wasn't exactly in peak condition.' He felt not only royally pissed off at having been cheated of the information he was to have had, but ridiculously sorry about Herbie. Ridiculous because Herbie had been an old villain, and there was no doubt he had caused much misery in his time; but there was something about this penned and helpless death that disturbed him. Herbie's eyes were open. He had seen it coming, like the stalled ox awaiting the blunt end of the butcher's axe.

'I wouldn't be at all surprised,' Slider said, interrupting his thoughts, 'if this were the missing lock and chain from the park.'

'Good heavens! Do you think so?' Atherton played up.

'They wanted him found,' Slider said. 'They left the lights on deliberately. And the street door on the latch. I think this – leaving the chain like this – is their idea of a joke. Like leaving Lenny sitting on the swing in the playground. Taunting us.'

'In which case,' Atherton said, 'they'd have to have known he was meeting me, and what he was going to tell me. How would they know that?'

'Not necessarily. They might have seen him as another weak link and the timing was coincidental. On the other hand they might have tapped his phone. Or overheard him. Or got it out of him with threats. Or he might have told someone else what he was going to do, and they grassed him.'

'I can't see him doing that.'

Slider shrugged. 'One thing's for sure, we know there's some powerful business behind it somewhere. Organisation like this doesn't exist unless someone's making a healthy profit.'

'Your Mr Big?'

'It's looking that way.'

'A Mr Big with a sensayuma,' said Atherton, looking again

at Herbie Weedon. 'What's work if you can't have a laugh?'

'I could do without it,' Slider said.

Joanna caught up with them again in the canteen for break-fast.

'You look tired.'

'Didn't get any sleep, did we?' Slider said. 'Are you having the full house?'

'Why not?' she said. 'Makes a change from endless bread and jam. What kind of a breakfast is that, I ask you? It's no wonder we always beat them in wars. I mean, Napoleon's Old Guard – *café au lait*, two croissants and a dab of apricot jam; British Grenadiers – porridge, kippers, ham and eggs, sausages, toast and tea. No contest.'

While forking in the big fry-up – or scrambled eggs on toast in Atherton's case – they told her about the new developments.

'So now we know where the lock and chain went,' Slider concluded, 'but not how it got there.'

'Presumably whoever killed Lenny took it away with them,' Joanna said.

'But why?'

'Maybe they were going to strangle him with the chain the same way they killed the old man, and then as it happened they used the knife instead.'

'Then why take the chain away?'

'Forgot they were carrying it, perhaps,' Joanna offered. 'You can do that in the heat of the moment.'

'Or maybe they were going to use it to incriminate some-body,' Atherton said. 'I don't see that the chain and padlock are very important, except that they suggest the same person did both murders. Or at least they were ordered by the same person.'

'What, the big boss?' Joanna said. 'Have you started believing in him now, then?'

'There's been another development,' Atherton said. 'Another witness – of sorts.'

'Why of sorts?'

'She didn't see much.'

A woman working late at the BBC Television Centre had been leaving via the back gate into Frithville Gardens in a taxi at about two o'clock on Tuesday morning and had passed two men walking down the road, in the direction away from the park gates. She hadn't seen them coming out of the park, but they looked suspicious types to her. They were both wearing dark glasses, baseball caps, blouson-type leather jackets and dark trousers, and had given her the impression of being young and of muscular build. One was talking on a mobile phone. The other had something thrust into the front of his jacket. The woman, Elly Fraser, had said he was 'sort of supporting it with his hand as if it was heavy'. It was what had attracted her attention in the first place.

'The chain?' Joanna suggested.

'Might be. The bad news is that she's sure she wouldn't be able to recognise them again. Only got a glimpse – dark glasses etcetera. And they might not be anything to do with it, of course.'

'Or they might,' said Slider, 'especially as Lenny was seen talking to two similar characters earlier that evening. But the chain definitely suggests the two murders are linked. And the unfunny joke in each case was a warning to anyone else who might think of talking. Whoever he is, he's got a tight hold on his people.'

'But was Herbie Weedon one of his people?' Atherton

said. 'I definitely got the impression he was an independent operator.'

'Doesn't matter, does it? If he'd ever done any business, if he'd merely rubbed shoulders with this big boss socially, he was going to tell you who he was, so he'd have to be silenced.'

'I wonder why he wanted to tell,' Joanna said.

'Get rid of a rival, maybe. Or pure public-spiritedness.'

'Please!' Atherton protested. 'Not while I'm eating!'

'I'm serious,' Slider said. 'Herbie Weedon was obviously as straight as a pig's tail, but there's villainy and villainy. You often find that people like him resent it when someone a lot worse than them comes clodhopping over their patch and—'

'Giving criminality a bad name?' Joanna finished for him.

'I suspect Herbie stopped at murder,' Slider said, 'and thought other people should too.'

'Well, it's all academic now,' Atherton said. 'And it leaves us an idea short of *Mastermind*.'

'We'll have a look through Herbie's house,' Slider said, 'though I'm not hopeful of finding anything. I tend to agree with you, I don't think he was actually working for them—'

'—and if he was they'll have been there before us, like they were with Lenny.'

'It occurs to me,' Joanna said, 'that if that was a gang punishment killing as you're suggesting, it might explain why they didn't take the money.'

'Then what did they go through his pockets for?' Slider asked.

'His keys,' she said. 'So they could let themselves in at his house.'

'You're brilliant,' Slider said.

'I have my moments,' she said, fluttering her eyelashes at him.

'If I can interrupt the love fest, where does it leave us?' Atherton said. 'Sonny Collins won't talk, and everyone else can't talk.'

'There's Everet Boston,' Slider said. 'We'd better try and get to him before they do.'

'And what about Lenny's girlfriend?' Joanna said. 'She must know something about what was going on.'

'Yes, but it's a case of *cherchez la femme*. She's gone AWOL,' Atherton said.

'But Everet seemed to know her from somewhere,' Slider said. 'I think he's got to be our lead to her as well. He's definitely next in the big black chair.'

'Looks like I won't be seeing much of you,' Joanna said.

'I'm sorry,' Slider said. 'This had to happen just when you manage to get over for a few days.'

'Ah well,' she said philosophically. They scraped back their chairs and got up. 'I'll push off. I've got dirt to scratch and eggs to lay.'

He gave her a grateful look. She would not burden him with her needs, even though she wanted to have a Serious Talk with him and had been twice baulked. 'You're a gentleman,' he told her.

She smiled at the compliment. 'Ring me when you can,' she said, and left them.

'You know what the definition of a gentleman is?' Atherton said conversationally as they headed for the stairs. 'Someone who knows how to play the piano accordion, and doesn't.'

'I wonder why they always play one of those things in the background of films set in Paris.'

'Shorthand,' said Atherton. 'Like onions, berets and

bicycles.' They both had things to keep the mind away from.

Atherton staggered into Slider's room, his hands over his face. 'The shining! The shining!' he moaned.

Slider looked up from the paperchase with bare interest. 'Jack Nicholson. Too easy. And if you've got time to play charades—'

'No, no,' Atherton said, resuming normal service, 'you're way out. It was the light of his countenance that dazzled me.'

'His who?'

'Him what sent me to summon you unto his presence. I am not that light—'

'Now you're getting blasphemous,' Slider warned. '*Who?*'

'Detective Chief Superintendent Palfreyman has descended from the clouds and wishes to bless you.'

'Oh Nora! That's all I needed.'

Palfreyman was the head of the Homicide Advice Team, whose decision it had been in the beginning to leave Lenny Baxter's murder with them rather than give it to the over-stretched SCG. The arrival of the HAT car followed the discovery of a corpse as summer follows the swallow, but Slider was not pleased to be revisited. It was never good news when top brass got interested in what you were doing. They were lucky at Shepherd's Bush to have Porson as their Det Sup, for he was old-fashioned enough to see his job as standing between his men at the sharp end and the demi-gods at Hammersmith – those blessed ones whose exalted rank and sheer weight of salary left them with nothing much to do all day but think of ways to make the working copper's life more burdensome. Their previous Chief, Richard (or 'God') Head, had vaulted from their shoulders clean to the stars, otherwise known as SO19, the firearms unit at Scotland Yard, where he could deploy troops and shout 'Go! Go! Go!' into a radio mike to his heart's content.

'I suppose I'll have to go and see what he wants,' Slider sighed, getting up.

'He's in Porson's room,' Atherton said. 'Better run, lad. And stick a book down inside your trousers!' he called after him. 'The Head's looking batey!'

Actually, Palfreyman was looking, as he always did, super-ficially genial. He was a tall man in his thirties, quite good-looking, and slim, except for his hips and upper legs, which seemed disproportionately thick. Slider had noticed many times that tall, slim men with fat thighs were often to be found in managerial positions, and that they were generally popular and successful with their peers and seniors, and ineffectual at their jobs. There must be a fat-thigh gene that marked you out for the top-of-the-range Mondeo, the exec-utive swivel chair and the 'Mr So-and-so's in a meeting, can I take a message?' Now he came to think of it, DCS Head had had fat thighs too. The difference was that Head deliv-ered his life-complicating 'initiatives' with a snarl, while Palfreyman did it with a smile. Palfreyman wanted everyone to like him; but that was in any case a function of manage-ment style these days. He would vault to the stars just like his predecessor, but not having Head's predilection for kicking down doors, would probably find his resting place in a 'think-tank' or policy unit. It was the third law of thermo-dynamics in the Job that bollock-brains always ended up where they could do the most harm.

'Ah, DI Slider?' he said as Slider appeared in the doorway. 'Come in, close the door. Bill, isn't it? May I call you Bill?'

Slider's lips said yes, yes, yes, but his eyes said no, no no.

'Sit down.' Palfreyman gestured genially, and sat down himself behind Porson's desk. 'Just thought I'd pop in and have a little chat.' He was as conciliatory as an old-fashioned ward sister with an enema in mind. 'See how you're getting on. In Detective Superintendent Porson's absence. That causing any problems, at all?'

'Is there any news from him, sir?' Slider asked. 'Do we know when he's coming back?'

'I'm afraid not. His wife's rather poorly, apparently.'

'*Poorly?*' Slider couldn't help himself. As if The Syrup would stay home just to mix the Lemsip and pass the tissues!

'Not well,' Palfreyman translated kindly, as if Slider perhaps did not know that 'well' and 'poorly' were antonyms. Actually, Slider would have bet a substantial chunk of his dinner money that Palfreyman wouldn't know an antonym if it sat in his lap and peed on him.

'In what way, not well?' Slider asked stonily.

Palfreyman flushed a little. 'I'm not at liberty to say,' he said. 'I didn't come here to answer questions, but to ask them. This big case of yours – there's been a rather serious development, I understand.'

It wasn't a question, so Slider didn't answer it. He knew it was foolish to provoke a demi-god, but he couldn't help it. Palfreyman was so young, and so pointless.

'There's been another death, hasn't there?' Palfreyman went on.

'Yes, sir.'

'It doesn't look good, you know. Not good at all. Do you think they're connected?'

'I think the second victim was killed to stop him giving us information,' Slider said.

'I see. And does that point to any particular individual?'

'I believe we may be dealing with a criminal organisation, and that the first death was a punishment killing.'

'Ah, yes, I see. An organisation, eh? It's a gang thing, then.' He pondered a moment, tapping his fingers on the desk. 'Perhaps you should look into the operations of all the criminal organisations in your area and see if there aren't similarities of method.'

'We have done that,' Slider said patiently, and added in language Palfreyman would understand, 'It's an ongoing process, but to date it has not yielded any significant data.'

The DCS looked happier. 'Ah, clearly you are keeping on top of things. There has been some discussion – I've been talking to Peter Judson—'

'Is the SCG taking the case over, sir?' Slider asked quickly. 'Because if so, I'd sooner they did so now, before I commit any more effort to it.'

'I'm sure you're doing your best,' Palfreyman said. 'But a second death – and connected to the case – it just doesn't look good.'

'Is the SCG taking the case?' Slider insisted.

Palfreyman's eyes slithered away. He disliked directness. Directness never built any empires. Well, actually, directness had built most of the empires in history, but that was in the bad old days, before interactive human resource management residential training seminars had been invented.

'Mr Judson would like to, but the manpower situation is critical at the moment. He has so many men tied up in court, now the terrorist business has gone to the Old Bailey – well, you know how it goes. He just hasn't a man to spare. But if your case is stuck and you can't get any progress on it, we may have to think of bringing in some people from outside the borough. And I don't think I need to tell you how Mr Wetherspoon would feel about that.'

The honour of the school is at stake, Slider. Ten to make and the last man in.

'We have some lines to follow up, sir,' he said. 'I don't think we can say the case is stuck at this point. It's only been a week.'

'But this gang – if it is a gang: there's nothing in records to help?'

'Either they're very new, or they're very good, and they seem to have a powerful hold on their people. But that's the very reason I'd really like to get at them. I don't like new kids on my block throwing their weight around.'

'Very well,' Palfreyman said. 'You go ahead and do what you have to do. Get a quick result on this one, and a lot of people will be very pleased indeed.' By which Slider divined he didn't mean the good burghers of Shepherd's Bush. 'And of course if there's any help I can give in Mr Porson's absence, my door is always open.'

'You're staying here, sir?' Slider said, surprised.

'Oh – well – no. I was speaking metaphorically,' Palfreyman said hastily. Olympians couldn't breathe the air down here for very long. 'But you can always telephone me. You've got my direct line number.'

Slider was on his way out when Palfreyman, having relied so far, as HR guidelines dictated, on the carrot, decided there was no harm in a wave of the stick. 'I'll need to see some concrete progress very soon, though. We're under a lot of pressure over our clear-up figures, and you don't need me to tell you that any murder is a high-profile case, whoever the victim.'

No, Slider thought as he headed downstairs, I don't need you to tell me, so why do you? Obviously, because everyone knew that Slider had so little understanding of the seriousness of murder that he wouldn't exert himself to clear up the case unless he was chivvied – and chivvied, moreover, by an expert who'd been on all the right courses and was a fully qualified chivvier.

He didn't get all the way to his office. On the stairs he encountered WPC Asher who said, 'Oh, sir, they're looking for you in the front shop.'

'No point in looking for me down there when I'm up here, is there?' Slider said reasonably.

Asher's rather hard blue eyes did not soften. She hadn't much sense of humour. 'No, sir, I mean Sergeant Paxman was looking for you. There's a man come in with some information about your case, sir.'

'Thank you,' Slider said meekly, and went. The man waiting for him in the reception area could only be American. It wasn't just the height and the air of having achieved a perfect diet, but above all the immaculateness. He was wearing a blue chambray shirt, open and with half rolled sleeves, over a white teeshirt so gleaming bright it would have had an oncoming motorist flashing his lights in annoyance. His blue jeans managed to look brand new and yet softly worn at the same time; his pale leather desert boots were unscuffed and unmarked and his socks – dead giveaway – were white. Everything was exquisitely clean and perfectly ironed. When the Last Trump sounded and all hearts were opened, the American nation was going to have to give up the secret of laundering to everyone else.

He seemed to be in his thirties, though it was getting harder to tell these days. He had the shining hair and supple tan skin of lifelong good nourishment, and the straight white teeth of expensive orthodontics. He was also wearing, for reasons Slider hoped to discover, a faintly hangdog look.

'I understand you have some information for me, Mr—?'

'Garfield. Tom Garfield. Yes, I have, but – could it be in private?'

'Of course,' Slider said. He led the way into one of the interview rooms.

Garfield looked about with a keen interest that seemed hardly warranted by his drab surroundings; and then explained it when he said, 'This is all new for me. I haven't been inside a British police station before. But it's just like the TV programme. Do you watch *The Bill*?'

'I never seem to get home in time to watch the television,' Slider said. He could have added that what you didn't get on *The Bill* was the smell, but desisted on the grounds that in the present circumstances he was an ambassador for his country. He invited Garfield to sit down and asked, 'What have you got for me?'

'Well, it's a little embarrassing.' Garfield crossed one leg over the other and smiled nervously. 'You see, I don't know whether what I've got is important anyway, and I really don't want to get myself into trouble . . . ?' He added a tempting question mark to the pause so that Slider could leap in with an amnesty.

Slider regarded him solidly. 'Do you know something about the murder of Lenny Baxter?'

'Lord, no, not about the murder. But I did know Lenny. Only slightly. In a business sort of way.'

'Your business with him was not of a legitimate type, I take it?'

The smile became ever more winning. 'There's an expression, "victimless crime"?'

'Mr Garfield, if you know anything that may help us solve

this terrible crime you have a duty to – tell me.' He just managed to stop himself using the words 'disclose it'. What was it about talking to well-brought-up Americans that made his vocabulary slip back fifty years?

'And my own little – misdemeanour?' Was Garfield like-wise struggling against the word 'peccadillo'?

'I will turn a blind eye to anything I can. It's not in my interests to make life difficult for witnesses.' He had to get him started somehow. 'Why don't you tell me a bit about yourself?'

'Oh. Well, okay. I work at the BBC – you know, at the TV Centre – as an assistant programme editor. I started out in journalism back home, working on a local paper.'

'Where's "back home"?'

'The States. I thought you'd – oh, you mean where exactly. In Springfield, Massachusetts. My folks come from Vermont but we moved there when I graduated from high school. I started out on the *Springfield Messenger*, and then I went over to broadcasting. I moved to Boston, to a radio station there, and then I met a guy from IRN. He was over from London on secondment and I got pretty friendly with him and his wife and, to cut a long story short, they got me in with a news agency – Visnews – in London, and from there I went to the BBC. End of long story,' he added with a nervous laugh.

'So if you work at the Television Centre you must know that we have had enquiries out for the best part of a week for information about Lenny Baxter.'

'Yeah. I kind of—' He shrugged. 'Okay, I hoped someone else would come forward and I wouldn't have to. And, like I said, I didn't know if it was important anyway. I couldn't see how it could be. But then my girlfriend kept on at me, and – well, here I am. You see, they're saying you want to know about Lenny's leather jacket, and it was me that sold it to him.'

He looked at Slider to see what effect this news had. Slider guessed that the leather jacket was not the source of Garfield's embarrassment. In fact, he had a pretty fair idea what it was Garfield didn't want to tell him. He confined himself to raising an eyebrow and saying, 'Where did you get the jacket?'

'From a guy back home. I went back to see my folks at Christmas and I spent a couple of days in Boston, checking out old friends. One of them had these jackets.' He spread his hands ruefully. 'Okay, maybe I should have asked more questions, but Sparky swore they weren't hot and – well, I wanted to believe him.'

'These jackets? How many did he have?'

'A boxful. Maybe about twenty, I don't know. He said they were a discontinued line, but they looked pretty good to me, and the price he wanted for them, I suppose I should have guessed he'd knocked them off. But I knew I could sell 'em over here and make a few bucks. So I took four. I'd have taken more,' he added frankly, 'only I couldn't have got 'em in my baggage.'

'Describe them to me.'

'Oh, you know. You've seen one of them. Three were black leather and one was tan suede, and they all had this tartan lining, but not Scottish tartan, just shades of brown. And the label was Emporio Firenze. That's a top smart label in Boston. I should have cut the labels out, really, but I didn't want to spoil the jackets.'

'And you sold these jackets to Lenny Baxter?'

He looked embarrassed. 'I thought if I offered them to people at work questions might be asked. Lenny was always selling stuff anyhow, and he said he'd take all four off my hands. I thought it'd be easier that way. I didn't make a whole lot when you come right down to it, but I was kind of regretting I'd bought 'em by then. You've got to have the right kind of contacts if you want to go in for that kind of thing. I mean, it's okay for guys like Sparky and Lenny, but when I offered one to a friend of mine he looked at me as if I was peddling human flesh or something.' He gave Slider an engaging smile. 'I sure have learned my lesson. From now on I buy in a shop or nowhere.'

Slider remained unengaged. 'How did you come to know Lenny?'

This was the question Garfield didn't want asked. A blush spread across his fresh, boyish cheeks. 'Oh – I don't know. I kind of saw him around, you know.'

'Around? I can't think Lenny Baxter moved in the same circles as you.' Garfield didn't speak. Slider decided to put him out of his agony. 'Did you buy something from Lenny, was that it? You said he was always selling stuff. Did you buy something from him that you don't want to tell me about? Maybe a little something to smoke, or a little something to sniff?'

'Hey, listen, I don't do cocaine, okay? I mean, I know a lot of people who do, but I don't touch that stuff.'

'So it was cannabis, was it?' Garfield blushed more richly, but said nothing. 'Look,' Slider said, 'what you say to me on that count is not going to get you prosecuted. It would be pure hearsay, and I am too busy with other matters to take it any further. I just want the facts, okay?'

'Okay,' Garfield said, but he sounded a little resentful. 'But you guys over here are so stiff about it. I mean, my folks used to smoke grass at college, and they didn't think it was so bad. Okay, they didn't exactly *encourage* me to take it up, but I know damn well they still like to toke a little weed just to wind down at the end of the week. There's no harm in it.' He laughed. 'Hell, American TV is such shit you've got to have *something* while you watch it.'

'So how did you meet Lenny?'

'A guy I know put me on to him, when I said I wanted to get hold of some hash. He introduced us at a pub. After that Lenny gave me a mobile number and when I wanted something I gave him a ring and we'd meet somewhere.'

'In the park behind the Television Centre?'

'Yeah, once, but I didn't like it. I was scared stiff someone would see me going in or coming out. I know he did stuff there, but, frankly, I didn't want to meet any of his other customers. Mostly it was in pubs. A different one each time. He was very careful.'

'And was cannabis the only thing you bought from him?'

'Yeah. He was always offering me other stuff – watches, cameras, videos, you know? That's why I offered him the jackets. But I wasn't tempted.'

'Did you meet him alone?'

'Of course. You think I was going to take witnesses along?'

'Was he alone?'

'Sometimes he had his girlfriend with him. Tina. She's gorgeous,' he added with enthusiasm. He seemed to hesitate on the brink of something.

'Yes?' Slider prompted. 'What about Tina?'

'He – Lenny—' He stopped again, with an expression of distaste, and met Slider's eyes with a renewal of the blush. 'She was one of the things he offered me.'

'Did you accept?'

'What do you take me for?' Garfield said angrily. 'For Chrissake! He offered her to me right in front of her, and she's sitting there listening while he tries to tell me what she does, and what I can do to her. It nearly made me throw up.'

'Do you think she was willing to be offered like that?'

'Willing? Poor kid, she looked like a frozen mummy or something, staring at the wall, like she wouldn't dare make a sound or a movement. I don't know what he did to her, but he made her do what he wanted, I know that. Lenny was a bastard, and he deserved what he got, as far as I'm concerned.'

'Why do you think he did it?' Slider asked curiously. 'Just for the money? I suppose he wanted a good lot from you for the pleasure?'

'I never got as far as finding out,' Garfield said with dignity. 'I told him to shut up right away. But as to why he did it – I suppose it must have been the money. I guess he'd sell anything to anyone if the price was right.'

Slider pondered a little. Lenny was a bad gambler and had been mixing up the money he collected, trying to pay his debts. Maybe he was desperate enough for money even to sell his girlfriend. But of course, he had sold her before, hadn't he, to Ken Whalley in exchange for the park keys? And that hardly constituted grave need. Was there something else going on there?

But at least now he knew where the leather jacket came from. Four of them, eh? Probably not important, but where did the others go? And he had confirmation that Lenny sold whaccy baccy, both in the park and elsewhere.

'Tell me,' he said, 'what did you think of Lenny Baxter? Apart from his attitude to his girlfriend.'

'How do you mean?'

'Did you think he was a real hard man? A top-notch crook? The sort no-one could get one over on?'

'He was a crook all right,' Garfield said. He paused,

looking back into memory. 'He was a kind of good-looking bastard, the sort who gets women running after them and treats 'em badly. And he was tough all right. He could take care of himself. I mean, I wouldn't have wanted to get into a fight with him.'

'But?'

Garfield hesitated. 'I don't know. It's hard to put into words, but there was a sort of—' He paused again. 'I don't know,' he said, shaking his head at the impossibility of explaining it. 'All I can say is that I wouldn't have been surprised to find out he'd made a really stupid mistake. You got the feeling he had a bit missing, a common sense bit.'

'You mean he was reckless?'

'I don't quite mean that. I don't really know what I mean. It was just a feeling – that he'd trip up one day, and it would be something really stupid that tripped him. I wasn't surprised to find out he'd been murdered.'

Herbie Weedon's house was a nightmare.

'The old geezer must have lived there since Moses was at primary,' McLaren said. 'And he never threw anything away.'

'Papers everywhere,' Mackay supported him. 'It's going to take for ever to sort through that lot. I mean, you never saw anything like it. It's even stacked up the stairs. You can hardly see the carpet.'

'You wouldn't want to,' McLaren interpolated.

'It was a death-trap, I tell you that, guv. He hadn't had his wiring done since before the war—'

'Hadn't had anything done. Blimey, you should've seen the kitchen!'

'—and with all that paper hanging around—'

'The only clear space is a sort of track leading to the piano.'

'Herbie Weedon played the piano?' Slider said.

'Half the stuff lying about everywhere's piano music,' Mackay said, 'and old song sheets from God knows when, Queen Victoria's time or something. You know, all curly writing and drawings on the front of geezers in penguin suits with big moustaches.'

'A suit with a moustache? That'd save a lot of time,' said Atherton.

There was something faintly disturbing, Slider discovered, about the thought of that mountainous old villain going home at night and playing the piano to himself, all alone in his unreconstructed house with his one social grace.

'Well, I suppose we'll have to go through the motions,' Slider said, 'but I don't believe there'll be anything in the house to help us. These people knew what they were doing, and if Herbie had incriminating documents they'd have taken them away.'

'More likely if he'd had something like that he'd've kept it at the office,' Hollis said reasonably.

'And we know they've been there,' Atherton concluded.

'So where are we going next, guv?' McLaren asked.

'Keep watching Eddie Cranston. I'm not convinced he knows anything – I think he knew Lenny Baxter as a freelance rather than as Mr Big's runner – but you can't be too careful. And keep watching Sonny Collins.'

'If I have to drink any more of his pissy beer—' Mackay began.

'No, your face will be getting too well known by now,' Slider said. 'We'll have to put someone else onto it.'

'Why don't we just do him for something?' Anderson said. 'We must have enough on him to nick him.'

'Yes, but where would that get us? He won't tell us the name of the big man.'

'We could lean on him.'

'Not nearly as hard as the big man leans,' Slider said. 'You saw what happened to Herbie Weedon. Collins is tough, but he's practical. He knows it'd be better to go down for a spell as a martyr than to end up dead. No, our only hope's to watch him and pray he gives us a clue to follow up. Anybody who comes in looking like a courier, we put a tail on.'

'It's all long-term stuff,' Swilley commented. 'No quick result there.'

'Yes, I know, and Mr Wetherspoon doesn't want jam tomorrow. I want all of you to keep asking around. Try and find Lenny's girlfriend, Tina. And look for Lenny's ex-customers, both on the bookie side and the drugs side. I know,' he added to their murmur of protest, 'that it's not easy to get people to incriminate themselves, but all we need is a hint, a start in the right direction. Use your powers of persuasion.'

Atherton followed him back into his office. 'That was it? That was your best Billy Graham-style rouser?'

Slider turned in frustration. 'What kind of a gang is it that no-one knows about? Tidy Barnett's come up with nothing. He's asked everywhere and no-one knows anything.'

'Or they're not saying.'

'Tidy knows everything that happens on the manor, but he can't get any handle on who the two heavies were that were seen talking to Lenny. All he gets from people is that there's a big game going on, but they don't know who's running it. Whoever the top banana is, he seems to be well insulated from the underworld.'

'Well, Lenny Baxter and Everet Boston can't be the only runners. There must be more of them if the business is all that big, and if we pull them in one by one, someone's bound to squeak sooner or later.'

'I'd almost put a bet on Everet squeaking,' Slider said, 'if I could just get hold of him.'

But Boston was not to be found. His address was a flat in Harlesden, but no-one had answered the door, and the locals who were watching it reported no movement in or out. And he had not been to any of his known haunts.

'Maybe we should get a warrant and search Boston's place,' Atherton suggested.

Slider rubbed distractedly at his hair. 'Yes, maybe. I'm just worried that if we show too much interest in him, what happened to Herbie Weedon will happen again.'

'You can't proceed on that basis,' Atherton said reasonably, 'or you'll never do anything. That would be letting them win.'

'If Everet Boston gets offed, they win.'

'Maybe they've done him already,' said Atherton. 'Maybe that's why there's no answer to his door.'

'You're such a comfort to me,' Slider said.

CHAPTER TWELVE

Not Buried But In Turd

One-Eyed Billy was distinctly nervous. He had got himself right up the end of the bar in the British Queen where he could keep his back to the wall and watch the door.

'I don't like it, straight I don't,' he said, and tipped the rest of his pint down his throat in two swallows. Nerves seemed to make him extra thirsty.

Slider nodded to George, the barman, who sidled up and refilled Billy's glass, his eyes darting from face to face from under his Neanderthal brow. George was a short, long-armed, potato-faced bloke who looked as though his descent from the apes had been via a handy short cut. He had worked at the Queen just about for ever, and was invaluable to the management because most people were scared of him; though Slider knew him well enough to know that he was really a gentle, inoffensive man who was very good to his mum and by no means as dumb as he looked.

'Look, Mr Slider,' Billy went on when George had moved away, 'I want to help you. Me dad said I had to help you. But what's going to happen to me? I mean, Ev said he couldn't go home 'cos they were watching his drum. He's frit for his life. I mean, what if they're watching me? What if they see me talking to you?'

'Do you know who they are, Billy?' Slider asked patiently.

'No! Course I don't. I don't work for 'em. I'm straight.'

'Then why should they mind you talking to me?'

'They killed old Herbie Weedon just for talking to you.'

'Obviously Herbie knew something. And we suspect he'd done business with them. Like you said, you don't work for them. Why should they kill you? These are professionals, and believe me, professionals don't go round killing people unless there's a really good reason – from their point of view.'

Well, it sounded good, and Billy seemed to buy it. He lowered a quarter of his pint, wiped the foam off his upper lip with the back of his hand, and seemed a notch calmer.

'Just tell me what Everet said,' Slider urged.

'I told you, he said he couldn't go home 'cos they were watching.'

'Yes, and what else? Did he say where he was? Any clue at all?'

'No, he just said he was laying low for a bit.'

'What could you hear in the background?' Billy looked blank. 'When Ev was talking on the phone, what was going on in the background? People talking? Music? The sound of urinals flushing?'

A long gawp ensued. 'Nah, none of them. Maybe – traffic. No, I'm not sure.'

'All right.' Slider cancelled that line of enquiry. 'What else did he say?'

'Like I told you, he said to tell you to lay off him, 'cos otherwise the Man'd have him rubbed out, an' that he didn't know nothing about Lenny being offed so there was no point in trying to find him. And he said to tell you to find Tina. That's Lenny's bird.'

'Yes, I know.'

'"Find Tina," he said, like that, all urgent. And he said he'd ring me again when he could and see if I'd heard anything from you.'

'Why is he so keen on this Tina?' Slider asked.

'I dunno. He knew her from before, that's all I know. Maybe he fancied her.'

'All right, Billy. Look, if Everet phones you again, tell him to phone me. Take this number, and give it to him, and tell him he *must* phone me, all right? It's really important.'

As Slider got up to leave, George caught his eye with a look of significance. Slider raised an eyebrow and was given an infinitesimal nod, and a flickering glance sideways. Slider left the pub and loitered casually round the corner into Thorpebank Road, and in a moment or two George appeared at the staff entrance.

'You got something for me, George?' Slider asked.

'Billy's mate Ev Boston,' George said without preamble. He had the enviable ability to speak without moving his lips at all, and the rest of his face was so inexpressive it was like sound issuing from a stone.

'You know him?'

George shrugged, indicating that this was not a deep and abiding friendship. 'I play snooker up the Snookerama in Harlesden High Street. Well, I live up Craven Park, don' I? So I seen him there. He used to come in with this bird Billy's talking about. Tina.'

'When?' Slider asked.

'Not recently. A while back. Couple years.'

'Girlfriend?'

'Nah. She was a lot younger than him.'

'Was Ev working her?'

'Nah, I don't think she was a tom. I think maybe she

was a relative. Cousin or something. From the way they talked to each other. That's all I know. Any good?'

'Thanks, George. That is a help.' He slipped a note across to George's ready fingers under cover of the drying-cloth he was holding. As an afterthought he said, 'You don't know anything about this man Ev was working for?'

'Nah. Sorry. I know you got the word out. Whoever he is, he keeps himself private. All I've heard is it's big business.'

'Yes, well, I guessed that. If you do hear anything—'

George gave a curt nod and sidled away. He was not one of Slider's regular informants, but Slider had known him a long time and did not underestimate him, for which George was in a quiet way grateful. This was not the first piece of information George had given him.

Slider called Swilley in. 'I've got a job for you.'

'Now or tomorrow?'

'Oh Nora, is that the time? Well, it's going to take a while. You'd better start in the morning.'

'Okay. D'you want to tell me about it?'

'It's a bit of a long shot anyway,' Slider sighed, and told her about Everet Boston's putative relationship with the missing Tina. 'I want you to go through the records. Start with the toms register, but don't restrict yourself to that if nothing comes up. Try the name Boston. Of course, cousins don't always have the same surname, but it's a chance. And if that doesn't work, just look for any possible connection with Everet. Tina's probably not her real name, which adds to the fun for you. Get onto Everet's old school, get them to look up what his address was when he was there, see if that yields anything. A lot of these Harlesden families live close together. I know it's a tenuous brief, but that's why I want you to do it. Use your intelligence.'

'Thanks,' said Swilley; and then, 'It's that bad, is it?'

'Oh, I don't know,' Slider said. 'We're bound to get a handle on them sooner or later. I'd just prefer it was sooner.'

'You think this Tina's in danger?'

Slider met her eyes. 'Everet thinks she is. And he knows them better than we do.'

Passing the door of Porson's office, Slider saw to his surprise that Porson was there, standing by his desk, reading.

'Sir,' he said.

Porson turned. He looked worn out. 'Just looked in,' he said hoarsely, cleared his throat and tried again. 'Make sure everything's all right. I've been on the dog to Mr Palfreyman, so he's filled me in *vis-à-vis* the status quo. But you don't always hear everything when it's coming down from above rather than up from below.'

And with Palfreyman it had a long way to fall, Slider thought. Porson met his eyes and there was a sudden sympathy between them.

'I expect you've come in for a bit of the brown shower,' Porson said. 'That's usually my job, to intersect it. Act as a sort of umbrella for the pony. Otherwise you lot'd be buried up to your navels and never get anything done.'

'We do appreciate it, sir,' Slider said. Porson looked bleak, and he added, 'It's a lonely job.'

That was going too far. Porson's face tightened and he said briskly, 'So what leads are you following as of this instance?'

Slider gave him a précis. 'It seems at the moment that Everet Boston is our one hope, and he's disappeared. We're watching his house but I can't see him going back there in his present state. What we have got is his mobile number. It's switched off at the moment—'

'He is being careful,' Porson remarked.

'Yes, sir. But he has said he'll phone Billy Cheeseman again and he may phone me. What I'd like is a warrant for the mobile service provider so that if he does use his mobile again they'll pinpoint where he is, and we can pick him up.'

Porson considered a moment, and then said, 'Well, it's a long shot, but this is a bastard of a case. I'll authorise it. Get it typed up and I'll sign it.'

'I've got it here,' Slider said. 'I was going to send it over to Hammersmith, but—'

'Glad I'm useful for something,' Porson barked. He fumbled at his pocket for a pen, then went behind his desk to get one out of a drawer. As he bent over to sign, his rug slipped forward, and he pushed it back with a careless hand. Was it possible to lose weight on your actual skull? Porson straightened up and Slider moved his eyes hastily.

Porson passed over the warrant. He fixed Slider with a steely gaze. 'We haven't got long on this one. It's going to turn into a political problem if we don't break through and they'll have to bring in an SCG from another borough.'

'I've half expected it before now, sir.'

'All right, it's no shame to us. Normally they'd have had it off us from the start. We've only been left holding the bathtub this long because of the manpower situation. But they'll bring in people who don't know the ground, and I'd as soon not have 'em treading mud over my carpet. Mud or worse. Capisky?'

Slider nodded. 'I'll do my best, sir.'

'I know, laddie, I know. You always do. I'm not just

breathing down your parade to annoy you. You've got my full support. Any warrants you want, as much overtime as it takes. Whatever you need.'

Slider thanked him. 'Does that mean you're back, sir?'

The old granite face seemed to harden a fraction more. 'No, laddie, I'm not back. I just popped in, like I said. I've got to get back to the hospital.'

Hospital? Slider started to say, 'I hope——' and then realised there was no way to finish that sentence. *I hope it's nothing serious?* But he wouldn't be away from work if it weren't.

Porson seemed to appreciate the reticence. He nodded. 'If you need anything, call me on my mobile. And you can send someone over with anything that wants signing. Come to me, not Mr P.'

'Yes, sir.'

'And keep leaning on every bit of lowlife in the borough. This lot may be well organised, but somewhere out there there's a weak link, and I want us to put our foot through it before they do.'

Joanna opened the door of Atherton's house to him, with a cross-eyed teenage Siamese clinging to her scalp.

'Gosh, you're late,' she said.

'Doesn't that hurt?' Slider asked.

'Like hell,' she assured him mildly. 'I can't detach it until you're inside.'

'Sorry. Shall I do the honours?'

'Yes please – *gently*!'

He lifted it, freed the curved claws from the chunks of hair, and placed it on his own shoulder.

'He jumped on me from the top of the kitchen door as I came through,' Joanna said.

'Which one is it?'

'Vash,' she said. 'But it makes no conceivable difference. They're both bonkers.'

Sredni Vashtar teetered on Slider's shoulder, purring like an engine; then, as his brother's voice was upraised plaintively in the kitchen, scuttered straight down Slider's front and disappeared in two flouncing leaps towards the smell of food. Slider took the cat-free window of opportunity to kiss Joanna.

'Mm, you taste nice,' he said at half-time.

'It's Jim's sherry.'

'No, it's you,' he assured her, and sank back in.

'God, you two!' Sue said, coming in from the kitchen. 'You're like horny teenagers.'

Slider straightened up. 'We haven't seen each other in a while.'

'I haven't seen my gran for years,' Sue said, 'but all she gets is a peck on the beak and a box of Quality Street. Have a bruschetti.'

'Thanks. Isn't that plural?'

'You want waitress service *and* a Linguaphone course?'

'I'll get you a drink,' Joanna said indistinctly, having stuffed the smallest slice whole into her mouth. She went into the kitchen, leaving Slider alone with Sue. She fixed him with a penetrating blue gaze. Tinted contact lenses, Slider thought absently as doom fell on him.

'He wasn't working overtime last week, was he?'

'What do you mean?' Slider said. That was feeble. He'd never been good at this confrontation thing.

'Wednesday and Thursday. Oh, it's all right,' she said, waving away any possible answer he might have been going to give – which from where he was standing was not likely to have arrived until next week some time. 'I won't ask you to perjure yourself. I know the symptoms. That's where you men always get it wrong. You think we're stupid.'

'I don't think you're stupid,' Slider said, which could have meant very nearly anything, so wasn't the height of tact.

'I just thought,' she went on, 'that we'd got all that nonsense over with.'

Slider felt a looming trap. 'Look,' he began, and she flapped a hand to stop him.

'For God's sake don't say anything that starts with "look". Sentences like that lead anywhere and they're always fatal.'

'Sorry.'

'No, I'm sorry,' she said, and Slider saw she was. Sorry and angry and also afraid.

'He really cares about you,' Slider said awkwardly. Doing the old bosom-baring on your own behalf was bad enough, but having to talk girly about a male friend was as easy as eating a sand sandwich.

'I can't keep going through this time after time.'

'Talk to him,' Slider said.

'Talk to him who?' Joanna asked, coming back in with a tumbler of gin-and-tonic. It was a beauty – long and cool, blue with gin, clinking with ice, and with a floating demi-lune of lemon beaded delicately silver on the upper side. Slider wanted to dive in and stay under till the coast was clear.

But Sue rescued him. 'Jim,' she said easily. 'About the case.'

Which showed, Slider thought, that a lady could be a gentleman as well as a bosom friend.

At the table, over a starter of baked goat's cheese and rocket, Atherton said, 'I don't think we're ever going to solve this one. No witnesses, no info. We haven't even got a weapon.'

'What about the old man who was strangled with the chain?' Joanna asked.

'Herbie Weedon? Same story. No-one saw anyone go up. The hardware shop was closed at the time but the deli was still open, but they said they never took any notice of people going in and out of the door to Golden Loans. And why should they?' Atherton finished in frustration. 'People just don't look at each other any more. Everyone wanders round in their own little bubble as if no-one else on the planet exists.'

'But how could the killer know Herbie was going to talk to you?' Joanna asked.

'Maybe his phone was bugged,' Atherton said with a faint shrug. 'He said it wasn't safe to talk on the phone.'

'Is it really that easy to bug someone's phone?' Sue objected. 'Outside of a James Bond film, I mean.'

'Oh, it isn't difficult, if you've got the know-how. The gear exists, and it's very sophisticated and very compact these days. It doesn't even have to be inside the actual phone. They've got radio bugs that are so powerful they can pick up what's said on both sides of a telephone conversation from anywhere in the room.'

'Wouldn't you have found the bugging device if there was one?'

'Not if whoever killed him remembered to remove it,' Atherton said. 'And I suspect they might have.'

'But then,' said Joanna, 'you're talking about a very sophisticated killer. And if the same person who killed Herbie Weedon killed Lenny Baxter—'

'Which we assume is the case because of the lock and chain,' Atherton said.

'—then that means Baxter wasn't killed by one of his drugs customers or his betting customers—'

'Or any other of the assorted lowlife, like Eddie Cranston, that we think he associated with,' Slider concluded.

'But the killer himself needn't have been sophisticated,' Sue said, reaching for the bottle and pouring more Chablis. 'If it was a gang thing, he could be just a crude tool given orders by a sophisticated boss.'

'Not too crude,' Atherton said.

'Everet Boston is smart enough,' Slider said. 'And so is Sonny Collins. The trouble is we just don't have any evidence to point to anyone.'

'Or even a motive?' Sue suggested.

'Murders, very generally, are done for one of two reasons,' Slider said. 'Money, or passion.'

'But in this case, the money was left in the victim's pocket,' Sue said.

'Well, there's money as in wads of folding, and money as in don't jeopardise my business,' Slider said. 'Robbery from the person isn't the only option. What we need is a witness. Some helpful passer-by with a description we can act on. Or, failing that, we could do with laying our hands on someone who knows something from the inside. Like Lenny's girlfriend.'

'Or Everet Boston,' Atherton said, standing up and beginning to clear plates. 'It's a pity you didn't keep hold of him when you had him.'

'Yes, Mr Atherton. Sorry, Mr Atherton,' Slider said.

Sue followed Atherton out of the room with her eyes. 'Do you let him talk to you like that?' she said in mock amazement. 'He's only the cook.'

'You just can't get the staff these days,' Slider apologised.

*   *   *

In the car on the way home, Joanna asked out of the blue, 'Is Jim up to his old tricks again?'

'I don't know,' Slider said. She looked a protest. 'Really, I don't know.'

'Sue seems to think he is.'

'Is that what she said?'

'Not directly. It's just the impression I got.'

'From what?'

'Stop being a detective for a minute. What is wrong with him?'

'If he is up to something – which I don't know that he is – he probably wouldn't think there was anything wrong with him, or it. They're not married.'

She gave him a hostile glance. 'That's beside the point. Either he wants a relationship or he doesn't. He's got to make up his mind.'

'Why? I'm not defending the position, just asking.'

'In a spirit of pure enquiry? All right, because he expects her to have made up her mind. He wants what she's got to offer him, but he doesn't want to give her anything back.'

'I don't know that that's true,' Slider said. 'It's just—' He couldn't phrase it, and fell silent.

At last she prompted. 'It's just what? He doesn't even really try very hard not to get found out. That's insulting.'

'No, it isn't. It's the one hopeful thing, that he *wants* her to find out.'

'So she'll punish him? But she's not his mum. He'd better shape up soon or that'll be that. Can't you talk to him?'

'Not possibly,' Slider said firmly. 'But if he should open the subject with me—'

'Yes?'

'I'll tell him he's not Peter Pan,' Slider concluded. 'Good God, there's a parking space!'

'Grab it, quick,' she said, allowing the subject to be changed.

Later, sharing the bathroom basin for tooth-cleaning, she said, 'I understand, really. He doesn't want to stop chasing women because that will be the end of his merry days of youth. And he's afraid of feeling too much for Sue because she can hurt him, where none of his casual dollies could.'

'Are you sure he's that deep?' Slider said. 'Maybe he just can't help it.'

'If that's what you say about your friends, heaven help your enemies,' she said, without heat.

He rinsed his brush and watched the water swirling away down the plughole. He wasn't a bit sleepy now, and as personal problems were the flavour of the moment . . . In for a penny, he thought. Might as well get it over with.

'You wanted to have a serious talk,' he suggested.

She turned back in the bathroom doorway. 'Oh that. No. Not now. I'm not in the mood.'

'Is that good or bad?' he asked tentatively.

'Depends on your point of view.'

'What are you in the mood for?'

'No more talk,' she said. 'Let's just go and have some really rampant sex.'

'There are no two points of view about that,' he said, following her and putting out the light.

During the morning one small piece of comfort in an otherwise unpleasant case arrived on his desk: the PM report on Herbie Weedon suggested that he had not actually choked to death. His neck, which Slider remembered as being about the same width as his head, had been so well-covered that the chain had dug in and restricted his breathing but had not actually stopped it altogether, and none of the delicate bones – the cricoid, hyoid etc – had been fractured. Perhaps, eventually, sufficient force would have been administered to achieve these effects but, in Freddie's opinion, Weedon's heart, which was in a shocking condition anyway, had given out before that happened. Why Slider should find any comfort in the fact that Weedon had died of heart failure rather than being strangled he didn't know, but it seemed just marginally better. Not a ray of sunshine, precisely, but a small one up to them. Herbie had slipped under the net. They had not got him – *he* had got him.

Swilley interrupted his thoughts. 'Guv, have you got a minute?'

'Where would I get one of those?' Slider asked.

Swilley took that for an invitation. 'I think I may have something.'

'Really? That was quick.'

'Well, I don't know if it is anything,' she backpedalled, 'but, look. I didn't find any match for a girl with the name Boston—'

'I didn't really think you would,' Slider said.

'But I got onto Everet Boston's old school, and they put me onto his old form teacher. He remembered Everet very well. A bright lad, but always in trouble. And when Everet's mum was unavailable – which was often, because she was apparently a bad lot – they used to have to call in his auntie, a Mrs Angela Coulsden who lived in Wrottesley Road. That's just round the corner from Furness Road where Everet lived with his mum. So I ran the name Coulsden through the records and came up with a Mary Coulsden, who had two minor busts a couple of years ago, one for underage drinking and one for shoplifting a lipstick from Woolworths. Cautioned for both and nothing recorded against her since.'

'Same address?'

'No,' Swilley said apologetically, 'and the appropriate adult that was sent for was her dad, a Neville Coulsden. But the address was All Souls Avenue, which is only two minutes from Wrottesley Road. They could easily have moved.'

'True.'

'And Mary was the name on his tattoo.'

'Which Doc Cameron says is fairly recent.'

'*And*,' Swilley concluded, as one coming to the fruitiest bit last, 'when the store dick in Woolies nobbled her, she gave a false name to begin with. She called herself Teena Brown – spelt T, double e, n, a. Only gave her real name when they got her down the nick. Which was Mary Christina Coulsden. Maybe she didn't like the name Mary,' she concluded, looking at him hopefully.

'So if she is the same person, she might still be going under the name of Teena Brown,' Slider said. 'Did you—?'

'Yes, I checked, but there are no busts against a Teena Brown, spelt either way. But that doesn't mean anything. She might have been careful, or lucky—'

'Or Lenny Baxter might have been doing everything for her,' Slider concluded. 'Well, it isn't much, but it gives us another line to follow up. Put the word out for a tom using that name, and see if you can find the parents. They might still be at the same address—'

'The father is. He's on the current voters' register.'

'Oh?'

'No mention of Angela, though. He's listed as living alone.'

'All right. Go and see him. If it is the same, maybe the girl's run home; or if she hasn't, he might know where she might go to hole up. Good work, Norma. If this works out there could be a sainthood in it for you.'

She smirked. 'Something like a golden ha-lo?'

'Don't you start,' Slider said.

'For you, Jim,' Hollis called across the room. 'Line two.'

Atherton took it. At first he thought he was getting an obscene phone call: there was nothing but heavy breathing. But when he said 'Hello?' again, there was an instant response.

'Hello, hello, Mr Atherton? Sorry, I thought someone was coming in. It's James Mason here – not the actor of course.'

'I should hope not. Yes, Mr Mason, what can I do for you?'

'I hope maybe it is what I can do for you,' Mason said. 'That leather jacket you brought to show me.'

'Yes? You've had some thoughts on it?'

'Better than that, I've seen its twin. One of my regulars came in this morning to bespeak a new suit. A very nice gentleman, and a very good customer. Appreciates fine cloth and good tailoring just as you do. I showed him that cashmere-mink cloth I showed you, and he said yes right away. Couldn't wait. Of course, there will be enough there for two suits, if you should change your mind—'

'Not at the moment, thanks. What about the leather jacket?'

'Ah, well, he wasn't wearing that himself, of course. A very good dresser, always, and never casual, not in town. Knows the value of matching the outer shell to the inner strength. We are what we wear. No, I don't think I would ever see him in town in a leather jacket. There are places—'

It struck Atherton that Mason was more than usually rambling, and it sounded like nerves. 'So who was wearing it, then?' he asked with a hint of impatience.

'His driver,' Mason said. 'He was waiting outside with the car – there's no parking outside my shop, as you know – and while we were in consultation he came in and said that there was a traffic warden coming, and asked my gentleman if he was ready. My gentleman said he should drive round the block and come back. That was when I noticed the jacket. It was the same quality, the same cut and style, and the lining was the same – that very fine tartan wool in the shades of brown. I couldn't see the label, of course, because he was wearing it.'

'So you don't really know—'

'One moment please, Mr Atherton. There is more. I took my gentleman into the back to consult on the style of the suit – his measurements I have already, of course; those I did not need to take. Later the shop bell rang, and I put my head out just to see who it was. It was the driver come back. I said we would be a few moments longer, and he nodded. But he seemed to feel it warm in the shop, and he slipped the jacket off. That's when I saw the label. It was the same.'

'I see. That's very interesting,' Atherton said. 'Did you say anything to either of them?'

'No, indeed! For one thing, I did not know how important the jacket might be. To be making a fuss for nothing – and for another thing, I should not like to upset a very good customer by asking impertinent questions. Also—'

'Yes?'

'If it is a serious matter, I should not like to do the wrong thing. Perhaps you would not like me to ask anything. So I let it go, and I pondered. And now I have rung you. *Is* it important?'

'I don't know,' Atherton said. 'When I first came to you, it was a question of identifying someone—'

'The dead person, yes.'

'But we know who he was now. On the other hand, we still know very little about him. The jacket might be a lead. If your customer's driver bought it from the same person, it might give us an idea of what he was up to. Do you have the driver's name?'

'Oh, no. I've never made for him,' Mason said simply.

'Then I had better have your customer's name,' Atherton said. 'I notice you've been careful not to let it drop so far.'

Mason hesitated. 'The thing is, my dear sir, that the gentleman is a very good customer of mine, and I should not like him to think I had been talking about him behind his back.'

'I'll be tactful,' Atherton said. 'All I want is the name and address of his driver. He can't object to giving me that, surely?'

'Oh, no. No, no. Of course not. No, any respectable citizen must want to help the police in any way they can, and he is a very respectable citizen.' He sounded deeply doubtful.

'Don't worry, Mr Mason, I'll treat him with kid gloves. What's his name and address?'

'It's Mr Bates. Trevor Bates. And he lives in Aubrey Walk in Holland Park.'

'He's well-to-do, then.'

'Oh yes, indeed.'

'I'm not surprised you don't want to upset him.' He wrote down the full address. 'Telephone number?'

'It's ex-directory,' Mason said unhappily. 'I *really* don't think I can give you that. It would be breaking a confidence.'

'All right,' Atherton said, 'I'll manage. Thank you for telling me this. It might not turn out to be important, but you never know.'

'My pleasure, my pleasure, sir. And if you would like to pop in some time, I should be extremely happy to make you a suit, or a pair of trousers—'

'I'll see what I can do,' Atherton said. Never let it be said that he had broken a tailor's heart.

CHAPTER THIRTEEN

How Grim Was My Valet

All Souls Avenue was a wide road, once respectable but now brought low, blighted by traffic from having become a through route. The terraced houses were shabby, and most had been broken up into flats and rooms. Mr Neville Coulsden had a ground-floor flat in a three-storey house whose front garden had been concreted over and had its fences removed so that cars could be parked on it. A bile-green Fiesta sat inches from his bay window, two of its wheels up on blocks and a confetti of rust all around it. On the other side of the path were several hunks of rusting metal – car innards of some kind, Swilley deduced – and the gay multicoloured gleam of crisp bags and sweet wrappers blown behind and underneath them showed how long they had been there. The top-floor windows of the house were open and the beat, but not the melody, of heavy rock music issued forth past the dirty net curtains, as if someone up there were regularly whacking something springy with a wooden mallet.

Mr Coulsden opened the door to Swilley with a searching look and a rather flinching mouth. Expecting bad news, she thought. Inside his flat the music noise was both worse and better. The slight upper-register jingle perceptible outside, like change rattling in someone's pocket, was here inaudible; but the regular thump was closer and more personal. Transmitted through the fabric of the house as a vibration, it seemed to assail the skin rather than the ears, like a physical threat.

'Won't you sit down? I'm sorry about that,' he said, raising his eyes to the ceiling. He had a mild but musical West Indian accent. 'It don't do no good to hask. They just turn it up even more. Can I make you a cup of tea?'

'No, thank you, nothing for me.'

Coulsden nodded gravely and sat down in the armchair opposite her, but well forward, elbows on thighs so that his hands hung over the space between his knees. He was a very big man, tall and bony, with large chalky-nailed hands and a massive head. He was neatly dressed in grey trousers and a white shirt open at the neck, a home-knitted sleeveless Fair Isle cardigan and tartan bedroom slippers. His close-cropped hair was quite white, so it looked like sheep's wool, and his brown eyes were appropriately mild, but the overall impression was of a still strength, quietly contained and waiting – though for what?

The sitting room was tidy and clean, furnished with a hideous brown brocade three-piece suite with fringe edging, and one or two pieces of early MFI finished in wood-style veneer. The carpet was crimson cut-pile, the wallpaper patterned with brown and cream cabbage roses, the curtains grey with a yellow and turquoise zigzag motif. Spotless nets shut out the view of the rusting Fiesta and the migrating mastodons of buses and lorries beyond, and in front of them, on a small table, stood a fern in a pot, its fronds trembling to the rhythm of the Garage beat from above.

On the wall in one fireside alcove was a large framed print of the Sacred Heart of Mary, and on the narrow, low, tiled mantelpiece over the gas fire a tiny statuette of Pope John Paul II stood amid a collection of well-polished brass ornaments. There was a large, elderly television, Swilley noted, but no video recorder, and no books anywhere, no reading matter at all except for the *Radio Times* folded open on the set-top. There was an air of stillness about the flat, into which the disco thump intruded like an unpleasant menace, like the evil men starting to break down the door of your hiding place in one of those pursuit dreams. Stillness and emptiness and the unstoppable thud. How did he live here? It made Swilley shiver.

'Thank you for letting me come and talk to you, Mr Coulsden,' she began. And then – she had to ask. It was her job. 'Is Mrs Coulsden—?'

'My wife is dead,' he said calmly, but the dry old lips trembled again. 'Eighteen monts ago. We'd been married forty-five years. We married in Kingston the year before we came over. She was a wonderful woman. Forty-five years and never a cross word.'

'I'm sorry.'

'You weren't to know,' he said kindly. He looked round the room in a rather lost way. 'It hard without her. I try to keep things nice, the way she did, but I can't get used to it. I keep thinking she going to come in the kitchen door and tell me tea's ready.'

'So you live here alone?'

He inclined his head, and the faintest gleam of humour came into his eyes. 'Doesn't sound like it sometimes, eh? Hall day long they go on like that. Young people! Why don't they go out to work? I wish I went out to work, then I'd get a bit o' peace. I'm retired now.'

'What did you do?'

'Train driver. I drove trains for London Underground.

Hit was quieter in the tunnels than it is in here when they playing that stuff.'

'I believe you. Does your daughter come and visit you?'

'Mary? No. I haven't seen her in nearly two years. She used to phone sometimes, but since her mother died, she hasn't phoned me once.'

'Oh dear. Why is that?'

The lines of his face grew stern. 'It that man she live with. That wicked, evil man. I suppose that's what you've come about.'

Bullseye, Swilley thought with relief. They had got the right Mary after all. 'You mean Lenny Baxter?'

'Our Lord forgive me, but I hate that man for what he did to Mary. I saw on the TV he'd been murdered. So he got what he deserved. Just not soon enough.'

'I'm sorry, but I have to ask. What did he do to Mary?'

'Put her feet on the path of evil. Took her from us, and from the Church. Now she living in a state of sin, and if—' He stopped and swallowed, and then asked with a quiet, desperate courage. 'Have you come to tell me something bad happen to her? Is she dead?'

'No – I mean, we don't know anything about her, except that she's not at Lenny Baxter's flat. Some of her clothes are missing and we assume she's gone into hiding. We'd like to find her and we hoped you might know where she is.'

'I don't know anything about her life since she left us. But she in a state of sin. If anything happen to her now—' He shook his head, unable to articulate the awful possibility.

'How did she meet Lenny Baxter?'

'Her cousin Ev introduced them. You know Everet Boston?'

'We have talked to him.'

'That boy always getting into trouble, from the time he could walk. But Angela – my wife – she had a soft spot for him. She thought he was a good boy underneath. Otherwise we wouldn't have let Mary see him.'

'Did they go out together?'

He frowned, evaluating the question. 'No, it wasn't like that. Everet older than Mary. He like a big brother to her. He was round here a lot when he was a boy. His ma – Angela's sister – lived round the corner, but she was a bad mother, so Angela tried to do her best for the boy. Teresa wasn't married, you see. The black sheep of the family.' He looked to see if she disapproved, and she pursed her lips in what she hoped was a noncommittal way. 'She was a bad mother, so I suppose hit no wonder Ev went wrong too. He not a bad boy really, but he got mixed up with bad company.'

'Like Lenny Baxter?'

'I wish to God Ev never introduced Mary to him. Ev used to go down the snooker hall couple of times a week. He always fond of Mary, an' he took her sometimes. We didn't approve of that, but Ev said it was a respectable place. What could we do? If we forbade her to go with her cousin, she might do something worse. And Ev swore he'd look after her. But Lenny Baxter play at the same snooker hall – that how Ev knew him – so of course Mary get to know him.'

'They went out together?'

He bowed his head in assent. 'We think nothing of it at first. But we see a change come over Mary. She wouldn't go to church any more. Then we find she smoking that weed. Lenny Baxter give it to her. I don't know what else he getting her into.' His eyes were distant now, reliving the old misery. 'But she a different girl. Disrespectful to her mother. Paying no heed to her father. It was row, row, all the time.' He focused suddenly on Swilley. 'She not a bad girl, you understand? But she was yong and full of life and she wanted fun, and she got into bad company.'

'Yes, I understand. It happens all the time.'

'I never thought it would happen in my house,' he said sternly.

'Was that when she got into trouble with the law?'

'You know about that?' He seemed pained. Swilley nodded. 'She stole a lipstick. The police were very kind. They know we not that kind of people. They let her off with a warning. But it a terrible shock to Angela and me. We just couldn't understand how she could do such a ting. Then one day she tell us that she moving hout, going to live with Lenny Baxter.' He shook his head slowly, goaded by memory. 'It broke our hearts. Angela was never the same afterwards. We always been church-goers. After Mary left, Angela wouldn't go to church any more. Said she too ashamed, with a daughter living in sin with a bad man like Lenny Baxter, God forgive him.'

It was odd, Swilley thought, how believers could say 'God forgive him,' as if it meant the exact opposite. 'Do you know what line of work Lenny was in?'

'I don't know what he did at first. But Ev working for this bookmaker – we didn't approve of that, but at least it a job, and Ev did pretty well at it, enough money to dress nicely and buy a car. Hanyway, he got Lenny Baxter into it, working for the same boss.'

'Do you know the name of the boss, or the company?'

He shook his head. 'I wonder sometimes,' he said painfully, 'if it all legitimate. I wonder if they not mixed up with some criminal hactivity.'

It was fortunate he didn't know the half, Swilley thought. 'Is Mary your only child?' she asked.

'Angela and me had tree sons. Much older than Mary. She was our little afterthought, Angela always say.'

Menopause baby, Swilley translated.

'But we loved her all the more because of that. She was a gift from God. That's why we called her Mary.'

'But when she was arrested for shoplifting she gave a different name.'

'Yes. She made up a name. I don't know why she did that. Maybe she was a bit ashamed.'

'Is it possible she's going by that other name again now?'

'I don't know what she doing hany more,' he said with bitter dignity. 'At first she used to phone her mother sometimes. But when Angela died—' He paused, coming with difficulty to perhaps the hardest part. 'She didn't come to her mother's funeral. After that I never hear from her again.'

'What does she do for a living?'

'Nothing that I know of. That man give her money, I suppose.'

So he didn't know about the prostitution, Swilley thought; or knew and wasn't allowing himself to believe it.

'Did you ever meet him?'

'No. She knew better than to bring him here. But Everet talk about him sometimes. Said he very free with his money. Maybe that's what Mary liked about him. He gave her a watch one time – expensive one. Angela and me never wanted for anything, but we couldn't afford loxuries. We thought we'd brought Mary up to know that the things of this world are a snare and a delusion. All our boys turned out straight. Good, hard-working boys, married with families, always paid their way, like we did. But Mary stole a lipstick. It was like she slapped me and her mother in the face. How could a child of ours do such a thing? It was never the same afterwards. It was like something in us died. And then she went away with that man . . .'

He stopped talking, as if it was all too much effort, lowering his head and staring at his hands. Swilley was beginning to get a picture of a lively teenager fretting against the restraints laid on her by staid and elderly parents and the heavy hand of the Church. Yes, if every minor peccadillo – things her contemporaries didn't even think were wrong – was portrayed as a dagger of ingratitude through the heart of her mother *and* the BVM, one could see why she might prefer to hang out with the street-cool Ev and, ultimately, his friends. Every influence in her life other than her parents would be pulling her in a contrary direction. Maybe it just got too much for her.

'Well, we really need to find Mary,' Swilley said, interrupting his reverie. 'Would she perhaps have gone to stay with one of her brothers?'

'I don't think so. She never had much to do with them. They were grown up and left home before she was born.'

'I think we'd better check, just in case. Can you give me their addresses?' He nodded. 'And also, can you give me a recent photograph of Mary?'

'I haven't got a recent one, not since she went away. The last one I have must be two years old at least.'

'That would be better than nothing,' Swilley said.

He got up and went over to the piece of furniture in the corner, a mixture of display shelves, drawers and cupboards usually called, with unconscious irony, a unit. A moment later he came back cradling a photograph in his big palm, which he bestowed on Swilley as if passing over a baby bird.

In front of a grim, modern urban church a stout, bespectacled black woman in a yellow print dress, white hat and handbag beamed at the camera; beside her was a slim young girl, mini-skirted and skinny-jumpered, leaning on her mother's shoulder as if on a lamp-post, legs crossed, other arm outstretched in some obscure gesture. She was remarkably pretty, from what Swilley could tell, but in her age, her clothing, even her pose, she looked like the woman's grandchild rather than daughter.

'You'll let me have it back?' Mr Coulsden asked.

'Yes, of course. Thanks. Now can you think of anywhere at all Mary might have gone? An old friend? Another relative?'

He shook his head. 'She dropped everyone when she went off with that man. Everyone except Everet. If he doesn't know where she is, no-one does.'

A sense of futility came over Swilley. Nothing in this case seemed to lead anywhere. Every little rivulet ran out into the sand. And this place was beginning to get her. Though there was no smell of damp the room struck cold, despite the bright sunshine outside. Cold as a tomb. Swilley wanted to be gone. She knew now what this quiet old man was waiting for.

He showed her to the door, and said suddenly, 'There was a woman. When Mary get to know Lenny Baxter, they went out as a foursome with Ev and a woman called Susan. I remember because when Mary came back one time after she moved out to collect some more of her things, this woman drove her, waited for her outside in the car. She was older, more Everet's age. Did he tell you about her?'

'No.'

'Maybe it nothing then. Just a casual acquaintance.'

'Still, it might be worth checking. Did you get her surname? Can you describe her?'

He shook his head. 'I only caught a glimpse at the door.

And I never heard another name. Mary just said, "I've got to go, Sue's waiting," or "Susan's waiting." And then I remembered that she'd mentioned her before. That's all.'

Swilley thanked him, shook his cold, old hand, and left. As she filed between the Fiesta and the rusting junk, she felt his eyes on her, and resisted the urge to turn back and look. She didn't think she could bear the sight of him, standing all alone in his doorway, a dry rock out of the flow of life.

Atherton assured Slider that he needed his company when he went to interview Mr Bates. 'I'm the one that knows about schmutter.'

'I'm only going to ask him the name of his driver,' Slider said. 'I already know the name of his tailor.'

'Well, I promised James Mason I'd take care of him, and it makes it more natural for me to ask this Bates bloke, since he and I have a whistle or two in common.'

'Feebler and feebler. Why don't you just admit you want to see your rival face to face?'

'Rival?'

'You're afraid he's better dressed than you.'

'I have no rival,' Atherton said. 'I am the nonpareil. Anyway, there's no need for *you* to go at all. Why don't you just admit you want to see the house?'

'Certainly, if it will make you happy,' Slider said genially. Architecture was a passion of his – or an interest that would be a passion if he ever had time to indulge one. 'All right, you can come with me, if you think you can control your-self.'

'Do what?'

'I don't want you dribbling on this bloke's lapels.'

'Ditto his parquet flooring.'

Aubrey Walk was a posh small street in the posh area of Campden Hill, which itself was the priciest part of Kensington; but the house Slider and Atherton found themselves standing in front of was far beyond expectations. It was detached, a mid-Victorian villa standing in a small square of ground entirely surrounded by high walls. The only ingress was through a stout and high pair of electronically operated gates topped with a security camera; the ten-foot-high walls were embellished with revolving spikes and an almost invisible wire which Slider guessed would trip an alarm if touched.

Through the gates they could see a gravel sweep up to the front door. Doors and windows were all hard shut and there was no sign of life. The upper ones seemed to have blinds pulled down over them. The square, handsome villa had a false parapet around the top of the façade which partly concealed the pitch of the roof, and Slider caught a glimpse of a satellite dish lurking there, together with a cluster of tall and powerful radio aerials and a telephone mast that looked like the upturned fitment from a giant rotisserie. Apart from the electronics and security, the condition of the house alone – the attention to detail, the quality of the paint job, the immaculate state of the gravel – would have been an indicator of the real-estate value, which, added to the location, the size and the detachedness, made it a seven-figure job.

'This bloke must be earning serious biccies,' Atherton remarked.

'Unless he inherited it,' Slider suggested.

'Either way, it makes me like him more.'

'How's that?'

'Because for a really seriously rich man it would be very easy for him to get his clothes from a posh outfitter up in

Jermyn Street, or even from Paris or Milan or whatever. And of course,' he added fairly, 'he may do that as well. But he must have real taste and judgement to go to a funny old geezer like James Mason; and taste and judgement like that do not come automatically with the large bank balance.'

'You talk such unreconstructed cobblers sometimes,' Slider said. 'It's quite refreshing.'

On pressing the bell and announcing their business, they had the gate opened for them by some unseen remote hand. The front door did the same ghostly gape just as they reached it, snapping to behind them with a heavy clunk of dropping tumblers, leaving them in a small vestibule. Before them glazed doors gave a view of a beautiful hall of black-and-white marble tiles, pillars, gigantic chandelier, and a splendid staircase. A man was approaching them through the hall, and opened the glazed doors with a slight bow of the head. He was dressed immaculately in a butler's jacket, but he had a security guard's eyes, and there was something definitely un-Gordon Jackson about his build. Hudson over a lifetime of cleaning cutlery never lifted as much metal as this man must have had to, to achieve that boulder-in-a-bag look.

'Mr Bates is expecting you,' he said, and gestured for them to follow him across the hall. All three of them were wearing rubber soles – probably for the same professional reasons – and in the absence of their footfalls Slider could hear through the white silence of air conditioning the very faint whine of a security camera tracking them. Rich man's toys? But a house like this must be something of a target to burglars. And there were one or two fine pieces of furniture in the hall and old paintings on the staircase wall.

They climbed in Indian file on the crimson carpet which

ran up the centre of the staircase. On the first floor the
man opened a door and admitted them to a room which
was rather surprising in its modernity. The floor was of
bare, shining pale wood, the walls distempered white – the
better, Slider supposed, to show off the modern paintings
hung all around in plain polished steel frames. He didn't
know anything about modern art, but he could see they
were originals and therefore, presumably, valuable. A
modern settee covered in scarlet cloth was against one
wall, a spiky halogen standard lamp angled over it like a
predatory bird. A massive glass coffee table stood before
it, and on the other side were two leather-and-steel chairs
so determinedly modern it was impossible to think of
anyone sitting in them. They looked more like hide-covered
Zulu shields bent in the middle.

The windows were completely covered in a thin white
material which let in light but kept out the sun (for the sake
of the paintings, perhaps?); not in the form of blinds but
actually stretched taut and fixed somehow to the window
frames themselves, so they were obviously a permanent
fixture. It was not unattractive, though Slider thought it
claustrophobic; but this was not the sort of room one would
linger in anyhow. In the bay of the window was a desk of
blonde wood, with a computer terminal standing on it, and
the rest of the room was bare but for two enormous parlour
palms in brushed-steel pots. The empty space, the blonde
wood and the sunken halogen ceiling lights all made it look
like a modern art dealer's gallery, and Slider wondered
briefly if that was how Mr Trevor Bates made his money.

It was a room for having meetings in, that was all. Or
perhaps it was an observation cell? There was no large
suspicious mirror, but there were security cameras: three,
small and discreet, tucked into the angle between the wall

and the ceiling and covering the whole room; and Slider wouldn't have given a tenpenny piece for the chance that there weren't hidden microphones too. He drew Atherton's attention to the cameras with a flick of his eyes, and he nodded slightly. Neither of them was tempted to speak or move around. They stood where they had been left, looking at the pictures; and a few moments later the door opened again and a man came in.

Atherton could tell immediately from the suit that it must be Trevor Bates. He was not above medium height, but carried himself very upright. His body was well muscled but not out of proportion: the sort of figure a tailor would enjoy making for. His face was lean and firm, with a good straight nose, strong chin and prominent cheekbones, a face remarkable enough to have been called good-looking, though it was not conventionally handsome. His skin was pale and curiously clear, stretched lucently over those good bones like an advertisement for inner cleanliness, and deco-rated with one or two small freckles.

His suit – everything about his dress – was expensive, smart and conventional. The only unusual thing about him was his hair, which was a vigorous, dark red, brushed straight back from his face, and grown – thick, glossy and neatly trimmed – to shoulder length. The effect was star-tling, and probably it was done deliberately to put the oppo-sition at a disadvantage: it was not what any chief executive would expect to have come walking in at his office door.

'Gentlemen,' Bates said, pausing inside the door and surveying them. Posing so they could look at him? Slider wondered. 'I am Trevor Bates. What can I do for you?'

He walked past them and stopped again, turning to face them so he was now cut out against the diffused light from the window. Good entrance, Slider thought. Definitely theatrical. Bates had what horsemen call 'presence', that indefinable quality that commands your attention and makes you keep looking. And indeed there was something horselike to Slider, the countryman, about that fleshless, clean-cut head and the thick backswept mane of hair. But there was nothing horselike about his eyes: grey, hard and intelligent, a businessman's eyes.

Slider introduced himself and Atherton. Bates nodded but did not ask them to sit down. 'I shan't take much of your time,' Slider said. 'I'm sure you must be a very busy man.' He moved his gaze round the room. 'Wonderful paintings. Is this your line of business – fine art?'

'I collect paintings. Sometimes I sell them.' He had a strong and vibrant voice like an actor's, and a neutral accent which told nothing about where he came from; but he spoke very precisely, as though he had often to talk to people whose English was not their first language. 'Call it investment rather than business. Investment and a hobby.'

'Oh, I see,' Slider said. 'You obviously know how to keep them and display them, so I wondered. What is your line of business, sir, if I may ask?'

Bates made a tiny movement of impatience, which Slider knew he was meant to see. 'Property, mostly. You had something you wanted to ask me?'

'Yes, sir. The name and address of your driver, if you'd be so kind.'

'My—?' Bates looked astonished, his eyebrows making perfect arcs above his eyes; but the eyes themselves were unmoved.

Atherton took over the tale. 'When you went to visit your tailor yesterday morning, the man who was driving your car was wearing a particular leather jacket, and we're rather anxious to ask him where he got it.'

'I hope you're not suggesting he stole it?' Bates said. 'I trust my driver implicitly.'

'No, no, nothing like that,' Atherton said. 'It's just that it is very like the jacket worn by the victim in a case we are investigating, and we hoped that if we could trace the jacket to its source we might find out something more about the victim.'

'Victim? Do you mean he's dead? It's a murder case you're talking about?'

'Yes, that's right,' Slider said. Bates waited with still eyes and Slider supplied the data silently requested. 'Lenny Baxter was the man's name.'

'Oh, yes, I saw something on television about it.'

'Did you know him, sir?' Slider asked.

'No, I've never met him,' Bates said with calm indifference. 'I recognise *you*, though, now I come to study you.' He looked at Slider thoughtfully for a moment and then said, 'Well, I doubt whether the information you want about the jacket will help you. You see, I gave that particular item of clothing to my driver.'

'Did you, sir?'

'Yes, I bought it for myself in a rash moment, but when I got it home I knew it wasn't really me. I very rarely dress casually – I prefer a suit, whatever I'm doing. So I gave it to Thomas.'

'When would that be, sir?'

'About two months ago, perhaps. Does it matter?'

'It may do. Where did you buy the jacket?'

'In the States. I can't remember where exactly.'

'Could you please try?'

'It was somewhere in Boston. A small shop in a side street. I had some time to kill between meetings and wandered in just to amuse myself. I bought the jacket on a whim, almost instantly regretted. I took it home with me but never wore it.'

'Why *did* you buy it?' Atherton put in, with an air of frank, clothesman to clothesman enquiry.

Bates frowned just slightly, as though the question were an impertinence, and then said, 'I liked the smell. There's something about new leather, don't you think?'

'It's the best reason for buying a new car,' Atherton said.

Bates smiled, but did not thaw. 'Quite. Well, gentlemen, if that's all?'

'Almost all,' Slider said apologetically. 'You wouldn't happen to have the receipt, I suppose?'

'I'm sure not. Why?'

'So that we can trace the shop or perhaps the maker. It seems a coincidence that our victim was wearing a jacket just like it—'

'Hardly,' Bates said shortly. 'These things are mass produced, after all.'

'But not in this country. And we have been given to understand that this jacket was not made for export.'

'Even if you're right about that – which, frankly I doubt,' Bates said impatiently, 'America is not exactly inaccessible, is it? Your man probably went there on holiday like thousands of others.'

'I'm sure you're right,' Slider said. 'It's just that we have to check all possible avenues. I'm sorry if it seems pointless to you, but there it is. We have to be thorough.'

Bates gave a perfunctory smile. 'Of course you do. It's your job.'

'Can you remember the name of the shop? Or even the street?'

'I'm sorry.'

'Well, if it should come back to you, perhaps you'd let

us know. And if you could just give us the name and address of your driver – Thomas, you said his name was?'

'No, I don't think I can do that. I have a duty to protect my employees—'

'From helping the police?'

'From needless annoyance. I've already told you that I gave the jacket to Thomas. He knows nothing more about it than that.'

'He may have known the victim, Lenny Baxter.'

'Why on earth should he?' Bates said impatiently. 'That's a nonsensical thing to say. Like suggesting that all the people who wear Marks and Spencer shirts must know one another.'

'Nevertheless,' Slider said steadily, 'we would like just to speak to him. I'm sure you can have no reason to want to prevent that?'

The still grey eyes met his for a moment, and then he seemed to shrug faintly. 'Of course, if you insist. His name is Thomas Mark, and he lives in my staff quarters here.'

'May I see him now?'

'He is not in the house at present,' Bates said. 'He is out on business for me. However, if you really feel you need to see him, I can send him down to the police station when he returns.'

'Thank you, sir,' Slider said.

'And now, if you will excuse me,' Bates continued, stretching out his arm in an ushering gesture, 'I am a very busy man, and there is obviously nothing more I can do to help you.'

At the door Slider said, 'If you should find the receipt, sir, or remember the name of the shop—'

'Yes, I'll telephone you.'

Bates opened the door, and the butler type was standing

outside, waiting to see them out. How had they arranged that? Slider wondered. Perhaps he had been watching the meeting on camera somewhere nearby.

When they were outside in the street and away from electronic eyes, Atherton turned to him and said, 'Phew! Sent away with a flea in our collective ear.'

'No use in being a high-powered businessman if you can't face down a couple of coppers.'

'Well, the jacket seems to be a dead end,' Atherton said. 'Another dead end, I should say, in a Hampton Court Maze of them.'

'What did you think of him?'

'Mr Bates? Bit of a poser. But sharp. Well, he must be to have done so well for himself, considering there was a time in his life when he must have been called Master Bates.'

'Yes, a handicap for any child. He had a lot of security equipment.'

'So does every house in that bracket.'

'And a security guard for a butler.'

'Better he takes care of himself than gets burgled or done over and wastes our time.'

'True again. Still, I confess to just a teensy touch of curiosity about Mr Bates. You go on back to the factory. I'm going to see a bloke I know in the property world.'

'It's no use setting your heart on that house,' Atherton advised. 'You'll only be disappointed.'

CHAPTER FOURTEEN

Lifestyles of the Rich and Shameless

Ben Tarrant was tall, good-looking, in his early thirties, and an estate agent, but still Slider liked him. He gave Slider an excellent cup of coffee, leaned back comfortably in his swivel chair and said, 'Oh, the Aubrey Walk house? Yes, I know it well. I didn't sell it myself, more's the pity, but I had a look at it for another client of mine. We were outbid, though. Quite handsomely. It's a very nice property. Eight bedrooms, all *en suite*, plus staff bedrooms on the top floor. Four recep, not counting the entrance hall – including a thirty-foot drawing room – and a swimming pool and gymnasium in the basement.'

'So Mr Bates has plenty of money?'

'Oh, yes. He undertook extensive renovations, and put in all the latest security electronics. Heavy stuff.'

'I saw some of them. Why so particular?'

Tarrant shrugged. 'He's a rich man, which makes him a target. And I think it's rather a thing with him, anyway.'

'Privacy?'

'Yes, that, but also the gadget side of it. Boys' toys, you know? You often find your wealthy bachelor goes in for that sort of thing.' He laughed. 'I'm a bit of a hi-fi fanatic myself.'

'So Bates is unmarried?'

'As far as I know. Mind, this is all hearsay – I don't know the man personally. But for a mega-rich guy, his name has never been linked with any famous woman, as far as I know. I mean, he doesn't turn up at gala openings with a Liz Hurley on his arm, as you'd expect.'

'But he does turn up at gala openings?'

'Oh, yes. You'll find pictures in the newspaper morgues,' Tarrant said intelligently. 'How else he takes his pleasure I don't know, but what with his business, the gym and the electronics, I don't suppose he's short of something to do with his time.'

'And what is his business?'

'Oh, I dare say he's got fingers in a lot of pies. When you get to his level, the divisions between one branch of business and another are extremely permeable. But his home branch, from what I understand, is property. Buying and selling. Developing. There's money to be made there if you get the right start. He buys run-down houses and does them up, and he's got a knack for spotting where the next yuppification is going to happen, getting in while the prices are still low and selling when they soar.

'Is Aubrey Walk his permanent home?'

'I think it's his main place, but he's got houses all over the show, here and abroad, and in the US – though he may only be holding them until the price is right to sell. He seems to have a fondness for this area, though. He's got a house in Loftus Road he's just done up. He's a big QPR fan, apparently.'

'I think I know it,' Slider said. 'I've passed a house that's been done up to the nines.'

'Yes, he doesn't cut corners. I think he's got a genuine feel for houses.'

'You seem to admire him,' Slider suggested.

Tarrant shrugged. 'Oh, I don't know the man at all, but I admire anyone who can make a fortune from his own efforts, and of course property's my field so it's close to my heart.'

'So you've never heard anything to his detriment?'

'No, I can't say I have. Why, do you want him to be a villain?'

'Not at all. I was just wondering.'

'Well, he's a businessman, and I suppose there must be areas of all big businesses that are less than snowy white. But I haven't heard anything, that's all I can say.'

'Are you sure it's all right for you to take time out to drive me to the airport?' Joanna asked. 'I don't want to get you into trouble.'

'Oh, I've got minions toiling away at the factory, covering my back,' Slider said.

'Mixed metaphor. It's a tricky one, this one, isn't it?'

'We'll be all right once we get on the M4,' Slider said, threading his way round Hammersmith Broadway.

Joanna smiled. 'I meant the case.'

'Oh. Well, it's not obvious, that's for sure. No blunt instrument covered in fingerprints matching those of the nearest and dearest. The thing that puzzles me most,' he added, 'is that there's no word on the network about it. We've got a lot of good informants between us, but no-one seems to know anything about this particular gang.'

'I suppose they're very well organised,' Joanna suggested.

'Well, we know that. But even if they're well kitted and

sophisticated, someone ought at least to have *heard* of them.'

'You'd have thought so.'

'And it's not as if Lenny Baxter was doing anything very high-powered,' Slider added in frustration. 'An illegal bookie's runner doesn't amount to much. If his boss was only a tax-evader, was it worth murdering two people to cover that up?'

'Tip of the iceberg,' Joanna said. 'Maybe the boss had other businesses too, that were worth protecting.'

'I suppose he must have. He certainly put the fear of God up Everet. *And* Sonny Collins, who doesn't look as if he usually had trouble sleeping at night. But that brings us back to the question, why doesn't anyone know who he is?'

'Oh well,' Joanna said, 'you'll crack it. I have every faith in you.'

'It's not faith in me that's needed, it's a few witnesses. But we've still got doors to knock on and reports to filter from the TV appeal. Maybe something'll come up.' He stopped talking while he threaded the needle through the traffic emerging from the Fulham Palace Road and accelerated hard round the corner onto the Great West Road. Then, 'I'm sorry,' he said, 'that we haven't had much time together.'

'Luck of the draw,' she said. 'Couldn't be helped.'

'It was good seeing you, though. It was worth it from my point of view, even for those few hours.'

'Mine too,' she said. She seemed on the verge of saying something else, but did not.

He felt it was time to face trouble. 'About that serious talk you wanted to have.'

She laid a hand on his leg. 'It's all right.'

'We've got half an hour now.' She didn't say anything, and he pushed on bravely, 'Was it the usual? I mean, about us – your job and mine?'

'In a way,' she said. 'But don't worry now. It's not the time and place. It can wait.'

He felt a craven relief, but also a nervous doubt. If it could wait, did that mean she was becoming indifferent, giving up on him? The man in him wanted to put off that sort of 'talk' as long as possible, preferably for ever, while the detective in him wanted to know what was going on. 'I love you, you know,' he said, which was not what he meant to say, but worth a mention anyway.

'I know,' she said. 'I love you too.'

He slipped a sideways glance at her, and she appeared calm and untroubled. Oddly, this did not reassure him. She might look like that if she had got another man and wasn't coming back, just as much as if everything really was all right.

She caught him looking, and turned her face to him. 'Look, you've got this case to think about and I don't want to compete with that. It's something we need to talk through together, but I'd like to have your undivided atten- tion when we do. But really, it can wait.'

One more thing to add to the seething pot, he thought.

Atherton waylaid him when he got back. 'Yon Thomas Mark came in, and guess what?'

'He said his boss had given him the jacket.'

'And?'

'He didn't know Lenny Baxter.'

'You're getting good at this. So that's another dead end.'

'Is it? We're looking for a big boss.'

'And you think Trevor Bates is it?'

'I haven't got as far as that yet. But the jacket bothers me.' They reached his office and he sat down behind his desk while Atherton propped himself as usual on the radiator, folding his long, long legs at the ankle. 'It's just such a coincidence.'

'Is it? I thought he had a good point, about Marks and Spencer. Yes, I know this jacket isn't mass produced in this country, but we've only got James Mason's opinion that it isn't made for export. And you might just as well say it's a coincidence Bates and I both go to the same tailor, therefore I must be in it with him.'

'All right, fair point. But why did he buy the jacket at all? If, as he says, he never dresses casually—'

'Weak moment. Every man has his off day.' Atherton cocked an eye at his boss. 'What's your idea, then?'

'If – and it *is* a big if at the moment – Trevor Bates is our Moriarty, he wouldn't want it known that several of his employees were connected through these jackets. So maybe said he had given it to Mark to stop the investigation dead in its tracks. To turn it into the dead end you greeted me with.'

'That's a very long shot.'

'I know.'

'He'd have done better to deny all knowledge, surely? And why "several"? Mark and Lenny make two.'

'Everet Boston had a new suede jacket when I interviewed him. I noticed the smell.'

'You didn't mention that before.'

'It didn't connect, being suede and not leather; but it had the same lining, and Tom Garfield said one of the ones he sold Lenny was suede.' He pondered a moment, drumming his fingers softly on the desk top. 'You didn't get any joy from the Americans on Lenny Baxter?'

'The Cultural Legation? No, nobody recognised the mugshot or the tattoo.'

'How are you with them? Are you in?'

'I'm getting on very well with a nice young woman called Karen Phillips. Archivist. We talk books – she collects crime fiction first editions. Why?'

'I didn't want you to be stepping on toes, but if you've got a reasonable in, you might try them again with Trevor Bates, see if he's got any connections there.'

'Why should you think he has?'

'Oh, it's just a hunch, nothing more. We know he goes to the States a lot, and he lives in Holland Park, not far from the Legation building.'

'Pure propinquity, then?'

'Than which nothing propinks better. You could try them with the jacket as well.'

Atherton shrugged. 'You're the boss.'

'Yes, I am, aren't I?' Slider said pleasantly. 'In that case, you might get someone to fetch me a cup of tea – and tell Norma I've got a job for her.'

McLaren stuck his head round the door. 'Guv,' he said urgently. 'It's Everet Boston on the blower.'

'Right. Put him through. You know what to do.'

McLaren nodded and disappeared. Slider's phone rang and he picked it up. 'Slider,' he said.

There was a long, static-creating sigh of breath. 'Wha's happenin', man? Billy said to phone you. You gotter make it quick. It ain't safe.'

'I know,' Slider said. 'They're after you. That's why you've got to help me get them before they get you.'

Everet moaned. 'Oh man, I can't do this, awright? If I talk to you I'm dead, like ol' Herbie Weedon.'

'If they're half as good as you think they are, you haven't got a prayer. I'm your only hope, Ev. You've got to tell me who the boss is.'

'But I don' know. Straight! I'm tellin' you. That was the way he ran it. Hardly nobody never met him. It was all done froo contacts. All I knew, we called him the Needle.'

'Why was that?'

'I dunno. That was what we called him. I dunno what his real name is, and that's the honestroof.'

'So who was your contact?'

'Sonny Collins, o' course. Me an' Lenny bof.'

'Does Sonny know who the boss really is?'

'I dunno. He might. But if he does, he'll never tell you.' He sounded quite sure about that at least. 'It don't matter what you do, he won't talk.'

'Why did they kill Lenny?'

'Lenny, he wasn't a team player. He done fings on the side – stuff for himself. But the Needle like everfing tight, everfing done exactly the way he said, right, and no argu-ment. Control freak, right? That way he reckoned we was all safe. But Lenny don't like to be told. I reckon he was a mistake, and that's why they rubbed him out.'

'Did Lenny know who the Needle is?'

'Maybe. I got him the job 'cos he was short of money, but he was a lot furver in than me. Maybe that's anuvver reason they done him. 'Cos he knew.'

'And Herbie? Why was he killed?'

Everet moaned. 'Oh, man, it was me put the bug in ol' Herbie's office. I was just doin' what I was tol', but I wish I never. He was all right, ol' Herbie.'

'Why did they want him bugged?'

'I reckon he must've knew somefing. Guessed it maybe. He's been around a long time, he knows a fing or two.

Or maybe it was 'cos Lenny worked for him, and they knew Lenny was trouble. Like they was gettin' rid of anyone 'at might lead the fuzz to the Needle, you know?' This seemed to remind him of a deeper concern. 'You found Teena yet?'

'Not yet, but we're doing all we can. She's your cousin Mary, isn't she?'

There was a breathy pause, then he said on a failing note, 'Yeah. How d'you find out, man?'

'We're not as dumb as you think.'

'She was a good kid. Lenny ruined her. I fought he really loved her, you know? The bastard.'

'Ev, you've got to help us,' Slider said. 'It's not just you that's in danger, it's Teena as well.'

'Shit, man, I know that. D'you fink I don't know that? I seen what happens to girls wiv 'im. But I dunno where she is. I've been lookin' for her. That's why they're lookin' for me. Listen, I gotta go.'

'Wait a sec,' Slider said quickly. 'Where did you get that suede jacket you had when I saw you?'

'Oh, man! You wanna talk about *cloves* now?'

'It's important. Where did you get it?'

'I bought it off Lenny. He had 'em in the Phoenix one day, four of 'em, going cheap. Shit, man!' His voice changed, and there was an indeterminate scuffling sound from the background. 'I gotta go. For Chrissake find Teena, okay? If they get her – oh, shit!' Another scuffling noise, and the connection was broken.

Slider put down his receiver. He hadn't had a chance to ask about Susan. 'Shit, man,' he said in sincere imitation.

After a bit, McLaren came to the door. 'There's good news and bad news.'

'Isn't there always?'

'The good news is they've pinpointed the origin. The bad news is it's in Soho, and they can't get it down closer than three or four buildings.'

'Soho, eh? If I was running from the Needle I think I'd go a bit further afield,' Slider said.

'Bashy boys like Everet Boston wouldn't go out in the fields,' McLaren said. 'He'd be lost out of London.'

'He wanted to be lost. Well, let's get on with it.'

McLaren followed him out. 'Who's the Needle?' he asked belatedly.

'Your head's running about two minutes slow,' Slider told him.

The most likely candidate out of the possible buildings was one of those narrow brick houses turned into bedsits where toms plied their trade. Slider ruled out the Chinese restaurant. Of the other two buildings one was a hardware shop, with storerooms on the upper floors and a single flat at the top which was occupied, according to the proprietor, by a very nice man who worked as a waiter in Claridges. Slider couldn't see him harbouring Everet Boston; and besides, he was at work and there was no reply at the door. The other building had one of those weird shops on the ground floor that sell candles and tarot packs, joss-sticks and cushion covers decorated with sun and moon motifs, and a selection of daffy books on the occult, obscure eastern religions and feng shui. The upper floors were flats, but of a more decorous and permanent sort. Two elicited no reply and the occupants of the other two seemed respectable and genuinely puzzled.

So with the help of the local lads, they went through the tom house and waded through the ocean of lies, insults, righteous indignation and sheer bullshit, looking for even a square foot of firm ground. Prostitutes were a different breed nowadays from when he had worked Central in the balmy days of his youth, and with the hiving off of vice into a discrete unit the local boys had much less of a relationship with the toms than had been possible in his day. Many of the girls were shockingly young (had they been that young in the past? Maybe his memory was at fault) and many of them were not Londoners, while two at least were drug users. It was hard to tell if they were lying or not, as they would probably lie whatever you asked them. Slider's suspicions coalesced eventually on a tall and spectacularly ugly woman with dyed black hair who was somewhat older than the rest – nearer Everet's age – and had a West London accent you could have sliced and bottled. She also said she didn't know what they were talking about and she'd never heard of no Everet Boston, but when Slider caught her eye as she said it there was a flicker of consciousness there.

He looked permission to his colleagues and took her a little to one side. 'Look, love,' he said confidingly, 'it was me Ev was talking to on his mobile. I want to find him to protect him. I don't know how much he told you, but it's not me he's on the run from. If his ex-boss gets to him before I do, he's in deep trouble, you know what I mean? He was here, wasn't he?'

She looked uncertain, which was enough for him.

'Where's he gone? What scared him off? Did someone come for him?'

'Nah, he fought someone was coming, the tosser, but it was only a customer for one of the girls downstairs,' she said with the usual ripe contempt of a pro for anything in trousers. 'But he went anyway. He said you'd trace his call.'

'So where did he go?'

'I dunno. He never said.'

'Come on, love. It's for his own safety.'

'Straight up, I don't know where he went. And I don't care neither,' she added. 'It's nuffing to do with me.'

Slider sighed and tried again. 'Look, if you know where he's gone, or even where he might be, it'd be better for you to tell me. Don't forget, if I could trace his call, his ex-boss might be able to. He might be round here soon asking the same questions, only he won't be nice about it, d'you know what I mean?'

She looked alarmed. 'Oh, blimey, I told him not to come here! But I had to let him in. He was good to me in the old days. Now what's he gone and done, the silly sod? What's he got me into?'

'Tell me where he's gone. It's the only way to help him.'

'I don't know. That's the trufe. If I knew I'd tell you.'

Slider believed her now. 'Well, you might want to get away from here for a few days. Have you got somewhere you can go?'

'Me sister's,' she said after a moment's thought. 'I can stop wiv her for a bit.'

'All right. But just think for a minute – did Everet ever mention anyone called Susan?'

'I dunno. Maybe.' She shook her head, evidently trying to be helpful now. 'I'm tryna think.'

'Was she a working girl?'

'Susan.' More brow furrowing. 'Wait a minute, was it Susie Mabbot? She run this posh house down Notting Hill, introduction only, you know the sorta thing? Businessmen an' escorts. I never worked for her, but Ev knew her from way back. Maybe that's who you want.'

*   *   *

'I've checked with all the main renting agencies for central London,' Swilley said, 'and there's two that specialise in letting to American service people and embassy staff. One of them – Hughes Garvey – pricked up their ears all right when I mentioned our Mr Bates. He apparently has quite a few nice properties they handle for him on short leases, mostly flats but one or two houses – including that one in Loftus Road, which he's only just given them.'

'And what do they think of him?'

'I didn't get the impression they knew him personally, only that he's a respectable businessman and very astute. Yanks are favoured tenants and letting to them's the top end of the market, so you're looking at nice properties and everything done above board. The US Government's very particular about the way their people behave when they're abroad, so when you let to one of them you've got Washington and the Pentagon standing guarantee.'

'Yes, I see,' said Slider. 'You couldn't want a better reference than that, could you?'

'No, boss,' Swilley said. 'It looks as though Mr Bates is squeaky clean.'

'Yes,' said Slider.

'And the business with the jacket is just coincidence.'

'That's right,' said Slider.

Swilley eyed him. 'All of which convinces you that he must be a villain, right?'

'Right.' Slider smiled ruefully. 'Am I just being perverse?'

'I've known your hunches to come off before,' she said politely.

'But?'

'But just be careful, eh, boss? If this bloke is clean and he finds you've suggested otherwise – well, he doesn't sound the sort to let bygones be bygones. If he hasn't got a tame lawyer up his sleeve I'm a monkey's uncle.'

'Nothing simian about you,' Slider said. 'I wonder who paid for David Stevens to appear at Sonny Collins's elbow?'

'Wondering's free.'

'If we could establish some link between Sonny Collins and Mr Bates . . .' Slider mused. Swilley waited. 'Look, if this bloke's that big, there must be some biographical information about him somewhere. Try the newspaper morgues, *Who's Who* – you know the form. All the usual places. Anything about his past and his private life you can dig out.'

'Okay.'

'I wish we could find the girl. No nibbles on her yet?'

'The usual number, I should think.'

'Nibbles, not nipples.'

'No, we haven't scored with the name Teena Brown, but of course she might have changed it again. You think she's important?'

'I don't know. Maybe. Boston's certainly worried about her, and it may not all be family feeling.'

'Well, we'll keep looking.'

'Right. Meanwhile, Atherton's out being urbane at the Cultural Legation, and Sonny Collins is being watched. Not that I think that will produce anything. If they're as careful as Everet Boston thinks, nothing will be passing through Sonny Collins for the time being. They'll have frozen that bit of the operation.'

'If Collins is the key, why not just get him in and lean on him again?' Swilley suggested.

'It wouldn't do any good. He'd just sit us out. We've got to get more information, something we can really hit him with – something that scares him more than the Needle does.'

'And what might that be, I wonder?' Swilley speculated.

'Maybe it doesn't exist,' Slider admitted.

CHAPTER FIFTEEN

A Time to be Bald and a Time to Dye

'All right, settle down,' Slider said. The sunny spell had broken at last, and outside the windows the sky was a uniform blank off-white, depthless, as though the whole world had been enclosed in Vitrolite. It was still warm though, and the troops had all taken off their jackets, letting loose a faint prickle of male sweat into the air to compete with six different aftershaves and Norma's *Eau de Givenchy*.

'First of all, I've got some sad news. I've been informed by Mr Palfreyman that Mr Porson's wife died in hospital last night.' There was a murmur of comment. 'I know he has the deepest sympathy of every one of us. I think we should send him a card to that effect.'

'I'll do it, boss,' Norma said.

'Thanks. Get everyone to sign it and come to me for his home address. Now, I imagine that means we won't be seeing anything of him for a day or two more, but it would probably cheer him up if we could get a result on this Baxter business, so let's see what we've got.'

Hollis took over. 'Our first suspect was Eddie Cranston,

because he'd had a fight with Baxter. But we've got no evidence against him.'

'I think Eddie's too much of a plonker to have done it and not give himself away,' said McLaren.

Swilley performed an introduction. 'Pot – kettle. Kettle – pot.' McLaren made a face at her.

'I can't believe it's Eddie,' Atherton said. 'I think he just stumbled over the corner of the operation because of his beef with Lenny Baxter. Remember the very first interview with Collins? He didn't mind giving up Eddie's name, while he denied all knowledge of Lenny. He was happy for us to go and investigate Eddie's little games because it led us away from the real danger.'

'Also,' Swilley said, 'his alibi is Carol Anne Shotter and she seems to be completely straight. Not that women haven't lied for men before now—' She waited for the whoops to die down. 'But she comes across all right and everyone I've spoken to who knows her thinks she's honest.'

'All right, let's put Eddie aside,' Slider said. 'Next up is Everet Boston.'

'His alibi checks out as far as it goes,' Hollis said. 'He was definitely in the Snookerama snooker hall – half a dozen witnesses – but nothing to say where he was after one o'clock. He could have got back to the park by about half past, and we don't know for sure exactly when Baxter was killed. And we know he had a motive – some kind of ill-treatment of his cousin Mary, aka Teena Brown.'

'As against that,' Slider said, '*he* came to *us* with information, which he'd hardly have done if he'd offed Lenny. And he's apparently now scared for his life and in hiding.'

'I don't think he did it,' Swilley said. 'What you said is right, boss. He wouldn't have come forward if he had. He came forward because he had a beef against Lenny that he wanted to air. And there's no evidence against him anyway.'

'There's no evidence against anybody,' Anderson pointed out.

'Which makes it more likely that it was a professional killing, punishment by the gang,' Swilley went on, 'which is what Everet said.'

She looked round to gather opinion, realised that no-one was looking at her and swivelled in her seat. Detective Superintendent Porson was standing in the open doorway. The sight of him had frozen the entire room in shock. It was not that he looked utterly drawn and about a thousand years old – anyone might have expected that – but that he was not wearing his wig. His high bald dome was pale and strangely bumpy, and the few wisps of grey hair round the edges seemed only to emphasise the nakedness, as pubic hair contributes to pornography. It was somehow indecent. All these years he had toted the appalling rug about, denied its existence and vented his fury on anyone who so much as looked at it, let alone mentioned it; and now he had simply abandoned it. If he had stood there totally starkers with his dangly bits on parade it could not have caused more consternation.

Slider rallied himself. It was too bad for everyone to be staring at the old boy. He scraped up a voice and said, 'We weren't expecting to see you in here today, sir. We heard the news. I know I speak on behalf of everyone when—'

'None o' that,' Porson said sharply, cutting him off with an imperiously lifted hand. His pink-rimmed eyes swept the room. 'Consider it said. We've got work to do. I've had Mr Palfreyman on the dog, chewing my ear off. He's not as compunctionate as you lot, apparently. He's agitating to take this case away, given I've taken my hand off the steerage. Fulsome apologies and all that, but wouldn't it be better under the circs, de-dah-de-dah. So let's get on with it. I haven't lost my marbles yet. I can still out-copper any bastard with a degree in sociology.' He quelled Atherton's rising comment with a look and nodded to Slider. 'Carry on where you picked up.' And he sat down on a desk at the back of the room, forcing them all to turn their heads away from him.

'All right,' Slider said, and with an effort caught hold of his thread. 'That brings us to Sonny Collins, who on the surface of it looks very tasty. However, he has no criminal form.' He looked at Hollis. 'Have you managed to get anything on his service record?'

'Yes, guv. That was interesting. He was in trouble a few times for fighting, but nothing major. The best bit comes at the end. He was in a shore-based posting in Hong Kong and got in a fight one night outside a bar with a local. The other bloke produced a knife and stabbed him. That's when he lost his eye, apparently. In retaliation Sonny hit him under the chin so hard it broke his neck. Well, all hell let loose as you might expect. There was the civilian police enquiry as well as the naval one, and questions asked right up to the Governor and the diplomatic bag.'

'Be more respectful of the Governor's wife,' Atherton said sternly.

Hollis resumed. 'Anyway, the other bloke was a known troublemaker and already wanted by the Hong Kong police on several other counts. So, given that witnesses saw him get Collins with the knife, and his mates swore Collins wasn't carrying – which he was known not to – it was brought in self-defence. When Collins came out of hospital he got his discharge on medical grounds and there was no court martial. Otherwise he couldn't have stopped in Hong Kong, o' course.'

'Did he?' Slider asked.

'Opened a tattoo parlour in Kowloon, ran it for a couple of years before coming home and going into the licensed trade. Must've tattooed a few tars in his time there. Maybe he did his own neck. I'm wondering what other services he offered as well as the skin pics.'

'Yes, that might be worth knowing. Any way you can follow it up?'

'I'll have a go,' Hollis said. 'I might be able to trace some of his mates.'

'Okay. Well, Collins is tasty, and he denies knowing Lenny Baxter, though Eddie Cranston was sure enough that Lenny was a regular at the Phoenix to wait for him there; and of course Eddie says Collins called Lenny by name. And there's Everet Boston's statement that Collins was the gang control for both him and Lenny Baxter. Which all looks nice and suspicious.'

'But Collins has got a good alibi,' Anderson said.

'Not for the whole night,' said Mackay.

'For the likeliest bit,' Anderson asserted.

'Yes, what about that alibi?' Slider said.

Atherton looked at him patiently. 'I know you don't like it, but if Collins actually did the killing he's not likely to have arranged himself an alibi up to four o'clock and then gone a-murdering afterwards, is he?'

'And besides,' said Anderson, 'we've got that Elly Fraser bird's statement about the two heavies walking down Frithville Gardens at two o'clock, which is right in the middle of his alibi time.'

'We don't know they were the killers,' Swilley said. 'And

don't forget there was a report from one of the residents saying there was no chain on the gate when he came home from the pub just after midnight.'

'Yes, but that's not what he said the first time his door was knocked on,' Mackay pointed out. 'He only came up with that after the telly appeal. Probably just wanted to make himself important. You know how they do.'

'I don't think Sonny Collins actually did the killing,' Slider said to Atherton. 'But I still don't like that alibi.'

'Guv, I think it's genuine,' said Anderson. 'Liam the barman at the Shamrock remembers very well, because he said Sonny Collins hadn't been in for months, and when he did come in, he never stayed that long, just had a couple of drinks to unwind and went away. And Liam was the one called the cab for him, so he knows what time he left. And the cab company confirms the booking, and the driver identified Collins and said he dropped him outside the Phoenix about ten past four.'

'That's exactly what I mean,' Slider said. 'It's all so perfect. He hadn't been to the Shamrock in months, so why suddenly did he go there that particular evening and stay so long, with extra precautions to establish the time he left?' He answered his own question. 'Perhaps because he knew Lenny was going to be eliminated. Maybe he was warned to make sure he was covered.'

He looked round, and saw no absolute resistance to the idea. 'Let's look at the sequence of events,' he continued. 'Lenny goes into the Phoenix, as we're told he often did, and if we believe Everet Boston he had every reason to because Collins was his contact. He goes in just before eleven, let's say to transact some business with Collins or to give or receive a message. He's not expecting to be molested by Eddie Cranston. An argument starts. Collins tells him to take it outside. Eddie tries to make a fight of it but Lenny knows he mustn't get involved with that sort of thing, so he slugs Eddie a good one and instead of following it up, legs it like one John Smith, and heads home.

'We next find him talking to some professional minder types outside his own home at about half past eleven. Shortly after that Sonny Collins pushes off to establish himself an alibi. And later that night Lenny is killed very neatly and efficiently by a single stab wound to the heart by some one or some ones who go through his pockets to remove something but leave his wad of money behind. Later again, Lenny's house is expertly turned over and his girlfriend hastily packs her bags and runs for it – we don't know whether before or after, or whether the people who searched the house also took her with them, either by force or otherwise. Everet is sure they're after the girl – presumably because she knows too much about the outfit, maybe even who the Needle is.'

'Guv,' said Mackay, 'if it was the minders who done Lenny, why didn't they do it when they met him at half eleven? Why wait until later?'

'Well, they wouldn't want to kill him in a public street, would they?' Anderson said.

'They could have taken him inside his house and done it there,' Mackay said.

'Yes,' Slider said. 'That's a point. Any suggestions?'

'Maybe he wasn't due to be done then,' McLaren said. 'Maybe the minders reported back something he'd said, and it was that that made the Needle put the order out on him.'

'Or maybe he'd said something to Sonny and Sonny reported it,' Swilley said. 'And got his orders to get himself an alibi at the same time.'

'Maybe what Sonny reported was the fight with Eddie,' Hollis said.

'That's certainly a possibility,' Slider said. 'According to Everet, Lenny wasn't a team player and that was what the boss objected to. We've got him running for Herbie Weedon and crossing money to fund his gambling habit. We've got him selling dope in the park on the side. And we've got a lot of iffy goods in his flat which he may have been processing outside of his job for the boss. If he was seen as the weak link and likely to bring police attention down on the gang, that would be good reason to get rid of him.'

'They got rid of Herbie Weedon just for wanting to talk to me,' Atherton said. 'And Everet Boston is running for his life. Could it be that the boss is determined to stop us making any connection between the lowlife and him?'

'Maybe what was lifted from Lenny's pocket, apart from his keys, was some kind of paperwork that would link him with the boss or the gang,' said Swilley. 'His betting book, for instance, maybe with a telephone number or something in it. He must have written down the bets somewhere, and we never found anything like that.'

'Yes,' said Slider, 'and there was an inkstain on the inside of his empty pocket. Maybe he habitually carried his betting book in there, along with a Biro, which leaked at some point, as they always do.'

'Brilliant, boss. And we thought something was lifted from beside his telephone at home – which could have been an address book or something similar.'

'But why kill him in the park like that?' Mackay said. 'I mean, it's a public place. Anyone could have seen them.'

'Well, evidently anyone didn't,' Atherton said. 'When you think about it, it's one place they could be sure there'd be nobody around, and it's not overlooked. They've only got to walk up the street and through the gates – no suspicious climbing over because they know Lenny's got the key. And we know nobody notices anyone walking up the street, particularly late at night, because he's been doing business there for years and we've never had word of it. And the woman who *did* see the two heavies walking away didn't think anything about it. She didn't come forward for a week, thinking there was nothing in it.'

'There's people coming and going to the BBC's back door all the time,' Swilley said. 'I suppose that's cover.'

'I've said before,' Slider continued, 'that the way Lenny was left, sitting on the swing, looked like a joke. That and the park chain round Herbie Weedon's neck could point to the boss having a nasty sense of humour.'

Porson spoke up suddenly, surprising them all: they'd forgotten he was there.

'All this is all very well, but it's all supperstition. Maybe, maybe, maybe. You've got no murder weapon, no witnesses, no suspects. If it was a gang killing, it'll have been orders to some hood to carry it out. There'll be nothing to connect the killer with the victim.'

'Except the boss,' Slider said. 'We'd have to trace it back from the boss.'

'Ah yes, the boss. But you don't know who he is. You've got no evidence he even exists, apart from the word of one villain on the run.'

'I think he exists. I think Everet Boston is telling the truth,' Slider said steadily. 'He's got no reason to lie; it makes sense of a lot of things; and he's genuinely scared, both for himself and for his cousin.'

'Well, as it happens,' Porson said, 'I agree with you. But it doesn't get you any further forward. Who is the boss?'

'Everet called him the Needle.'

'And you think it's this Trevor Bates bloke?'

Slider hesitated. 'There's nothing to connect him except the leather jacket, and that could be a coincidence.'

Porson eyed him cannily. 'But you don't think it is?'

'It's just a hunch,' he admitted.

'Well, I'm all for hunches,' Porson said. 'You can't learn hunches at bloody Keele University.'

Palfreyman really had got up his nose, Slider thought. 'Four jackets,' he said aloud. 'Garfield sold Lenny four. He wore one himself, sold one to Everet and one to Thomas Mark. Who had the other one, I wonder? And why did Bates lie about it? To cut us off at the pass? But how much did he know about the jacket's origin? I suppose there's no reason Mark shouldn't have told him, just idly in conversation, that he bought it from Lenny. That would be enough to make him want to stop that line of enquiry.'

But Atherton shook his head. 'You don't know for sure that's where Mark got it, guv. Anyway, Bates apparently makes a fortune out of property. Why would he want to mix himself up with stuff like illegal bookmaking, and small-time crooks like Boston and Baxter? Why would he risk it? It doesn't make sense.'

'A lot of fingers in a lot of pies. Diversification. Running a huge empire. Pulling the threads and manipulating people. Pulling the wool over our eyes.'

'A Moriarty complex, in fact,' Atherton said. 'But we've no evidence at all that he's crooked.' He stopped.

Slider looked at him. 'Something just occurred to you.'

'My contact at the Cultural Legation,' he said, a little unwillingly. 'When I asked her if she knew Trevor Bates, and described him, she said no, but,' he shrugged unwillingly, 'I think she was lying.'

'A hunch, eh?' Slider said innocently.

'It was just a look in her eye. But I'll swear she was straight. Apart from anything else, the Americans are very careful about the people they send over.'

'All right,' Porson said. 'Here's what we do. Sonny Collins is your man. Turn his drum over. Check his phone records. I'll okay the warrants. And go into his past with a tooth-comb. Also this Trevor Bates. Find some connection between them. We can't touch Bates as it is. Until we find out he's not pure as the driven, he's sacrospect. But if we can get anything on him at all, we can look into his finan-cial affairs, check his bank accounts, and I think we'll find enough to start putting pressure on him. There's not one of these entry preeners can stand being put under the microphone. And,' he added on a different note, 'go up and down Frithville Gardens, ask everyone who they saw coming and going. Yes, I know you've asked 'em already, but ask 'em again!' He looked round them, and the anima-tion faded from his face, leaving a bleakness as embar-rassingly naked as his head. '*That*'s police work,' he said. 'Ninety-nine per cent perspiration, and one per cent sheer bloody luck. Get on with it.'

Since Sonny Collins lived in the flat above the Phoenix, there was some urgency in getting there with a search team before the pub opened. So when the warrant was forth-coming, Slider and Atherton went round there with half a dozen uniform PCs and Porson's promise that if they found anything at all interesting he would order up a Polsar team to take the place apart.

What they found when they got there was no answer at any door or to the only telephone number they knew. The pub was silent, the curtains were drawn upstairs, and the youth with a ring in his left nostril who acted as barman (cash in hand – no National Insurance, no pain, Slider would bet) was hanging around, knocking at the door and peering up at the flat. As soon as the cars drew up he had it away on his tiny toes. To chase a fleeing man is as instinctive to a copper as to chase rabbits is to a dog, and PC D'Arblay was out of the car before it had come to a complete halt; but chummy had too substantial a lead. He shot down the cut between Evans House and Davis House and was lost to them. Slider consoled D'Arblay as he came panting back that they could find him if they needed him.

'But I expect,' Slider said when their own knockings had gone unanswered, 'he was just trying to report for work.'

'But work there is none,' said Atherton. 'Where's our Sonny? Gone away?'

Slider looked up at the curtained windows and shivered a little in the May warmth. Somewhere nearby – in the park probably – a blackbird was singing, and the chippy in the parade of shops had started frying the first batch of the day. Those were the sounds and smells of life; but the closed curtains gave him a premonition of death.

'All right,' he said. 'Force an entry.'

There was a separate door round the side for the flat. Renker and Coffey burst it in, while the others held the gathering crowd at bay. Inside was a tiny lobby with a locked door into the bar and stairs straight ahead. Slider listened, and then with Atherton at his shoulder started up the stairs.

The flat consisted of a sitting room, bedroom, kitchen and bathroom, all with the unrelieved flat walls and mean proportions of the sixties. It was sparsely furnished, and unexpectedly clean and tidy, the walls painted cream, the floors lino-tiled, everything stowed away in cupboards as if the owner were still at sea and under orders. There was also a spare room which was set up as an office and contained, as well as what was needed to administer a public house, a powerful two-way radio. So that, Slider thought, was how information and orders were passed without bothering British Telecom.

Mr Colin 'Sonny' Collins was in his desperately tidy bedroom, lying naked under a sheet on the hard single bed. On the locker beside the bed was an empty pint glass which seemed to have held water, and empty pill bottle with the label removed, and a bunch of keys with a luggage label attached on which was written in capitals HW. Collins's eyes were closed, his hands folded together on his chest as if he had composed himself with an easy conscience for sleep, but he was dead and cold.

'Pipped at the post,' Atherton said. 'Blast and damn it! So they decided to sacrifice him?'

Or did he sacrifice himself? Slider wondered. He liked that possibility even less.

'But how did they know we were on the way?' Atherton went on. 'You don't think they're bugging us, do you?'

'I hope not,' Slider said. 'But I dare say they're bugging Everet Boston. Mobiles are relatively easy to hack into. He pointed us at Sonny. Don't forget he said he was the control for him and Lenny.'

'So they didn't trust Sonny to keep his mouth shut?'

'Maybe. Maybe he didn't trust himself. Whatever he might have told us, we'll never find it out now.' He looked at the pill bottle – sleepers? Probably. You could force a person to take sleepers by threatening a worse death, but Slider couldn't see Sonny Collins caving in without a fight, and there was no sign of a fight, on him or in the flat. But if he took them voluntarily, what order of loyalty did that suggest? It wasn't nice to think about. 'Maybe the pill bottle's a ruse and we'll find there was a different cause of death,' he said. 'Mustn't pre-empt the post-mortem.'

Atherton nodded. 'What about those keys, left prominently for our attention?'

'I shouldn't be surprised to discover that HW was Herbie Weedon, would you?'

'Not overwhelmingly. We're being led by the nose to the supposition that Sonny killed Herbie.'

'Well, maybe he did,' Slider said. 'Anything's possible.'

Porson looked even more haggard than in the morning. 'This is getting out of hand, God damn it! What the hell is going on? We've already got two murders on our hands and now this! We can't have our ground littered with bodies like Amsterdam after an England away! And not a suspect for any one of the three!'

'I think we're meant to take it as confession and suicide,' Slider said cautiously. 'The keys are the keys to Weedon's office and house. We're meant to assume that Collins did Weedon and then topped himself.'

'Then why no note?'

'Maybe they thought that would look too obvious. This way is more natural-looking – more subtle.'

Porson gave him a ripe and goaded look. 'Subtle? A subtle criminal? This is not Ealing Studios! What are you going to give me next, the cockney char? The tart with the heart of gold?'

Slider withstood the blast. 'They left the keys in case we wanted the evidence. The way I see it, it's an invitation to us to let it go.'

'An invitation?'

'It won't be hard for them to guess we're over-extended – it's all over the papers every week – and here's a way for us to clear up something, get the Brownie points and release some manpower.'

Porson's frown was terrific, but he was following, however unwillingly. 'That still leaves Lenny Baxter.'

'Maybe they're just hoping we'll write that off, let it go by default. After all, we've got no evidence and nothing to link him with anyone.'

'Except Everet Boston.'

'Yes,' said Slider.

'What price his life now?' Porson moved restlessly, the light from the window throwing his head into planes and his face into shocking hollows. How much weight had he lost, for Pete's sake? 'I've put out an all units on friend Boston, but if he keeps using his mobile like the plonker he is, I don't stack any hope on us finding him before they do. But what kind of bloody people are they? This isn't Chicago!' He paced about a bit, thinking. 'Where do we go from here, if it's not a rhysterical question. We've got no concrete evidence on either the Baxter or the Weedon murders,' he continued, 'which is what you'd expect if they're professional. No forensic, no witnesses. And Collins either was or wasn't suicide, and there'll be no evidence there either, you can bet your bottom boots. So unless we can pick up Everet Boston, we've got nothing to connect any of this with the gang or the boss – Needle, or whatever they call him. What a bloody shambles! So what are you working on?'

'Trying to trace the Susan or Susie Mabbot we think may have been the friend of Boston and Baxter, in the hope that she may know where Baxter's girlfriend Teena is.'

'What good will that do if you do find this Teena?' Porson snapped suspiciously.

'She lived with him, so she may know who the two

minders were who talked to him that night, and she may have seen who searched the house.'

Porson snorted. 'May and might butter no parsons! I can't see any future in wasting effort trying to find her. If she knew anything they'll have done her as well. You said yourself she might have been lifted when they searched Baxter's gaff. What else?'

'We're trying to find out more about Trevor Bates.'

'But you don't know he is the Needle. You've no reason even to think so, except for that bloody jacket.'

'And the sophisticated electronics equipment and the radio and telephone masts on his house.'

'Anyone could have those.'

'Anyone could, but he *has* got them. I think he's worth looking at.'

'All right. But carefully. We don't want a case against us. What else?'

Slider shrugged. 'Keep slogging on, looking for witnesses.'

'Right,' Porson said gloomily, and turned to stare out of the window. 'Someone saw something. Sometimes it takes months. Sometimes it takes years. Look at the Dando and the Russell murders. But we're not rolling over. I'm not having some bastard smart alec villain treating my manor like his own private playground.'

Death, Slider thought, had suddenly become personal to Porson. 'We'll get him, sir,' he said, which was as near as he could go to offering sympathy.

Porson turned. 'See you bloody do!' he barked, but there was understanding in his red-rimmed eyes.

CHAPTER SIXTEEN

Intimations of Mortality

The search of Collins's house had revealed in the store-room a vast stock of cigarettes, including Lenny's own favoured brand Gitanes, for which there was no paper-work upstairs in the office, and which it was pounds to peanuts had been brought in illegally from the low-tax continent; ditto various cases of spirits. Evidently Sonny, either on his own behalf or for the Boss, had been used to augment his income by the sale of these private stocks without involving the brewery. Slider wondered if the smuggling was itself another of the gang's operations. With cigarettes retailing at £4.50 a pack here and purchasable for £1.20 in Spain, there was plenty of leeway in between for a healthy profit to be made. Perhaps Sonny's pub was a distribution centre? The brewery was not going to be happy about that.

The brewery had of course been told that Sonny was dead and that the Phoenix was closed while the investigation went on. It was agitating for more information and for a date when it could reopen with a new manager, and the phone calls were coming from progressively further up the hierarchy; to which Slider had responded at last by leaving orders for all such calls to be re-routed direct to Mr Palfreyman.

Palfreyman got the big money, let him have the nuisance, Slider thought. He had enough to do without that.

The rest of the search had revealed a very Spartan lifestyle for Mrs Collins's son Colin. The bed was hard and narrow, the floors uncarpeted, the kitchen sparsely stocked. Even the soap in the bathroom was Wright's Coal Tar. Personal possessions were few, with the notable exceptions of an old and beautiful piece of scrimshaw work, and a ship in a bottle which Slider thought might be late eighteenth century or early nineteenth. But these two rather exquisite esoterica only seemed to sharpen the question of what Sonny spent his money on. There seemed little point in a criminal career if you didn't enjoy yourself with your ill-gotten gains. Maybe he was stashing it away for a comfortable retirement? But the kind of spare living exemplified in the flat did not argue a disposition that craved comfort. Maybe it was just the power he had craved. That at least made sense. But why, then, had he so obligingly killed himself?

One gratifying thing emerged from the search, however. Sonny's clothes were generally few and monotonous, leaning heavily towards the black trousers and teeshirts. Everything was spotlessly clean, beautifully ironed, and squared neatly away in true Bristol fashion. The man even ironed his underpants, Slider discovered, with a sense that it was more than he really needed to know. But hanging in the wardrobe (the first wardrobe he had ever seen in a private house where you could actually push things back and forth along the rail) was a black leather jacket with a rather distinctive tartan wool lining in caramel shades; a jacket new enough to make the wardrobe smell like the inside of a Rolls-Royce.

'The fourth jacket!' Slider had exclaimed happily when they discovered it; at which Atherton had warned him sternly not to jump to conclusions. But it was a perfect match with Lenny Baxter's. It gave Slider great satisfaction to have this small part of the puzzle sorted.

'But it doesn't help,' Atherton pointed out. 'All it proves is that Lenny knew Sonny, and we knew that already.'

'I know,' Slider said, 'but when little things like that trip up the mighty, it makes it all seem worthwhile. Lenny Baxter has four leather jackets and sells one of them to Thomas Mark, driver to the great mogul Trevor Bates—'

'Who we have no reason to suspect is the Needle,' Atherton interpolated.

Slider waved that away. '—and thus provides a link without which no-one would ever have looked in Bates's direction. It's the mad bitch Chance at her most trivial. It's beautiful.'

'So you're determined to believe it's Bates?' Atherton asked.

Slider tapped his chest. 'I feel it. In here. He lied about the jacket, you see. That was his mistake.'

'But you don't *know* Mark got the jacket from Lenny,' Atherton said, frustrated. 'Bates could have bought it in Boston. After all, how did he know it was American if he didn't buy it there himself?'

'I suppose Lenny told Mark and he told Bates.'

Atherton shook his head. 'You're more obsessed with jackets than Spud-u-Like.'

Slider looked at him, amused. 'You're determined it isn't Bates, aren't you? What is it, his suits?'

'I've no feelings about the man either way. I just don't like to see you run ahead of your data. It's not like you.'

'What's a man without a hunch?' Slider said lightly.

'Tall,' said Atherton.

*   *   *

Freddie Cameron telephoned.

'Working on a Saturday?' Slider wondered.

'So are you,' Cameron pointed out. 'Got to catch up with the workload somehow. Besides, we've got builders in, and it offends my delicate sensibilities to watch them spend all day drinking tea and listening to Kiss FM on my penny.'

'What are you having done?'

'We're having the bathroom refitted, God help us. Of course the brunt of it falls on Martha, but what drives me mad is that they could have finished a week ago if they'd just got on with it. If it was me, I'd sooner work hard for a week and have a week off than slop around for a fortnight for the same money. But what do I know?'

'Start taking your work home,' Slider suggested. 'That'd have 'em out in no time.'

'The speed one of them moves, I suspect he's clinically dead anyway,' Cameron said bitterly.

'So what have you got for me?'

'The Collins PM. The report's in the post, but I thought you'd like to know that it was the pills that killed him.'

'That's something, I suppose.'

'It was a short-acting barbiturate, secobarbital. He'd had a large dose – blood levels were 20mg. Death would have occurred within about half an hour, from respiratory collapse.'

'Any idea where he might have got hold of it?' Slider asked.

'Well, as you know, old boy, barbiturates haven't been prescribed in this country for twenty years, or in any of the other civilised countries, but they're more or less freely available in places like Mexico and China, so they leech in across the borders onto the illicit market. My personal preference for country of origin in this case would be China. I found remnants of the capsule cases in the stomach, and they were coloured a shade of blue that I've come across before with Chinese drugs. There's a large Chinese population in every major city in the world, and half the cargo ships on the high seas are crewed by Chinese, so distribution's no problem. That's only an opinion, mind; I can't prove it.'

'Your opinion's usually good enough for me.'

'By the way, I didn't find any evidence of force – no bruises or chipped teeth – so it does look like suicide. And, unusually, there was no alcohol in the bloodstream. He did it stone-cold sober in the clear light of morning. Odd, that.'

'It's not just odd, it's creepy,' Slider said.

'Greater love hath no man?' suggested Freddie.

'Yes, but love for what?' said Slider.

The Chinese restaurant Karen Phillips chose for her rendezvous with Atherton was down one of the little side turnings off Holland Park Avenue. It had ground-floor and basement dining rooms, and the latter was low-ceilinged and divided into a multitude of secret little booths by bamboo screens and large palms in pots. The lighting was dim, from low-hanging bulbs shrouded in red paper lanterns, and monotonous Chinese music from a loop tape added to the authentically mysterious atmosphere of an opium den in a *Carry On* film.

Miss Phillips herself, a strikingly pretty young woman with thick, dark, curly hair and innocent brown eyes, was evidently deep into the character of conspirator. She had chosen a booth in the darkest corner and looked round constantly and nervously in a manner guaranteed to draw attention to herself, should anyone actually be watching them. Atherton found this rather endearing. Most of the women he knew were so briskly capable that her ineptitude at intrigue had the attraction of novelty.

'I shouldn't really be here, you see,' she said in a low, thrilling voice. 'I mean, not talking to you like this. Not that we're not allowed to meet people, but there are things we're not supposed to talk about.'

Atherton gestured towards the menu. 'Shall we order lunch and get that out of the way?'

'Well, I don't really want anything to eat,' she said, in faint surprise that he hadn't twigged that.

'Yes, but it would look rather more like a secret meeting if we didn't have any food, wouldn't it?'

'Oh! Yes. You're smart! I guess your training makes you think of things like that.' She smiled self-deprecatingly. 'I'd never make a detective, would I? Or a spy.'

'Oh, I don't know,' he said. 'You've got a distinct advantage to begin with.'

'Why's that?'

'Somehow one never suspects beautiful women of anything underhand.'

To his surprise she withdrew a little. 'Now you're making fun of me.'

He backpedalled. 'Sorry. That sounded a bit patronising. I didn't mean it like that. It's this place going to my head.'

She giggled. 'Yeah, it is kind of goofy, isn't it? I keep expecting Inspector Clouseau to jump out and do a karate chop or something.'

The waitress came and hovered, and they ordered some food, more or less at random, and tea – Karen said she didn't drink at lunchtime. While they were thus engaged some more people came in and took tables: a young man and woman; three giggly twenty-something females; an older woman with two younger ones, mother and daughters who'd been shopping. Another waiter appeared to attend to them. Everything looked like normal enough lunch trade to soothe Karen's nerves, and they chatted easily about books and movies until the food arrived.

When they were alone again, she said, 'So, what did you want to talk to me about?'

'I think you know that,' Atherton said. 'Trevor Bates, of course.'

She looked round with an instinctive, guilty movement to see that no-one was listening. 'I told you, I don't know him.'

Atherton smiled. 'Yes, you told me. But I know that isn't true. And if you didn't want to tell me the truth, why are you here? Have a prawn ball.'

'Look,' she said, leaning forward a little, 'I do want to tell you, but I don't want to get into trouble. Do you promise me no-one will know I've been talking to you?'

'Scout's honour,' said Atherton.

She frowned. 'I'm serious.'

'So am I. This is a very serious matter. Two people have been murdered.'

Now her eyes widened. 'Murdered?' she gasped. 'I didn't know that. I thought it was about—'

'About what?'

She shook her head. 'That's awful. You think he did it? Oh God, that's awful! I kind of guessed he was a bad guy, but I never thought . . . Were they women?' she asked suddenly. 'The people he killed?'

'We don't know that he killed them. And, no, they weren't women. But we have our reasons for suspecting he's involved and we need to know everything we can find out about him. So, tell me, how do you know him?'

'I don't really know him,' she said. She seemed shocked. The prawn ball between her chopsticks slipped out and fell back into her bowl without her noticing. 'I've seen him coming and going, and I know his name. I mean, I know the man I've seen is Trevor Bates because he was signing in one day when I was passing through reception and I heard the security guy call him by his name.'

'So he comes to the legation? Often?'

'I've seen him around a few times. I don't know how often.'

'What is his business there?'

'I can't tell you that.'

'Can't, or won't?' She hesitated, looking down unhappily at her lunch. 'What does a cultural legation do, anyway?'

'Oh, all sorts of stuff,' she said automatically. 'Promoting United States goods and cultural exports, protecting our intellectual property, liaising between artists and governments, dealing with the media and British Government agencies—'

'I see,' said Atherton ironically. 'And what has Trevor Bates to do with all this?'

'He – he provides some kind of goods and services. I can't say what,' she said. Still her eyes were down.

Atherton waited for more, and eventually broke the silence by saying, 'Well, if that's all you've got to tell me, it was a bit of a waste of time meeting, wasn't it? Or was it just an excuse to date me?'

She looked up. 'I said he was a bad man. I don't mean in his business – though he may be a crook for all I know – but I mean in his private activities.'

'Which are?'

'He – he has strange sexual tastes.' It seemed an effort for her to get it out, and Atherton's interest quickened.

'Tell me about it,' he said more gently. 'How do you know? Has he done anything to you? Or said anything?'

'Oh, no! Not me. But there was this girl – she's gone back now. She worked in another department but she and I got friendly. We used to lunch and go to the movies together, that sort of thing.' Atherton nodded, to encourage her, and she went on, with gathering fluency. 'Well, sometimes we talked girl talk, you know the way it goes. And one evening when we went out Mr Bates had been in the building and, I don't remember how it came up, but I said I thought he was good-looking, in a weird kind of way. Kind of charismatic, you know, with all that auburn hair and that pale skin. And a great body. And terrific clothes. Well, Katy – this girl – she looked at me kind of sideways, and said I had to be joking, and she asked if I'd spoken to him. I said no I hadn't, and she said I should keep it that way. "If he comes on to you," she said, "you run a mile. He's bad news," she said.'

'Bad news in what way?' Atherton asked.

She shivered a little, unconsciously. 'Katy said he likes hurting women. She said that's how he gets his kicks. She said he's got this house not far from our place, built like a fortress, with all kinds of creepy security guards and stuff to keep people out. She said he takes women there and does stuff to them and takes movies of it so he can watch it all again later on his own.'

'Had Katy been to his house?'

'I don't know. I guess not.'

'Had he done anything to her?'

'I don't think so.'

'So how did she know about his strange tastes?'

'I don't know. I didn't ask. She just said what I've told you, but she sounded like she knew what she was talking about.' Karen looked apologetic. 'I guess it doesn't sound like so much now I tell it. But I believed her, and if ever I saw him round the building I made sure to stay away from him and not catch his eye, you know? I still believe it. I mean, there must be something wrong about him, or why are you here asking me questions?'

Atherton didn't follow that by-way. 'You said this Katy had gone back? You mean to the States?'

'Yes, about a year ago. Her tour was over – or, wait! No, it wasn't. She went early, now I come to think of it.'

'Do you know why she went early?'

'I never knew anything about it beforehand. One day she just wasn't there and when I asked someone from her office they said she'd gone back. But it does happen. People get moved for all sorts of reasons. Only, later, someone said she'd been sent home under discipline for talking too much.' She looked an appeal at Atherton. 'So you see how important it is that you don't split on me? That's why I didn't say anything when you first asked me. If you get disciplined it ruins your whole career.'

'Well, that was just a waste of time,' Atherton reported, swinging through the door.

'It took you a good long lunch to find that out,' Slider commented.

'I couldn't rush away. She was so worried about anyone guessing she was talking to me, I had to make it look as though we were lunching for pleasure. I had to cover her back.'

'As long as that's all you were covering.'

'Wot, me? I'm not on the pull any more. I've got my hands full with Sue.'

'And Sandra Whitty?'

Atherton eyed him defensively. 'If it's about saying I was working late—'

'My own excuse on many occasions, I know,' said Slider. 'Who am I to complain? It's none of my business anyway.'

'But?'

'I thought you were settled with Sue, that's all.'

'I am. Look, it was just a one-off. I'm not seeing her again. Apart from anything else, she smells faintly of formaldehyde. Very off-putting.'

'So why did you do it?'

Atherton tried for an insouciant smile and almost made it. 'Sheer force of habit. I couldn't help myself.'

'I think we'd better book you in at the vet's,' Slider said gravely.

'I know, I know,' Atherton sighed. 'It takes time to alter the customs of a lifetime, that's all. I'm getting there slowly.'

'But with all that rampant totty out there practically gagging for it—?'

'I have never expressed myself so vulgarly,' Atherton said with dignity. 'Do you want to know what Karen Phillips had to say or not?'

'It'll be charged to expenses, I suppose, so I might as well,' Slider said.

Atherton told him. 'But it's all pure hearsay,' he concluded. 'Even the unknown Katy didn't give a source.'

'Yes,' said Slider. 'It sounds like one of those "everyone knows" rumours. That doesn't mean it isn't true, in some form. But of course we can't use it.'

'I'm glad you acknowledge that much.'

'There's been a development here while you've been hard at it, lunching your socks off.'

'Purely in the line of duty.'

'That goes without saying. Well, my news is that Swilley's been pulling together the various morgue pieces on Bates and there's precious little of it. But one interesting fact did emerge. It seems his background is in electronics.'

Atherton perked up. 'So all that gear in his house wasn't just rich men's toys?'

'He did an electrical engineering degree, then a post-grad in his special area of audio-electronic systems, and then he joined a company called Shenyang.' He looked hopefully at Atherton, but Atherton shook his head. 'No, I hadn't heard of them either,' Slider said, 'but apparently they're a very big name in micro-electronics – they're the Sanyo of surveillance devices.'

'Bugs.'

'Not to put too fine a point on it. Much of their work, naturally, is both funded and consumed by the Chinese Government.'

Atherton nodded. 'We all know governments are the biggest buggers of them all. Well, that's a nice pointer, given the bug in Herbie Weedon's office. And the masts on top of Bates's house.'

'That's not all. The capitalist face of Shenyang,' Slider went on, 'is their prestige Shenyang Tower building in Hong Kong. Which was where Trevor Bates worked in the research and development department in those far-off days when he was young – and when, by coincidence, an ex-tar called Colin Collins was running a little tattoo and we-know-not-what-else parlour in Kowloon. Interesting, wouldn't you say?'

'Provocative,' Atherton agreed. 'But *did* they know each other?'

'That's what we're trying to find out. Hollis is tracking down some of Sonny's old service pals, while Swilley is trying to work it from the other end and find someone who knew Bates in those days. That bit's harder. Now that we don't own Hong Kong any more, Shenyang is effectively behind the Great Wall, and getting anything out of the Chinese is like trying to lift paving slabs with a nail file.'

'Still,' said Atherton hopefully.

'Yes,' Slider agreed.

'Well,' Atherton acknowledged generously, 'it looks as if you might have been right about Bates after all. It all begins to add up against him.'

'Even if we prove he knew Collins, it doesn't prove he's the boss we're looking for,' Slider said.

'Now you're just being perverse,' said Atherton.

There was a repeat appeal on the six-thirty regional news programme, for witnesses who saw anyone entering or leaving the park or walking along Frithville Gardens late on the Monday night or early on the Tuesday morning. It was done by the news team themselves, with an OB shot of the street and the park gates to jog sluggish memories, so Slider was not obliged to expose himself again. He watched it on the television in Porson's room, without too much hope that it would yield results. They had pretty well come to the end of the crop from the previous appeal, and nothing had turned up. In a place like Shepherd's Bush, people didn't notice each other much, unless someone was trying to draw attention to himself; and whoever killed Lenny Baxter was too professional to do that.

He was back in his own room, thinking about going home, when the phone rang. Blimey, that's quick, he thought, picking up. 'Slider,' he said.

'It's DI Priestfield here, Harrow Road. You put out an all units on a male IC3, name of Everet Boston? Well, I think we've found him. We've got someone who fits the description and the e-fit you sent out, but there's nothing on him to ID him.'

'Thanks very much for letting me know,' said Slider. 'Keep hold of him, will you, until I get someone over there? I don't want him to go walkabout again.'

'You can take your time. He's not going anywhere,' said Priestfield laconically. 'We fished him out of the Grand Union Canal. He's in the morgue at St Mary's now. He's well dead.'

CHAPTER SEVENTEEN

A L'Eau C'est L'Heure

Slider had to go himself to identify the body of Everet Boston, remembering at the last moment that he was the only one of the team who had met him face to face. Boston had been dispatched efficiently with a blow to the back of the neck, fracturing the cervical spine at the level of the second and third vertebrae – the 'hangman's blow'. A quick death, he thought, for what comfort that was, which was very little. The whole thing sickened him. Gang wars were bad enough when it was pot-headed youths or rival pushers knifing each other in the heat of the moment, but this calculated removal of people merely out of greed, for threatening a livelihood, was disheartening and disgusting.

Back at Harrow Road nick, Priestfield gave him tea and talked him through what they knew, which was virtually nothing, while eyeing him with the interest and sympathy accorded to one visibly on the brink of disaster.

'So what's this now – four?' he asked.

'It doesn't take long to get round on the grapevine, does it?' Slider complained. 'Anyway, this one's on your ground, and I'm no poacher.'

'Thanks,' Priestfield said shortly. 'But it *is* connected with your ongoing, I take it?'

'I wouldn't be a bit surprised,' said Slider wearily. 'I'll give you what we've got, but it's not much. They're all professional hits, and you know what that means.'

'No forensic evidence.'

'Right.'

'And unless you can get to the brains behind it—'

'Right.'

'Ah well,' Priestfield said, 'at least they're not innocent bystanders. It makes me sick when some old keff gets blagged for his pension.' He stretched until his shoulder muscles crackled. 'God, it's been a long day.'

'Are you finished now?'

'Yes, I was only hanging on to see you. The DCI's at the scene and there's nothing for me to do here tonight. I'm going home, see if my dog still recognises me. You can bet the wife won't. You?'

'I haven't got a wife,' said Slider.

'Oh well, you're all right then,' said Priestfield.

Slider thought of the cold empty flat and another tepid take-away meal congealing in its container even as he forked it. 'Yes, I'm all right,' he said.

When he got back to the station, Nicholls warned him that Porson was in. 'Came through looking like a ghost.'

'Say anything?'

'Not a word.'

Slider climbed the stairs and went quietly to the door of Porson's room. It was open, as always, and through it he saw the man himself sitting at his desk, bowed a little forward, hands clasped on the desk-top, staring at nothing. He was so still he might have been asleep, except that his eyes were open.

After a moment, Slider said gently, 'Sir?'

When Porson looked up, Slider realised he had been looking at the framed photograph that always stood on his desk. He also realised that he had never actually seen the photograph, though it was not hard to guess who it was of.

'Did you want something?' Porson said. His voice came out so unused he had to clear his throat.

'I was just going to ask you that,' Slider said.

Porson made a throwaway gesture of one hand. 'Got to be somewhere. Can't settle at home. Keep seeing her out of the corner of my eye. Think I hear her calling me from another room.' He met Slider's eyes with a kind of shyness. 'Maybe that's what gives rise to ghost stories.'

Slider thought of what Nicholls had said, and remembered that someone – was it C.S. Lewis? – had said that a ghost was a person out of his place. To him, of course, Porson's place had always been here. It had been impossible to think of him having a home life – but then it nearly always was with senior brass. By definition they were inhuman. But now Porson's heart and mind were plainly elsewhere, and he was out of place here in his office.

With a visible effort, Porson roused himself. 'Any developments?'

It seemed inhumane to drop it on him; but then Slider thought perhaps it would serve as a useful counter-irritant. 'We've lost Everet Boston.'

'What do you mean, lost him?' Porson asked sharply. 'I didn't know we'd found him.'

'Somebody else found him,' Slider explained, 'floating in the Grand Union Canal.'

'Oh, bloody Nora,' said Porson. 'Go on, then, give it to me.' Slider told him what he knew. 'Well, that's it then!' Porson said with large exasperation. 'Finito. We've got no evidence against anyone, and we've lost every witness we had who might have led us to this so-called big boss. We might as well pack our towels and go.'

Pack our towels? Slider wondered. Was that a Germans-and-deckchair image, or had he caught the tail of 'throw in the towel' as it wandered across his line of vision? He shook the thought away. 'There's still the girl, sir. Lenny Baxter's girlfriend. She might know something about the boss, or at least point us towards someone else in the organisation. If we could find her,' he added fairly.

'If she's still alive,' said Porson. 'What chance they won't have cleared her up like they've cleared up Boston?' Slider didn't answer that. After a moment Porson asked, 'What are you doing to trace her?'

Slider almost shrugged. 'The only lead we've got is the Susan who used to be friends with her and Lenny, who may or may not be Susie Mabbot, who ran a house in Notting Hill.'

'That's not bloody much!'

Slider admitted it. 'We're trying to trace her but we've had no luck so far. And we still might get some witnesses coming forward from the repeat TV appeal tonight.'

Porson hauled a sigh up from his boots. 'Palfreyman's been leaning on me, you know that. And Mr Wetherspoon's leaning on him. Now there's a fourth body—'

'Not on our ground,' Slider said quickly.

'We may get out on a technicality with that one, but three is four too many as it is. They won't leave it with us much longer.'

'How long have we got, sir?' Slider asked.

'The Murder Review Team will be here on Monday, or Tuesday at the latest. If we've got nowhere, they'll bring someone in from outside. Well, I wish them joy of it, that's all. A case like this is a bugger. When you lift the corner of the carpet, you never know what you'll find looking back at you. Do what you can in the time available, Slider, and I'll authorise any overtime you want for your team. If you can get a result, well and good.'

Slider could not hold out the slightest hope that they'd get anywhere by Tuesday morning, so he remained silent. Porson was staring at nothing again, deep in a reverie. Suddenly he came back and said, 'If they take it away I'll have a few days off. Go down and visit my daughter.'

'I didn't know you had a daughter, sir,' Slider said – foolishly, since he hadn't known anything about Porson's life.

'Lives down in Devon. Married, two boys. She's an artist. Paints views for the tourist trade – but good stuff, mind!' he added sharply as if Slider had sniggered. 'None of your tat! She's a real painter. I used to make a joke about it. I used to say to her, "Moira, I may be a superintendent but you're a right Constable."'

Porson making a joke? Slider thought in astonishment. And then, *Moira?* He tried to smile.

Porson went on. 'I'll stay with them for a few days and we can all come up together for the funeral on Friday.'

'If anyone deserves a few days off it's you, sir,' Slider said in a kind of desperation. All this personal revelation was terrifying. He was afraid any minute Porson would ask him to come too.

'So don't beat yourself up, Slider, that's what I'm saying,' Porson concluded in a wholly normal voice. 'If it doesn't come off, let someone else worry about it.'

This was worse than anything, Slider thought. If the old man gave in to the Palfreymans of this world without a struggle, it really would be the end. If the great granite Porson was defeated there was no hope for any of them:

the world would crack in two like a saucer and fall into the void.

'But it's *our ground*, sir,' he said, trying to infuse some urgency into the old man.

'Is it?' Porson said. 'I wonder sometimes. I wonder if it's not theirs.' Theirs? Palfreyman's and Wetherspoon's, did he mean? 'Your Lenny Baxters' and your Sonny Collinses',' Porson elucidated. 'Whoever said the meek shall inherit the earth was talking out the back of his head.'

This didn't seem to be the moment to tell him that it was the Lord. Slider kept schtumm.

All the same, someone had to do something, and when he got back to his office he rang his old friend Pauline Smithers. She was now with the National Crime Squad, and he found her still in her office at the West London headquarters.

'Hullo,' she answered him. 'What do you want?'

'That's a very hurtful conclusion to jump to,' Slider said. 'I phoned to say congratulations.'

He had known Pauline Smithers his whole career, ever since he was a probationer in uniform and she had had the stern glamour of five years of seniority over him. There had been a time when something might have started between them, but he had held back through diffidence, and in the end he had married Irene and she had married her career. The gap between them had widened exponentially since that point. He was a detective inspector working seventeen-hour days at a local nick. She was a detective chief superintendent and second in command of a team that had been investigating Internet paedophile rings and had just made a spectacular and widely publicised bust, with a hundred arrests and several lorryloads of porn confiscated.

'I saw you on the telly,' he said. 'You looked very good, Pauly. The grapevine says you're destined for great things.'

'Well, that's what we all thought, but it was splashed in the papers for one day and then forgotten, like everything else. Fifteen minutes of fame, you know? Now we've got to slog it through the courts. A hundred arrests but how many will we get down? Still, it was nice while it lasted.'

'Now don't you let me down,' Slider complained. 'None of that defeatist talk. You're always bullish and positive. I phoned you for a bit of backbone stiffening, and here you are, *c'est-la-vie*-ing me.'

'Hah! I knew it! You did want something.'

'Well, only a bit. I really did phone to congratulate you, and I should have done it sooner only—'

'You had stuff to do. I know. So what's your problem this time, chum? I don't know but what having a go at yours wouldn't be a nice temporary relief from my own. I'm sick of paedophiles.'

'I bet you are.'

'Sometimes I find myself trembling with rage and wanting to go down to the cells and simply beat them to death. Not good for the soul, that. We've got to keep our objectivity. Like surgeons. We're the last rational people in the whole legal system.'

Slider sighed happily. 'Ah, that's the stuff! Come on, more! Pump it in – I can feel it doing me good already.'

She laughed. 'What do you want, you bastard? I've got stuff to do myself before I can get home to my cot.'

So he told her. Just saying it all out loud helped him to slot the pieces into place. She listened, putting a question now and then, and he imagined her at her desk with the lamp making a puddle of light over her hands, taking notes in her quick, small script. He felt an enormous surge of affection for her, a familiar and comprehensible person in a wild and woolly world.

At the end she said, 'Well, I see why you want this Bates person to turn out to be the Needle, but you really haven't got anything to go on, have you?'

'No, I know. That's where I need you.'

'Oh, is that where?'

Slider missed that one. 'These high-powered people are difficult to get information on. His house is like Fort Knox and I've exhausted the normal routes. But if he's providing some kind of goods or services to the American cultural legation, someone official must know about him.'

'Don't you think that makes it unlikely that he's a criminal?' she asked him kindly.

'What better cover could there be?' he said.

'Yes, but why would he bother?'

'Some people just can't get enough. Look, if he turns out to be pure as the driven, so be it. At least it stops me wasting my time – and I've got little enough of that to waste.'

'All right, I'll see what I can do. But I don't know why you can't just let it go, Bill. After all, there's plenty more criminals where that one came from.'

'Why do you bother catching a hundred paedophiles when there's a hundred thousand more out there? Crime's a Medusa head. Every snake you cut off, another ten spring up. But what's the alternative? You can't let them do it right under your nose without so much as a challenge.'

'All right, I said I'd do it,' Pauline interrupted him.

'Thanks. Right away?'

'By yesterday, if that's soon enough for you.'

'Thanks, Pauly.'

'Is your mobile number still the same? All right then, I'll call you as soon as I know anything. Don't call me, okay?'

'Okay.'

'Okay. How's what's-her-name – your friend?'

'Joanna? Absent.'

'Ah. I smell a story. Well, you can buy me lunch or some-thing and tell me all about it.'

When he had rung off from Pauline, he phoned home to get his answering machine messages – two from Joanna, the second saying she was just going in to play and she'd try again after the concert. He hadn't realised it was so late. He was hungry, too, he discovered. He quite fancied a ruby. Hadn't had one of those for ages. He'd stop on the way home at the Angla Bangla for a nice chicken tikka with saffron rice and a big greasy naan: a thinking man had to keep his energies up.

That decided, he felt more cheerful and embarked on his last task – ringing round his team to get them in tomorrow. Two days. A lot could happen in two days. Even a result wasn't out of the question.

Hollis's quest for people who had known Sonny Collins had led at last to one of those raw new estates built beside the M1 to take the overspill from Northampton. Here he was received on Sunday morning by one Stanley Rice who lived with his wife in retirement at number 5, Meadowview. Despite its name, it looked out at the front only on the houses opposite, across the narrow road and the open-plan front gardens, and at the back on the high wooden fencing that divided the estate from the motorway.

Hollis had driven to Meadowview through Orchard Way and The Glebe, passing such side turnings as Haystacks, Willow Close and Primrose Dene. When he got out of his car and the roar of the traffic hit him, he almost staggered. It thundered past just beyond the flimsy barrier with a noise like a waterfall driving hydro-electric turbines; it battered the air in a way that surely was literally unendurable. It must be like living in the exhaust pit of a rocket launcher. He half expected his nose and ears to start bleeding.

But it was amazing how quickly he got used to it once he was inside the house where, though constant, it was not at killing pitch. It was a mean little house, with low ceilings and tiny rooms, as if built for a smaller race of hominids than your actual *homo erectus*. Hollis came from Manchester, and was reminded of things he had learnt in history lessons about the cramped and gimcrack housing that was run up for factory workers in the nineteenth century. How the wheel turned!

Mr and Mrs Rice had brought with them to their new castle their old furniture, which had been designed with normal-sized houses in mind. With the sofa in place along the only piece of wall long enough to accommodate it, and a footstool in front for Mrs Rice, who suffered from swollen ankles, there was only just room for a person to pass between it and the log-effect electric fire. An armchair placed at either side of the fire made it an obstacle course to get from the door to the far window, under which a gateleg table and two dining chairs filled all the remaining space from wall to wall. There was another window at the front of the room, looking onto the road, and beneath it stood a bookcase and a cupboard with two drawers underneath, which impeded the opening of the door from the tiny entrance hall to the 'living room'.

Every step they took, Hollis reflected, must involve sidling past something or squeezing through some gap. It was depressing. Still, they seemed an immensely cheerful couple and even, to his astonishment, said that this house was much nicer than their old one.

'We've got the hatch through to the kitchen here, for one thing,' Mr Rice explained, 'so I can talk to Mother while she's in there cooking or whatever, and she can see the television through it, so she doesn't miss things. She likes the soaps, you see, and if they come on when she's washing up or doing the potatoes . . . Mustard on the soaps, she is. Aren't you, love?'

Hollis had missed the television. It was behind one of the armchairs, between it and the wall. They would have to push the chair back up against the dining table to be able to see it.

On top of the television was a rather nice model ship, made of wood and ivory.

'I can see you were a naval man,' Hollis said, to get things rolling. 'That model, the painting and everything.' Over the fireplace was a large, cheaply framed reproduction of a three-master in full sail over a rollicking blue sea; while on the narrow, low mantelpiece, the top of the bookcase and the cupboard was a whole collection of ships in bottles, of various sizes and degrees of accomplishment.

'Oh yes,' Mr Rice said, pleased. 'I like my bits and bobs about me. Collect 'em, when I can find 'em. And I've got a lot more stuff upstairs, in the spare bedroom. I make model battleships from kits – the modern ones, you know, not like her.' He gestured towards the three-master. 'Mother laughs at me about my "kid's hobby", but I find it satisfying. She has her knitting, and I have my models, right? Where's the difference?'

'Oh, go on, Stan!' Mrs Rice protested. 'The gentleman doesn't want to know about your silly ships. Would you like a cup of tea, Mr – er? Or coffee?'

'Thanks, that'd be very nice,' said Hollis. 'Coffee, please, if it's no trouble.'

She bustled off and he heard her presently in the tiny kitchen just through the cardboard wall, making kettle-and-cup noises. It was hardly necessary to have a hatch, Hollis reflected. You could have put your hand straight through the wall without half trying. But he supposed if Mr Rice had been a sailor he'd be used to confined spaces and living on top of other people. As to Mrs Rice, women of her generation adapted themselves, in his experience, to absolutely anything.

At Mr Rice's invitation he sat himself in one of the armchairs and chatted inconsequentially until Mrs Rice came back in with a wooden tray on which reposed two cups and saucers of instant coffee made with milk, a sugar bowl, and a plate of mixed biscuits. The china all matched and was decorated with pink and silver roses, and there was a spotless embroidered linen tray cloth underneath. There was something about people like this that made Hollis almost want to cry. He thanked Mrs Rice warmly and admired the china, and she looked pleased, and took herself off with a puzzle book and a Biro to sit at the dining table and give them privacy, or as much of it as was possible at a distance of three feet.

'So, Mr Rice, you knew Colin Collins? Or Sonny Collins, as he was known.'

'Not when I knew him,' Mr Rice said. 'Not Sonny. Never heard him called that. Crafty Collins, we called him. We all had nicknames, o' course. Mine was Speedy. Not that I was fast, or anything – though I was a lot spryer in those days than I am now – but my initials were S.P.D., you see. Stanley Philip David. S.P.D. – Speedy Rice, you see?'

Hollis got it. 'So why was he called Crafty Collins?'

''Cause he *was* crafty,' Mr Rice said promptly, opening pale blue eyes wide. 'I mean, crafty as in handy with his hands, yes, that was one thing. He was what we called an artificer. He could *make* anything *out* of anything. But he was crafty the other way, too. On shipboard, even on a shore base, you live on top of each other, you know, Mr Hollis. And that means you have to get on, you have to trust one another. And if somebody's not honest, it messes up everybody's life. No, he wasn't popular, wasn't Crafty Collins. We knew he'd come to grief sooner or later, and there was no tears shed when he did.'

'Oh, Stan!' Mrs Rice protested, proving she was not as far out of earshot as she was pretending.

Speedy seemed to understand her objection. 'Well, I know it's a terrible thing to lose an eye. But it has to be said he had it coming, if not from one source, then another. A terrible *contentious* man, he was. Always getting into fights. He'd argue about anything. You couldn't say it was raining without he'd pick you up and say it wasn't. He just *wanted* to fight. Needed it, sort of. There are men like that – I've known a few of them.'

He looked enquiringly at Hollis, who nodded and said, 'Yes, I know what you mean.'

'*Thought* you did. After all, the police is a service, just the same as the navy. And men are men all over. And there are some that've just got to be getting their fists out and proving it, even when nobody's said "boo" to them.'

'So how long did you serve with Crafty Collins?'

'Well, let me see. We were two years on the base before he got in his bit of trouble and got discharged, and then it must have been another three years or so he was still there, but as a civilian. Then it was about six months after he left before I was posted back to England, home and beauty. O' course, we weren't *friends*, you understand. I mean, I was a good bit older than him, and I was a petty officer, while he was just a rating. And apart from that, you didn't make friends with Collins. He wasn't a friendly man. Not,' he added thoughtfully, and pausing to sip his coffee, 'that he didn't have a soft spot somewhere. I maintain everyone's got one. And Collins had this bird. We weren't supposed to have pets,' he went on, dismissing Hollis's immediate vision of a girlfriend, 'but on a shore base things are a bit different and blind eyes are turned now and then, if you know what I mean. Anyway, Collins had this little bird in a cage. A finch, I think it was. He bought it off a Chinee – they're big on these little cage birds, the Chinese. Walk through a Chinese section of Hong Kong and you'll see a cage hanging up on every balcony with some canary or whatnot whistling its little heart out.'

'Cruel, I call it,' Mrs Rice put in.

'She's not keen on birds, Mother,' Mr Rice explained for her. 'Give her the creeps.'

'It's not that,' she said. 'I like 'em well enough in the garden, but keeping 'em in cages is not natural. They just sit there hunched up all day and night, like they're in mourning.'

'Fanciful,' Mr Rice explained her to Hollis.

'No I am not,' Mrs Rice defended herself. 'Even when they sing, it's not happy singing. Makes me shiver.'

'I knew a man once had this parrot,' said Mr Rice. 'Or, well, it was a cockateel, to be absolutely accurate—'

Hollis felt they were on a banana skin to unfettered reminiscence, and coughed slightly. 'About Mr Collins?'

'Oh, yes,' said Mr Rice, quite unembarrassed. 'I was saying he had this finch or whatever it was – a little grey bird with a red cap, very smart. Looked like an MP. And, I will say, it whistled a treat. Well, you wouldn't think Crafty would care that much about it. He was built like a bag of boulders, and full of boiling oil, if you know what I mean, and this little bird was only about three inches from head to tail. But he looked after it like a mother. Used to go down the market to get it fresh lettuce and fruit and stuff. He loved that bird, which goes to prove what I've always said, that there's a soft spot in everyone, if you know where to find it.'

'What happened to the bird?' Hollis asked in spite of himself.

'Oh, it died. They don't live long, them sort, even in the wild.'

'And was he upset?'

Speedy gave a snorting laugh. 'I don't suppose there was anyone on the base brave enough or daft enough to ask him. He never showed anything, but I reckon he was upset. He never got another one to replace it, anyway. And I'll tell you something.' He leaned forward a little. 'He gave that bird a Christian burial. Put it in a cigar box and buried it somewhere up on the Peak. I'm the only person that knows that. I saw him put the bird in the box and I saw him leave with the box and come back without it; and later someone told me they'd seen him up there, so I worked it out.' He sat back. 'Nothing as queer as folk, is there?'

It certainly was an interesting, if unilluminating aside on the character of Sonny Collins. 'Tell me about the fight when he lost his eye. What was all that about?'

'Well, I can't tell you officially,' Mr Rice said, settling himself back for the long haul, 'but *un*officially a lot of us knew what was really going on. I told you Collins was crooked, but crookedness doesn't pay when you're practising it on people you live on top of. So he started to look outside, and it wasn't long before he built up contacts with the local people. Well, Hong Kong – you ever been there?'

'No, I haven't,' Hollis said. 'More's the pity.'

Speedy nodded. 'It's a special place, is Hong Kong. I expect it's different now, of course. Pity we ever gave it back, that's what I say—'

'Now, Stan!' Mrs Rice warned.

'I know, I know. Well, as I was saying, Hong Kong is – or was – the best place in the world to set up a bit of business and make a bit of money on the side. Anything you want, they'll get. And when you've got it, there's a stack of people to sell it to – tourists, service people, ex-pats; boats and planes coming in all the time with new customers, all of 'em with money burning a hole in their pockets. So Crafty gets in with a lot of shady characters. This particular one – can't remember what he was called – one of those wing-wang-wong names – he was a right wrong 'un, a real cross-eyed ugly little geezer and as crooked as a dog's hind leg. The local coppers had been after him for years for drug smuggling.'

'Was that what Collins was into with him?'

'I can't tell you as to that, not as a literal fact. But I wouldn't be surprised. Anyway, thieves fall out, as they say, and one night him and this Chinee start arguing, and before Crafty can get a swing at him, he outs with a knife and stabs him right through the eye.' Mrs Rice sucked her teeth in protest. 'The medico said he was lucky to be alive, because a fraction further and it would have gone right into his brain, which is probably what this Chinky was after. But he missed his shot, and Crafty came right back and swung a right hook at him, caught him under the chin and lifted him four feet in the air, so they said that saw it. Flew like a bird. He was dead before he hit the ground. Broken neck, neat as you like. Saved somebody a job, because he'd have been hung sooner or later, the sort he was, sure as eggs are eggs.'

'But Collins wasn't punished for it?'

'Well, it was self-defence, wasn't it? There were enough witnesses, and there he was without an eye and the medico saying he was lucky to be alive. Open-and-shut case. The enquiry cleared him, but he couldn't serve with only one eye, could he?'

'Nelson did,' Hollis couldn't resist.

Mr Rice smiled. 'Nice one! That's one to you! But Collins wasn't no Nelson and the Royal Navy's a bit different now. So he got discharged on medical grounds. Honourable discharge – funny to think of anything Crafty Collins did being called honourable.'

'And then what?'

'Well, everyone thought he'd go home. That's what any of us would've done. But I suppose old Crafty didn't have anything to go back to. No, he stopped on and set himself up in business.'

'A tattoo parlour.'

'That's right. You've done your homework,' said Mr Rice approvingly. 'Well, where there are sailors, you can't go wrong with a tattoo parlour, can you? He learnt how to do it off an old Chinee that was going out of business, and bought his needles and dyes and everything, and there he was. Service people and daft young tourists flocked to him. O' course, tattooing wasn't all he provided 'em with.'

'Now, Stan!'

'Got to tell him, haven't I? That's what he's here for,' Mr Rice said indignantly.

'What else did he supply?' Hollis asked.

'Whatever was wanted. Hashish, cocaine, girls. I dare say he'd find you a watch or camera or pearls if that was all you wanted. But that stuff doesn't pay as well as the other. It wasn't long before he had a very nice stash built up. But o' course that sort of activity attracts attention in the long run. In the end he had to pack up and get out before they clamped down on him, but I reckon he took a good bit back to Blighty when he went. Enough to set up in business.'

But he didn't, Hollis thought. He got a job in the licensed trade. He didn't buy a pub, he got a job as a manager. So what did he do with the stash? Spend it all in one wild debauch? Maybe – except that he didn't seem like the debauching kind.

'Did you,' he asked casually, but with great anticipation, 'ever know a man called Trevor Bates?'

'What, Crafty's friend?' Mr Rice said, little knowing what joy he brought to a policeman's calloused old heart with those three words. 'Well, I didn't know him personally, o' course, but I knew *of* him.'

Thank you, God! Hollis offered inwardly. 'Tell me about him,' he said aloud, settling himself comfortably to listen.

CHAPTER EIGHTEEN

Susie Wrong

'Boss,' said Swilley as he crossed the office on his way back from the loo. He changed direction towards her. She was looking extremely fetching in a skinny powder-blue top that consolidated her assets magnificently. He was about to conclude that Tony was a lucky man when he remembered that Tony was at home alone in his slippers reading the papers while his new wife was here with them, which wasn't so very lucky after all.

'Life's a bitch,' he said.

She raised her eyebrows at him. 'You don't know what I'm going to say, yet.'

'It was a general observation. Go ahead.'

'Well, I hope you'll be pleased. I've found out about Susie Mabbot, and I know now why we had trouble tracing her.'

'Oh?'

'She's dead.'

'Oh, my God, not another one!' Slider sank into the vacant seat at Anderson's desk, next door.

'No, no, it's all right, she's been dead for ages. Before we started.' She spread out the sheets of paper under her hands for him to see, and walked him through it. 'She was pulled out of the river. She was right down at Creekmouth – that's the opposite bank from Plumstead Marshes – but they reckoned she'd gone in a lot further upstream. You know how far bodies can be dragged if the tide's set right. There was nothing on her to identify her, but fortunately one of her girls had reported her missing, and she got matched up as soon as they checked Mispers.'

'And how was she killed?'

'It was a bit strange and nasty,' Swilley said, turning down her mouth. 'I've got the PM notes and the inquest report. Apparently they found a whole lot of tiny holes all over her, only a couple of millimetres deep and so small in diameter they were hardly visible to the naked eye. The pathologist said they looked like the marks left by acupuncture needles.'

Slider frowned. 'Acupuncture's hardly life-threatening. You're not telling me the water rushed in through the holes and drowned her?'

'No, her neck was broken. The pathologist concluded it was some kind of sex game, because there was evidence of penetration, and semen in the vagina, but no sign of force having been applied, apart from the death blow. PM report said her head was probably pulled sharply backwards by someone standing behind her – which of course could be part of it. Naturally once they found out she was a tom they concluded she did it for a client. I mean, being stuck full of needles would be uncomfortable but they do worse things for their money. And then he got carried away and killed her.'

'So if it was a client, I presume they were able to find out which one?'

'No, that's the odd thing. No-one was ever charged. They questioned all the girls, but none of them had anything to say, not even the one who reported her missing. Her evidence says she was worried about Susie being missing because of the nature of their work. Later, with a bit of pushing, she said she knew Susie had a client who was into some weird stuff. Susie had apparently told her she was seeing him that night – the night before she was reported missing – and was apprehensive about it. Here, look, her words: "Susie said this bloke gave her the willies. I said to her, well, don't do it then, and she said it'd be the worse for her if she didn't. She said he wasn't a bloke who took no for an answer."'

'But she never said what it was the bloke did?'

'No. She said she didn't know – Susie never told her.'

'And *no* idea who the bloke was?'

Swilley shook her head. 'They hauled in quite a few of the customers but cleared them all. Well, they had a DNA sample from the semen so they could be fairly sure about it, and most of them were well known to the girls and just ordinary punters. Susie ran an expensive house. They were respectable (ha-ha) businessmen, most of them.'

'I bet that enquiry ruined a few lives,' Slider commented. 'Did the locals suspect anyone, even if he wasn't charged?'

'Nope. Not a clue. I rang Dave Tipper and he asked one of the officers who was on the case. They've never come near to looking at anyone. Of course, they ran the DNA but there was no match on the database. They're now thinking that the killer must have been either a foreign businessman or someone from outside London who visited occasionally and went to Susie for his jollies, went too far and had to dump the body. She was dressed when she was found in the water, so they reckoned he could have got her into a car by "walking" her with her arm over his shoulder and his round her waist, so that if anyone saw they'd think she was just drunk. But apparently no-one did see.'

'Yes, it's amazing how people don't see things,' Slider said. But of course a lot of the time they did see things, and simply wouldn't say. And there was, he knew, a stratum of thought that whatever happened to prostitutes was their own fault.

'So what do you think, boss?' Swilley asked. 'I mean, all this acupuncture business, and Everet's boss being called the Needle – do you think there's something in it?'

'It's certainly very suggestive,' Slider said. 'Whoever this boss is, his people are afraid of him, afraid enough not to grass him, and apparently Susie Mabbot was too afraid of him to refuse sex or to tell anyone his name.'

'But she'd dead and it doesn't really get us any further forward, does it?' Swilley said gloomily.

'Oh, it does,' Slider said. 'For a start we've got a DNA profile now, so if ever we do arrest someone we've got something to check against.'

'It's a big if,' Swilley concluded. 'What do you want me to do?'

'Get a picture of Susie Mabbot and take it over to Neville Coulsden, see if he can identify her as the Susan who came to help his daughter move her things. Take one of her in life, if you can. I'd rather not have that poor man faced with a mortuary mugshot.'

'Sure, boss. And if she is the same?'

'One step at a time,' Slider said. 'There's every chance she isn't – or he won't be able to say one way or the other.'

'But *if* she is—?' Swilley insisted.

'Then we know that she knew Everet, who worked for a man called the Needle and might well have introduced her to him.'

'Or vice versa.'

'Whatever. It comes out the same. And as she was killed

with those particular marks on her, it is very suggestive that her killer and the Needle are one and the same.'

'But we still don't know who the Needle is,' she pointed out with fatal logic.

'There is just that small thing,' Slider agreed. 'But link by link we're forging a chain.' And eventually, he thought, it might be long enough to trip somebody up.

When Swilley had departed – with a 'publicity' picture of the ex-madam – on her way to Harlesden, Slider took the papers on Susie Mabbot into his own room and went through them again, settling the facts into his head. When he got to the statements of the other girls in the house he slowed, then paused. Then he rummaged amongst the photographs, pulled one out, studied it, and smiled.

'Sassy Palmer, as I live and breathe,' he said. Toms were notorious for using false names, of course, but at the end of every string of aliases, like the crock of gold at the end of a rainbow, was a set of fingerprints and a birth certificate. The employee of Susie Mabbot who described herself as Suzette Las Palma had been pinned down by the patience of the Notting Hill squad as Suzanne "Sassy" Palmer, and Slider knew Sassy. What was more, he knew where to find her. That level of the underworld rarely moved far from its origins, and though Notting Hill came under a different borough, its station and his own were a bare mile apart.

He looked at his watch. This time on Sunday morning she ought to be in bed and asleep after her Saturday night exertions. Just the right time to catch her with her guard down and ask her a few questions.

'Trevor Bates,' said Speedy Rice. 'That was a queer thing, now, the way Crafty Collins took up with him. You wouldn't have thought they had a thing in common. I mean, Crafty, he had enough upstairs. He wasn't stupid by many a long mile. But this Bates bloke, he was college educated and everything. Smart as a whip. Well, he was an engineer – and I don't mean he was a greaser,' he added sternly, as if Hollis had expressed doubts.

'Electronics engineer, wasn't he?' Hollis said, to show he was on the ball.

'That's right. Motherboards and solder, that's as dirty as he got *his* hands.'

'How did they meet?' Hollis asked.

'Well, as I understand it, this Bates wandered into Crafty's tattoo parlour because somebody had told him that was where to go for a spot of the doings, know what I mean? He worked in one of them tower buildings on the island, you see. Anyway, him and Collins struck up a what-d'ye-call—?'

'A rapport?' Hollis offered.

'That's the thing. Like love at first sight, kinda thing, only this was more of an un'oly alliance. They were thick as thieves. They made quite a team, too. Collins had the brawn – and the violence – and Bates had the brain. He was a skinny runt of a feller, was Bates, until Crafty took him in hand. Like the bloke that gets sand kicked in his face in the advert. Sickly white, too, and with that red hair – not ginger, but more like Rita Hayworth, know what I mean?'

'Auburn,' said Mrs Rice, without looking up from the jumbo *EastEnders* crossword. Seven letters with two f's in the middle? What the blazes was that?

'If that's what it is,' Mr Rice conceded. 'Anyway, Collins showed him body-building techniques, acted like his personal trainer, not that they'd invented them in those days. Bates wasn't half badly built by the time Crafty'd finished with him. No Mr Atlas, but he looked the goods.'

'And what did Collins get out of the relationship?'

'Well, now,' Mr Rice said thoughtfully, 'as to that, I can tell you what I think, but it's only my opinion. I remember that little bird, you see. I think Crafty was fascinated by Bates. I think he sort of – loved him, in a way.'

'Now, Stan!'

'I don't mean in a queer way, not that,' Mr Rice amended hastily. 'But he protected him, looked after him just like he did that little bird. 'Course, he was older than him, Collins was, older than Bates. Maybe it was like an older brother thing, I dunno. Anyway, he kept him from being beaten up or killed, which he quite likely might have been, moving in the sort of circles they moved in. Anyone even looked cross-eyed at him, Crafty'd sort 'em out so's their own mothers'd have to look twice at 'em. On the other side, I reckon it was thanks to Bates that Collins stopped getting followed about by the police.'

'How's that?' Hollis asked.

'Well, Bates tamed him, kind of – taught him to keep his temper, or at least to use his violence a bit more cleverly. Bates was an organiser, and he thought things through the way old Crafty never had. Bash first, think later, that was Crafty. And Bates was clever – inventive, always thinking up new things. Collins was just a doer, know what I mean? Together they could get up to four times as much mischief – and they did, from what I heard. Well, Bates was a bit of a scholar and he got on well with the Chinese – into all the philosophy and Chinese medicine and them eastern therapies and everything. He kind of understood 'em, and they trusted him, so he could do business with 'em without 'em giving him away. That's how Collins made himself a nice fortune without getting caught by the authorities. If you want a solid reason for him liking Bates, that's what he owed him, keeping him out of legal trouble like *he* kept *him* out of physical trouble. But that wasn't what it really was, not to my mind. Bates was that little bird to him. He was his soft spot.'

Mr Rice shook his head slowly, gazing in wonder down the telescope of memory.

'I'll tell you an example,' he went on, 'of how soft Collins could be with this Bates bloke. Have you ever seen him – Collins, I mean?'

'Yes,' said Hollis.

'Well, you might have noticed a tattoo round his neck, a dotted line right round the bottom of his neck.'

'Yes, I've seen that.'

'Well, it was Bates did that to him. I told you he went to Crafty's shop first of all for some of the other things he sold, but the story I heard was he'd never been in a tattoo parlour before and he was fascinated by the needles and the dyes and the stencils and all that. That's how it all started. He might have gone away with his spot of hash and that would've been that. But he hung around to watch Collins working the needle, and kept coming back to watch some more, and they got friendly.'

'Did Bates get a tattoo himself?'

'Oh, no. Squeamish about it, as far as his own white skin went. But couldn't get enough of seeing it done to other people. Well, that's what I heard. Anyway, I was telling you – one day, this is what I heard, he asked Collins, could he have a go using the machine. And Collins let him do one on him. That's how far he'd let this bloke go, because it must've been a big risk, especially round his neck like that.'

'Why that particular tattoo?'

'I heard it was a kind of joke, that it was meant to be

like Boris Karloff – you know, the stitches holding his head on?'

'Frankenstein's monster?'

'That's the one! Bates was all brain and Collins was all brawn, like I said, and, what with him only having one eye – well, Bates used to call him that, Frankenstein's monster. Kind of affectionate, I suppose,' he added, but doubtfully.

Hollis thought that from what he had heard so far, it was evidence of Bates's desire to live dangerously. 'So when Collins went back to England, did Bates go too?' he asked.

''Course he did! You couldn't have one without the other. Gammon without spinach that'd be.'

Perhaps, then, Hollis thought, that was where the stash went. Perhaps the faithful Collins used it to set Mr Bates up in business. A capital sum to buy the first old houses to be done up? It was possible – though why would Collins give it all away? Wasn't that taking friendship too far? Most criminals displayed all the loyalty of a tart in a barracks. On the other hand, if they had made the money together, as a partnership, perhaps it was only nominally Collins's, because he had the legitimate business to pass it through: he was the laundry for their joint efforts. And perhaps they shared the profits. There was nothing in Collins's lifestyle to suggest he had money, but maybe that's how he liked to live. It was not impossible that there was a big deposit somewhere they hadn't discovered yet.

Speedy Rice seemed to have come to an end of his recollections. Hollis looked over his notes, thanked him, and asked if he'd be willing to have a statement taken, if anything should come of it.

''Course I will,' he said. 'Got to do our duty, haven't we?'

'I wish everyone thought like that,' Hollis said. He got up to go, thanking Mrs Rice for the coffee and biscuits, at which she beamed with pleasure and said he was welcome, it was nice to have company now and then, and come again.

The company removed itself carefully, stepping over furniture and squeezing through the doorway. Hollis was a thin man and no more than average height, but this place made him feel like the jolly green giant.

Mr Rice had leapt nimbly to his feet and said, 'I'll show him out, Mother, don't you move.' When they got out into the roaring, shuddering street – Hollis could swear the traffic bellow was bouncing off the pavement in lumps – it became clear this courtesy had an ulterior motive.

'I didn't like to say anything in front of the wife,' he told Hollis in a confiding shout, 'but there's some other stuff I could tell you about Collins and Bates.'

'Please do,' Hollis shouted back.

'Well,' said Mr Rice, 'when I said it was like a kind of love, Mother thought I was suggesting they were queer. But it wasn't that. They both had women – lots of 'em. They used to go hunting 'em together. Chinese women, mostly, o' course. There wasn't many of the other sort, and you could get into trouble chasing them.'

'Prostitutes?' Hollis asked.

'I suppose so. There *were* lots of prostitutes, B-girls and dancers, and then all those massage parlours and places that were sort of on the brink.' He made a rocking movement with his hand. 'Could go either way, get me? But there were plenty of women available. I dare say some of them were just poor and needed the money. And maybe some were too scared to say no. They had some funny habits, those two.'

'Such as?'

Mr Rice looked up at him with a sort of stern reluctance. 'It's only hearsay. But there was a lot of talk about Collins and Bates – Collins having been one of ours, you know. The talk was that they liked to hurt women. I'd hesitate to believe that of anybody if I could help it, but I've knocked around the world a bit, and I know what men can be. Even some of the decent lads in our unit, well, they thought Chinese women didn't count the same as white ones.'

'Yes,' said Hollis. 'I've known men like that.'

Speedy nodded, man of the world to man of the world. 'And if you start thinking like that, it's not a big step to thinking no women count.'

'Did both of them get their pleasure that way?' Hollis asked.

'The way I heard it, it was Bates liked to do the hurting, and Collins liked to watch, but he must have been part of it, mustn't he? I dare say he held 'em down or something. Nasty, I call it. People like that – well, I don't know what they deserve.' He paused and then added reflectively, 'So Crafty Collins is dead, is he? There's a lot of 'em gawn, from back then. I go to the reunions, and every time there's another one gawn. The old man with the scythe, you know. And what about afterwards? Collins'll be finding out about that. If there is an afterlife, your sins'll all be looked at pretty bloody close, I reckon. It makes you think, doesn't it?'

'Yes,' said Hollis gravely, 'it makes you think.'

Before Slider could get out of the office, his mobile rang. It was Pauline Smithers, so he sat down again to talk to her.

'Blimey, that's quick,' he said. 'I didn't expect to hear from you for a day or two.'

'Yes, well what I found out I thought you'd better know ASAP,' she said. 'You do like to shove your hand into hornets' nests, don't you, old pal of mine?'

'What have I done now?'

'I hope you haven't done anything. That's why I'm calling you on a Sunday morning when I should be in a deep bath with a glass of Chardonnay.'

'Stop it, you're making me dribble.'

'I'm not fooling, Bill,' she said sternly. 'Do you know what this cultural legation is?'

'Not what it seems?' he hazarded.

'I shouldn't be telling you this, and the person who told me shouldn't have told me, but it's one of those secrets that aren't so secret any more since the end of the Cold War, and in any case I want to stop you hurting yourself.'

'Oh, it's like *that*, is it?' Slider said, enlightened. 'Atherton half thought it might be. He's been chumming up to one of the employees and found her exposition of what the cultural legation did less than convincing.'

'Yes, well, apparently that particular branch specialises in listening, and given that they're willing to share what they hear – or some of it, at any rate – with us, it's one of those situations it's worth turning a blind eye to, as long as no-one does anything that has to be noticed.'

'Like someone drawing attention to himself?' Slider said.

'Never mind himself,' Pauline said. 'I'm thinking of you. If everyone's ignoring everything like billy-oh in the national interest, how grateful do you think they'll be to someone who asks so many questions some of them have to be answered?'

'Oh, Pauly, been there, done that,' he said. 'If I were to tell you how many times I've been threatened—'

'Not by this lot,' she said shortly. 'I know you have to

do what you have to do, and in any case, I'm not speaking to you now and this conversation never happened. But for God's sake be careful.'

'I will. I promise. But what about Bates? Did you find out anything about him?'

He almost heard her wince. 'Must you name names? How secure do you think this telephone is? All I know about him is that he supplies some systems and hardware, again with tacit consent – which makes it even more dangerous to mess with him. But I can tell you that according to my source they've got their doubts about him. He's been under investigation for some time. He's got his finger into too many pies, and they think he may be a security risk.'

'Because of the pies, or for some other reason?'

'I don't know specifics. Is there another reason?'

'There may be. That's what I'm trying to find out. Any particular flavour pies mentioned?'

'She didn't say, but I'd guess they were criminal or at least questionable, or why the worry?'

'And are they doing anything about him?'

'Yes, they're going the Al Capone route. The Inland Revenue has got a special investigation team liaising with one of our squads, trying to find out where his money comes from and where it goes to.'

'Ah, yes, softly softly finee monkey,' Slider said bitterly. 'And we've got four corpses and counting.'

'It's no use complaining to me. If you're so keen on him, get some evidence the CPS can't ignore. All I'm saying is be sure you know what you're doing. He doesn't exactly have friends in high places, but high places eat up little chaps like you and me.'

'Yes, okay. I understand. Thanks, Pauly.'

'No sweat. Or not much, anyway. So now you owe me – again!'

'When all this is over I'll take you out for a meal. A real blow-out, okay?'

'When's this lady of yours coming back?'

'Why d'you ask?'

'I'm wondering how she'll feel about you and me and the candlelit dinner.'

'She can come too.'

'Oh. I see.'

He hesitated, and added, 'She may not be coming back at all. This job – she's been trying to tell me something for the last week and not managing it.'

'You think she's found someone else?' Pauline asked with gruff sympathy.

'It's possible,' he admitted painfully. 'I mean, what have I got to offer her?'

'Don't trail your coat. You know what I think of you.' Before Slider, startled, could say 'No, what?' and embarrass them both, she went on quickly, 'If she says she's found someone she prefers, have her certified, that's my advice. And now I've got to go. Take care, Bill.'

'You too,' he said, but he was talking to the air. He sat a moment lost in thought, trying to sort out the strands, to put the personal things aside where they wouldn't interrupt him. Pauline – Joanna – his future, possibly alone. Work was nearly everything, but not quite. It took it out of you – put it back in, too, of course: the pleasure of getting a result; the intellectual satisfaction of sorting out tangles and finding where the truth had been buried, usually at the bottom of a festering pile of profiteroles. But you needed more, you needed the human dimension too, otherwise you became lop-sided. You could end up as twisted as the people you investigated. That was it, wasn't it? Crime was a lop-sidedness They talked about a person being well-balanced, didn't they? Well, how well-balanced could you be doing a thirteen-hour shift and going home to a take-away and a cold bed, day after day? He wanted Joanna, but he needed her too. If she didn't come back – if what she had been trying to tell him was that it was just too hard and she was going to let him go and look elsewhere – could he do the Job without her? Could he ever, now, care for anyone else? He thought he knew the answer to that one, helped to it by kind Pauline. The answer was, not enough.

Forget it for now, he told himself firmly, knotting the whole bundle together and putting it aside. Right now he had more immediate things to think about. And if he didn't get out of the office toot sweet, the phone would ring again and he'd be here all day.

CHAPTER NINETEEN

Deja Vous

Slider had to knock and ring at the door of the flat just off
Portobello Road for a good long time before it opened.
Sassy Palmer, in a cotton dressing-gown that was not really
man enough for the job, looked at him blankly, then said,
'Oh, fuck me! You again!' and tried to shut the door.

'Don't be like that, Sassy,' Slider said, stopping it with
his foot. 'I just want to talk to you.'

'I ain't Sassy to you,' she said irritably. 'Show some
respec', for Chrissake. And whut make you think I want to
talk to you?'

'Miss Palmer, then,' Slider said placatingly. 'Come on,
let me in. You know I'm one of the good guys.'

'You a honky bastard, like all the rest,' she said, but with
less heat.

'Better to talk to me than someone else, isn't it? I do
respect you, Miss Palmer, I really do. And I'm on your
side. I just want some information.'

'Yeah, like that *all* you want!' she said, but she stopped
pushing at the door, though she didn't yet abandon it. She
seemed to be considering.

He pushed again his main credential. 'If you don't talk
to me someone else will come. You don't want a squad of

heavy-handed coppers pounding at your door, do you?'

At last she said, 'I ain't alone.'

'You've got a customer with you?'

'At this time o' day?' she said scornfully. 'No, I got my sister stayin' over.'

'I didn't know you had a sister.'

'There a lot you don't know 'bout me. Hanyway, she asleep. Don't you make a noise an' wake her.'

'I won't,' Slider said. Taking this for an invitation he pushed the door again, gently, and she yielded and let him in.

The narrow hall, hardly more than one human wide, had been painted purple by an amateur hand, and an ugly cast-iron chandelier much encrusted with candle wax made the headroom hazardous. Sassy, walking away before him, seemed to fill the space. She was a tall woman, taller than Slider, well-bosomed and slim-hipped, though with a fleshy behind that twitched in what might have been an inviting way under the thin cotton, except that Slider knew she was dog-tired and invitation was the last thing on her mind. Her feet were bare except for toe-rings, and silver anklets that clinked at every step. Her hair was grown long and stood out in a great mass round her head and shoulders, too wiry to do anything as pedestrian as hang down.

She led him into the sitting room and flung herself down on the sofa, one foot tucked under her, giving the cotton wrap even more pressing problems to solve. Her eyes were bleared with her interrupted sleep, and one of her long talon fingernails was missing. They were falsies, he supposed, since they were painted black and the short nail on the odd finger was a natural pink. She seemed to like black. One of the walls was painted black – the other three were red, a depressing combination, he thought – and there was a black 'throw' over one of the armchairs. Chairs and sofa were old, probably bought second-hand, and reno- vated in the cheapest way by hanging a piece of cloth over and tucking the slack into the creases. There were a lot of candles around, and paper flowers, and objects that had been painted with silver paint, or decorated with stuck-on sequins or squares cut from mirror-flex. Everything in the room was cheap and the decoration was home-made, but it was certainly individual. There was a smell in the air which he thought at first was joss-sticks, but realised after a moment was old perfume – hers, presumably – whose brand he knew but couldn't for the moment place.

Sassy yawned mightily, showing the gold cap on one of her front teeth. 'So whut you want, anyhow?' she said uninvitingly. She went to pull her robe together at the front, and noticed the missing nail. 'Shit! How'd I do that?' She pronounced the expletive with extra vowels, like an American. Her accent wandered quite a bit, from Harlesden to Harlem, but leaning more towards the latter. When Slider had first known her she had been pretending to be American (that's where she had got the nickname) on the grounds that it was good for trade, and old habits died hard.

'I want to talk to you—' Slider began, then snapped, 'Sassy, pay attention! This is important.'

She looked up resentfully from examination of her finger- nail. 'I listening. I don't have to look at you as well.'

'Yes you do. I want to see your face.'

''F you think I gonna lie to you, why you botherin' t' ask me?'

He didn't answer that. 'Until three months ago you used to work in the house run by Susie Mabbot.'

Now he had her attention. 'Shit! Not that again,' she said. Now in her apprehension her accent had come home to

London. 'I told 'em everyfing I knew. It's ancient history. What're you draggin' it all up again for?'

'Not that ancient. And I don't think you told quite everything. I don't think any of you girls told quite everything.'

'Listen, Susie was good to us! We was all heart-broken over what happened to her! What d'you think?'

'I know you were. I think you were also scared to death that what happened to her might happen to you. So you did the sensible thing and kept your mouths shut.'

'Yeah, well if we did, we had good reason, didn't we? So what makes it any different now?'

'Like you said, it's ancient history. Over and done with. You're out of the loop, aren't you? So you can talk to me quite safely.'

'I don't want nuffin' to do with it,' she said with finality. And then she added, bethinking herself, 'I don't know nuffin', anyway. I don't know what you're talking about.'

'Yes, you do, Sass, don't say that. This is heavy stuff, and I need your help. You working girls have got enough to worry about without creeps like him. Look what he did to Susie! Don't you want to get revenge for that?'

'I hate him for that,' she said with low anger.

'And now there's another girl in danger. I've got to get him put away.'

'You can't,' Sassy said. 'He's untouchable.'

'No, he's not. We've got his DNA profile. If we can arrest him for anything, we can match it and prove he killed Susie.'

'How d'you get that?' Her eyes widened, her nostrils flared with distaste or distress. 'Not from her?' He nodded. 'After all that time in the water?'

'He miscalculated,' Slider said. 'The river cheated him. The way the tide was she oughtn't to have been found for days, even weeks. She might have gone right down to the sea and never been found. But just by chance she got washed up within hours.'

Sassy wasn't listening to that. She was staring at memory. 'I hate that bastard.'

'He was a customer of Susie's, yes? Why did she keep seeing him? He must have had some powerful hold over her.'

'Money,' Sassy said bitterly. 'He was a rich bastard, and he paid big. Plus she was scared of him. She was scared he'd kill her if she didn't do what he said. I said to her, get away, girl. Jus' get away. But she said he'd find her and kill her.'

'Well, he did kill her,' Slider pointed out.

'Yeah.'

'So you've got to help me.'

'What, an' get myself killed?'

'He can't hurt you if he's inside, can he?'

'He'd find a way. He'd get someone to do it for him. He had people around him. He'd come to the house with a couple of bodyguards, and we'd have to entertain 'em while he was wiv Susie. Bastards!'

'They're just the fleas on a dog,' Slider said. 'They'll go down with him. Help me get him, Sassy. Just give me his name, for a start.'

'I never knew his name,' she said. 'No, straight up, I ain't kidding. Most of the punters didn't use their own names. Susie knew 'em, most of 'em, 'cause a lot of the regulars had accounts. Put it down as business entertainment. But she never told us the real names.'

'So what was this particular man known as?'

'He was Mr Lee. Bruce Lee. I s'pose that was a kind o' joke,' she added. 'Very funny, I don't think.'

'But he wasn't Chinese?'

'Nah, he was English all right. But he'd been out east. That's where he got his funny ideas from. He was into all that Eastern shit, Chinese medicine and—'

'Acupuncture?' Slider suggested.

She had been slipping into it bit by bit, but at this interpolation she started and looked at him with alarm and dislike. 'I told you, I ain't talking. You fink you can trick me into it, you bastard?'

'No, I don't think that. I think you want to help me get back at this bloke, for Susie's sake.'

'An' get myself stuck full o' fuckin' holes?' She started to rise. 'Go fuck yourself,' she said. 'I'm goin' back to bed.'

'Please, Sassy—'

'Don't call me that! You ain't got the right.'

'Miss Palmer, then. Please just talk to me for a bit.'

'I gotta get some sleep. I got a livin' to earn.'

'I'll pay for your time. What do you charge nowadays?'

A little calculation entered the atmosphere. 'A cent'ry, or I go back to bed.'

'I haven't got that much on me,' Slider said. 'I think I've got fifty. I'll give you fifty for an hour of your time. Come on, Sass, fifty pounds an hour's not bad. Only lawyers and accountants get more than that.'

'All right,' she said, flopping back down. Her face was still closed. 'I'll talk to you for fifty, but only 'alf a hour. And I ain't tellin' you anyfin', okay?'

'Blimey, that sounds like a real bargain,' Slider said.

In spite of herself she thawed a little. 'You a funny bastard,' she said.

'I think I must be to go on doing this job. Go on, Sassy, tell me about Susie's special customer.'

It had been going on for a couple of years before Susie's

death, Sassy said. He only visited about once a month, but it was pretty regular. They never saw him. He would go straight up the stairs to Susie's private room, while she brought his companions – usually two, and obviously minders – into the lounge for the other girls to entertain.

'What about other customers?' Slider asked.

'Not when he was there. That was the rule. He took the whole house for the whole night. Paid well for it, an' all. That was how Susie got into it in the first place, I s'pose.'

'Do you know how Susie first met him?'

'Nah, I dunno. Maybe someone told him about her. All I know, she said he never went wiv white girls. He only liked black and Chinese. Well, we never had no Chinese girl but there was Susie an' Michelle an' me all black.' She shuddered. 'It could have been me, man,' she said quietly.

'Did Susie have many special customers?'

'Nah, just a couple of others apart from him. She was still gorgeous, but she mostly just done the management an' everyfing.'

And who could blame her, Sassy went on. No sane person would want to earn it on their back if they could make more getting someone else to do it. Not that he should get her wrong. Susie had always been good to the girls, and generous. They all got a bonus when Mr Lee visited, or they did one of them big corporate parties. And Susie kept the customers in order and never let any harm come to the girls. None of that S&M stuff. She said there were other houses they could go to if that was their bag. Which was what made it all the more strange about her and Mr Lee.

And he never had any of the other girls? He never had Sassy?

No, fank God. He didn't like tall girls, Susie said. He only ever had Susie. She didn't say at first what his bag was, but over the months they could see Susie didn't look forward to his visits. She would get quiet and kind of depressed when the day came. Well, not depressed, exactly, but kind of thoughtful. Eventually they all knew she didn't like Mr Lee and wished he wouldn't come, but when Sassy had asked her why she didn't refuse him, she said, 'It wouldn't be wise.' Just that. And she kind of tried to shrug it off and said it wasn't so bad what he did, just creepy.

What did Sassy know about the man?

Not much. Susie said at first he was a rich businessman. Always wore real expensive clothes. But Sassy reckoned his business wasn't legit. Susie hinted as much later on. In any case, why else would she be afraid of him?

Could Sassy describe him?

Like she said, she had never seen him. No, Susie never described him either, 'cept that he had a good body. Oh, and he was very white – his skin. Susie said once, kind of joking, that he must never step out of doors. That was in the middle of a heat wave when they was practically sleeping over in the park. Susie said he lived in the dark like a mush-room. Sassy remembered that because it gave her the creeps. She reckoned it gave Susie the creeps an' all.

No, his goons never talked about him either, not that Sassy ever heard. Well trained. They were real tough guys. You could see it in their eyes. Not cheap-smart tough, like a lot of blokes, all mouth and muscles for show, but the real thing. You wouldn't mess with them guys.

This seemed to be a dead end, and Slider turned to another tack. 'Do you know a man called Everet Boston?'

She answered with barely a pause, but Slider got the impression of wariness in the sudden cock of her atten-tion. 'Yeah, he was a mate of Susie's.'

'A customer?'

'A mate from back home. They used to go out drinking once in a while. It was like her evening off.'

'Did you meet him?'

'Couple o' times. He come in for a freebie once or twice.'

'Did you like him?' Shrug. 'Was the freebie with you?'

'Nah. Another girl.'

'Did he ever bring another man called Lenny Baxter with him?'

'Lenny never come in for it. He wasn't into it much. I see him once or twice when him an' Ev called for Susie to go out. See, she and Ev and Lenny used to make a four-some wiv anover girl. But Susie used to talk about him. Ev thought he was all right, but Susie reckoned he was a wrong 'un.'

'In what way?'

She seemed to have difficulty putting into words. 'He was trouble, she reckoned. Kind of stupid-smart, know what I mean? The kind'd try and be too clever, do somefing stupid, get himself into trouble, and then chuck someone else in it, tryin' to get himself out. She said he'd get Ev into trouble one of these days. She was fond of Ev, Susie was.'

'Was it Susie who introduced Everet to Mr Lee?'

'Ev never met him. No-one never met him. I *told* you that.' She yawned again, gaping like a hippo. Now her acute apprehension had worn off, the sleepiness was returning.

'But Ev did work for him, didn't he?'

'Maybe.'

'You know he did.'

She looked goaded. 'If you know, why d'you ask me?'

'I need confirmation. You know how the game's played, Sassy. Did Susie introduce them?'

'Ev needed the money, and Mr Lee was looking for a smart guy. But they never met. That was the way he done things. Ev would've been contacted by a fird party, all right?'

'A control.'

She shrugged.

He changed tack again. 'Did you ever hear of a man called Trevor Bates?'

'Nah.'

'Are you sure? Think, Sassy.'

'Sure I'm sure. Who is he?'

'I think he might be the big boss Everet worked for. The boss of a criminal ring, a man with the nickname of Needle. Lenny worked for him too. I think he might be the man who killed Susie, and I need your help to pull the two ends together. He's a hard man to pin down.' She was not looking at him, but at her nails again. 'Come on, Sassy,' he said, 'try and help me. There must be something else you can tell me about this Mr Lee. Remember what he did to Susie, and try and help me.'

'Remember? I'd sooner forget!' In her indignation she lost some of her reserve. 'That's what she called him, the Needle. Said it was his nickname from when he was out east, the creep! I'll never forget what she told me. He'd stick them needles in her, one by one, all over, till she look like a porcupine. And then he'd do it. That's what give him his kicks. He couldn't get it up any other way. I hate that bastard.'

'But why did he kill her?'

Sassy paused on the brink a moment, and then lowered her voice and said, 'I'll tell you what I fink, but you must never let on I told you, or I'm dead. Promise me!'

'I promise.'

'Swear it.'

'I swear. Just tell me, Sass.'

'All right. She found something out about him.' She swallowed, and lowered her voice still further, as though she could lessen her guilt that way. 'The week before he came that last time, she told me. She said he told her he'd killed someone by mistake that way, a girl he'd had, only he'd never got found out. He told her while he was doing it, all that needle stuff. You know, to give himself a thrill by scaring her, the filthy bastard! Only she reckoned he might be sorry he'd said it. She was scared. That's when I said to her, get out, girl! Get out while you can. But she said he'd find her, and it'd be the worse for her.' She shook her head in grim wonder. 'How could it be worse? Me, I'd sooner run away an' have a fightin' chance than stand still and wait for it. If she'd only listened to me! But I reckon she was like hypnotised by him, you know? Like one of them snake things.' She made a circling motion with her finger. The allusion escaped Slider.

He tried one last tack. 'What about Ev's cousin?'

'*What* about her?' It was unwarily said, and at once Sassy seemed to realise she had betrayed something. 'I never knew he had a cousin.'

'Then how did you know it was a she and not a he? Come on, Sassy, give me a break! Ev's cousin Mary, or Teena as she called herself, was the fourth in the foursome, Lenny Baxter's girlfriend.'

'You know it all, don't you?' Sassy said sourly.

'So tell me about her.'

'I never met her. She never come in the house. She was just a kid.'

'What did Susie say about her?'

'Oh, she was just a kid,' Sassy said dismissively. She

seemed to think of something, and went on more confidingly, 'Susie said she was in over her head with this Lenny character. She was nuts about him – Teena was – but Susie reckoned he'd treat her bad in the end. He was using her, Susie said. And he was a bloke that'd always look after himself, whatever it took, know't I mean?'

This, Slider suspected, was either a smokescreen or a lure, but he didn't know what it was meant to conceal or lead him away from.

'So where is she now?'

'I don't know. How should I know? I ain't seen her since Susie was killed,' Sassy said with emphasis.

Slider noted that she had said before that she had never met her. Was it possible that Sassy knew where Teena Brown was? If so, how could he get her to tell him?

'Look,' he said, 'I think Teena is in trouble. She's disappeared, and I need to find her.' Sassy looked unimpressed. 'I've got to get to her before the Needle does. I think she knows something about him – maybe even who he is – and if he finds her first he might kill her.'

'I told you, I never met her,' Sassy said impatiently. 'I don't know nuffin' about her.' And then, 'Why'n't you asked Ev? She's *his* cousin.'

'I can't ask him. He's dead.'

Evidently she hadn't known that. It was a shock. She stared a long time, perhaps debating whether to ask more, and deciding she didn't want to know. 'I shouldn't a let you in,' she said at last. 'I knew you was trouble. If you've led 'em to me—'

'No, no, I wasn't followed. They're not watching me.'

'You fink they aren't.'

He spread his hands and looked helpless. 'They think I don't know anything. They think I'm harmless. And anyway, why should they bother you? You've never met the Needle. You were just one of the girls. If they were worried about you they'd have done something about you before now, wouldn't they?'

'Yeah, you take chances wiv your own life. I want you out, now.'

She was on her feet. Slider rose too, but slowly. 'One last thing, and then I'll go.'

'Now, I said. I ain't talkin' to you no more.'

'Okay, but you want your money, don't you?' He fumbled in his pocket, as if looking for his wallet, and brought out the interview room photos of Colin Collins and Thomas Mark. 'Just look at these while I'm sorting it out, will you. Tell me if they are the men who came with Mr Lee to the house.'

He held them out, and when she didn't take them, flapped them a little, to indicate that he couldn't search efficiently for money without both hands free. So she took them with a shrug, and looked at them. The picture of Collins she rejected with apparent indifference, but at Thomas Mark she nodded and said, 'He was one of 'em. One of his minders. I dunno the uvver bloke.'

Bingo, Slider thought with deep satisfaction. A link at last! He could have kissed Sassy, had it not been for various hygiene considerations, and the fact that she was bigger than him and could have decked him with one blow. 'I want you to come back to the station with me and make a statement, saying you recognise this man, and where you saw him,' he said.

Sassy recoiled. 'You crazy? I told you you can't let anyone know I've helped you. He'll find out and he'll kill me.'

'No he won't, because we'll have him banged up.'

'I ain't saying nuffin'. You promised me! You swore!'

'I swore I wouldn't tell anyone you told me about him killing another girl,' he reminded her. 'And I won't. All I want is for you to make a statement about this man.' He tapped the photo.

'It's the same fing. I ain't coming.' Her face seemed to crumple. 'Oh Christ,' she said, 'you gonna get me killed. You've led 'em straight to me! I'm dead.'

'If they were following me, you'd be safer at the station than here, wouldn't you? But they aren't. Look, once we've got this man under lock and key, we'll have plenty more evidence against him. I promise I won't use your statement unless I absolutely have to. And it won't have your name on it. Your identity will be protected.' Still she refused, and he allowed a touch of impatience to show. 'I can force you to come, you know. You don't want a big fuss at the door to draw attention to yourself, do you? Come on, Sassy, get it over with. Better me than the local lot. They don't like working girls at Notting Hill.'

'You tellin' me!'

'But you know I'll look after you. Go and get dressed.'

She shrugged at last, and said, 'All right. But I gotter tell my sister where I'm goin'.'

She went out, and down the passage towards a room at the back of the flat. Slider considered the possibility that she might try and escape, but it was the fourth floor, and he knew these death-trap old conversions had no fire escape. Besides, Sassy's real desire was not to go anywhere. Still, he listened carefully for sounds of windows being thrown up, and was just a touch relieved when she reappeared in a short, tight red dress that left everything to be desired, red spike heels and a fake leopardskin jacket. Once a tart, always a tart, he thought with no little affection. He held the front door open for her, and she stalked past him with stunning hauteur.

It was mischievous of him to choose that particular moment to thrust out the small wedge of notes at her.

'I nearly forgot your fifty quid,' he said.

'I don't want your money,' she said scornfully; but she took it all the same.

CHAPTER TWENTY

The Eye of Childhood

The team was assembled in the office. Slider sat on the edge of Anderson's desk.

'There's bound to be a visit from the MRT tomorrow or Tuesday morning at the latest,' he said. 'We'd better get our ducks in a row now, so that we'll have something to present them with.'

'If only they'd called it the Homicide Review Team we could all have had HRT,' Atherton said laconically.

'A lot of people have been suggesting we could do with some extra hormones to pep up our performance,' Slider said.

'I just hope this is worth giving up my Sunday for,' said Atherton. 'I could be at home now with the *Observer*—'

'Make you go blind, that shit,' McLaren warned him cheerfully. The *News of the Screws* was sticking out of his pocket.

'Oh, it's worth it all right,' Slider intervened. 'We've got, at long last, the one thing we've been searching for – a link between Trevor Bates and the Needle. So let's look at the story as a whole.' He checked that he had their attention, and began. 'Colin Collins and Trevor Bates met out in Hong Kong and formed an unholy alliance. Collins had a tattoo parlour and some very shady contacts. Bates had an over-fertile imagination and managerial skills. Together they built up an illegal supply-and-demand business – drugs, girls, whatever. Bates, meanwhile, was developing an obsession with needles and skin; Collins, I suggest, with Bates.'

'Is Collins homosexual?' Atherton asked.

'Certainly not overtly,' Slider said. 'He and Bates shared girls. Let's call it more a fascination – which Bates apparently held for other people, too. Collins was fiercely protective of him, and probably very strongly influenced by him—'

'As those of less nimble minds often are by clever people who take time and trouble with them,' Atherton concluded. 'Well, it makes sense.'

'Fiercely protective and fiercely loyal,' Slider went on. 'They came back to England when Hong Kong started to get too hot. Collins had – and this is all assumption now – quite a bit of money to bring with him. But he took a job, while Bates went on to found a business empire on renovating property.'

He looked at Hollis, who took it up. 'My idea was that maybe Collins gave the money to Bates to get him started.'

'Out of devotion?' Swilley asked with some disbelief. 'I wish I had friends like that.'

'Maybe. Or because he was under his influence, or because Bates was the businessman and could make something of it where Collins couldn't. We don't know that Bates didn't share the proceeds with Collins.'

'And we don't know that he did. Why would Collins go on managing pubs if he had money coming in from Bates?'

'Well,' Hollis said apologetically, 'maybe he liked it. I can't think why anyone would want to own a pub but lots of folk do, because they like the life.'

'Let's not get too poetical,' Atherton said. 'We know that

Collins ran two small-time crooks for his boss, and we can assume it was more than two. Maybe the pub was just very good cover.'

'Then why not buy one?' Mackay asked. 'Why risk interference from the brewery?'

'I can think of two reasons,' Hollis said. 'In the first place, running your own pub is a lot more work than managing one. If it *was* only a cover, you wouldn't want it to take up too much of your time. And for a second thing, it'd be much easier to move on if you had to. Changing jobs is easier than selling a pub and buying another one.'

'All right, let's get on,' Slider said. 'We turn now to Susie Mabbot, a tom who ran a high-price house in Notting Hill, catering for rich businessmen. Somehow or other Trevor Bates finds her, or is recommended to her. He has strange sexual tastes which he wants to exercise in strict secrecy.'

'Exercise or exorcise?' Atherton asked.

'He pays her well, she keeps his identity secret – if she knew it at all.'

'I can't see why he'd ever tell her who he was. Presumably he paid her in cash,' said Mackay.

'You'd think so, wouldn't you?' said Slider. 'She calls him Mr Lee. He visits her, in company with two bodyguards, about once a month.'

'Boss, d'you think that's significant?' Swilley asked.

'What, the once a month bit? It's possible. Strange mental urges can run in cycles. I'm not up on all the latest research, but—'

'You don't believe that bollocks about going mad at the full moon?' Mackay protested.

'Linking it to the phase of the moon may well be self-suggestion,' Slider said, 'but it doesn't mean it doesn't happen. However, that's not for us to debate at present.

Bates is visiting Susie Mabbot. He mentions he's recruiting – or she brings the subject up, we don't know which – and it results in Everet Boston being taken on by Bates.'

'Boston said he got the job through a friend,' Anderson observed.

Slider nodded. 'Boston and Mabbot were old friends from back home. Boston had another friend, Lenny Baxter, whom he met playing snooker. He introduced Baxter to his cousin Mary, and the four of them – he, Mabbot, Baxter and Mary, who called herself Teena Brown – became friends and went out together. This friendship was broken when three months ago Mr Lee, alias Trevor Bates, murdered Susie Mabbot and dumped her in the river.'

'And if we can arrest him for anything at all,' Swilley said, heartfelt, 'we can cross-match his DNA and get him for that.'

Slider nodded. 'So now we come to Lenny Baxter.'

'Our number one corpse,' said Atherton. 'The first but not the last.'

'Baxter was an unreliable type. He was a prolific villain but a rotten gambler with a taste for the ponies. He was working as a runner for Herbie Weedon's loan firm, but he was short of money, and about a year ago Everet, perhaps with his cousin's welfare in mind, got him taken on by the big boss, whom he only knew as the Needle. But Baxter still kept on his other job with Herbie Weedon. Baxter had gambling debts, and was blacklisted by legal bookies. Getting a job running for an illegal bookmaker must have been like letting Billy Bunter loose in a cake shop. He started placing his own bets as well as the customers', and, when they went down, crossing money collected for Herbie to cover them.'

'And getting himself in a right old two-and-eight,' McLaren concluded.

'Eventually,' Slider went on, 'and here we are in the realm of supposition again, the Needle decided he was too much of a risk and that he should be eliminated. He was conducting business of his own on the side, which included selling drugs in the park. One evening the fiat went forth—'

'I can't see a rich bloke like Bates driving one of them,' McLaren objected. 'He'd have something a bit posher.'

'I see him as more a Beamer type,' Mackay agreed.

'Don't encourage him,' Swilley said witheringly.

'Now here a piece of blind chance intervenes,' said Slider. 'Baxter's going about his normal business when he's waylaid by Eddie Cranston, who's got a beef with him about one of his sidelines – preying on females that Eddie feels are his own legitimate feeding ground. Eddie tries to get into a fight with him, but Lenny know his boss doesn't like attention drawn to any of his outposts, and makes a getaway. Later he meets with two heavies in a conversation in the street, and later still he's murdered very efficiently in the park, presumably by the two heavies seen walking away from the park down the street at two in the morning, carrying something which I feel we have reason to suspect is the missing lock and chain.'

'Which later turns up round the throat of Herbie Weedon, who was about to tell me something interesting,' Atherton said. 'How did he know, though?'

'We don't know what he knew, but I suspect it was something he gleaned from Lenny Baxter, who doesn't seem to have been the world's most reliable crook. Probably Baxter told him something and he put two and two together out of his vast experience. And the Needle, in the course of clearing up Lenny Baxter's mess, had Boston put a bug in his office and soon found out he was talking to the police in the form of Mr Atherton.' Wolf whistles. 'So Herbie was killed.'

'Which put the wind up Everet Boston and made him run for it,' said McLaren.

'Later again,' Slider said, 'Boston seems on the brink of telling us something, and is murdered.'

'And chucked in the canal,' Hollis mentioned. 'Like Mabbot was chucked in the river.'

'A watery motif,' said Atherton. 'I wonder if he got into the habit of throwing people in the harbour in Hong Kong?'

'And when,' Slider continued, 'it looks as though we are going to lean heavily on Collins, he takes his own life.'

'Why?' Swilley mused. 'Was he afraid he'd break down and start talking? It doesn't seem likely. He was as tough as old boots.'

'I think maybe it all just got too much for him,' Slider said. 'Running one bit of the crime network for his great idol – perhaps stashing away some of the proceeds for his old age – presumably enjoying the odd night out, or in, with Bates, like in the old days – was one thing. But the body count was mounting. Mabbot, Baxter, Weedon, Boston – what next? Maybe he thought Bates was out of control. Disillusion,' he said, looking round his team, 'is a powerful emotion. It can lead to anger or despair. And if in the middle of that he got the idea that Bates didn't trust him any more and was maybe putting him on the list for removal – well, he'd have nothing left to live for.'

'He jumped rather than waited to be pushed?' Atherton said. 'Hm. I suppose it's possible.'

'And there the trail ends,' said Slider.

'But what have we really got against this guy?' Swilley asked. 'He may have killed Mabbot with his own hands but he won't have personally offed the other three. It will have been his minders. And Collins killed himself.'

'It's the old gangland conundrum,' Atherton agreed. 'The bloke with the motive has clean hands and the bloke who actually does it has no connection with the victim.'

Hollis enumerated, holding up his fingers. 'We know he knew Collins in Hong Kong. We know from Ev Boston that the boss was called the Needle. We know from Rice that Bates was fascinated by needles. We know Mabbot's lover and killer was called the Needle. We know one of her killer's bodyguards was Thomas Mark. We know Thomas Mark is Trevor Bates's driver.'

The chain, Slider thought, forged link by link, connecting all the scattered pieces of lives. 'And then there's the whole business of the jackets,' he said aloud.

'Yes, Bates and Mark deny knowing Baxter, but Mark is wearing a jacket identical to one of the four Baxter bought from Tom Garfield. Bates says he bought it and gave it to Mark but can't prove it.'

'And we can't prove he didn't,' Atherton pointed out. 'We can't really prove anything. It's all suggestion. We still don't know who killed Lenny Baxter, even if we think we know who ordered it done.'

'My guess would be that the actual deed was done by Mark and that butler type we saw in his house,' Slider said. 'However well Bates pays and however much he's feared, he's not going to give jobs like that to just anyone. It would have to be done by those closest to him that he trusts the most. And they looked like professionals. So we show their pictures to Elly Fraser and see if she can ID them as the men she saw leaving the park.'

'And if she can't?'

'There's still Susie Mabbot,' Hollis said. 'If we can get him for that on the DNA, it makes the others look more credible. Then they might start rowing for the shore, him and his minders, and shopping each other in the hope of a comfier cell.'

This idea seemed to go down well. There was a murmur of conversation, out of which Swilley spoke up.

'There's still one thing that bothers me.'

'Only one?' said Atherton.

She ignored him. 'If the minders were going to kill Lenny in the park at two in the morning, they must have arranged to meet him there at that time. So why was he there two hours earlier, at midnight? We know the chain was off the gate then, so he must have been in there.'

'We don't *know* the chain was off the gate,' Atherton said. 'A very dodgy witness says it was.'

'He might have been doing a spot of business,' Mackay said. 'Why not?'

'It wasn't his regular night.'

'He wasn't much of a regular guy,' Hollis pointed out.

'But two hours? Hanging around in the park for two hours? And there are no reports of a stream of customers going in and out of the gate.'

'When were there ever?'

'Anyway,' Swilley said, 'I can't believe there'd be that much trade for him on a Monday night, when he wasn't known to be there selling. Maybe for an hour after the pubs closed, but not through to two in the morning.'

'Well, maybe he wasn't there,' McLaren said. 'Maybe he did a bit of biz, then went home and came back at two.'

'Leaving the gate unlocked all that time?'

McLaren shrugged. 'Why not?' Swilley couldn't answer that.

'There is one other loose end,' Slider said. 'Baxter's girl-friend being missing.'

'She's probably in the river too,' Atherton said.

'Some comfort you are,' said Swilley.

'Well, if he's been getting rid of anyone who could finger him, he'd hardly leave her out, would he? She was just as much a threat as Everet and Baxter.'

'She probably wasn't anything to do with it at all,' Mackay said. 'She's just scarpered, and who wouldn't?'

'All right,' Slider said. 'Things to do. We want full statements from Rice about Collins and Bates, and from Neville Coulsden about Mabbot, his daughter, Boston and Baxter. Get Tom Garfield formally to identify Baxter's jacket as one of his. Get Elly Fraser to look at Mark's picture, see if she can identify him.'

'Guv, won't we have to give the Mabbot stuff to Notting Hill? It's their case.'

'First I want to get everything lined up to see if Mr Porson thinks it's enough to get Bates in to answer questions. If he does, we can get the name of his butler bloke and a mugshot to show Sassy Palmer, see if he was the other minder that came in with Mark.'

'If Bates is as bonkers as he sounds,' said Swilley, 'we could probably get him to crack by telling him everything we know about him and Collins.'

'It did cross my mind,' Slider said.

Slider was having a very late cheese and pickle sandwich at his desk and working on assembling the paperwork when the phone rang.

'Oh, Mr Slider? It's Andy Barrett – from the Boscombe Arms?'

Slider wrenched his head back into the present. 'Oh, yes. What can I do for you?'

'Well, it's like this.' He sounded a bit furtive. 'There's someone here wants to say something to you, but he's scared of coming into the police station. I wondered if you could pop down and have a word with him?'

'Can't you put him on the phone?'

'It's a bit awkward. You'll see why when you come.'

'All right, I'll send someone down.'

'I don't think he'll talk to anyone else,' Barrett said anxiously. 'Couldn't you come yourself? It's about this Lenny Baxter business,' he added, with the air of speaking without moving his lips.

'All right, I'll try and make time later today,' Slider said unwillingly.

'Oh dear. The thing is, can you come now?'

'Why now?'

'Well, we're closed now, so it's quiet. You'd have a bit of privacy. And – well, it's the wife, you see.' He came to the real reason with a little rush. 'She doesn't like me to get mixed up in anything, and she's out at the moment, so she wouldn't have to know if you came now. Only I know she'd say to leave well alone if she was here, but I don't think that's right, not when it's a case of murder, you know?'

Slider sighed. 'I'll be there in about ten minutes,' he said, abandoning the sandwich. It was stale anyway – yesterday's left-overs, from the taste of it. Not much of a Sunday lunch. Oh, it was a glamorous life in the CID!

The Boscombe had a small snug behind the main bar, and Andy Barrett, having let him in from the street, ushered him in there.

'All right, Bernie, here he is,' Barrett said with a large-lipped, talking-to-idiots emphasis. Passing through the door, Slider saw why. Sitting side by side on the banquette facing the door were Blind Bernie and Mad Sam. 'They've been here since opening,' Barrett added, as though they couldn't hear him. 'I thought there was something on his mind. When it came to closing I didn't realise they were still in here till I'd shut the outside doors. Then he said he had to talk to you.'

'What's all this "he" and "him" malarky?' Blind Bernie said suddenly and angrily. 'I'm not deaf, you know. Nor daft, neither. Is that you, Mr Slider?'

'Yes, it's me. You've got something to tell me, Bernie?'

'Yes, I have,' he said definitely. He turned his face towards the sound of Slider's voice, and then back to where Andy Barrett had last spoken. 'It's for Mr Slider's ears only. I don't want anyone else listening. You clear off and give us a bit of peace, you hear?'

'Now look here,' Barrett said, annoyed. 'You can't talk to me like that in my own pub! I let you stay here on sufferance—'

Slider touched his arm to stop him. Mad Sam, who had been staring about him with his usual vacant expression of goodwill, was growing upset.

'Sufferance, my eye!' Bernie cried. 'Go on, clear off! This is police business.'

'All right,' Barrett said, more to Slider than to Bernie. 'I'll leave you alone. But don't take long. If you aren't out of here by the time the wife gets back we'll all be in the soup.'

Blind Bernie turned his head this way and that, listening. 'Is he gone?' he asked.

Slider sat down opposite them. 'Yes, he's gone. It's just me here now.'

'Is he gone, Sammy?'

'Yes, Dad.'

'Where's my glass? I meant to get him to fill it up again before he went,' Bernie grumbled.

'Drinking out of hours?' Slider said.

'Don't count if I don't pay,' Bernie said promptly. 'I know the law. Ah well, too late now, I suppose.'

During this exchange Slider had been examining the strange pair before him. Bernie was in his sixties, but looked older: a gaunt and grizzled man, sparse white hair mostly concealed under a greasy brown trilby that was never off his head, indoors or out; white whiskers like a horse's; gnarled and blue-veined hands knotted round the end of his old-fashioned white cane, the wooden sort with the crook handle. He always wore the same clothes: a dirty mackintosh that had once been tan, over a grey suit, with a collarless shirt under the jacket and a button-necked vest under the shirt. In the winter he interpolated a pullover and cardigan between the shirt and jacket, and all the layers peeped out from under one another in a stepped *décolletage*. Blind Bernie, the human onion. Slider didn't know why he was blind, whether it was congenital or the result of an illness or accident. There was no sign of it on his face. His eyes were rather small and round and pale blue, and the lack of focus gave him a vacant look, just like his son's. Otherwise they appeared normal, except that the pupils were rather too large and dark which, for some reason Slider could not fathom, gave him the faint look of a budgerigar.

Mad Sam must now be nearly forty, though he looked younger until you studied his face closely. He was hardly taller than his father, but round where Bernie was gaunt; a chubby fellow with a rolling gait and the unlined cherubic face of a choirboy. His hair was thin now, though still dark, and his eyes were blue and round, his expression amiable and harmless. He dribbled slightly from time to time, when his mind, distracted by the necessity to think about something hard, was forced to let go of his jaw to compensate. He always wore the same greenish old tweed overcoat, buttoned up and with a yellow muffler filling in the neck-line, winter and summer alike. Slider had no idea what he wore underneath it and was not eager to make the discovery. The two lived together and managed somehow, had done so since Sam's mother died thirty years ago. They spent most of their lives walking about the streets, Bernie's hand on Sam's shoulder: Sam leading, Bernie directing; Sam describing, Bernie explaining.

They lived, as Slider had known but dismissed from his thoughts, in Frithville Gardens – about halfway up, on the right – in the ground-floor maisonette of a two-storey terrace house conversion.

'I'll buy you a pint afterwards,' Slider said to Bernie now. 'And something for Sam,' he added, smiling at the lad (it was impossible not to think of him as a lad, despite the deeply grooved fine creases round his eyes).

'No beer for him,' Bernie said sharply. 'He's not to have alcohol. It's not good for boys.' He had never lost his slight northern accent, and from talking almost exclusively to his dad, Sam had it too.

'I don't like beer,' Sam said easily, in his rather childish voice. 'I don't want beer, Dad.'

'You'd better not,' said Bernie. 'Orangeade's good enough for him, Mr Slider, when he's done telling you what he saw.'

'If it's something important, I can do better than orangeade,' Slider said. 'How about a Coca-Cola?'

Sam's eyes lit up. 'I like that, I do. Can I have Coca-Cola, Dad?'

'It's too good for you,' Bernie grumbled automatically, 'but if Mr Slider wants to waste his money . . .'

'So what's all this about?' said Slider. 'Something to do with that nasty business in the park, is it?'

'Nasty,' said Sam.

'He saw something,' Bernie said. 'That night, the night it happened. Someone coming out of the park.'

'Why didn't you come to me with this before?' Slider asked.

Bernie spread his hands. 'I didn't want to get mixed up in it,' he said defensively. 'Don't hold it against me, Mr Slider. You know what people are like. They want to put me and him in a home. Any chance they'd get to say I was a bad father, they'd use it to put us in a home. If I was to get mixed up with the police . . . Always after us, the social people, ever since Betty died.'

Sam was looking at him in alarm. 'Dad, Dad!'

'Take him away, they would, and then what'd happen to me? Him in the asylum and me in an old folks' home, and we'd never see each other again.'

'Don't let 'em, Dad,' Sam said. 'Don't let 'em take me away.' He began to rock a little.

Slider intervened hastily. 'They won't take you away. Don't you worry, Sammy. They wouldn't punish you for doing your duty, coming forward and helping the police. That's the right thing to do. That's good.'

'Oh, you don't know,' Bernie moaned. 'Any excuse, that's what they want. They'd blame me for taking the lad to a pub. Bad influence, that's what they'd say I was.'

'Well, they won't say that because they won't know,' Slider said firmly. 'I shan't tell 'em. And they can't touch you for taking Sam to a pub. He's over eighteen. It's perfectly legal.'

Sam looked at him across the table, blue eyes as round as an owl's. 'I don't want to leave me dad. I love me dad.'

'You won't have to, don't worry. I'll make it all right, Sam. Just tell me what it was you saw.'

He didn't understand the question, and only stared, a

drop of drool elongating at his mouth corner.

Bernie, recovering himself, took up the questioning. Slider saw him pinch the back of Sam's hand sharply. 'You ready to tell, Sammy? Like we talked about? That night we were down the Red Lion, and we got talking to Mrs Wheeler, and we walked home late? That was the night of that trouble in the park,' he added to Slider. 'I may be blind, but the lad isn't – and he's not daft either, whatever people say. He doesn't know much, but what he knows, he knows. He told me right there and then what he saw, but I was afraid of the fuss and bother, and the social people saying I couldn't look after him.'

'All right,' Slider said soothingly, 'just start at the beginning. You were coming home from the pub. What time would that be?'

'It'd be half eleven easy 'fore we left the Red Lion,' Bernie answered. 'Mrs Wheeler'd tell you, and Sid Field, the barman. And then twenty minutes or so to walk home. Near on midnight it must have been. We was just coming up to our front gate when Sammy says, "There's a lady," he says. "Coming out of the park."'

Sam's face suddenly illuminated, as though someone had just switched him on. He bounced a little in his seat with pleasure at understanding something. 'That's right, that's right!' he said excitely. 'A lady, I saw a lady. She came out of the park.'

'Was the gate open or closed, Sam?' Slider asked, not from a need to know but to focus him on the memory.

'Closed, it was closed. She closed it behind her. I saw her. She didn't see me, though. She was too upset. She just ran by. She didn't look at us.'

'How do you know she was upset?'

'She was hurrying along and all like hunched up. And

she was crying,' Sam said. 'I was sorry for her. She was a pretty lady.'

'Can you describe her to me?' Slider said. 'What did she look like?'

'She was pretty,' Sam said. 'And she smelt nice.'

'What was she wearing?'

'She had a dress on, a nice blue one, like Oxford and Cambridge.'

'Light blue,' Bernie translated. 'The boat race. We're Cambridge, but he always calls it Oxford and Cambridge. He thinks it's the same thing.'

'What else, Sammy?'

'She was a black lady,' Sam said helpfully.

'If you saw her again, would you recognise her?'

Sam nodded his head. 'I would. I would know her. I would.' Then his mouth turned down. 'Because of the nasty thing.'

'What nasty thing was that?'

Sam looked at his father. 'I don't have to say, do I, Dad? I don't like saying it.'

'Aye, you must,' Bernie said. 'Like I told you, you've got to say it to Mr Slider, and you've not got to get upset, or they'll come and take us away and put us in a home. Now get on and tell what the lady did.'

Sam's lip trembled, and his eyes were moist. He rocked again, gently. 'She had something in her hand, something nasty. I saw when she went past. It was all covered in blood. It was nasty.'

'Was it a knife?' Slider asked. Sam nodded, near to tears. 'All right, Sammy, go on.'

'Go on, son,' Bernie encouraged. 'Tell what she did.'

'She threw it away,' Sam said. 'In the house with the weeds, down the area. She went across the road and threw it in there. And then she ran all the way down the street and turned the corner that way.' He made a gesture of turning right.

'I understand,' Slider said. 'Is that all?'

Sam nodded.

'That's all,' Bernie said. 'But when we heard about the murder, I couldn't decide whether to say anything or not. You won't let them hold it against me, will you, Mr Slider? I know I'm old, but we manage all right. We look after each other. If they split us up, I don't know what would become of the boy.'

'I won't let it make any trouble for you,' Slider said, with more conviction than he felt. It wasn't that anything they had done or not done was reason for institutionalising either of them; but Bernie knew with the instinct of self-preservation that in their situation you did not draw attention to yourself. Journalists might get hold of the story and decide to splash it for 'human interest'; or simply being in court might direct official eyes in their direction. And then questions would be asked, and appalling things done to them for their own good. A social worker would only have to smell them to know they ought to be put in a home; and God knew what the inside of the maisonette was like.

'That man was killed,' Sam said suddenly and confidingly. 'I know, I heard it. I saw our street and our park on the telly. That man was killed with a knife, a sharp knife, a pointy knife, and there was all blood and he fell down dead. Bang!' It was sudden and loud and made Slider jump, which in turn made Sam flinch. He was getting too excited.

'Never mind about that,' Bernie said sharply. 'You sit still and be quiet or I'll give you what-for.' And to Slider, 'I don't like him watching telly. It's not good for the lad, but they have it on sometimes when we're down the pub.

He saw you on the telly, Mr Slider—'

'I saw you on the telly, Mr Slider,' Sam nodded.

'He's not daft, whatever people say. He wanted to tell you about the lady and the knife—'

'It was a sharp knife, all covered in blood! It was nasty!'

'But I was afraid. I told him to forget about it, but then my conscience wasn't easy.'

'Well, you did the right thing, Bernie, and I'm grateful to you. To both of you. And I'll make sure there's a little something for you both to say thank you.'

'Oh, no, that wouldn't be right,' Bernie said gravely. 'Not a reward for doing your duty.'

'I'd like to give you something anyway. There's nothing wrong with that. You didn't do it for the money, so it's quite all right.'

'Well,' said Bernie, but less doubtfully.

'Now I want you both to come with me to the station, and we'll take down what Sam saw in writing, to make it all official. And then I'd like you, Sam, to sit and look at some pictures and tell me if any of them look like the lady you saw. Can you do that?'

Sam looked sly. 'Can I have a Coca-Cola if I do?'

'You can have the back of my hand if you don't do as you're told,' Bernie said fiercely, and Sam collapsed like a pricked balloon. You could have blown Bernie away with a puff of wind, and Sam was twice his weight at least; but in the minds of both of them Sam was still nine years old and in short trousers.

CHAPTER TWENTY-ONE

Content – Liable To Settle

'The house with the weeds,' Mad Sam had said, and Slider, having been up and down Frithville Gardens often enough in the past week, had no difficulty in identifying it. One house on the left-hand side going up (the side opposite to where Blind Bernie and Mad Sam lived) had been empty for some time and was boarded up and semi-derelict. Weeds had sprung up with mongrel vigour from the small patch of earth on the side of the area, ragwort and grass was sprouting from cracks in the steps and windowsills, and the gutters were gay with buddleia so that the house looked as if it was wearing an Ascot hat.

Atherton looked with distaste down the area, which was choked not just with weeds but with rubbish, carelessly discarded tins, bottles and fast-food boxes, and the inevitable skeleton of a pushchair. The rate of attrition of children's buggies was so abnormally high, he thought, it was something to bear in mind when looking for shares to invest in.

McLaren was equally unimpressed. 'You want me to go down there?'

'Well, I'm not trousered for it,' Atherton said.

'And there's got to be some advantage to my higher

rank,' Slider added. 'If it's not that, I can't think what else it can be.'

'You're breaking his heart,' Atherton warned. 'Come on, Maurice, you're the one who'll feel most at home among all those KFC cartons.' He nudged McLaren towards the steps. 'Be careful, though. There might be rats.'

'Not at this time of day,' Slider intervened. 'Get on with it.'

McLaren donned his gloves and descended gingerly. It was fifteen minutes before he straightened up and said, 'I think I've got something.'

'I wouldn't be a bit surprised,' Atherton murmured.

McLaren was clambering back up. He displayed his booty: a paperknife in the shape of a stiletto, sharply pointed and narrow, double-edged, and with a blade about five and a half or six inches long.

'Probably a souvenir of Toledo,' Atherton commented.

'It's still got blood on it,' McLaren noted happily.

'And with any luck,' Slider said, 'fingermarks.'

'It'll take time to get it processed and get a match on either,' Atherton observed.

'Doesn't matter,' Slider said. 'Mad Sam picked her photo out without the slightest hesitation.'

'Mary Coulsden, aka Teena Brown,' McLaren said with satisfaction. 'Well, at least we know we've *got* her prints on record, so we've got something to match the finger-marks with, when we get 'em back.'

'But if Teena killed Lenny, what does that do to our lovely house of cards?' said Atherton. 'Doesn't it all come tumbling down?'

'No, no,' Slider said distractedly, 'it all makes perfect sense.'

'All we've got to do, of course, is find her,' Atherton mentioned.

'I think,' said Slider, 'that I know where she is.'

Sassy Palmer was dressed this time when she opened the door – not in the red dress but in a pair of mauve Lycra leggings and a tight, low-cut top of ocelot-printed cotton.

'Not a-bloody-gain,' she said with enormous, theatrical exasperation. 'I already spent half me Sunday down the cop shop. Can't you buggers leave me alone?' She eyed Atherton professionally and slipped abruptly into her Harlem persona. 'How you doin', honey? I hain't seen you befo'.'

'I'm sorry to have to bother you again,' Slider said, slipping his foot into position, 'but I'd like a word with your sister.'

'My—?' Sassy's eyes narrowed as she recollected. 'She's not here. She's gone.'

'Oh, I don't think so,' Slider said.

'Yeah,' Sassy assured him earnestly. 'She was only stoppin' over the one night. She lives up – up Birmingham,' she added inventively.

Slider looked at her sadly and kindly. 'The game's up, Sassy. I know Teena's here. I smelt her scent when I was here before. She wears *Paris* and yours is *My Sin*. Come on, love. We've got the evidence now, and we have to take her in. But you know I'll be gentle with her. Better me than somebody else.'

'You always say that,' Sassy complained, but she seemed near to tears.

'You've been a good friend to her,' Slider said, laying a hand on her wrist. 'Come on, be a good girl and let's get this over with.'

She seemed to consider resisting, but then to realise it was pointless. She did not, however, *let* them in: Slider had to push her gently out of the way, understanding that it was her way of salving her conscience.

They could see through the open door that the kitchen and living room were empty. Atherton looked in one bedroom, Slider in the other. There was a sharp cry and a scuffle, and Slider reversed hastily and ran to help Atherton, who was holding Teena Brown by both wrists while she screamed at him in a mixture of anger and fear.

She was wearing a white teeshirt and a pair of pink pedal-pushers, and her pretty face was drawn and exhausted with fear and distress. 'Let me go! Let me go!' she cried. 'I ain't done nothing! You don't understand!'

'Yes, I do,' Slider said. 'Calm down, Teena. Stop struggling – you'll only hurt yourself. I know what's been going on. I know you killed Lenny, and I know why. It's all over now.'

She stared at him a moment and then burst into tears, and feeling the struggle leave her, Atherton released her so she could sit down heavily on the bed behind her and sob into her hands. Behind Slider, Sassy was swearing softly and continuously under her breath, but she made no move to intervene.

Slider had hardly ever been sorrier than when he began, 'Mary Christina Coulsden, otherwise known as Teena Brown, I arrest you for the murder of Lenny Baxter. You do not need to say anything . . .'

'Hullo. Am I disturbing you?'

Slider looked up sharply. Joanna was standing in the doorway of his office, her overnight bag slung over one shoulder, her handbag over the other. It took him a moment of wondering what was strange about her – apart from her actual presence here – before realising that she did not have her fiddle case in her hand. It didn't look natural, somehow.

'I got tired of having my phone messages ignored,' she added, seeing his brain was still catching up, 'and since I haven't got any work to do until Wednesday morning I thought I'd hop on a plane and come and see how you're doing.' She cocked an eyebrow at him. 'Say something, even if it's only "bleh".'

'Joanna,' he said.

'Well, that's a start. At least you recognise me.' She crossed the room and he stood up hastily, sending a plastic dispenser cup tumbling to the floor, where it bounced hollowly but fortunately drily. Then his arms were round her, and she was pressing against him, warm and real and full of the usual interesting bumps.

When he released her she smiled and pushed him gently backwards and said, 'Sit. You look fit to fall down.'

'I feel it. What time is it?'

'Nearly seven. When did you last go home?'

He thought. 'Saturday night,' he said.

'You do realise it's Monday night? No wonder you're tired.'

'Everything's happening,' he said. 'We've made an arrest on one murder and we're about to make an arrest on another, and what with one thing and another—'

'Yes, I get the picture. That accounts for why you haven't picked up your messages.'

'You could have called me on my mobile,' he said.

'I'd have loved to,' she said drily, 'but it's turned off.'

'Oh yes,' he said vaguely, 'I did that to stop it ringing.'

'That'll do it,' she agreed. 'Have you eaten anything?'

'Not for – oh, years and years,' he said, managing to smile.

'Come and eat, then. You can spare the time for that. Even Wellington took time out at Waterloo for a snack.'

'Station buffets can be handy.'

'They haven't knocked the cheek out of you then,' she noted, taking his hand and tugging, gently but insistently, like a child.

The canteen was quiet, and they took a corner table well out of earshot of anyone else. 'You're right, of course,' he said, unloading his tray. 'I'm famished.'

'And the brain needs food to operate properly,' Joanna said. He'd chosen the all-day breakfast, heavy on the beans; she had a piece of quiche and some salad. She wasn't really hungry, but knew he wouldn't eat if she didn't. She talked inconsequentially while he stifled the first urgent pangs; then, when his fork-work slowed below warp speed, he told her about the case, and about Mary Coulsden.

She had always admired her cousin Everet, the slick, street-wise, ineffably sophisticated yet kind cousin Ev, her hero and icon of naughtiness. When he had introduced her to Lenny Baxter, she was predisposed to like him, as she would have liked anyone Ev recommended to her. But Lenny was handsome and well-built, smartly dressed, appeared to have money, and was generous with it. He had an air of edgy dangerousness that was missing from the more familiar Ev, which thrilled her; and he had charm, too, something that of course could not be known to anyone who had only ever met him dead.

She fell instantly into infatuation with him, and after only a few dates was ready to move out from her parents' home and into his.

'She was finding life at home too stifling anyway,' Slider
said. 'A lively youngster with old parents, and church-going
parents at that. All children want to rebel at some point.'

'I bet you never did,' Joanna said.

'I grew my hair long in 1968,' he mentioned.

'*Ruat coelum!*' she said, but he didn't understand her
pronunciation. 'Go on.'

'Well, things seemed all right at first for her with Lenny.
She found him exciting, she liked spending money, smoking
and drinking, and going about with him and his wicked
friends to the sort of places she knew her parents would
disapprove of. She was in love with him and thought he
was in love with her. The first shock was in the course of
a drunken party when he proposed to share her with two
of his friends. She was drunk too, and rather excited by
the wickedness, and went along with it, but the next
morning she felt bad about it. She told Lenny she would
never do anything like that again. Lenny told her not to be
so narrow-minded and that it was just a piece of fun – and
Lenny, after all, must know best.'

'Yes, I can see how it would have gone,' she said. 'I bet
he made fun of her parents' religion.'

'How did you know?'

'Figures. Religion isn't cool these days.'

Not long after the incident at the party, Lenny told her
he wanted to 'lend' her to Ken Whalley in return for the
key to the park.

'She argued about that one; but he pressed her, saying
old Ken was harmless and it would all be over in seconds.
Then he was offended and said he'd thought she loved him
and why wouldn't she do this one little thing for him. In
the end he wore her down, and she did it.'

'What a bastard,' Joanna said.

'Yes. Of course, she began to realise in the end that he *was* a bastard, and to guess that he didn't really love her. But if ever she got close to rebelling he'd charm her back again and tell her he loved her and buy her a present.' He shook his head at it. 'I've noticed time and again that women don't seem to care how badly a man behaves, as long as he *says* he loves her. And vice versa – they'll leave a good and loving man because he doesn't use the words often enough.'

'We're so shallow and fickle,' Joanna said, and he managed a troubled smile.

'Sorry. All generalisations are false—'

'Including that one,' she finished for him.

So the truth was that Teena, who had first been mentioned to Slider as the tom Lenny lived with, was not a prostitute in the proper sense. It was all at Lenny's insti-gation, sometimes for money – as time went on and his affairs became more involved, always for money – but there was another motive which Teena, from her innocent upbringing, only ever sensed and never clearly understood. Lenny *liked* lending her; he liked having her in company, and he liked to watch other men having her. She didn't like it, felt besmirched and humiliated by it, but Lenny's hold over her was absolute. She quickly learnt about his temper, and that the air of dangerousness which had thrilled her – and still did – was in fact the leading edge of a real violence. So out of fear and infatuation she stayed with him. Life was at least more exciting with him, and where else, after all, could she go? Certainly not back home. Lenny offered her soft drugs, and she relied on them more as time went on to soften the edges of her world and lend an air of unre-ality to the things her childhood conscience still told her were wrong.

She had no idea he was in money trouble, though she knew he spent freely and was losing money on the horses. Still his 'business' interests seemed so wide and varied she assumed they would cover his lifestyle. But as his money troubles got worse, and he got himself into more of a muddle, his temper grew worse and she grew more afraid of him. Sometimes now she wanted to get away from him, but the one time she had hinted at leaving him he had grabbed her by the neck and said if she ran away he would find her and kill her. It was what men like him said, and not all of them meant it, but she believed it. Who would take the risk that he didn't? It was what accounted, said Slider, for so much abuse of women.

Then one day Lenny told Teena that the boss – the Needle himself – had seen her and fancied her.

'How?' Joanna asked. 'I mean, where did he see her?'

'In the Phoenix. There were CCTV cameras in there. We thought they were just for ordinary pub security, but of course they'd been put in by – or at least at the order of – Needle Bates, who liked to spy on his employees. Lenny had taken Teena in there several times. She is very pretty, of course; and it might have occurred to Bates that being under Lenny's thumb she'd be compliant about his strange ways; and also, of course, he could be sure Lenny wouldn't object.'

'What a sweetheart,' said Joanna.

'Which?'

'Both.'

'Yes, Lenny wasn't exactly above his company. Well, anyway, what he didn't know was that Teena knew something about the Needle's proclivities, having heard it from Susie Mabbot during one of those ladies' loo confessions when they were out in foursome with Lenny and Everet.

Susie made light of it, but Teena could see she hated it
and feared the Needle. And of course Susie was now dead,
and Teena had her suspicions about who had killed her.
The evidence about all the tiny holes had not been generally released, but that only gave her imagination room to
run riot. So she refused point-blank to do what she was
told. First Lenny argued and cajoled – this was so important to his career, he would get into trouble if she didn't
do it, et cetera. Then he smacked her around a bit – but
carefully, so as not to damage the goods – and told her if
she didn't obey, Bates would kill him, but not before *he*
killed *her*.'

'Poor kid.'

'Yes. Anyway, then things all came to a head at the same
time. This is speculation, but I think Bates had decided to
get rid of Lenny, partly because he was unreliable, and
partly as a way to get Teena for himself. Lenny must have
been dragging his feet about "lending" her, hoping to talk
or bully Teena into it. Teena, meanwhile, had worked
herself up into a pitch of terror. Lenny had told her he was
going to force her to do as she was told and be nice to the
boss, and she couldn't see any way out. She apparently
tried to get Everet to help her but he didn't understand or
didn't believe what she was trying to tell him.'

'Everet didn't know about the Needle killing Susie?'

'Not then. It was only afterwards he began to put two
and two together with his buried suspicions and make
ten.'

On that Monday night, Teena had been out to the all-
night supermarket and on her way back saw Lenny outside
the flat, talking to two of the Needle's men. She assumed
they were arranging her fate between them, and that it was
imminent. She concealed herself and watched. When they

went away and Lenny went into the flat, she rang him on her mobile and told him that she had something important to tell him and he must meet her in the park.'

'Why there?'

'She knew the flat was bugged. Lenny had told her. It was one of the conditions of employment. And she knew, of course, that Lenny did his own business in the park so it must be private there.'

'And what was she going to tell him in the park?'

'She wanted to plead with him one last time. Her idea was that they should both run away and start a new life somewhere else.'

'How traditional.'

'But when she'd seen him leave the flat, she dashed in and grabbed the paperknife from beside the telephone, in case he wouldn't listen to reason. She'd got to the point when she felt it was him or her. And,' Slider added thoughtfully, 'she probably wasn't far wrong.'

Joanna reached across the table and laid her hand over his, and he chafed her fingers as he spoke, as if it comforted him.

'So she followed him to the park, to the children's playground where he used to conduct his business. She said when she saw his face, she knew straight away that it wasn't any good, and she just walked up to him and stabbed him before he could guess what she was up to, and before she lost her nerve. I thought that single blow straight to the heart was professional,' he said, 'but it turns out it was just lucky. One of my many misjudgements.'

He must have gone down like a felled horse, he thought: a dreadful thing, and yet giving small, slight Teena a terrifying sense of power. Then horror overcame her, and she ran for it; ran sobbing back the way she had come, a murderess now, and still afraid for her life; too upset to notice Blind Bernie and Mad Sam – though if she had noticed them she probably would have ignored them.

'They were street furniture, practically,' Slider said. 'And anyway, who would think of them as witnesses? Not the CPS,' he added, 'that's for sure.'

Finding herself still clutching the bloody weapon, she flung it away as she passed the empty house. Later she had thought that was the wrong thing to have done, but it was not surprising if she hadn't been able to think clearly at a moment like that. She thought that the Needle's men would be after her, and she certainly feared them more than the police. She went back to the flat, packed a bag in jittering terror, and left.

'She didn't know where to go. She thought of Everet, but didn't know how far he could be trusted. He still worked for the Needle, and suppose he just gave her up to him? She couldn't go home to her parents – certainly not now she'd killed a man. In the end she thought of Sassy Palmer, whom she'd met at Susie's house and knew had been a friend of Susie's.'

'Always trust a girlfriend when you're in trouble,' Joanna said. 'How did you know she was there?'

'I guessed. Sassy said she had never met Everet's cousin, but she knew the word "cousin" was female in this case. And she said she had met Lenny with Everet when they called for Susie to go out as a foursome, but not Teena. Why would they have left Teena outside? So if she had met Teena and was lying about it, there must be a reason. And finally I realised I had smelt her scent in Sassy's house – *Paris*. I'd smelt it first in Lenny's flat.'

'God bless your nose,' Joanna said. 'You're so clever.'

'No, I'm slow, too slow. There were indications I ought

to have picked up. Right at the beginning, Freddie Cameron said there was a fresh pint of beer in Lenny's stomach. That ought to have told me he was killed earlier than two in the morning.' He paused, thinking. 'Funny thing, Nutty said to me that there was a woman at the bottom of most things. There were enough hints I should have picked up. If I'd got onto the true line earlier two lives might have been saved.'

'I doubt it,' she said, but he only shook his head, unable to be comforted by her. She knew this mood of his after a serious case. It was reaction to the tremendous mental effort and the awful responsibility. 'You're tired,' she said. 'When are you finishing tonight?'

He looked a little blank, and then dragged in a sigh. 'I hadn't even thought about going home, but now you're here . . .' The food was making him sleepy now. 'Give me another half hour at the desk, and then we'll go home together.'

In the car, going home, he told her the rest of the story: conjecture still, but he hoped capable of proof. Bates's goons had gone to the park later, at the time previously arranged, the time for which Sonny Collins would have fixed his alibi according to orders. Finding Baxter dead, they had gone through his pockets for the keys to the flat, for any form of identification and, perhaps, for his betting-book.

'I imagine they rang the boss for instructions and Bates told them to sit the corpse on the swing as a kind of joke. It's too depressing to think of them having that sort of sense of humour for themselves.'

'What about the chain – why did they take that away?'

'I don't know. Maybe they picked it up on the way in with the intention of using it on Lenny, and then took it with them without thinking. Or maybe the boss told them to keep it for some other purpose. I don't know how devious his mind really is.'

After that it was a matter of clearing up behind them. Back to Lenny's flat to remove anything that might incriminate anyone.

'And, presumably, to take Teena. But Teena was gone. Bates must have been furious.'

Then the other strands of Lenny's life had to be unpicked. Herbie Weedon, his other employer, was bugged. When it looked as though he was going to be a nuisance, he was eliminated.

'Or perhaps he wasn't supposed to die, only to be frightened. But his heart gave out.'

And then Everet Boston, at last worried for his cousin and tending to put two and two together and to talk too much – Everet had to be silenced. But he had already revealed the importance of Sonny Collins in the network. So now Sonny was a danger.

'Did Sonny jump or was he pushed?' Slider wondered, waiting for the traffic lights to change. 'The thing I'd most like to know, and never will, is what was in his mind when he took the pills.' Maybe he wasn't up to all the bodies. To get rid of Lenny he might have seen as essential, but one murder was leading to another, and where would it end? And doing nothing might – was this the final betrayal? – lead to his being murdered himself, if Bates, who seemed to be getting more and more paranoid, decided he couldn't trust him. Maybe the Needle he had known and loved in Hong Kong was mutating into something even he couldn't contemplate. To live with the knowledge of his evil, or to give him up, were equally unthinkable alternatives. The only other way out was the Big Sleep.

Slider was silent until they moved off again, and then

he said, 'The most extraordinary thing of all was the sheer chance of it. Bates was so careful. If it hadn't been for the leather jacket, we never would have looked at him at all. And the Phoenix was just a little outpost of the empire. The whole towering structure of Bates's world, built up piece by piece over the years, was made to totter through the frailty of Lenny Baxter, and one American amateur smuggler.'

'Will you get him – Bates? For the other murders?'

'I think so. We'll get him for Susie Mabbot; and Teena can identify the two men she saw talking to Lenny outside the house. We know one is Thomas Mark, and we think the other is Bates's butler. Once we've got them tied in, and tied in with his visits to Susie Mabbot's, I think they'll give him up to save themselves.'

'And what about Teena?'

'Her fingermarks are on the paperknife along with Lenny's blood, which supports her confession, so we probably won't have to call on Mad Sam, which is a blessing. It's enough to convict her, but she'll turn Queen's evidence against Bates and get off with a reduced sentence for manslaughter, I should think. Well,' he added wearily, 'it's out of my hands now. Susie Mabbot was Notting Hill's case anyway, and the NCS has already got an enquiry in train on Bates. They'll take the whole thing over.'

'Including Teena Brown?'

'I should think so.'

'But it will be good for you, won't it? I mean, you got a result.'

He gave a tired smile. 'Oh, I should think I might get a commendation.'

'As much as that?'

'I'm glad you're here,' he said. 'How long can you stay?'

'If I get up at the crack of dawn, until Wednesday morning. That was our turning, by the way. You've gone past it. You really are tired, aren't you?'

'Bashed,' he said, indicating right at the next corner.

'But you got him,' she said encouragingly.

'They'll get him,' he corrected. 'We got her. Poor weeping thing.'

After some satisfying lovemaking and a hot bath, he found himself irrationally wide awake again, so he opened a bottle of wine while she put some music on and they got into bed to enjoy them.

'So what's going on with Sue and Jim?' she asked.

'Oh, I think they're all right,' he said.

'What about his wandering eye?'

'I think it's ceased to wander, really. He's discovered he doesn't really want to. It was just force of habit.'

'Fine excuse.'

'We had a bit of a chat earlier on. He was going home this evening to apologise and make everything right.' He looked at her sideways. 'Do you think she'll forgive him?'

'She'll have to,' Joanna said. 'They can't split up now they have two cats between them, can they?'

'No. Divorce is hell on pets – turns them into feline delinquents.'

He felt her come to it, an almost physical sensation, like an indrawn breath. 'And what about us?'

'*What* about us?' he gave the question back. 'You've been gearing up to say something to me, I know. You held off because of my case, but I can't hide behind that for ever. Maybe it'd be best to get it out and get it over with.' She was still silent, and he went on, 'Say something to stop me babbling. Can't you tell I'm scared to death?'

She gave him a strange look. 'Scared of what?'

Over the edge in a barrel. 'That you want to end it. That you've found someone else.'

'After the proofs of love I've just given you?'

'You might just have been being kind,' he said; but he almost grinned with huge relief. It wasn't that. He could tell. There was no-one else. Maybe she was just going to revive the question of his going to Amsterdam, a much less scary possibility. 'Go on, out with it. What did you want to talk about?'

'I'm going to tell you something,' she said in a rather strained voice, 'and you have to be very careful what you say in reply, because if you get it wrong it'll kill me. Are you ready?'

'As ready as I'll ever be.'

'All right then. Here it is.' She swivelled to face him so that she could watch his expression. 'I'm pregnant.'

He said absolutely nothing. His brain could not get to grips with it.

'Well, I suppose that's better than saying the wrong thing,' she said. She looked at him wryly. 'You hadn't guessed that's what it was? Some bloody detective you are!'

'How?' was all he managed to say.

'What do you mean, how? Didn't they do human reproduction in biology?'

'Not when I was at school. I suppose I mean when, really. On what occasion.'

'When I came back in February, as far as I can make out.' She looked a little conscious. 'I don't remember missing a pill, but when I got back to Amsterdam I found I must have.' She gave a lop-sided smile. 'It wasn't deliberate, I promise you, but – well, they say there's no such thing as an accident, don't they? Maybe subconsciously – look, I'm doing all the talking. You still haven't said anything. About it. About being pleased. Or not.'

'I'm pleased,' he said, taking her hand. February? She was three months gravid, then. The child was well on the way. His child, his-and-hers child. And what did he think about that? Children, to him, were Kate and Matthew. He'd been a father already, he'd done that bit, and he wouldn't have been normal if he didn't think, however fleetingly, of broken nights and nappies, responsibility and expense, and the curtailment of freedom children brought.

But it was only fleeting. Her dear face was close, and though she was trying to make light of it he could see her apprehension. *If you say the wrong thing it will kill me.* She had been alone with the pregnancy for nearly three months, alone and wondering, hoping for the best and fearing the worst, afraid to tell him in case he was not delighted.

Well, she should not be alone with it any more. He was delighted. A child, her child, their child, was already started and on its way, and the least it deserved was for them both to be wholeheartedly glad about it. It should not come into the world with any remembered coolness to blight it, no unwelcoming word, like the bad fairy's gift, to come back to haunt it.

'You really didn't guess?' she said, watching his thoughts flit about his face, and – more importantly – the slowly dawning smile.

'Not a bit. Call me dumb.'

'Dumb. But you really are pleased? I mean, I know it wasn't planned, and the situation is—'

He stopped her with a kiss. 'I'm dumb with bliss. It wasn't what I expected, but how could I not want our child?'

She almost sagged with relief. 'Bless you for that. I've

made a complete mess of this. I should have told you weeks ago. I just didn't know how to.'

'I understand,' he said. Matthew and Kate and – well, call him X. Him or her. He felt a surge of wild excitement grasp his loins. Their child would be special. What would Kate and Matthew think about it? He must make sure they never felt set aside for the new one. He would have to talk seriously to Irene to make sure she said the right things too. And what the hell was he thinking about Irene for at a moment like this?

'But what will you do now?' he asked. 'I mean, you're over there and I'm over here. We'll have a schizophrenic baby.'

'What would you think about my coming back?'

'What about the job?'

'I was only doing it on trial. I'd have to give it up, of course. Try and subsist on casual work, whatever I could pick up over here. For as long as I could work. I could keep going almost up to the day. And after the baby's born—'

'We'll manage,' he said.

'It'll be tight.'

'It'll be all right. Money's the least of it.'

'Oh brave man! You just wait.'

'I mean it,' he said. 'I know about babies and expense, remember. People expect too much, that's what makes the problems. You can always manage, if you have to.' He lifted her hand and kissed it. 'There is just one thing.'

'Oh?' she said suspiciously.

'One small proviso.'

'I smell a rat,' she said.

'Well, I think I'm entitled to one demand. After all, you did trick me into this—'

'You bastard!'

'Nail on head, as usual,' he said. 'I'm an old-fashioned sort of bloke, as well you know.'

'Hidebound,' she agreed. 'Practically ossified.'

'And if we're going to have a baby, I'm afraid I must insist on our doing it properly.' She looked at him. 'Will you marry me? And I warn you, it's one of those "Nonne" questions.'

'What questions?'

'Questions that expect the answer "yes".'

'Oh, those!'

The phone rang. They looked at each other and then burst out laughing. Slider picked it up.

'I thought you were still at work,' Atherton said.

'What are you ringing me here for, then?'

'I thought you'd like to know the result of your advised plan of action. You know, bottle of wine, nice meal, soft lights, heart-to-heart talk?'

'How did it go?'

'Well, apart from the cats going mad around us, very well. She forgave me.'

'I thought she would. And?'

'She still loves me.'

'Wise woman. And?'

'Brace yourself for a shock. I asked her to marry me.' Slider began to smile, slowly. Into his silence, Atherton spoke again. 'Are you there? Did you hear what I said? I said, we're going to get married.'

'Now there's a coincidence,' said Slider.